D1748302

MY CRAZY TALE

OTHER LOTUS TITLES

Ajit Bhattacharjea	*Sheikh Mohammad Abdullah: Tragic Hero of Kashmir*
Anil Dharker	*Icons: Men & Women Who Shaped Today's India*
Aitzaz Ahsan	*The Indus Saga: The Making of Pakistan*
Ajay Mansingh	*Firaq Gorakhpuri: The Poet of Pain & Ecstasy*
Alam Srinivas & TR Vivek	*IPL: The Inside Story*
Alam Srinivas	*Women of Vision: Nine Business Leaders in Conversation*
Amarinder Singh	*The Last Sunset: The Rise & Fall of the Lahore Durbar*
Hamish Mcdonald	*Ambani & Sons*
Kunal Purandare	*Ramakant Achrekar: A Biography*
Lakshmi Vishwanathan	*Women of Pride: The Devdasi Heritage*
Lucy Peck	*Agra: The Architectural Heritage*
Lucy Peck	*Delhi a Thousand Years of Building: An INTACH-Roli Guide*
Madan Gopal	*My Life and Times: Munshi Premchand*
M.J. Akbar	*Byline*
M.J. Akbar	*Blood Brothers: A Family Saga*
Maj. Gen. Ian Cardozo	*Param Vir: Our Heroes in Battle*
Maj. Gen. Ian Cardozo	*The Sinking of INS Khukri: What Happened in 1971*
Madhu Trehan	*Tehelka as Metaphor*
Monisha Rajesh	*Around India in 80 Trains*
Noorul Hasan	*Meena Kumari: The Poet*
Peter Church	*Added Value: The Life Stories of Indian Business Leaders*
Peter Church	*Profiles in Enterprise: Inspiring Stories of Indian Business Leaders*
Rajika Bhandari	*The Raj on the Move: Story of the Dak Bungalow*
Ralph Russell	*The Famous Ghalib: The Sound of my Moving Pen*
R.V. Smith	*Delhi: Unknown Tales of a City*
Salman Akthar	*The Book of Emotions*
Sharmishta Gooptu	*Bengali Cinema: An Other Nation*
Shrabani Basu	*Spy Princess: The Life of Noor Inayat Khan*
S. Hussain Zaidi	*Dongri to Dubai*
Sunil Raman & Rohit Aggarwal	*Delhi Durbar: 1911 The Complete Story*
Thomas Weber	*Going Native: Gandhi's Relationship with Western Women*
Thomas Weber	*Gandhi at First Sight*
Vir Sanghvi	*Men of Steel: India's Business Leaders in Candid Conversation*

FORTHCOMING TITLES

Shahrayar Khan	*Bhopal Vignettes*

MY CRAZY TALE

His Holiness
THE GYALWANG DRUKPA

Translated by
LOBSANG THARGAY

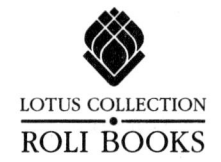

LOTUS COLLECTION
ROLI BOOKS

© The Gyalwang Drukpa, 2016
First published in Tibetan, 2013

This English translation published in 2016

All rights reserved. No part of this publication may be reproduced or transmitted, in any form or by any means, without prior permission of the authors.

The Lotus Collection
An imprint of
Roli Books Pvt. Ltd
M-75, Greater Kailash II Market, New Delhi 110 048
Phone: ++91 (011) 40682000
E-mail: info@rolibooks.com
Website: www.rolibooks.com

Also at Bengaluru, Chennai, & Mumbai

Cover Photo: Dan Paton
Other Photos: Collection of family and friends of the Gyalwang Drukpa
Editors: Diana Cook, Tessa Heror, Steve Todd, Angela Vargas
Layout: Bhagirath Kumar
Production: Yuvraj Singh
Cover design: Sneha Pamneja

ISBN: 978-93-5194-175-0

Typeset in Sabon LT Std by Roli Books Pvt. Ltd.
Printed at Printways, New Delhi.

Contents

Foreword		ix
Root Text		1
Introduction		19
1.	Invocation	27
2.	The Buddhist View: Is Mantrayana Possible Without Sutra?	69
3.	Blessings of the Lineage: The Origin of the Drukpa Lineage	93
4.	Innate Loving Kindness and Compassion	121
5.	Entering the Path of Dharma	129
6.	Retreat and Meditation	147
7.	Faith in Ultimate Reality	169
8.	The Essence of Guru's Kindness	193
9.	Defilement of Black Offering	227

10.	Recognition as a Reincarnation of Drukpa	233
11.	Grave Consequences of Black Offerings	239
12.	Remember the Guru's Kindness	263
13.	Nirvana is Within Your Hands	271
14.	Meeting a Qualified Guru	289
15.	Root and Branch Teachers	341
16.	Appearances as Example	367
17.	The Ultimate Great Bliss	373
18.	Crazy Thoughts	379
19.	Supplication	391

A compilation of the explanations given by His Holiness the Gyalwang Drukpa at different places and on different occasions, at the request of his disciples, on the verse composition *My Crazy Tale* by His Holiness, narrating his life story and experiences of spiritual practice. The original Tibetan transcript of the teachings was transcribed and compiled by Jigme Tingdzin Zangmo, and was translated into English by
Lobsang Thargay.

ಐ ಡಿ

The narrator of the content in this book is His Holiness the Gyalwang Drukpa, the reincarnation of Tsangpa Gyare Yeshe Dorje, founder of the Drukpa Lineage and the unmistaken reincarnation of the eleventh-century great Indian Saint Naropa.

ಐ ಡಿ

In order to improve one's life one has to improve it on both the spiritual and mundane fronts. One has to be aware of everyday activities, from drinking tea and having meals to improve relations with other human beings, animals and the environment. Improving one's own life should be the main focus of our life story.

Foreword

This book is a collection of the explanations I have given about my life story entitled, *My Crazy Tale*. At the request of my disciples, I have given them the permission to publish it. I hope it will serve as an entertainment for the readers.

Gyalwang Drukpa
Pema Woeling Abode
Hemis Monastery, Ladakh, India

Root Text

Text Text

A HO!
The mind is the door to everything:
Free from the net of errant duality
The primordially liberated dimension –
To this, the ultimate Guru
I sincerely pay homage.

To the Lord of Compassion, Avalokiteshvara,
To the sole protector, Mahaguru,
To Glorious Naropa and Tsangpa Gyare,
And to the continually incarnating teachers of the past,
I pay homage.

To the great teachers of the snowy realms
And emanations of former times,
To their play of knowledge and compassion,
Like the dancing reflection of the moon in water,
I pay homage.

They are the world's eyes,
And I take shelter in the blessings
Of their three secret dimensions (of body, speech and mind).
This, my humble tale, was composed
At the request of my friend Kunzang Tenzin.

These crazy ideas of mine
Are not important to recount,
But I jot them down anyway
As a joke, just to ruin your eyes.

The Lotus Lake in India
Was my birth place,
The great sacred spot of the Mahaguru
And the dance floor of the dakinis.

Who was present when I was born?
Padmasambhava's regent Dudjom Rinpoche was there
Surrounded by many male and female wisdom holders
Turning the wheel of the profound Dharma.

At sunrise on the auspicious tenth day,
During the performance of Padmasambhava's
Dance of the eight aspects,
At this wonderful moment,
Due to prior prayers,
I issued forth from the defilements of the womb.

Due to favourable karma
I emerged onto the lap
Of Zhichen Bairo, my father,
And so met the Dharma at the moment of birth,
And was blessed by a sign from Dudjom Rinpoche.

Due to past good karma ripening at this time,
I was quite happy as a child and,
Without instruction, I naturally had
A little kindness and compassion.

I have met many great teachers and studied many texts,
Easily getting the ultimate meanings,
But I still do not get many conventional meanings.
Maybe that is why it is said there is no end to what can be known.
Anyhow, I am glad to study and learn about everything,
But especially about my own practice.

If I do not become certain about it through listening and reflection
It is like having no hands and trying to scale a rock –
If I cannot grasp hold of the meaning,
I cannot properly practise.

So if you do not first listen and reflect,
But just stay in retreat to meditate,
You are like a lost helpless prisoner,
Knowing neither what to meditate on nor how.
Not knowing even the meaning of the word faith,
The chance of insight arising from practice
Is as rare as seeing a star in daylight.
These defects I have experienced myself
So I am quite motivated to listen well and reflect.

Whatever virtuous actions I have done
Are for the benefit of others and the next life,
So I avoid actions of self-interest and the eight worldly motivations[1]
Glad that I am strong enough to resist such obsessions.

Whoever bestows teachings and empowerments
Should be cherished as your very own eyes.
If you insult the teacher's consort or attendants
It is obvious your realization is far away.
Watching the actions of your teacher
And hoping they will coincide with your wishes –
This will be the source of every misfortune,
So regard every action of the teacher as perfect.

This "perfect view" sounds great,
But it is rare to find anybody correctly practising it.
That is why the "Practice Lineage" is degenerating
And just adding numbers to the ranks of the vow breakers.

It is essential to grasp a vital point – What is it?
In the Pure Realm, Buddhas appear in perfect form
To train pure beings.
But impure beings like us
Have no chance to see a perfect Buddha,
Nor to hear his voice.
For beings like us could not be tamed
By the Buddhas of the past,
And that is why our present teacher was reborn
In ordinary human form –
To help tame us.
That is why our teacher's kindness
Is far greater than that of other Buddhas –
A kindness beyond reason and logic.
The point is this:
Buddha activity is beyond conception.
The import of this vital point really astounds me!

---

1. The eight worldly motivations or dharmas: pleasure and pain, loss and gain, fame and shame, praise and blame.

Lord of Great Kindness,
Sole Protector dwelling in my heart,
For a mind free from doubt, blessings come,
But for one plagued with doubts, there is no chance.
On this it is said, "The Tantras and Upadesas both agree."
That is the counsel of Choje Ongpo,
And I have complete trust in it.

It is as if I have been given the wish-fulfilling jewel
By the saviour of beings,
Kyabgon Ontrul of Zhichen
Who is inseparable from my heart,
Filled with the three forms of faith.
This is my understanding.

These things are just a sketch of what I know,
Today's crazy ideas.
So please do not be bored by all this
And listen some more:

Toward the Great Lord Guru – my father and mother –
And towards his spiritual descendants and lineage holders,
I had natural single-minded faith, even as a child.
As a child, whenever I had good food and nice clothes
I thought they were bestowed on me
By my Great Father Padmasambhava.

These days, due to hindrances of *Kor*,[2]
My devotion is not as pure as when I was a child.
Repeatedly receiving this poison *Kor* is bad,
And I will have more to say about this presently.

---

2. *Kor/Kor-nag* (dkor-nag), lit. "offerings", "black-offerings"; a key point throughout this tale. It refers to offerings and requests poisoned by the impure motives of devotees and the spiritual obligations placed on the guru who receives such poisonous "gifts", yet is obliged to respond to requests of blessings. It also refers to the negative karma which results from accepting offerings but neglects to perform the requested spiritual activities.

In my own life I have met no enemy
Worse than such *Kor*;
I have been with this enemy a long time
And I know his faults,
So it is appropriate for me to remark on these faults.
I will explain how I got caught up with such *Kor*.

Though starting with a store of good karma,
I ended up with bad results.
But somehow, prior karma and prayer
Created this guru form of mine.

Around the age of three or four I had some memories:
The messenger of demon deceit entered me,
Going straight into my infant heart.
Thus before I could talk,
I began to give blessings with my hands,
And was thrilled when I was put on a high seat;
Even though my father struck me, trying to stop such action,
I continued to do it behind his back.

When I was able to speak, I proclaimed that
I had a monastery and a guru's residence,
And I spoke of many pointless silly things.
Just before my actual recognition (as an incarnation),
I blurted out that it was now time to depart for my monastery,
Saying farewell to my family and offering scarves.
Through such behaviour,
this 'guru' form was created without true Dharma.

Set on the throne of the eight worldly dharmas,
These hands of mine collected offerings and bestowed blessings.
At the age of eight I gave a public empowerment
Without having the proper qualities of a teacher.

At sixteen I gave a teaching on Hevajra, the king of Tantras.
I gave teachings before knowing the meaning of the words.
Before doing any practice I gave empowerments:

Doing these things was like a child's game for me
And I am not interested in recounting everything.
This is how I got involved with *Kor*,
The poison *Kor* which gradually burned my mind.

Even though others said, "This guru is really good",
They exaggerated:
These days a "good" guru is anybody
Skilled in the eight worldly dharmas.
Whoever is known as "authentic" is just
Skilled in deception.
Whoever is known as "learned" is merely
Expert in oratory –
Learned, authentic, and good
Are the three qualities of a sublime guru
Which are so loudly praised.

Thus the stream of poison *Kor* pours down like rain
And the door to hell is wide open.
So whoever lacks the three qualities
Cannot be counted among the sublime gurus –

"You are a bad person, have a bad temper,
And are from a bad family."
Thus, on and on, the mountain of abuse crashed down upon me
And I gathered the bad karma of having rejected true Dharma.

As the glorious Great Guru said:
"The times do not change, people change."
It is very sad that this is coming true.
It is really sad that the power of evil forces is increasing.
So I pray that I will not be praised and honoured with the
Poisonous virtues of being falsely learned, authentic and good.
For this praise and honour is the cause of being dragged into
Samsara.
They cause pride to increase
And disturb the development of true qualities.
Without recognizing the smell of my own rotting head
Yet pretending to help someone else,

Both of us are doomed.
This is how I have gathered terrible karma.

There are many ways to accumulate the poison *Kor*, but mainly two:
Offerings from devotees and offerings for the deceased.
When I received these, I laughed and enjoyed myself,
But neglected (my obligations) – both to the dead and to the devotees –
And this is terribly sad.

To block the development of the three kinds of wisdom;
This is the worst, isn't it!
To block the development of the three kinds of faith;
This is the worst, isn't it!
To block the development of the three kinds of training;
This is the worst, isn't it!

I cannot explain it all, but in short,

Kor is the real enemy and demon of practitioners.
It will not give a moment's peace.
It will torment the body with strange diseases,
Ruining chances for practice.
Yet when not practicing, the body and mind are fine,
Being quite healthy while doing unwholesome things
And not caring about the next life.
So whether one receives poison *Kor* oneself,
Or "benefits" from the poison *Kor* of someone else –
Teachers say it is the same thing.

So *Kor* heaped on top of *Kor*,
A guru's *Kor* is multiplied over and over,
Until even dogs start "honouring" you.

If I really think hard about the meaning
Of this poison *Kor*, then I am doing
Neither real Dharma practice nor worldly work.
I am in between, wearing Dharma robes
Which cover this body of mine infested with poison *Kor*:
I am like a pretend lion, having no essential qualities.

A TSA MA!
O dear, this really upsets me!
I have some idea how to avoid this poison *Kor*,
Which I have discovered through my precious Lord Guru's kindness.
This kind teacher is truly a Buddha,
His supreme qualities of three secret aspects
(of body, speech and mind)
I, his fortunate student, can remember,
And with great respect I can follow his way.

Oh precious Lord Guru, I call on you
To bestow your compassion!
Please do not let me fall into the pit of poisonous *Kor*!
May I be able to practise the Dharma like you!
Grant me blessings to accomplish my Dharma practice!

I have been nourished by the kindness of my father Guru
And many other teachers.
I have found the wisdom eye to discern
The difference between defects and qualities.
This achievement I realized through the kindness of my teachers.

However, regarding the path shown by the Buddha,
It is said: "Liberation depends totally on us."
So, accordingly, I understand that it is up to me
Whether I go for it or not.

Whoever does not take this path is no better than an ox.
Whoever does take this path is the best among humans.
I have the complete freedom to choose whatever I wish to do,
This is an amazingly rare chance I have got.

The habit of noting others' faults is completely wrong,
And for many years I have had this terrible custom.
For far too long I was plagued by this,
the source of all wrong actions,
Until my kind mother showed me that all the faults of others
Are one's own faults: the more one has,

The more one finds them in others –
Like reflections in a mirror.
So rejecting one's own faults is best.

Fault finding is the cause of broken Samaya between Dharma friends.
It creates terrible karma, resulting in the rejection of the Dharma.
This and much similar advice I received from my mother.
Her tender council was absorbed into my heart,
So that whenever I notice someone's faults,
I have vowed not to mention them.
This is my tale.

There are both good and bad stories,
And I should speak of them equally.
But I have far too many bad stories,
Some almost as bad as those of dogs and pigs –
So I do not want to elaborate on them.
Talk about visions of deities and the like
Is the business of worldly gurus.
I keep silent about my experiences.
If one leads a simple and happy existence,
One can actually accomplish great things
For this and future lifetimes.

In brief, (a word about my teachers):
The regent of the Lotus Born Lord,
His Holiness Dudjom Rinpoche;
And the lineage holder of the Drukpa Order,
The kindest teacher, Lord of Speech (Drukpa Thuksey);
And the Vajra Holder of the three vows, Trulshik Rinpoche;
Lords of the Mandala, actual Buddhas who eliminate all delusion –

They introduced me to the nature of existence
Through the direct experience of the Base.
The kindness of these Vajra Masters was measureless.

His Holiness the Dalai Lama is sole refuge
And protector of our social and spiritual welfare.

From Guru Khyentse Gyatso,
I received the oral transmission of Mahamudra,
Opening the Eye of Wisdom,
Discerning the difference between Dharma and non-Dharma,
Through vast kindness bestowed on me,
Great holder of the three vows,
Lord [Zhichen] Ontrul, you are the eyes of the world.

The kind spiritual father Do-Drubchen
Passed on the droplets of authentic thoughts of Longchenpa
Into the heart of this devoted son.
May you always remain as the jewel of my heart!
The great translator (Vairochana) – the Eye of the World –
Emanated as the father of this degenerate son.
The Guru, whose kindness extends to this life and the next.
May Zhichen Bairocana remain victorious!
The emanation of Vajrapani and Chakzampa (Thangtong Gyalpo),
Holding the life-line of the Oral and Treasure teachings
At the divine seat of Kathok,
May the truly fearless Moktsa excel in your activities!

I was fortunate to receive transmissions from these Buddhas,
These root and branch teachers.
Although I have not achieved
Confident realization of their teachings,
I have not displeased them.
And although I have not had prophecies induced by trance,
I am sure that I have received the blessings of their compassion.

As it is said:
"You do not need to visualize the Guru,
For he is inseparable from you;
You do not need to remember anything,
For he is always in your heart."

Although I cannot boast I have that view,
I always remember these teachers with longing –
Sometimes by recalling them, ordinary thought ceases.

Recalling their qualities often increases my faith.
Recalling my faults with remorse, I confess and renew my vows:
Reaffirming my vows with prayers,
This is my natural style.
Apart from that, I do not have much more to say.

In order to make favourable conditions purposeful,
One needs the eye which discerns and does not confuse
The actual intent of the causal and resultant vehicles.
Being clear and applying the meanings according
To the (particular) vehicle,
Through deep analysis, the essence of all the teachings
Is shown to be emptiness and compassion.

The fruit of realising this meaning comes
As the spontaneous fulfillment of benefitting others.
Until now I have not come to that,
Because of my endless busy work;
So I yearn to be in a remote hermitage
And to practise single-mindedly the Dharma I have understood.

I would like to practise in a remote place
By myself or with a Dharma friend;
Although I do not have the favourable situation of physical seclusion,
Whenever I have the chance,
I do practise in the seclusion of my mind.

Being amongst many "friends" who are contrary to the Dharma,
Does not provide the context for mental seclusion,
So I wish to avoid such "retinues" with their many activities
And just practise alone on the ultimate essence.
Friends who are uncertain about Dharma practice,
Disciples who are not enthusiastic about receiving teachings –
Such acquaintances damage both teacher and student,
And I never want to be in such a situation.

At first they see the guru as a Buddha,
Then they see the guru as a helpful human;

Finally they see the guru as their enemy, and use harsh words of abuse;
I want to avoid such disciples and go into a remote place.

Expert in praising if it benefits oneself,
Clever at avoiding what benefits others,
Clever at sowing the seeds which break Samaya –
I wish to avoid such friends and go to a remote place.
Unless I am hoping for fame, I do not need the entourage of today.
And unless they are looking for misery, they do not need a teacher like me.
As long as it is not the time to benefit others,
It is not right to have disciples:
This is repeatedly said in the Sutras and Tantras.

Therefore I wish to live in a remote place.
I wish to observe the real nature of things free from thought.
I wish to crush the shell of deluded ideas.
I wish to contemplate measureless compassion.
I wish to realize Buddha nature which is naturally present.

I should not practise Dharma for fame or profit,
And should dedicate the merit of doing practice to all beings.
Whether or not it is difficult depends on one's attitude –
If a decision is made, it is easier.

I have too many opinions;
It is impossible to write them all down.
Since so many past teachers have said:
"All appearances and existence should be seen as a teaching,"
I need to really think about the meaning of this,
Even though I do not have the sharpest of minds.

Yet knowing my own emotions create both pleasure and pain,
With conditions and companions always changing,
Impermanence and suffering, karma and its results,
Interdependence and the union of appearance and emptiness –
These I know as true teachers, showing what is real.
These I know as true teachers, pointing out defects.
These I know as true teachers, crushing arrogance.
These I know as true teachers, driving one towards Dharma.

These I know as true teachers, causing compassion to grow.

When I sometimes have a little insight about this,
According to my training, I feel this is truly
Receiving the guru's blessings.
So, to the gurus I intensely pray,
And am quite happy when I feel their kindness.

Apart from this, receiving a guru's "blessing"
Is merely like the pleasure of sex,
Or the bliss of being drunk or dizzy,
And this kind of "blessing" is not useful.
I have never received a blessing like this from my teachers,
And do not expect to in the future.

In fact, all appearance arises as the bliss state;
And the essence of this bliss being emptiness,
How can the net of attachment and aversion trap it?
How can the lasso rope of grasping and clinging tie it up?
Common bliss binds one through attachment and grasping –
Even dogs and pigs have this kind.

Common emptiness is like an empty cup.
But real emptiness means there is nothing whatsoever
To establish (as empty),
And yet the internal pulsing of
Real emptiness vibrates everywhere:
This is the union of emptiness and clarity, as I understand it.

A RE TSAR!
The bliss state is amazing!
But the union (of bliss and emptiness) is even more amazing!
Well, actually it is not so amazing.
We should really wonder about our assumptions,
For the really amazing thing is our habit of inquiry:
We perceive as dual the non-dual state.
We perceive as separate the unified state.
We perceive as existing, things which do not exist
And we perceive as non-existing, things which do exist!

Existing and non-existing things are creations of the mind
And these magical things are truly amazing.
Their ultimate view is the extreme of eternalism;
Their meditation is trapped in the shell of clinging;
Their conduct according to the eight worldly dharmas is quite active –
Such yogis are truly amazing!

We are the real magicians,
For in actual fact nothing exists.
Pleasure and pain are created by attraction and aversion,
Grasping attractions magically creates things,
And if we analyse this thoroughly,
We cannot be certain that even we exist.
I laugh when I think about daytime happenings;
I laugh when I think about continual change;
I laugh when I think about attachment and aversion;
I laugh when I think about pleasure and pain –
Maybe I am possessed by demons, I am not sure.

I call on you, my teachers – regard me with compassion!
I sincerely wish to receive your blessings.
Please regard your child's longing desire.
Please bless me with the resolve (to attain realization).
Please bless me to have a steady and smooth mind,
So that for this life and those to follow,
As a true practitioner whose heart and mind are in accord,
The special intention (to help others) is spontaneously present.
May I be able to benefit measureless beings.
Without the toxic stains of a competitive mind,
Without the intoxicating liquor of anger and lust,
May I be able to practise the peaceful and soothing Dharma.
May I be able to give teachings diligently.

Through listening and thinking and examining,
Especially about those teachings I practise,
May I be able to precisely determine their meaning;
Raising the victorious banner of ultimate practice,
May I be able to accomplish great service to the Dharma.

This is the way I pray, all the time,
And I request all of you to support my prayers.
These are my insane suggestions,
These are my crazy ways of thinking,
The shapes of a madman's musings.

The words are boring,
And the composition is lousy.
So there is nothing admirable here
For all those learned ones.

Since there is no mix of the eight worldly dharmas,
It is difficult to satisfy worldly-minded people.
This chatter is neither for the learned, nor for the worldly –
It is only suitable for crazies like me.

By spreading this kind of nonsense
May all innumerable beings be freed from their endless activities.
May they reach the state free from birth.
This, my own tale, is a lunatic's sketch, drawn from the heart,
I wrote down whatever came to mind, without distortion.
It has nothing to do with "benefitting beings"
It is pure gossip.

This was done in the Maratika Cave (in Nepal)
Known as Great Bliss Dharmadhatu
By one holding the name Kyabgon Drukpa XII
Commonly called Padma Wangchen,
At the age of twenty-eight.

On the 25th day, the feast-day of the dakinis,
I wrote this during a break in my practice.
May it transmit the auspicious
Union of bliss and emptiness!

Translated from the handwritten original, at the request of His Holiness the Gyalwang Drukpa, by Bhakha Tulku Rinpoche and Steven Goodman, on the 25th day of the first month of the Water Monkey Year (28 March 1992) in Berkeley, California.
May it benefit all beings!

Introduction

A HO!

"*Aho!*" is an exclamatory term used to express surprise, amazement and, sometimes, sadness. But in the present context, I may have used the term to call out to friends sharing the same fortune as I, asking them to listen to the song of amazing illusions that appear in the mind of a crazy man.

According to tradition, before we start anything, we invoke the higher beings remembering their graciousness and qualities. Doing this brings auspiciousness, benefitting oneself as well as others, whether one is undertaking mundane or spiritual activities. It helps in preventing the influence of anger, pride and arrogance, caused by ignorant clinging, during the activity one is involved in.

IDENTIFYING QUALITIES AND FAULTS

The differentiation between higher and lower beings is based solely on the qualities and faults of the nature of mind of those beings. This differentiation cannot be based on race, birth or social status. If the qualities or shortcomings are based solely on religious or worldly criteria, then instead of understanding, it will lead to controversy and conflict and ultimately there will be no grounds from which the qualities can be interpreted. Something that religion regards as weakness could be seen as a quality from the worldly point of view and vice versa.

Even within religions there are many different philosophies and views, and no religion can be singled out as the perfect one. Objectively speaking, even our religious views are coloured by our worldly outlook, and as such, until and unless one breaks the shackles of selfishness it would be very difficult to attain any profound or ultimate result. So long as one insists that one's tradition is the best, and with a strong sense of attachment and aversion, describes all other religions as bad and wrong, I believe there would not be any difference between the worldly attitude and the spiritual view. Respecting religious traditions, followed by oneself and others, that have been established on the basis of temporary requirements, if one follows and practices them with diligence, one will understand not only that having different names for the teachers and traditions is like childish play, but ultimately attains the equanimity view. Reaching such a stage of understanding makes one a true spiritual practitioner.

In practical terms, by understanding mundane thoughts and one's own views, one will get rid of the two poisons of attachment towards one's views and hatred or aversion towards others' views. One's mind will then undergo a definite change, transcending the mundane view and attitude. Gradually, misconceptions and discomfort will cease among the various religious traditions and this will usher in the noble behaviour of mutual respect, love and mutual appreciation.

I do not see much difference between such spiritual practitioners, whatever religious tradition they may follow, because such a practitioner would naturally have equal love for all beings in this world, without discrimination, like a mother who loves her child. Such a person would only think of helping beings and not of harming them and become what is known as the "unknown benefactor".

PRIDE LEADS TO ONE'S DOWNFALL

Generally speaking a spiritual practitioner should not have any feelings of hatred. However, in our world we see different religious traditions criticizing each other and destroying and plundering the shrines belonging to other traditions. History shows that wars have been fought, killing innumerable people and destroying towns and villages, in the name of religion, fostering anger and hatred in the heart of the people for generations. The disfigured images of gods and deities that we see today are a disgrace to religion. Seeing these images the youth today will naturally abhor religion. When I see such images I too wonder why people do such abominable and stupid things in the name of serving one's religion.

There are so many religions in the world and some religions may teach that it is right to hate other religions or to totally destroy other religions and their followers, and regard anyone who does so as a person of high standing. All that I have learned so far is that all religions teach abstinence from selfishness and anger, and advocate helping others. Whether this is being practiced is another matter. If all that is being taught is put into practice, all spiritual practitioners in this world would be like siblings of one family, helping and supporting one another, and all beings would live happily. Then one would not see the tragic situation of today, with people resorting to violence in the name of religion. An objective analysis, by people with wisdom, could reveal how this situation came about. It would be pointless for someone like me to dwell on this.

MISTAKING NON-SECTARIANISM WITH IMPRUDENCE

There are many written works stating that lay people should be broad-minded and tolerant. Elderly people also give the same advice. So I see no reason why spiritual practitioners should not be broad-minded and adopt a broader perspective. Broad-mindedness certainly does not mean confused indifference. Nowadays, some people consider following a guru[3] and practicing a particular tradition with dedication, as being rigid and a weakness and opt to stay aloof and alone, not following any teacher, guru or their parents, just like a stray dog following whoever feeds them, claiming to be non-sectarian. Such people can be seen in society in general and also among neo-Buddhists. I asked some Buddhist "practitioners" who was their guru and what practice they did and with great pride they told me that they were non-sectarian and, as such, they did not have any root guru and did not do any particular practice.

It is difficult to say whether such a non-sectarian attitude is beneficial or harmful. Just as we need to use the staircase to go to the roof of the house, whatever one's birth and religion may be – due to one's karma – it is common knowledge that one should be groomed in a traditional value system in order to lead a happy life, benefitting oneself as well as others.

The teachings of all religions, Buddhist or non-Buddhist, are based on altruism. On this basis, prayers are said, offerings made and non-violence practised in order to improve upon the religious view, ultimately leading to one's spiritual development. Such a spiritual development becomes apparent when one is able to live harmoniously in society, uphold one's religious views with intelligence and yet show respect and tolerance to other religions. Such a person will stand out in society for his/her humility, broad-mindedness and good relations with everyone. Such a person will be

---

3. Guru is the Sanskrit word and also equivalent to the Tibetan word "Lama" (bla-ma) in Tibetan, which means "none higher" and denotes a spiritual preceptor who guides others on the path of enlightenment.

genuinely non-sectarian. All these qualities are achieved through the development of the mind.

The suffering that all sentient beings do not want and the happiness that all beings seek are the results of one's physical actions and speech. All physical actions and speech are preceded by emotion. One indulges in non-virtuous activities like killing, stealing, lying or using abusive language *etc.* at the instigation of, what is called, one's non-virtuous mind or non-meritorious mind. As a result, one has to unwillingly experience the unspeakable sufferings of the hells, the hungry ghost and other realms. Even if you do not accept such realms exist, the sufferings caused by wars, famines, floods and earthquakes can be seen in this world. These can be called "the suffering of misery". Even though one has gross obscurations caused by selfishness, by the influence of the virtuous mind, one can engage in virtuous deeds like saving lives giving alms. As a result one can enjoy temporary happiness such as a good physique, health, wealth and long life. These are what the scriptures call, "the suffering of change".

The one-pointed mind that is not distracted by other influences is called the meditative mind, non-fabricated by hope and doubt of the highs and lows, the good and bad or joy and sorrow, and is a form of contemplation. The outcome of such contemplation is rebirth in the higher or god realm. Although gross suffering is absent in these realms, it is said that the beings there are not free of their mind, so they experience subtle "suffering of conditioning". There is no need to insist that this is true because the Buddha said so. Even scientists, who are the main protagonists of materialism, have not been able to point their finger to anything other than the mind. Today, the scientists are showing interest in this subject and they may have found something.

BUDDHA: THE REAL SCIENTIST

I always say that Buddha is a great scientist. Buddha calls the mind "the king of all activities". A bad king does not bother about the well-being and happiness of his subjects and a good king will always keep his subjects happy. Similarly, a bad mind will instigate bad activities, leading to sufferings and a good mind will engage in good deeds, leading to happiness as mentioned earlier. Diligent practice of the three-fold trainings and the Six Paramitas,[4] inspired by the pure unusual mind, greater than any other kind heart, and mentioned in the Mahayana Sutras, leads to the attainment of a temporary state of happiness of gods and human beings and the ultimate bliss of omniscience. Similarly, the practice of compassion leads to the development of exalted wisdom, and meditating on the union of these two, according to the instructions of one's guru, leads to the attainment of nirvana or enlightenment. At this stage there is no selfish effort for a higher state of birth or happiness in this life or the next as there is in the lower vehicle.

By practising ethical behaviour as the foundation and contemplation as the path, with the sole purpose of attaining enlightenment for the well-being of all sentient beings, one achieves wisdom and generates it further through meditation. As such it is called "unusual" since it is different from the other paths.

What then makes the good mind and the bad mind? The affliction of selfishness generates the bad mind and the altruistic mind, with a lesser affliction of selfishness, generates the good mind. Affliction can be described as suffering, or as if someone is causing pain, because this affliction does not leave one alone and makes one do a lot of things, causing rebirth in various realms, experiencing suffering and without being liberty.

The good news is that when you investigate the origin of affliction you find that it is caused by the illusory mind that believes in the existence of the "I" – that actually does not exist. Once you begin to gain an understanding of the non-existence of "I" and ultimately gain experiential confidence, just as there is no darkness where there is light, the cause of suffering vanishes and one attains the realization of selflessness. For this reason, affliction is called incidental defilement. Uttara Tantra and other scriptures mention that the mind is not inherently defiled by affliction. Therefore, as the mind becomes purified of the affliction of selfishness, one begins to gradually experience mundane happiness and ultimately develop all the profound and vast qualities – completely. As the incidental afflictions, such as selfishness and other illusory defilements, and

---

4. Transcendent Perfections, namely generosity, discipline, patience, diligence, meditative concentration and wisdom; comprise the training of a Bodhisattva, which is Bodhicitta in action.

their residues, become purified, they will no doubt be replaced by the inherent qualities of "the ten powers"[5] and "the four fearlessnesses".[6]

It is said: "The mind free of ego is the Buddha" and this mind is called the precious nature of mind. In some Tantras it is called the primordial mind. Beyond this, there is no basis for the designation of quality and hence the invocation is made to the primordial mind as the precious guru. If one ponders over the immeasurable compassion, as mentioned in the common practice, or the secret ultimate guru mentioned in the secret Vajrayana, one definitely gains new confidence that the Buddha is a unique teacher. I say new confidence because the meanings of the root texts such as "Praise to the Noble One" *etc.* were explained to me by my tutors and by many khenpos since I was young. What the materialistic scientists today proudly declare as their findings, after years of research using modern technology, was known to the Buddha over 2500 years ago. This fact gives a new feeling of amazement and confidence.

---

5. The ten powers of Tathagatha are: 1. the power of intention; 2. the power of resolute intention; 3.the power of retention; 4. the power of concentration; 5. the power of perfect application; 6. the power of confidence; 7. the power of conduct; 8. the power of prayers; 9. the power of great love and compassion; 10. the power of the blessings of all the Buddhas.
6. The four fearlessnesses of a Buddha with respect to the assertion of: 1.one's complete and perfect extinguishment of all negativities for the purpose of oneself; 2. one's complete and perfect accomplishment of knowledge for the purpose of oneself; 3. revealing the path of antidotes for the purpose of others; 4. revealing the eliminations for the purpose of others.

CHAPTER 1

Invocation

> The mind is the door to everything:
> Free from the net of errant duality
> The primordially liberated dimension –
> To this, the ultimate Guru
> I sincerely pay homage.

Just as it is said, "Previous to the guru, even the name of Buddha did not exist," all Sutras and Tantras agree that in order to gain complete knowledge of the path one has to rely on a guru. This fact can be proved by intellectual investigation also. For example, if a person is travelling in the wrong direction he or she will continue to go in that direction until he or she meets an experienced and knowledgeable person. Once this experienced person shows them the right direction, the traveller will realize that they had been going in the wrong direction so far, and which path to follow to go in the right direction. They will then make an effort to follow the right direction.

Similarly, until and unless we meet a spiritual teacher, a guru or a master to show us the right path, we will cling to the illusory phenomena as the truth, and be bound in an endless cycle of attachment and aversion. Instead of us controlling wealth and fame, we will become their slaves and work day and night to gain them. This is how we have been for life after life.

After the guru introduces the illusory nature of appearances and all grasping as misconception of existence of self, where no self exists and shows the path of union of compassion and emptiness one begins to look at life from a different angle and develops wisdom through learning and reflection. As the vague new perception gradually becomes more stable through experience, a special sense of joy grows in one's mind. As one's aversion to grasping of mundane wealth, pleasure and fame increases, one begins to gain control over all temporary worldly phenomena such as power and wealth, not to mention the ultimate fruit; and when they cease to control you, an immeasurable joy and pleasure can be experienced. As a consequence of this joy, when one applies the precept heard earlier to one's daily life and persists with its familiarization, one is able to reverse the wrong path, that of the attachment to illusion as the truth, and instead one follows the correct path to a state of happiness.

ALL EXTERNAL APPEARANCES AND EXISTENCES ARE TEACHERS

The guru is described in three forms: external, internal and secret. The external guru is the teacher in human form who shows us the path. It is also known as the external guru of conventional symbol. However, the guru in human form is not the only external guru. The rotation of the earth around the sun and the moon around the earth, seasonal changes, the appearance of trees, leaves and fruits, the happy and sad emotions and moment to moment changes in one's life are all teachers of impermanence, teachers of emptiness, and teachers of cause and effect. But in order to understand this, not just verbally but experientially, one has to approach a guru in human form and receive blessings and teachings.

RECOGNIZING THE VIRTUOUS AND NON-VIRTUOUS TEACHERS

The guru in human form can be one of two kinds: virtuous or non-virtuous. The non-virtuous teacher and a non-virtuous friend are the same.

A person in the garb of a spiritual master who gives the profound teachings, empowerments and transmissions of the secret Mantrayana casually without testing or checking the students, simply to gain offerings or fame; someone wearing the mask of religion, who teaches selfishness through sectarianism, wrong views and competition; a person who does not know the essence of the two truths or the attributes of disciples; a person who looks at the path as contradictions and mixes the teachings of Sutra and Tantra texts, the higher and lower vehicles and Dzogchen;[7] a person who has superficial knowledge of spiritual terms like Mahamudra,[8] Dzogchen, Middle Path and omnipresent

---

7. Dzogpachenpo or Great Completion is a term exclusive to the doctrine and meditation of Nyingma School of Tibetan Buddhism. It is the spontaneous and natural perfection of fully enlightened qualities possessed by the three kayas within the reality of mind: the primordially empty nature of Dharmakaya, the naturally luminous Sambhogakaya and all-pervasive compassion Nirmanakaya.
8. Mahamudra, the Great Seal. The Great Seal of emptiness, an exalted meditation on the nature of mind particularly associated with the Kagyudpa School of Tibetan Buddhism.

self-perfection, and teaches non-existence of cause and effect, that all appearances and stirrings are Dharmakaya or Dzogchen, and that one can indulge in any irregular conduct, and shows the non-virtuous path is called the non-virtuous teacher.

A person who fulfills others' material needs and appears as a friend, but in reality encourages others to engage in unethical activities for the sake of wealth and fame, and turns the mind towards negativity, is a non-virtuous friend. There is not much difference between the non-virtuous teacher and non-virtuous friend.

BE SMART WHILE LOOKING FOR A GOOD FRIEND

Just as when looking for a genuine spiritual teacher, it is equally important to find a sincere and true friend with the genuine qualities of a kind heart, instead of mistaking someone with good looks, or someone who gives you money, as one's friend. Otherwise, one will be doomed in this life as well as the next, if one believes in life after death. Even if one does not believe in life after death, one can see that most of the youths who indulge in unethical behaviour have been influenced by bad friends. We are born in the realm of desire and the male-female relationship exists even among small insects. However, importance should not be given to good looks or financial standing.

In the beginning of a relationship, everyone talks about how much they love each other and how they would give their life for love. The good looks, the charming voice, their sweet fragrance, the softness of their touch and expression of passion and love by one's partner seem unreal and dream-like. It is the first big step in life to not be deluded at that stage, and to investigate how that expression of love is, from the point of view of the mind. It is important to check one's mind, check the nature of the object of love, analyse the object of beauty, part by part, and ponder on the impermanent nature of appearance. It is important to check in various ways.

Love can be of two types: long term and short term. Long term love can be described as the wish to share one's life with the other person, both in this life and in many lives to come. For a Buddhist, for example, it would be the wish to share one's life with that person, life after life, through happiness and sorrow, until enlightenment. Such friends will not discuss wealth and looks, but give importance to encouraging each other to follow the virtuous path and accumulate merit. In the short span of their lives they will share, they will talk about the importance of good health, and peace of mind, taking medicine and the right diet, and try to become a good person in society. At the same time, they will support and help each other in earning wealth.

Whether it is long-term love or short-term love, one should not be self-centred but have a genuine wish to help one's friend. Today, most people blindly follow whatever they hear or see at the beginning of a relationship and ultimately have to face a lot of trouble.

A GURU MUST HAVE ALL THE QUALITIES DESCRIBED IN THE TEXT

It is the same with a guru. One has to keep on searching until one meets someone with the qualities described in the scriptures of the lower and higher vehicles. Buddha has described the qualities of a guru in the common Vinaya as well as in the higher Tantras, such as Dzogchen and Mahamudra. It would not be correct to behave like a hungry, wild animal when it sees meat. That is why the Buddha has described the qualities systematically. Today, when people follow a guru they do not look at the qualities of the guru but instead go after the fame, the large following, the external behaviour and endearing manner of speech. As a result, in the Sangha community today, we see a lot of confused people who, after practising Dharma for a long time, end up with disbelief in the Dharma, or sectarian feelings, criticizing the guru and abusing others, look down on spiritual friends of the same mandala, scorning the law of karma and creating disunity. This is one reason the Dharma is degenerating.

INTERNAL UNITY WILL MAKE EXTERNAL WORK SUCCESSFUL

If the members of a family remain together and united they are bound to make progress. If instead the father abuses the mother, the mother looks down on the father, parents deceive their children and children deceive their parents; if the mother of the house exploits her servants and scolds them and the servants lie and steal: such a family will not prosper. If there is no unity within, it will be difficult to face external problems. If one believes in life after death, then such a situation will not only lead to unhappiness in this life but also to birth in the lower realms. This can be understood if one looks back at the situation of Tibet and Tibetans.

The same can be seen in the histories of the world, East or West. One need not look at ancient history. When the Muslim fundamentalists destroyed a huge statue of the Buddha using explosives, recently in Afghanistan (Bamiyan), the Buddhist community in the world could not do anything. The UN said something about protecting heritage but actually did nothing. There may have been protests in some remote corners of the world but nothing global happened. The reason is lack of unity.

UNITY MEANS UNDERSTANDING AND RESPECT

I don't think unity means living under suppression and fear. It means an atmosphere of mutual friendship and love, and this depends on education. It is important to have a proper understanding of the worldly or spiritual tradition that one follows. After all, knowledge can bring about the power of unity when it comes to religion and culture, and whether individually one is a good or bad person does not matter. This is an important positive condition. Unity is extremely important.

UNITY THROUGH MONEY, POWER AND ELOQUENCE

Deceiving others through the use of eloquent speech, or winning over others by bribing them is not unity. Such an act may be superficially useful like a pain killer. Such methods have been adopted for centuries in both the mundane and the spiritual world. One can see this happening in the world even today.

UNITY MEANS RESPECTING OTHERS THROUGH INTROSPECTION

So then how should unity be defined? It means mutual respect irrespective of social status, wealth, scholarship or foolishness. There seems to be many types of respect: respect for others' wealth, knowledge, looks, beauty, or power. The respect we are talking about here is an introspective appreciation of others' good thoughts and deeds and seeing others' negativities as being due to the influence of ignorance, just as with oneself. A new understanding based on wisdom is needed.

Developing internal qualities and the correct external behaviour in society, through practicing loving kindness and showing effective respect for wealth, religion and culture, can bring about true unity. Acharya Dignaga[9] said that Buddhism should be practised and taught through scripture and logic. It means that violence is no justification. I feel knowledge is very important, not only for Buddhism but in the spiritual and mundane world as well. The great scholar-saint Mipham[10] has said, "If they don't resort to using sticks and stones to beat me, than I can't be beaten in terms of scriptural knowledge and logic."

So violence and suppression of others may work for some time. World history shows that suppression and exploitation has been used to achieve political ends. The use of violence and suppressive measures may work for some time. Political rulers have used suppression and exploitation over the centuries to remain in power. Similarly, even in the monastic set up, except for some of the genuine masters and abbots, many others have used authority, eloquence and money to retain power in the name of religion. However, ultimately they fall down and cause a lot of social damage.

SCHOLARS SHOULD USE SCRIPTURAL CITATIONS AND LOGIC FOR UNITY

Looking back on past history makes one feel ashamed. Instead of holding and spreading the spiritual path through scriptural citations and logic, and promoting unity through mutual respect, violence has been used. The saddest thing, it seems, is that instead of helping and benefitting others, their lives have been wasted through suppression and oppression. Many people have studied the scriptures and logic extensively and many have used the scriptures and logic as a weapon, like stones and sticks, to settle internal feuds or bully others into subjugation, instead of using the scriptural citations and logic to guide those lingering on the philosophical borders, or causing harm

---

9. An Indian Buddhist scholar of the fifth century, famed for his mastery of logic.
10. Ju Mipham Jamyang Namgyal Gyatsho (1857–1912).

to innumerable beings out of ignorance of the law of karma, onto the path of enlightenment.

Today, it seems very few are able to use Buddhist scripture and logic to lead beings onto the right path. The great work done by the Six Ornaments[11] and the Two Supreme Ones,[12] and especially Dignaga and Dharmakirti,[13] during their time, is common knowledge. These days we can hear, reflect and contemplate with confidence, thanks to them. Those who have studied the scriptures and logic should follow their example. Using debating skills to crush one's opponents, followers of other vehicles or other traditions within the same religious system, is a shameful thing to do. Similarly, those who are skilled in explaining the scriptures should use their skills to explain that the common purpose of the different religions and traditions is to tame the beings according to their disposition and intellectual capacity, and that the ultimate goal is the same, and to generate devotion and pure vision in the mind-stream of the disciples, instead of fanning the differences among various religious traditions. Those with literary skills and familiarity with grammar and poetry should use their skill to explain the Buddha's philosophy, the theory of cause and effect, how to accumulate virtue and abandon moral wrong doings. In short, they should explain the relationship between the view of dependent origination and non-violent conduct, and how to practise it. Praising one's own tradition and criticizing others' may fulfill selfish ends, but it will create disunity and a loss to the community. I am just saying whatever comes to my mind. There may be a bit of truth in it. Otherwise, it's just pure gossip.

CHECK BEFORE FOLLOWING A GURU

How does one check whether the guru is genuinely qualified? It is said that we should check from both the worldly and spiritual point of view. However, the most important way is to check the guru in accordance with the Vinaya, Sutras and Abhidharma as the

---

11. The Six Ornaments are: Vasubandhu, Asanga, Nagarjuna, Aryadeva, Dignaga and Dharmakirti.
12. The Supreme Ones are: Nagarjuna and Asanga.
13. A great Indian Buddhist scholar of seventh century who composed "Extensive Commentary on Valid Cognition".

testimony. But for people like us who do not have extensive learning, the criterion should be to check whether the guru's mind is blended with Dharma or not.

GURU OF THE LOWER VEHICLE

The teachings of Buddhism are divided into various categories, such as the Lower Vehicle of the Shravaka and Pratyeka Buddha, the Mahayana, or Great Vehicle, of the Bodhisattva and the Secret Vajrayana *etc.*, according to the motivation of the practice. A guru of the Lower Vehicle must have the Praktimoksha and other basic vows as prescribed by the scripture, completed ten years after full ordination, and kept the vows intact. In brief, he or she should possess the qualities of nobility and skill in teaching.

GURU OF MAHAYANA

Generally speaking, the important qualities that a Mahayana spiritual teacher should possess are altruistic motivation, a compassionate mind and never abandoning beings. The qualities or flaws are based on the degree of selfishness. Earlier, while discussing a good or bad friend, qualities and flaws were mentioned and it was stated that love has to be judged by the degree of selfishness present. Similarly, a guru too would have qualities and flaws, but the key theme is the degree of selfishness. However many qualities such a teacher may possess, if there is a strong presence of selfishness then all other qualities turn into flaws. In addition to knowledge of the three Pitakas,[14] many texts mention the necessity of the Bodhisattva's absence of selfishness. One can also understand this through inferential perception. Such a teacher must possess ten qualities, such as avoiding harm in every way, being peaceful, disciplined and having an appeasing disposition.

GURU OF THE HIGHER TANTRAYANA

With vows of individual liberation as the foundation, a guru of the secret Vajrayana must possess love and compassion for others as well as the other qualities described above for the Hinayana and

---

14. The three baskets of scriptural collections: Sutra, Abhidharma and Vinaya.

Mahayana, but tens of thousands of times greater, undimmed, and in addition, the qualities mentioned in the Four Tantras[15] and other texts. His or her mind must be ripened with empowerment and the lineage of the empowerment must be excellent. He or she must have pure devotion for their own guru, looking at him as the Buddha, and the secret commitment (Samaya) between them should be spotlessly clean, in body, speech and mind. His or her explanation of the profound view of Mahamudra or Dzogchen should not be mere verbal expounding, like the sound made by the river flowing in the valley, but based on genuine experiential understanding and realization. It must be checked whether he or she is willing to give the teachings to anyone who requests them, without discriminating on the basis of wealth, eloquence or behaviour of the disciple, out of love and compassion. It is important to check whether selfishness is present. The Samaya between the said guru and his or her guru must also be checked to see whether it is pure and unbroken. Many past masters have said that if the Samaya in the lineage of the guru is somehow adulterated or broken, then how much effort one may make in practising love and compassion, generation stage and completion stage, the Dzogchen view or Mahamudra meditation, or the profound middle way – no progress can be achieved on the path. Obstacles such as physical and mental illness, disharmony among disciples and inauspiciousness will follow in this life and the next. Considering the risks, it is paramount that one should be very careful when looking for a guru.

FUNNY UTTERANCES OF IGNORANCE

Today most of us deem that it may not be necessary for a Vajracharya of the secret Mantrayana to possess other qualities such as a peaceful and disciplined disposition *etc.*, if the Vajracharya knows the rituals of empowerment. It is also assumed that such a guru would eat meat and drink alcohol. Many people have told me so, some as a joke and some seriously. It seems that to cover one's own guilt about consuming meat and alcohol they say that they are not banned in secret Mantrayana.

Some have asked me, "Why is it that genuine gurus of Tantrayana

---

15. Kriya, Charya, Yoga and Anuttarayoga Tantra.

today do not consume meat and alcohol?" Such questions do sound accusative but you cannot blame them. You have the right to ask if you don't know something. It is also assumed that if a guru is in monk's robes that he has to belong to the new school, and one in the form of a householder has to belong to the Nyingma or old school of Buddhism; assuming that the old Tantra school does not have a community of monks, and that any practitioner of Vinaya is not included in the old school. Similarly, assuming that the new school does not have lay practitioners of Tantra because any lay practitioner of Tantra, however qualified such a person may be, is not accepted as a guru of the new school. One hears that some gurus have even been expelled from the monasteries, thereby accumulating negative karma. Looking back at history one comes across many dirty tales. There are instances of disciples first receiving teachings and initiations from a guru, and after having completed a certain stage of practice, the disciples then accuse the guru of having a consort and of lacking knowledge of the scriptures, and then he is killed and his monasteries, titles and followers are all taken over. It seems many are engaged in such uncivilised activities, immoral from both the spiritual and worldly point of view.

Maybe every part of the world has a similar story to tell. However, it is so inappropriate and shameful to hear of such things happening in Tibetan monasteries. We proudly claim to be Buddhists, Mahayana practitioners and Vajrayana practitioners, and engaging in such perverted activities, while making such claims is unseemly and sinful. This means accumulating the causes of the hell of endless torment. But then very few people believe in life after death today.

BROADMINDEDNESS THROUGH WIDER VISION AND AN ABILITY TO STAND ALONE BECAUSE OF EXTENSIVE KNOWLEDGE

So there is no need to discuss all this. The suffering everyone experienced after the turmoil in Tibet should be enough to understand this. I was born in India and in a way, I am an Indian. But Tibetan history shows that at one time Tibet was a very powerful nation, even more glorious and influential than the neighbouring countries. But the situation is different today. It is said that the 13th Dalai Lama wanted to start an English school and students were recruited for this. However, the heads of the big monasteries were not in favour of this school and gave the excuse that this would not help beings or the Dharma and shut the school down. One of the funniest excuses the monastic heads made, with a great fuss, was the claim that the children playing football, was like the act of kicking the head of the Buddha and that it was a subversive game!

I don't know to what extent that story is true, but there has to be some truth in it. Under such circumstances, even the Dalai Lama didn't have much power and the school had to be closed. Consequently, Tibetan children lacked exposure to modern education and the people had to suffer for many years. Our society has thus suffered extreme shortcomings, both worldly and spiritual, due to biased education and a narrow vision, scholarly pretensions without complete learning, and the pretence of discipline without reversing the worldly thoughts. In the future, too there is the danger of making such mistakes again, due to differing opinions. Therefore, it is important to have extensive learning and a broader vision, broad-mindedness and the ability to stand alone.

UNBIASED LEARNING, REFLECTION AND MEDITATION

Since we claim to be practitioners of the three vehicles it is important to undergo complete learning, reflection and meditation under the guidance of a good spiritual master. Regarding complete learning, my guru, the late Ontrul Rinpoche, used to say that since there is no end to knowledge there cannot be complete learning as such, but if you follow unbiased learning, reflection and meditation with diligence, after some time your mind will undergo an experience like taking off your hat, and an unobstructed inner knowledge of worldly and spiritual matters will emerge. Such an experience may be called complete learning.

A FULLY ORDAINED PRACTITIONER IS THE BEST TEACHER OF VAJRAYANA

Some of the novice disciples feel and say that a master with a consort is a teacher of Vajrayana and one without consort cannot be a Vajrayana master or, even if he is regarded as a Vajrayana master, he would not be as effective. I think this is a misconception. An acquaintance of mine once said to me, "I am not making much progress in experience and realization. Perhaps the reason for this could be that my guru is an adherent of the Vinaya codes. Would it be better to receive teachings from a guru with a consort? What do you think?"

I thought that the fact that he is asking such a question shows his interest in the Dharma, which is good. I told him that the Kalachakra and all the new and old Tantras mention that the teacher or practitioner of Tantra, besides possessing all the qualities described in the lower vehicles, qualities such discipline, love, compassion and Bodhicitta *etc.*, they possess, should have these qualities a hundred or a thousand times more so. A Vajrayana teacher in the form of a monk following the Vinaya codes is the best practitioner of Vajrayana. If one goes through the standard scriptures, it becomes clear that it is not right to appear surprised at practising the Sutras, or performing rituals with confidence just because one has some skill in holding the Vajra and bell, reciting prayers and making offerings. I realized that it is not easy for someone like me, who is neither a layman nor a monk, to be a Vajracharya or a guru of Vajrayana practices.

VAJRAYANA PRACTICE AND DRAMA

My root gurus often lamented that people these days run away when you talk about novice vows and full ordination, but swoop like flies on rotten meat whenever they hear about Vajrayana initiations and teachings being given. Yet the number of people paying attention to upholding the Samaya (secret pledge) afterwards is as scarce as stars during day time. My guru, Ontrul Rinpoche, used to say that today the practitioners and monasteries don't care about the three basic rituals[16] and fasting practice, indulge in consumption of meat and alcohol on the pretext of doing great sadhana[17] without any secret pledge, and people without devotion watch dancing gestures and mudras being performed without any meditative stabilisation. With only the eight worldly motivations in mind, they unabashedly compare whose ritual objects of religious service are more splendid, which chant master has a

---

16. 1. Bi-monthly restoration and confession ceremony; 2. Summer or monsoon retreat for three months; 3. The ceremony of lifting restrictions after the completion of the three-month retreat.
17. A tantric liturgy or liturgical manual, *i.e.*, the instructions to carry out a ritual.

more sonorous voice, which monastery is bigger and has more monks, etc. Looking at all these behaviours, perhaps the time described by Guru Padmasambhava as "the time of secret mantra becoming just a ritual chanting" has come about. This is a sign of our times.

My guru often used to say, "Before the Chinese came to Tibet, there was a time when everyone engaged in such activity. The ritual small drums were, for example, devoid of the quality and properties defined in the Tantra, heavily adorned with turquoise and coral and difficult to lift. Even though knowledge of the scriptures was lacking, the scripture holders were covered with brocade and decorated with silver on the sides and gold-plated engraved silver flowers on the borders. It was unbearable to even look at them." He recalled some elderly monks of his seat, Zhichen Monastery, telling him that once Terton Lerab Lingpa, popularly known as Terton Sogyal (1856–1926), the great Vajrayana master, teacher of the 13th Dalai Lama and recognized as the regent of Guru Padmasambhava, had visited their monastery and gave Guhyagarbha initiation to the monks. When the monastery's vase, which was made of gold and adorned with jewels, and which was kept in the Mandala, was handed over to him, he said, "This is too heavy. Leave it. This small vase which I had placed on the head of the Dalai Lama should suffice," and took out a small smooth bronze vase, measuring one *Khyi*,[18] from his pocket. So it seems that great yogis and genuine masters may indulge in splendour with special reasons to benefit the Dharma and beings. Otherwise, if gurus and disciples like us engage in such activity it would be stupid and meaningless and more like a drama.

In Darjeeling where I live, when local devotees request the monastery to send monks to do prayers and rituals at home, they ask for *Bajawala* which in their local dialect means monk musicians! The use of the term may be correct but when one ponders on it, it feels uncomfortable and funny. Similarly, in the sacred Vajrayana dances the deities come out to liberate the beings on sight, but today it is seen as an entertainment and is called a "Lama Dance".

Last year a Tibetan newspaper carried a report on a function held in Dharamsala on the occasion of Tsechu festival.[19] It said that "after

---

18. Breadth of the hand with the thumb extended.
19. 10th day of the 5th Tibetan lunar month observed as the birthday of Guru Padmasambhava.

all the guests were seated on the dais, the performance of the Eight Manifestations of Guru Rinpoche was presented for entertainment."

When I saw this report, I felt sad and thought, "Oh my... what a pity. They surely would have devotion to Vajrayana and Guru Rinpoche. The manner of reporting and use of expression is so condescending." I thought there was not even the slightest show of respect and devotion, and the time of secret Mantrayana becoming ritual chanting has certainly arrived. I still feel sad when I think about it. Maybe I am being narrow minded. You think about this. You may also feel the same as me. All this is due to limited learning or lack of knowledge.

GIVE UP MEAT AND ALCOHOL IF YOU HAVE CRAVINGS

There is much ado about the consumption of meat and alcohol. Though I am not well read, I don't think any of the old and new Tantric texts state that a teacher or follower of Vajrayana should blatantly indulge in the consumption of meat and alcohol or sensual pleasure. Many of the old and new Tantras explicitly explain the faults of sensual desire. It is said, "Meat should be consumed by the compassionate; alcohol should be consumed by the one with Samaya." Today people joke about it and do not take it seriously. If you think hard it has a deeper meaning. A person who has developed genuine love, compassion and Bodhicitta is highly praised in the scriptures as someone having a meaningful connection with whoever comes into contact with him or her.

"Meaningful connection" is not an ordinary quality. Seeing, hearing the speech, touching and just the thought of such a guru brings happiness, dispels suffering and fulfills all wishes according to the Dharma. In brief, if one follows such a guru and diligently practises the teachings received with full dedication, there is no doubt about achieving the state of Vajradhara within one life time. Even an ordinary connection by speech or body, or negative connection like hitting the guru, it is said, will end the samsaric cycle. This means that, as one's negative accumulations become less, one will meet this Bodhisattva guru with whom you had a connection of speech or body and he or she will compassionately take care of you and free you from cyclic rebirth. Since such a realized being has no selfish desire in his mind, the consumption of meat by him or her will not cause obscurations; instead this will benefit innumerable beings. Therefore, the consumption of meat by such a great being is more beneficial than not eating meat, for the beings that have no saviour. This is the reason why the consumption of meat by those with great compassion is described as a quality and not a fault.

All the actions of my root gurus are like that of the Buddha and we cannot embellish or discredit their activities or discuss them. For that would be like trying to measure the sky with outstretched arms. However, I remember one particular incident and I thought it might benefit you if I share it here. My gracious guru, Drukpa Thuksey Rinpoche was not well, and had to be hospitalized. I was with him at the time. Normally, the people who came to visit him would bring items of food but he wouldn't even look at them. One day he said, "There is a fish among the food the visitors brought. Bring it to me." The attendants, worried that it would be harmful to his health, replied that no one brought any fish. He laughed and said, "Don't say so. Bring it." So the fish had to be brought and offered to him. He said prayers and mantras for almost an hour and shedding tears he blew over it and then had it. Again he recited mantras and prayers despite his ill health.

We all know that generally speaking, elderly Tibetans are not fond of eating fish or seafood. At that time Rinpoche was not well and did not have an appetite for anything. But then Bodhisattvas like my guru have taken birth for the well-being of all sentient beings. The *Bodhisattvacharyavatara*[20] mentions that there is nothing a Bodhisattva would not do if it is for the benefit of others, and will happily brave every hardship for the benefit of other beings. If you think about this and the saying, "The compassionate should eat meat", one certainly feels a sense of devotion. I am absolutely certain that the root gurus, who are real Buddhas, consume meat not as a deliberate act of disregarding the faults or because they cannot abandon their desire for meat, but for a greater reason.

---

20. *A Guide to the Bodhisattva's Way of Life*: A fundamental text of Mahayana explaining a Bodhisattva's conduct composed by the seventh-century Indian saint-scholar Shantideva.

DO NOT CRITICIZE OTHERS SIMPLY BECAUSE YOU HAVE SOME VIRTUES

It seems many people let pride waste their own mind-stream. For example, people who are vegetarian criticize all non-vegetarians, some who are celibate criticize those who have consorts and some who have studied the scriptures look down on other practitioners and criticize them. I don't think just being vegetarian or celibate or having studied the scriptures is a matter for amazement. Some people become vegetarian to lose weight, some are vegetarians because of their caste, some become vegetarian because they don't like the taste of meat, and some become vegetarian to gain social recognition and proudly publicize that they are vegetarian. When they see a non-vegetarian dish they stare at the plate, with their watering mouths and wonder just what to do.

Then there are those vegetarians who prepare artificial chicken, fish, sea food, beef, lamb, pork and mutton dishes that look like the real thing and then cut them and eat. I wonder at the stupidity of this. Then there are men who have become monks because they do not like women, or are sexually dysfunctional. Similarly, there are women who have become nuns because of their dislike for men or are sexually dysfunctional. Some join the Sangha because they feel that they would not be able to lead a regular worldly life because of their looks or lack of ability. Some get the opportunity to study the scriptures in their youth for some years, due to positive circumstances. So, such acts are not of much benefit from the spiritual point of view, if you consider the precept, "Virtue or non-virtue follows the motivation."

Those who have a great desire for meat say that it is useless to give up meat and eat only rice and vegetables, since the extent of the sin is equal. Those who like eating meat of bigger animals say that the meat of one animal can satisfy the needs of many, and so it is a lesser sin and wonder at those eating chicken or sea food. Similarly, those who are used to eating meat of smaller animals insist that the sin is less because smaller-sized animals suffer less during slaughter and they relish sea food and insects. Those who don't eat meat but eat eggs say that eating eggs is not sinful because the egg is not a fully formed being. So, we see a number of situations. Everyone is simply trying to justify their desire without any genuine scriptural or logical basis for justification. The topic of the severity of the non-virtue is very complicated and confusing for someone like me. Can we accept one hundred per cent that vegetables and plants don't have life? Even if we accept that they do have life, there is the possibility of making a distinction between the presence and absence of consciousness. This can be learned by objectively studying the scriptures and, together with scientists, conducting investigations.

GENERALLY SPEAKING, EATING ANIMALS IS FRIGHTFUL

Leaving aside the gravity of the sin or the debate about big or small animals, the very act of eating meat itself is simply a heinous act. As human beings, we naturally think that we are hygienic and distinctively different. Just eating meat makes us outcasts, or pernicious beings who eat dead bodies. We talk of ghosts that eat meat and drink blood, and we fear them. But if you think about this properly, we are the *real* ghosts – the ones that can actually be seen or met. Eating eggs is also described as a seriously non-virtuous act in one of the scriptures. In short, as per the previous quotation, "Virtue or non-virtue follows motivation" and "Any deed resulting from desire, anger and ignorance is non-virtue". The teaching that "all phenomena are circumstances that dwell on intention," indicates that any act, such as eating, drinking, sleeping or sitting, when influenced by selfishness is not virtuous. The gravity of the non-virtue is also dependent on the degree of selfishness that influences the act. Therefore, you have to check your motivation behind your action.

It is not proper to kill animals and eat the meat with a sense of great pleasure. It is really good if one does not eat meat, out of compassion for the animals. It is in keeping with the Dharma. It also prevents one from becoming a carnivorous blood-sucking demon, and to remain clean inside and outside. If one physically abstains from eating meat and practises love in action, any being that comes into contact with you, will love you. Your love and compassion for all beings will grow in your mind. Scientists also have discovered this. Therefore, if one is able to gradually control the afflictive emotions, such as anger and pride that trouble our minds, one will be able to attain peace of mind. In this life one will be happy, and even for the next life there is nothing better than this. One must, therefore, ponder and do what brings genuine peace and happiness to all beings. It is important to use one's brain. For thousands of years we have been using our intellect to stubbornly pursue our desire and, with bias, we differentiate between types of meat, argue about eating or not eating meat, remaining celibate or not, shaving or not shaving our heads, dressing in a certain way or not, *etc*. These issues have been the cause of dispute amongst family members, villages and nations. No decision has ever been reached on these matters and will never be reached in the future.

THE PURPOSE OF ALCOHOL

As mentioned earlier, the texts say, "Alcohol should be consumed by the one with Samaya (sacred vow)". It means that a great being who has realized the essence of the three divine seats[21] and regards this as the solemn vow, remains in that state without wavering even for a moment, can consume alcohol.

Ordinary people like us may get drunk after drinking a few glasses of alcohol, vomit and get sick, cause embarrassment, and not know what one is saying or doing. Just as Aconite, which is poisonous to humans, makes the peacock glow, so alcohol stimulates meditative experience and the warmth of bliss in the great Tantric practitioner, instead of creating delusions.

Therefore, I believe, "Alcohol should be consumed by the one with Samaya," means that a practitioner with Samaya or sacred vow is allowed to drink alcohol since it aids meditative practice.

THE PRACTICE OF GANACHAKRA

Whilst discussing, as the main topic, whether a Tantric practitioner can or cannot consume meat and alcohol, we remain quiet about the rights and wrongs or permissibility of all other pleasures – because very few people dislike these three. For Ganachakra,[22] it is said, "Meat and alcohol are necessary," and this means that during the Ganachakra offering one has to cut off the dualistic thought of

---

21 1. Aggregates and sensory faculties as the seat for the male and female Tathagathas; 2. Sources of perceptions as the seat for male and female Bodhisattvas; 3. Limbs as the seat for male and female wrathful deities.

22. Accumulation of offerings of tantric sacrament.

what to enjoy and what not to enjoy, what is pleasant tasting and what is not, clean and unclean, the web of doubt and shame and embarrassment caused by pride, and enjoy, with the confidence of non-dualistic sameness of taste. Just as the text says, "Enjoy with the understanding that the inherent nature of Brahmins, dogs, outcasts and pigs is the same."

The Samaya or sacred vow of Vajrayana is bound by wisdom and method, and the view of the union of the two. Meat and alcohol should be used only as symbolic substances – meat as apparent method, symbolising bliss, and alcohol as the apparent wisdom, symbolising emptiness. Therefore, before talking about meat and alcohol, one has to check whether one has the confidence of realization of the view of sameness of taste, seeing no difference at all between a clean eighteen-course meal and the dirty excreta, and can enjoy both equally without any doubt or hesitation. If one is a practitioner lacking such a confidence of view, then one should take them only as symbolic substances. In the Kham region of eastern Tibet, a little amount is called *Dam-dze* or "symbolic substance". So only a small amount of meat and alcohol should be taken as symbolic substances and you should not eat meat until your belly is full, or drink until you are drunk. A practitioner with the confidence of realization of the view, on the other hand, can not only eat meat and drink alcohol, but can also enjoy anything. As the biographies of the Indian Mahasiddha Birwapa and Drukpa Kunleg[23] show, there is no limit to how much they can have. The Sutras and Tantras mention many sacred vows such as non-abandonment, earnestness to act, undertakings *etc*. All these have to be enjoyed and done with complete oneness of taste, not like us: eating meat because we like it or selecting the meat of our liking and leaving what we don't like; drinking alcohol because we like drinking and drinking only what tastes good and leaving what doesn't taste good; or having a relationship with a woman because we like it and just selecting the most beautiful one.

When I was about fourteen years old I participated in a Ganachakra offering, with my late Guru Kyabje Drukpa Thuksey

---

23. Also known as "Drukpa Kunga Legpa" (1455–1510), one of the three "Divine Madmen" of Drukpa Lineage, the other two being U-Nyon Kunga Zangpo (1458–1532) and Tsang-Nyon Heruka (1452–1507).

Rinpoche, in the nomadic Changthang region of Ladakh. Rinpoche picked up a piece of raw and rotten meat, and asked me if I wanted to have it. I replied, "I don't want it." He asked, "Why? This is a substance of Ganachakra offering." Because of my ignorance, I did not realize it was a blessing and that there was a special purpose, and my colleagues had said that it was rotten and should not be eaten. He looked disappointed and said, "What is the point of reciting *Ram Yam Kham* and *Om Ah Hung* if you cannot cut off such doubt?" Rinpoche had the offering meat and after sometime asked, "Do you know the meaning of *Om Ah Hung*?" I replied that I did not know it well. He stared at me and explained how to apply the external, internal and other suchness to the essence of the Three Ways,[24] how to connect this with the essence of the Three Samayas[25] and how the essence of all mantras is present in the three syllables. Although I don't remember everything, I have at least a partial memory. He must have wondered – "when will this boy realize all these essences?" Then he held my hand with loving kindness. A Buddha like my guru can explain the essential truth; someone like me can only give a vain literal explanation of the texts. I think even those claiming to be scholars with literal knowledge, will find it difficult to explain the deep profound meanings.

THE FAULT OF ALCOHOL

From the spiritual point of view, it is not right to drink on the pretext of Vajrayana practice, without any knowledge of the Samayas. Buddha said, "Those who drink are not my disciples; I do not presume to be the teacher of such a person." Quotations such as,

> A person who conspicuously loves drinking alcohol,
> Cannot benefit the self or give happiness to others.
> Alcohol causes ignorance and horrible acts.
> Like poison – abstain from drinking it.

---

24. 1. Taking all appearances as the body of a Buddha; 2. Taking all sounds as the speech of a Buddha; 3. Taking all thoughts as the mind of a Buddha.
25. The three-fold *Samayas* or pledges related to a Buddha's body, speech and mind.

can be found in many Sutras and Tantras. Even from the worldly point of view, the many faults of alcohol are explained in common sayings like:

> Alcohol is the cause of your disgrace,
> The stink of vomit and loose motions fills the air;
> A drunkard is shameless,
> He steals, robs and womanises;
> The pleasure of alcohol causes severe disaster,
> Blowing away the fortune and damaging the family.

We can see the many faults of alcohol. It does not look good when a practitioner indulges in alcohol. Guru Rinpoche has said, "Practitioners indulging in excessive drinking and gossiping, is an omen of degeneration of the Dharma." I don't remember in detail the faults of eating meat and drinking alcohol mentioned in the many texts and commentaries. You will understand them once you study them.

THE VIRTUE OF MALE-FEMALE RELATIONSHIPS

As mentioned earlier, a genuine Vajrayana practitioner, who, after taking the pledge of practice, has externally gained complete control over channels, energies and droplets of the body; has internally realized the nature of attachment, hatred and ignorance; and who has secretly attained confidence in the realization of the inexpressible meaning of great sameness, as a result of upholding the minutest of vows of individual liberation; correctly follows the path of the generation process and perfection process; and without wavering from the significance and essence of all the Tantric Samayas, even for a moment, with the genuine devotion of viewing the guru as Vajradhara – remains on the path of the three-fold Vajra holder.

It is said that, for such a practitioner, sensual pleasure manifests as enhancement. This means that the touch, fragrance, body and beauty of the consort, act to increase and develop the internal and external elements, and become the swift and blissful path igniting the secret inner heat of bliss; thus attaining the Mahamudra state of union of bliss and emptiness – or the seven-fold state of Vajradhara. This is clearly explained in the meaning of the scriptural quotation,

"Enlightenment is attained within a moment." It seems that all sensual pleasures, such as the touch of the female by the male and the touch of the male by the female, are needed. There are many stories of how practise, with understanding of the true nature of reality, leads to complete attainment without difficulty.

THE FAULT OF MALE-FEMALE RELATIONSHIPS

Many old and new Tantras repeatedly mention that for a person who has had no opportunity to understand the view, to engage in random indulgences driven by desire, on the pretext that the secret Vajrayana has no restrictions, would be the cause of endless torment. It seems such actions are not allowed. Emitting even a drop of seed-essence due to the selfish attachment to sexual desire, is described as being a root infraction of the Mantrayana, and so it can be understood whether it is permissible to actually have a spouse or partner, for someone like us. It is important not only to know what is allowed, and what is forbidden in the scriptures, but also to use one's awareness to understand the essential meaning of the rules of the Vinaya, and at the same time appreciate the level of one's own realization. It is a general practice for a layperson to have a spouse. Getting married and having children is seen as the proper thing to do. This general view is not based on any test or investigation.

LOSING YOUR FREEDOM UNDER THE ILLUSION OF SEXUAL BLISS

All beings in this desire realm, including humans, animals and insects, initially feel a sense of bliss and happiness at the start of relationship with a spouse or partner. But as a consequence of this relationship, one loses all freedom – the freedom to travel, to stay, to eat or drink as one wishes. Even after losing your freedom, if the partner takes care of you lovingly without subjecting you to abuse and insults, one will at least be able to lead a tolerable life. But most have to suffer the partner's nagging. As the saying goes, "Though the words do not have poisonous darts, they still pierce the person's heart." It becomes difficult to live together even for a day, let alone for months and years. As a result, one doesn't wish to stay home with the partner and wishes instead to find someone else. One finds oneself in a very difficult situation and this can cause unhappiness to all the family members, including the children. Under such circumstances, most people, it seems, look for extra marital affairs with other married people, as they are not able to find a good, younger partner. This can lead to quarrels or violent deaths.

SUFFERING DAY AND NIGHT DUE TO THE SHACKLES OF DESIRE

Even if one has a good relationship with one's partner, one still worries that the partner may fall ill or die, or may displease him or her. On top of that, if you have small children at home, their wailing and crying will keep you busy, and it's only for a few hours at night when they are asleep, that you get to relax and stretch your legs. You get worried that they are hungry or thirsty, that they are cold or will fall sick or die. Then you have to worry about their schooling.

Years and years of your life are consumed by these worries, making it difficult to do spiritual practice. Never mind spiritual practice, such people find it difficult even to take a break for a week or so. Then, those with a younger and good-looking spouse or partner worry that someone else may steal the partner from them, or the partner may fall for someone else. Even when going out to work, such people worry if the partner is sleeping with someone else. Consumed by such stresses, they can't eat or sleep or relax. And when they come home, all their conversations with their partners are tainted with doubt. Too much questioning then angers their partner. Even if it doesn't anger their partner, they find it difficult to trust the answers as the complete truth, and the mind loses its place.

Similarly, if the partner is someone who sits at home, their doubt about their partner will persist whenever he or she goes out. One can also see that people have extra marital affairs for years and keep it a secret, deceiving their spouse or partner by faking love. Such a person gets infected with various diseases because of the continued physical relations with others, and then transmits it to their partner, causing mental and physical agony. There are also people who secretly steal from home to give to friends, or do lots of meaningless things that ultimately makes everyone unhappy.

THE REASON WHY THE TATHAGATA PROHIBITED TAKING OF A PARTNER AND ALCOHOL

The Tathagata prohibited taking a spouse or partner because he saw the consequent sufferings. If it had led to genuine happiness he would not have prohibited it at all.

Alcohol, it seems, tastes good and makes one feel good after drinking. Drinking also seems to help one temporarily overcome minor mental problems, making one confident and fearless for the time being. However, addiction to drinking makes one an outcast, distancing oneself from one's family and friends and wasting whatever wealth one has. Ultimately, even death comes in a pathetic manner to an alcoholic. For these reasons drinking alcohol has been prohibited.

I DID NOT LIKE RULES

In my youth, when I heard the rules of the Vinaya being mentioned repeatedly, I used to wonder why there were restrictions on the things that one wanted to do, and why things that one was not very eager to do, had to be followed. Instead of feeling delighted to follow the precepts, I used to find them narrow-minded. Perhaps this was because, by nature, I love harmless distractions like song and dance, picnics and other forms of amusement. My horoscope states that I am a son from the realm of the gods. I don't know what this means exactly but I certainly seem to have the tendencies for the distraction of a lustful god. This is due to the fact that desire is the most influential of all the afflictive emotions. In addition, I had a strong attachment to the distractions of sensuous pleasures. I lacked experience and did not fully understand the purpose of the Vinaya rules set by the Buddha. Even today it is the same, not much has changed. However, thanks to the blessings and instructions of my root gurus, and using my contemplative wisdom, I later realized the need for mundane and spiritual laws.

As Nagarjuna said, "Like animate and inanimate ground, law is the foundation of all infinite qualities." I gained conviction through a dry understanding of its importance and why it is needed for practitioners of both the higher and lower yanas. The various Samayas and vows are especially meant for ordinary followers like us, because we are strongly influenced by attachment and aversion, and unable to loosen the knot of hope and doubt. If we did not have the robe of laws to uphold us, there would be no refuge, or saviour, or protector, except ethical conduct, when we are tormented by fire-like anger and icy desire. Being enslaved by attachment and anger, without any freedom, one's short life ends in exhaustion. The mind, being under the influence of attachment and anger, does not let the body rest; the mind does not reside in the body. Leaving aside the possibility of realizing the nature of mind and attaining enlightenment, one is not even able to lead a normal worldly life. Seeing these dangers, it seems, the rules were set.

ULTIMATELY THERE IS NO NEED FOR ETHICAL CONDUCT

Since the yogis who have reached the exalted stage naturally possess ethics, it seems they do not have anything to uphold separately. This is because, through the perfection of wisdom, they are able to recognize even the minutest affliction as inherently empty, and knowingly use such afflictive emotions, such as desire, for the benefit of other beings. The view and realization of the yogi bestows on them complete freedom; unlike us who jump blindly like dogs at the sight of a piece of meat, or we are like the moths drawn to the light. While explaining the qualities of a guru, I mention all these things incidentally. The topic of the external guru ends here.

FOLLOWING THE QUALIFIED GURU LEADS TO THE INTERNAL GURU

After finding the qualified external guru, who can guide you in this and the next life, you should follow him regularly, even at the cost of your life. Many ways have been described on how to follow the guru, but the crucial thing is to serve to the satisfaction of the guru, without being a disgrace to the guru or the Dharma. The *Fifty Stanzas of Guru Devotion*[26] and other treatises state that one has to do everything that pleases the guru, without choosing whether

---

26. Composed by Asvagosha, better known by the name Acharyavira, a *Tirthika Pandit* of great learning who was defeated in debate by Aryadeva, a disciple of Nagarjuna, and converted to Buddhism.

to do or not to do something. However, there seems to be some difference in the approach of the higher and lower Yanas. If you are interested in learning about these, then you can study the scriptures. In our tradition we follow the *Fifty Stanzas of Guru Devotion*. It can certainly be said that a qualified guru will appreciate non-harming behaviour, and so it is said that training in non-harming behaviour in accordance with the Dharma is the best way of serving the guru. I believe this is the meaning of the phrase, "Meditation accomplishment is the supreme service". If you place a bunch of grass in front of a dog it would not bother to look at it. Similarly, an unqualified guru would not find meditation practice by a disciple, very pleasing. A qualified guru will look upon any service of body, speech or wealth, by the disciple, as a means of accumulating merit and purifying defilements. He would not, however, regard this as supreme service.

ONE NEEDS TO UNDERSTAND THE THOUGHTS OF THE GURU

Many explanatory texts stress, "In the beginning, be skilled in testing the guru; in the middle be skilled in following the guru; and finally, be skilled in understanding his thoughts and actions", meaning once you have found the guru who is like a wish-fulfilling gem, you should be skilled in understanding his thoughts and actions. As the proverb goes, "Thirty people have thirty thoughts, their way of thinking is different", the guru will have a different notion for each obscured being like us. So this notion has to be understood. Without this understanding, if we pretentiously do things in the presence of the guru, you won't know whether it pleases or displeases him. These days the so-called practitioners actively do things intended to serve the guru, but end up displeasing him. This makes one unhappy and even impairs one's faith in the guru. There are many people facing this situation today. Therefore, it is important to remain patiently resolute to follow the path for the benefit of all sentient beings, in this life and the next, and to remain humble to ensure that auspicious coincidence (connection) does not go wrong from the very beginning.

One should, with humility, show utmost respect to the Vajradhara Guru's consort, children, attendants, manager, cushion, shoes or even the pet dog that the guru loves. This is clear from the explanation of this line from the *Fifty Stanzas of Guru Devotion*, "Respect whatever is dear to the guru as you would respect the guru."

My Guru Kyabje Ontrul Rinpoche, used to repeatedly say that if one sincerely follows these instructions with diligence, then the auspicious coincidence of the Vajrayana path is established. May the Guru Vajradhara embrace me with compassion!

ALL CONFUSIONS CLEARED THANKS TO MY GURU ONTRUL

When I started receiving teachings from Kyabje Ontrul Rinpoche, he said, "If the auspicious connection between the guru and disciple is established, then the purpose of this life and the next will be fulfilled. Therefore, how about starting with an explanation of the *Fifty Stanzas of Guru Devotion*? I don't have much to explain, but hopefully the words of the previous gurus still remain uncorrupted." His pure unusual attitude, untouched by pride and worldly motivations, and his radiant body inspired a strong natural devotion, and made one think that if one were to meet the eight great Indian masters, known as the Six Ornaments and the Two Excellent Ones, they would be like him.

His manner was humble, and as a gesture of reverence he placed his folded hand at his heart and recited *Praise to Manjushri* three times. After the stanza "The radiance of your wisdom, oh merciful one", he smiled and started giving instructions, starting with an explanation of correct motivation, in a simple and orderly manner. Sometimes he would give teachings by combining the texts and secret instructions in an amusing way. As my precious guru said, the auspicious coincidence of Dharma was established, and a new door of devotion opened in my mind. I didn't have to remain attached to a practice based on particular qualities of the body, speech and mind that one liked and revered. I understood that all phenomena are the same in true nature, and perfected the impartial pure vision. I gained a different feeling, similar to that of taking one's hat off.

From then on, I was able to connect the deity with the guru, and the guru with my own mind, during the recitation of mantras or the two stages of meditation. In the past, I felt that meditating on a particular root guru and lineage gurus; or male or female practice deities, wisdom or wrathful protectors; Buddha, male or female

Bodhisattvas; or a deity of wealth, would mean leaving the others out, and I feared that this would mean I would not gain accomplishment for that particular deity. I used to feel that I did not have the time to practice them all together. It was a difficult thing – like packing horns into a sack. But then, all such problems vanished. For example, I used to be scared while practising the female deities or protectors. Because of their jealous nature it was okay so long as you practised a particular female deity as a soul-mate, to the exclusion of all others. Even a simple meeting with any human or non-human females would cause disturbing dreams, unsound sleep, restless feelings or bad health, like nose bleeds. I used to get such signs.

Divinations and astrological readings would clearly state that such and such a female deity was unhappy, and I had to do ritual atonements and confessions. This would pacify her, and the problem would be resolved for the time being, but the problem would recur if I came into contact with any other female being again. I used to have similar problems with some of the male deities but they were not as serious as the ones with the female deities. Later, with the blessings and advice of my guru, I overcame these problems.

During teachings, he would often jokingly say, "All these offerings and rituals are important as the perceived traditions of a big monastery. Even I have studied this for many years. When I look at the way you practise I feel slightly proud that I know better. Ha ha. I am joking, seriously. Whether it is a deity or a ghost, one must know how to relate it to one's mind and purify the mind as the Buddha nature. There are many stories telling how: practising by beating drums and blowing trumpets, as though the deities resided in the drums and trumpets, reciting words that claimed one was right, and finding faults in others, has boomeranged and punishment befell the practitioner. One must be careful. There is no point in too much meaningless activity. The gods and local deities, along with their retinue, must naturally follow you. Having to keep on propitiating them is pitiful." On hearing this I realized that I did not know how to practice, and was able to correct the problems. He taught me how a male or female deity has to be understood as the manifestation of the guru, and how genuine masters of other traditions also, should be understood as inseparable from the root guru, and to see them as one's own guru, through devotion. I cannot repay his kindness. So, the main topic here is to first check the guru, then follow him, and finally be skilled in learning his thoughts. It would be difficult to follow the secret Mantrayana randomly without going through these three steps.

THE INNER GURU AND THE SECRET GURU

As one listens to the teachings on the Tripitakas[27] by such a qualified guru, and practises the path of the three-fold training, the karmic obscurations caused by afflictive emotions get purified, and one is able to understand quintessential points, such as: the creator of all the external and internal phenomena is one's own mind, and that the mind is unidentifiable as an entity. The cognition that realizes this is called the inner guru. This is what the texts call the inner ultimate cognitive guru.

The external and internal tantras and the new and old tantric traditions, have different interpretations of this. I don't know the details. My understanding, according to the teachings of my root guru, a real Buddha, is that the discriminating wisdom or cognition that correctly sees everything, from the ethics of abandoning the ten non-virtues, to the meaning of the ultimate truth of emptiness, can be called the Inner Guru.

THE SECRET GURU: ONE'S MIND, SELF-COGNIZANT, INHERENT GURU, ESSENCE OF THE THREE EXALTED BODIES

After cultivating familiarization with cognition, unmistaken intellectual understanding is attained and this wisdom breaks the web of illusion of the dualistic concept of subject and object; and in its place one sees the face of the primordial body of the great bliss of union. This can be called the secret Ultimate Dharmakaya Guru. As Milarepa said, "Look at your mind – that is the guru", this is inherent within us. As a result of purification having been practiced, we see the face, or recognize the face, that so far had remained

---

27. The baskets of Buddha's teachings is classified into three divisions according to their subject matter: 1. Vinaya Pitaka – basket of teachings on moral discipline emphasizing the training of ethics; 2. Sutra Pitaka – basket of teachings in discourses emphasizing the training of concentration; 3. Abhidharma – basket of teachings on knowledge emphasizing the training of wisdom.

unrecognized. Recognizing the primordially-perfected foundation, which is free of incidental conception of self and ignorant tendencies, naturally awakens the cognition, and the understanding of all branches of knowledge is fully developed. The result is attainment of Buddhahood or enlightenment.

FAITH IN BUDDHA MUST BE BASED ON REASON

The first condition on joining the Buddhist path is to understand what is meant by the Triple Gem, and why they are regarded as precious. It should not be based on bias because your friends or family members are Buddhists. Rather, one should understand what is so special about them; how does Buddha benefit us and on what grounds is this benefit based? The wisdom gained by learning and contemplating *Uttara Tantra* and the other scriptures naturally engenders vigorous faith, based on logical knowledge. As Je Tsongkhapa[28] prayed, "May the conviction of faith in the Teacher (Buddha), based on the understanding of the natural disposition of the path, always prevail"; one must develop the intellectual understanding of the guide to Dharma received from one's guru. Without falling victim to the demon of scholarship and competition, one should apply one's life experience to taming one's mind-stream. It is not enough to say, "My guru, the wish-fulfilling gem, is giving teachings during these days, on how to practise Bodhicitta and the Dharma. I seek refuge in him!" It would be good to also take the practical action of giving up non-virtuous deeds like killing, stealing, consuming meat and alcohol, smoking, and fighting *etc*. Even if you cannot give them up completely, try to cut down negative activities. If one makes a consistent effort then, as Shantideva said, "There is nothing that doesn't become easy with familiarization". Then, a profound, rather than superficial, confidence grows within you and you do more and more good deeds in your life, negative activities become fewer and fewer, leading to the happiness of one and all. At that moment you feel an infallible faith of devotion in the teacher who showed you the path in the first place. You will then receive what the texts describe, when they say, "The ultimate nature of refuge, is the inherently born devotion." At this stage you become a Buddhist.

---

28. Founder of Gelug tradition of Tibetan Buddhism (1357–1419).

As the Buddha said, "Neither by matted hair nor by carrying a staff", just changing one's external appearance, holding a rosary in your hand, doing prostrations or circumambulation – these alone do not make you a Buddhist. This is what I often heard my root gurus say. Buddhists and non-Buddhists alike talk about the term Supreme Being and why we should have faith in Him. I used to feel it was important to understand the unique distinctive features of the definition of a Supreme Being, and devotion. Being arrogantly and obstinately attached to one's tradition without reason and showering criticism, out of revulsion, against other traditions is simply an indication of one's ordinariness. There is no glory in such behaviour. On the contrary, it will be an obstacle to your spiritual practice or peace of mind and physical relaxation, and nothing positive will come of it. Buddhism does not have the tradition of converting others by use of force or deception, or through use of money.

The devotion that we talk about in Buddhism is not based on attachment to one's tradition and hatred of other traditions. The two are contradictory. Chandrakirti and many previous teachers have clearly explained this. However, Tibet has a history of such incidents. Our lineage alone has had many such experiences. For example, Drira Phug, Gyalwa Gotsangpa's meditation cave, an undisputed Drukpa Lineage monastery, was taken over and converted to Karma Kagyu with Chinese support, by giving a big feast to the gullible local people and telling them this was being done on the instructions of His Holiness the 17th Karmapa Ugyen Thinley Dorje, who is also known as Dharamsala Karmapa, who was then about ten years old or younger. I do not believe that he would give such instructions: firstly, an objective realized being would not even consider doing such a thing and secondly, a child of his age would never imagine taking over the monastery, land and followers of another lineage. Similar incidents have also taken place in the Kham region. The history of such incidents need not be retold here. This is something that those of us claiming to be spiritual heads must think about properly.

DEVOTION TO TEACHINGS ON TRUTH MUST ALSO BE BASED ON LOGIC

Continuing on from above, it seems that those extraordinary beings that have completed purification do not need to study the conventional texts, cite many reasons or carry out intellectual investigations to gain a new meaning. As Kunkhyen Pema Karpo[29] said, such a person is able to clear all doubts about phenomena internally, without having to insistently rely on words. It means such a person need not intellectually clear the doubts about the definition of devotion *etc.*, because all appearances and perceptions naturally appear as practice and Dharmakaya, without any obstacle or hindrance, just like looking down at a valley from a high peak. Some texts call it the "bursting forth of realization through the power of inherent wisdom." For people like me, following the path of Dharma and its rules without acquiring a certain knowledge of logic, through the study of texts, would be like an untrained soldier joining the army in battle; it is doubtful whether it will affect your mind-stream. This is why wherever I go around the world I tell people what we need is devotion based on logic, gained through study and reflection. Lack of it is the cause of all ills. In order to generate such devotion in one's mental continuum, one has to search for the root of all unhappiness, in this life and the next, caused by afflictive emotions like desire and aversion, under the influence of the wandering mind.

Nowadays, His Holiness the Dalai Lama is giving importance to science and holding conferences with scientists, Buddhist scholars, gurus and masters, with the instruction that there should be objective study of the thoughts and workings of the mind. This is not to seek refuge in science because Buddhism lacks substance. He is doing this because he knows that if the many distinctive features of Buddhism can be shown to the world through science, many people will be able to see the truth. Except for a few yogis, people in general lack genuine devotion, because the authentic truth has not been proved to them. A few years ago, His Holiness the Dalai Lama told me about his wish to reveal to the world, evidence of the control of internal channels and vital energy, through the Mantrayana practices, using scientific tools, as this would provide practical evidence to the world of the truth about the features of Buddhism in general and Vajrayana in particular. "Applying the experiences of energy channels, winds and droplets, we can explain and show the results of the five paths[30] and

---

29. The 4th Gyalwang Drukpa (1527–1592).
30. 1. Path of accumulation; 2. Path of preparation; 3. Path of seeing; 4. Path of meditation; 5. Path of no-more learning.

the ten *bhumis,* or grounds,³¹ achieved through diligent practice of the path. But for many generations these were kept secret, understood only by a few genuine yogis, and the world at large does not know these things. Therefore, very few people have any faith in this. Your lineage is special in this practice. So think hard. I feel it would be great if you can make everyone understand this in a scientific way." He said this to me. It is a profound idea.

Once, while I was in a strict one-year retreat I received a letter from His Holiness's Private Office asking me to go to Boston University in the United States – I think it was Boston, I can't recall clearly; it was a Science centre anyway – and show them the capacity of energy channels and winds, and gain their confidence. At that time I was in a strict retreat, and on top of that, my guru, from whom I had received the instructions, was very conservative. He would not have allowed me to show these practises in a foreign land like the United States. Hence I was not able to go. However, thinking about this with an open mind, I feel it is important that people at large should know the qualities that we call secret.

DEVOTION MEANS HAVING AN UNDERSTANDING OF THE DEFINITION OF CAUSE AND EFFECT

All of us who believe in the Dharma – lay men and women, gurus, monks, nuns and even renowned scholars – are of a low standard when it comes to devotion. Why so, one might ask? As mentioned earlier, this is because of the failure to provide practical proof. Because of the strong influence of gross grasping, we cannot be convinced of the truth unless there is practical evidence to prove otherwise. During the second turning of the Dharma Wheel, Buddha said that all external appearances are mere labels and exist only in our fancy. Those of us who have studied the scriptures can give explanations in a hundred different ways. But when we are amidst appearances that seem real – good looks, melodious voices, etc. – we are driven by afflictive emotions, and people like me who claim to

---

31. The ten stages of perfection according to Mahayana school: 1. extremely joyous; 2. spotless purity; 3. Luminous; 4. Radiant; 5. Unconquerable; 6. Manifest; 7. gone afar; 8. Immovable; 9. good intelligence; 10. spiritual cloud.

be Dharma practitioners, fail to use devotion as the antidote and we find it difficult to see our emotions as merely existing in our fancy. At a higher level, however much one might speak eloquently about the higher views of Middle Path, Dzogchen or Mahamudra, they face difficulty when it comes to the main point.

As His Holiness the Dalai Lama said, if we are able to carry out investigations together with scientists, we will not have to reason that Buddha taught that the dualistic concept of subject and object does not exist primordially; that this erroneous view is the result of mistaken awareness, and based on attachment to one's tradition and aversion to other traditions, we argue that this is in the scriptures. The truth could be revealed with proof. As a result, one would be able to realize that the powerful and invincible factor, known as mind, is simply backed by impressions it is accustomed to, since beginningless time in samsara, and that the afflictive emotions that cause sufferings, do not exist in the ultimate nature of the mind and can be gotten rid of. Then, one will gain a new understanding and a firm certainty in the reason given in Uttara Tantra and other texts, to explain that the nature of mind is luminosity. This is my understanding of devotion.

GAINING CONFIDENCE IN THE THREE JEWELS THROUGH THE FOUR NOBLE TRUTHS

Although it is difficult to say whether we have gained even a simple understanding of wisdom of the Middle Way and Dzogchen *etc.* on the view of selflessness, the root guru has, by his kindness, given the instructions, which are like a wish-fulfilling jewel, available to us to follow and practise with determination. If one is capable, then one can attain the primordial wisdom of selflessness, and realize the groundless and rootless condition of mind within one life time, thereby crushing the afflictive ignorant clinging to things as being true. Thus, one gains confidence that the truth of cessation of suffering can be realized. In its essential nature, nothing exists as it appears to be; the mistaken awareness sees what is apparent as the undeniable truth. For example, it sees humans as humans, animals as animals, gods as gods, ghosts as ghosts. Understanding that what appears as undeniable, is in fact just a product of dependent origination, leads to the understanding of Samsaric cause and effect, and a strong determination arises to renounce cyclic existence.

There are many explanations on the root of cyclic existence, but to my understanding, as I said earlier, the mistaken awareness caused by delusive ignorance, can be discarded by using the truth of the path as the antidote. For example, if the cause of a fire is blocked, then the resultant smoke can be prevented. Similarly, if action, along with affliction and residue, which is the cause, is negated, then there is no way for the various sufferings to emerge. Thus one gains certainty that ultimate happiness can be attained through purification of cause and effect. Thereby, making one aspire to achieve the state of liberation and omniscience, and to work towards this with intense application, without superficiality. In this way, one gains confident faith in the precious teachings, from the depth of one's heart. Consequently, one gains convincing faith in the Teacher of the path and confident faith in the noble assembly of ordinary monks and nuns practising the teachings. This helps us to practise pure vision instead of finding fault with our Dharma brothers and sisters, who are helping us in our spiritual practice.

As Maitreya pointed out, if one achieves confident faith in the two truths, followed by faith in the four noble truths, faith in the Precious teachings and then in the Precious Buddha and Precious Sangha, one would not have to seek refuge in the historical Buddha, or behave like those who believe in gods and spirits that reside in rocks, mountains, rivers, trees or sun whilst saying, "I seek refuge in the Triple Gem". All such shortcomings will be overcome and the meaning of the phrase, "The difference between Buddhists and non-Buddhists lies in refuge" will be understood. One may then call oneself a Buddhist. When Atisha[32] was in Tibet, he expressed his sadness by saying, "Even among the elderly white-haired monks facing the public are many who do not qualify as Buddhists." By this he had meant that they lacked pure refuge practice. It would be wrong if we, who claim to be practising Hinayana, Mahayana and Vajrayana simultaneously, cannot visualize a Buddha with four forms or bodies – Nature Truth Body, Wisdom Truth Body, Complete Enjoyment Body and Emanation Body – and not just the Emanation Body Buddha as the object of refuge. One should have certain knowledge of the process of the four bodies and be

---

32. Atisha Dipamkara (982–1054) who visited Tibet and founded the Kadampa tradition of Tibet.

able to bring to mind the four-body Buddha – the moment one says Buddha.

As I said earlier, one has to understand the apparent and real nature of all animate and inanimate phenomena, as explained in the Middle Path texts, through the two truths, by receiving the pure quintessential instructions: on appearance as mind, mind as emptiness, union of emptiness and clarity as fundamental wisdom beyond the sphere of intellect. This understanding has to be obtained from a qualified teacher, instead of simply relying on books written by skilled hands, or the speech of eloquent speakers. Unless one attains such a firm internal understanding, even if one pretends to have faith in the historical Buddha, it will be difficult to have fundamental faith, and hence it is difficult to have firm uncommon faith. To understand these thoroughly, a little study and contemplation is necessary. The teachings of past masters say, "Understanding the quintessence of refuge releases the essence of Sutras and Tantras." So it is really profound. When we hear someone giving teachings on refuge we typically don't pay any attention and rather engage in gossip and remain distracted. However, when we hear teachings on meditation and visualization, and especially teachings on meditating on a deity, or reciting of a mantra, demonstration of various mudras or yoga; then we listen with full attention, and even practise them with enthusiasm. But if one has proper knowledge, then the essence of all the Sutras and Tantras can be understood from refuge. If this essential point is not understood, then even if one pretends to practise any Sutra or Tantra, or claims to be a scholar, the salient point has been missed. As the text says, "Everyone has the vows, except those who have not sought refuge." Now this is a casual explanation I have given. As explained earlier, the inherent precious consciousness is the origin of Buddha and Bodhisattva; it is also called the Mother of the Victorious One. Since this is beyond the intellectual sphere or comprehension of ordinary beings, it remains secret and is called the "secret inexhaustible wheel of adornment" or "incomprehensible secret". Anyway, after recognizing the secret ultimate guru, one prostrates to the ultimate guru – the root or base of all foundation, path and fruit – instead of prostrating to any particular Buddha or Bodhisattva as the object of refuge.

NO NEED TO BE ATTACHED TO ANYTHING AS THE TRUTH

If you investigate the meaning of the sentence, "The mind is the door to everything", one will be able to solve many mental problems by analysing the meaning of the sentence. However, today, instead of looking at all phenomena as the creation of the mind, and not independently existing by themselves, most of us, from the beginning, close our mouths and eyes and try to look at the mind as non-existent in some sort of dark-room meditation, and finally fall asleep. Some see the mind as existing and follow every thought that arises, like dogs that run after sticks and stones thrown at them, instead of chasing the thieves. The stream of thought is endless and cannot be analysed; and in the process of chasing thought, afflictive emotions like pride lead one beyond the methods of taming the mind, and instead damages one's mind-stream. This can be seen among many neo-Buddhists. This is one of the reasons why practitioners have more attachment and aversion and worldly motivations than lay people today. It is said, "Calm and disciplined, devoid of afflictions, is the sign of learning and contemplation." But today, practitioners like me have pride and desire for prominence as the result of learning, and ignorance, and craving for wealth as the result of meditation, and the obstacles for spiritual practice just pile up. This is due to a mistaken way of thinking from the beginning.

LEARN THE PATH STEP BY STEP INSTEAD OF BEING AMBITIOUS

There must be great meaning to the Buddha's statement, "All phenomena exist only in our fancy." It is, therefore, important to understand that all external things, good and bad or big and small, are labels given by the mind. It is important that we practitioners respect and show devotion to this view while saying prayers or doing virtuous deeds, as well as in our way of life. Most of us, these days, are not able to understand this essential obstruction, and just blindly follow the chatter of dry scriptural citations, condescendingly describing as the lower view. To claim such superiority, one must have a certain experience concordant with the tenet. For example, by following a proper process of purification and training, one attains the true wisdom of seeing all good, bad or moderate things as an external reflection of one's deluded mind and nothing exists as it is.

After gaining confidence in this wisdom, one can clear the doubts, as the level of one's understanding of, and insight into, the nature of the mind, increases. This is a crucial point that those of us claiming to be practitioners of secret Mantrayana must understand. Vajrayana is also known as the path to fruition. As one trains on the path on the two stages of practice: the generation stage to develop skill, and the completion stage for complete wisdom – these form the foundation of the secret Mantrayana path – to familiarize oneself with enlightenment, or the primordial wisdom of the union of emptiness and compassion, or the precious nature of mind, commonly known as Buddhahood – the fruit of the practice. That is the ultimate fruit, which is personified by the two kayas or Buddha bodies, of the path. As Nagarjuna prayed, "May I achieve the two ultimate Buddha bodies, arising from accumulation of merit and accumulation of wisdom" – the Dharmakaya or the Truth Body is achieved as a result of accumulation of wisdom after perfecting renunciation of one's own interest, and Rupakaya or the Form Body is achieved as a result of accumulating merit after perfecting understanding for others' welfare.

When we practise, we recite the mantra OM SVABHAVA SHUDDA..., purifying all phenomena into emptiness. As one recites this, one has to transform the deluded idea of 'I' resulting from dependence of the body, mind and speech on the five aggregates, and clinging to apparent phenomena as solid reality, and develop a firm confidence within, that the external and internal phenomena do not exist as they appear to be. Then, contemplate on emptiness without letting anything influence the thought. Visualizing emptiness as the presiding deity, one meditates on the development stage of form body of the Buddha. At this stage one has to eliminate attachment to the view of seeing the face, hands, adornment and even the structure of the pure-land of the deity as solid reality, and meditate on the emptiness of the completion stage, to practise attainment of the Truth Body of Buddha. Continuing meditation in this state without wavering even for a moment, is what is called the union of the two stages. This is how my root gurus explained it.

All of us claiming to be practitioners need to meditate in this way, day and night. But these days most of us hold on to the apparent phenomena as solid reality and then look at something else to meditate on. From the very beginning, we look for something solid made of gold, silver, clay or any material that conveniently comes to mind, as meditation of the development stage. Some misunderstand the meaning of the term "firm pride in the deity", mentioned in the texts, and obstinately visualize a solid form and meditate on pride. As a result, most of them experience an increase in anger that causes rebirth as a ghost, and other than this, they achieve nothing. My gurus said that for anyone to practice the secret Mantrayana, one must have certain knowledge of the view of the Middle Path or Mind Only school. So, as I said earlier, according to my gurus, from the start of purification practice, one has to train the mind through emptiness according to the Sutra, and during the development stage meditation, an unshakable pride or confidence in emptiness is needed.

CHAPTER 2

The Buddhist View
Is Mantrayana Possible Without Sutra?

Someone who has mastered the Sutra in a past life may practise on Mantrayana without paying much heed to the Sutras in this life. For an ordinary being who has no knowledge or experience of emptiness and compassion as they are explained in the Sutras, to practise Mantrayana, visualizing deities with eyes shut and reciting mantras with a mouth wide open, may not be very beneficial, if not harmful. It seems that what is mentioned in the Tantras and the chastising words in the teachings of past masters, are now being experienced by some practitioners today.

An acquaintance of mine who is a kind of Dharma practitioner told me, "I have to practise the wrathful deities when I am alone. If my family members are around during such practice I have to beat them. I cannot practise the peaceful deities with lustful appearances at night before going to bed because I become stupefied with desire and cannot sleep at all. Next morning my mind becomes dull and I have a difficult time the whole day." He told me such funny and yet such saddening things.

I felt this was certainly due to some wrong way of meditation. Otherwise he would not have such experiences. As a sign of spiritual practice, even if one is not able to turn the sufferings of afflictive emotions into the nature of the two stages, one must be able to prevent one's freedom from becoming subservient to affliction.

THE MIND THAT GRASPS AT TRUE EXISTENCE IS CALLED IGNORANCE

Aside from leaving the externally apparent phenomena untouched – as existing as they appear, some practitioners pretend to meditate on the completion stage, emptiness, Dzogchen or Mahamudra as if there is something else to negate and, closing all the sense organs, they meditate on emptiness of mind. I believe this is "naming a child before its birth" as the proverb says, and this is not the correct way for people like us to practice. Though, it is possible that this kind of meditation may work for some types of beings. As I always stress, when we say that everything is made by the mind, you don't have to think that the whole external environment and its animate and inanimate inhabitants, such as mountains, rocks, buildings *etc.* are manufactured by a factory called mind. Similarly, as I just said, it would not be right to close one's eyes and all the other sense organs and forcefully meditate on nothingness, just leaving these phenomena alone as though they have no connection with mind. So then what should one do? There is a lot to explain, but I don't want to go into details here. I have already explained this a bit earlier according to our level of wisdom.

To distinguish between mind and the nature of mind: mind has to be understood as conceptual thought. What is conceived? It first conceives of an 'I', which does not exist in fact, and then this leads to the concept of 'mine', which in turn leads to desire, aversion and ignorance and all the positive and negative actions.

The familiar *Wheel of Life* is painted on either the right or left hand side wall of most temple doors. If one looks carefully in the centre there's the picture of the rooster, pig and snake following one another. You have to understand their significance. The pig symbolizes ignorance, the root of cyclic birth, which looks at the non-existent 'I' as existent. Today some people say that the pig is an intelligent animal and it is wrong to paint it as the symbol of ignorance. I feel that ignorance is not something unintelligible surrounded by darkness. On the contrary it is extremely *smart*. The rooster symbolizes desire, the master or cause of all the illusions in the world. The snake symbolizes aversion or hatred. They are called the three poisons. They symbolise the three basic defilements.

We can classify all thoughts into one of the three poisons – all positive thoughts come under desire, all negative thoughts come under hatred and all neutral thoughts come under ignorance. This is a unique spiritual term used by realized yogis. There's not a moment when those of us in this cyclic existence are not under the influence of these three thoughts, twenty-four hours of the day.

While under the influence of a positive thought we are attached to clinging to positive perception, while under the influence of a negative thought we cling to negative perception and have hatred, and while under the influence of neutral thought we grasp at ignorant perception. Thus starting with ignorance the whole cycle continues ceaselessly. If one thinks hard about it, ignorance is the most heinous root poison.

For example, all robbers are equal but the gang leader is the most influential and heinous, and the gang members follow the orders of the leader. Without their leader the gang members will not be as capable. Similarly, desire, hatred and ignorance are equally at the root of cyclic rebirth, but desire and hatred are set on the path by ignorance, and desire and hatred alone would not be able to continue on their own.

Ignorance sees the non-existent as existing. The scriptures mention, "ignorance that grasps as truly existing", meaning it is ignorance that sees something not true as the truth. It grasps at something, which does not exist primordially, as existing, and as a result all the perception of big and small, high and low, happy and suffering and good and bad appear. "Appear" does not mean something like the sun rising or a flower blossoming. It means clinging to the perception and to the perception as existing. It is important to understand this. Not just understand, but to practise by applying the understanding to experiences in everyday life. It seems that some people who spend their entire life as practitioner fall into cyclic rebirth due to their failure to cross this crucial point.

The description of perception can be endless. To give an example of a particular perception, two men may perceive the appearance of a woman in two different ways. One may find her beautiful but the second man may find her disgusting. When you investigate, you see that it was the second person's mind that found the woman disgusting. It is similar to saying "my mind perceived her as disgusting", because the woman's body by itself does not establish anything as disgusting. Likewise, the other person sees the woman as beautiful and it is his mind that perceives her as beautiful. Why do two men have two different perceptions about the same woman? It can be understood that it is the minds of the two men that perceived the woman as beautiful or ugly, and nothing about her body establishes her beauty or ugliness.

One will gradually understand that long or short, high and low, tasty and not tasty, sweet and bitter are all just perceptions and so is their nature. As Dharmakirti says in *Pramanavartika*,[33] "Clearing the web of perceptions, possessing the profound and extensive form, the light of Samantabhadra radiates completely", that the main cause of all the suffering is this grasping perception and if the perceptions are ignored the only result one can achieve is Dharmakaya, or the Truth

---

33. Commentary on Valid Cognition — Dharmakirti's main treatise on pramana, the most important of his "Seven Treatises on Valid Cognition".

Body of Buddha. Tilopa said to Naropa, "Son, you are not shackled by appearances but by attachment. Abandon attachment, Naropa." As Tilopa instructed, one has to break the shackles of clinging to perception. Clinging to non-existence of perception and blocking it, or meditating with fixation on vacuity is not needed for practitioners like me. Whether a practitioner or a family man, if one does not understand that all phenomenal existences are illusions, fabricated by one's mind, and one holds the wrong view or ignorant conception that all external phenomena exist as they appear, then the sense of joy and frustration, attachment and aversion, arising from spiritual practice will grow. This will eventually lead to sectarianism.

SECTARIANISM AND INFIGHTING

For example, criticizing other Bodhisattvas and spiritual masters on the pretext of serving one's own tradition; those with power misusing their power to capture the clergy and laity of other traditions, or occupying them through deception and encouraging the followers to do so, is the cause of rebirth in hell. I have heard of such incidents all over the world. Similar things have happened in Tibet and among Tibetan Buddhists in the past, and one can see some people doing so even today. It is despicable. Neither Buddha's teachings nor commentaries of his followers mention that one should resort to plundering and robbery to promote and preserve one's tradition. Dagpo Lhaje[34] chastised, "Not practising Dharma according to the Dharma will be the cause of cyclic rebirth." Buddha has taught against criticism of or harming not only other traditions within Buddhism but also other religious traditions. Whether one follows Buddhism or a non-Buddhist tradition, it is important not to start with wrong inauspicious foundations, but rather to undergo proper learning and contemplation.

A WRONG ATTITUDE CAN CAUSE PROBLEMS

Religion is a good thing that gives peace of mind and physical happiness to all. For this reason religion has survived for many centuries. However, not understanding that the objective of religion

---

34. Dagpo Lhaje Sonam Rinchen alias Gampopa (1079–1153).

is to improve one's mind, and influenced by the severe delusion of serving one's own religion through deception and use of force to recruit followers, religion has become the cause of most of the violence and social instability in the world today. Like the proverb says, "One evil person can destroy the kingdom." Due to the use of violence and deception by a few religions and a few religious practitioners, with a total disregard for the law of cause and effect, all men and women in the garb of spiritual practitioners of any tradition whatsoever, irrespective of whether they are proper practitioners or not, have suffered a loss of social respect as a result.

During a conversation with some friends a few days ago they said that nowadays, if your passport, or letter of invitation makes any mention of a title or profession related to religion, then you have to go through a lot of unnecessary interrogation and frisking at the check posts. This is really sad. Also, it was said that when receiving sponsorship money, the term monk or nun should not be mentioned, because if you do that the government becomes suspicious. I have never heard of anything like this in the past. It seems that many illegal money dealings were carried out in the name of religious practitioners. Today, all religious practitioners face problems. Any practitioner – excellent, middling or inferior – belonging to any religion, Buddhist or non-Buddhist, must possess such qualities as selflessness and the altruistic motivation to bring peace and happiness to society. Then he or she will become worthy of honour and be respected by others.

In the Sutras, Buddha has described the Sangha members as "Worthy of being greeted respectfully with folded hands, worthy of being saluted respectfully", and as being more equal than others. He further said, "However feeble my followers may be, a hundred ordinary beings will not be equal to one." This may be explained as following his body, following his mind and following his speech. But my understanding here is that a follower is one who applies his/her mind to the Buddha's teachings on not harming but loving all beings at all times, and practising this path regularly without being proud about the few qualities he/she possesses. So despite all your proclamations, if you do not possess any qualitative value then it would be very difficult to succeed. Some of the instruction texts say that just as the crows pick the eyes and intestines out of an animal that has lost all physical strength, even before the animal is dead, one will not survive unless one has the genuine spiritual qualities of kind heartedness. Even if one is able to meet one's selfish ends by deceiving others, ultimately it will not only have a negative impact in this life and the next, but will also harm the religion.

PRACTITIONERS SHOULD DO PRACTICAL SOCIAL SERVICE AND NOT ONLY PRAYERS AND MEDITATION

If we spiritual practitioners keep deceiving people, then they may lose faith in the body, mind and speech activities of the genuine masters as a result of seeing our behaviour and this will harm the activities of the spiritual masters, as I have said earlier. When people lose faith in the activities of the spiritual masters, they will have no field of activity in the world. The genuine spiritual masters who have freedom of birth and death say they will leave for the pure-land because they have no field of activity in this world. Then we become like orphans with no one to show us the right path. In essence, unless one attains true happiness from within the mind, there is no genuine happiness but only suffering in this world, and we would spent our entire life in search of happiness.

So how do we search for happiness within the mind? This can be shown only by a true spiritual path and a genuine spiritual teacher. So when the genuine spiritual practitioners and teachers are no more, it will be a great loss to the entire world community. I am referring to Buddhism here when I say spiritual path. Investigation shows that other non-Buddhist religions also have a socially beneficial view, behaviour and meditation methods. So long as beings are not harmed but benefitted I don't see much difference between religions, because it will be difficult to bring inter-faith harmony by being rigid about views, since there are few profound practitioners around today. Even if you look at the history of differences of views, things have not served well.

Differences of view remain even among Buddhists, not to mention between Buddhists and non-Buddhists. So I always say that life will be more convenient if you keep the view as your own secret practice, meditation as internal practice and behaviour or activity as the external practice. I say this at every opportunity I get, but since I am too small a person there are very few people who would listen to me. Non-harming behaviour is taught by Buddhist teachers and one can also see that even among Christians and Hindus, there are many who dedicate their lives in taking care of the poor, sick and disabled beings. Seeing their wonderful work I rejoice, and pray that such people have a healthy long life and prosperity.

A Buddhist like me stays in one place and prays to train the mind for the benefit of all beings. This of course is good. But adapting to the times, I appeal to you to learn to practically contribute whatever you can to groups that give food, medicine, clothes, shelter and education to the poor and needy, or even just one meal to the stray dogs.

BUDDHISTS MUST HAVE SOME UNDERSTANDING OF THE BUDDHIST VIEW

If those of us, in the form of practitioners, cannot consider that all perception, good or bad, is illusory and a fabrication of the mind and not a creation by perception itself, we will remain practitioners only physically, without any authentic quality within. Even if we give teachings or recite prayers one will feel a sort of reluctance in doing genuine practise, not knowing how to practise. Even ordinary lay people will have no choice but to engage in illusory activities, causing suffering in this life and the next, and having to return empty handed after working right up to their last – their last speech and last meal. For example, all of us have to ultimately die. As you lie on your sick bed and tears well up in your eyes, feeling sad that there is no escape from death, all that you have done in life flashes through your mind and you realize that you have done nothing meaningful for the benefit of human society or other beings. After having worked so hard for your personal interest, you are faced with death and you become disheartened. Faced with sickness and impending death, you are forced to put your thumb print on legal documents, and even before your death all your hard earned wealth is taken away by others, as rightfully belonging to them. Very few among your own children use your name with love and respect. We remain fooled until we reach this stage by our inability to understand delusion as delusion, and clinging to illusion as the innate truth, while walking, sitting or sleeping. This is what the scriptures describe as inherent ignorance and it has always been with us. Even the smallest insects have this inherent ignorance.

AN EXAMPLE OF HOW EVERYTHING IS CREATED BY THE MIND

If you think deeply, even if you don't have any extensive knowledge, you know that good and bad, joy and sorrow, fear and hope are all fabricated by the mind. For example, when you say "good", this is defined by the culture of the country, the traditions of the time, and especially by one's way of thinking. There is nothing good that is proven by the object itself. The object that you consider good may be found to be bad by thousands of other people. You cannot foolishly insist that what you find good *is* good. For example, the clothes that the older generation considered bad, are regarded as fashionable by the younger generation today, and are highly priced. We can understand that it is our mind that makes an object good or bad and that the object by itself is neither good nor bad. You spent a great deal of time and effort with high expectations of acquiring an object that the mind is attached to as good, but then you find yourself faced with impending death. Even if you acquire the object and are able to spend some time with it, it will be difficult to get the expected mental satisfaction and physical joy that you had craved for. It can also be concluded that you will suffer from mental agony caused by jealousy and competitiveness on seeing others' wealth and luxury. Similarly, given your aversion to a bad object you make every effort to avoid or evade it, and then you die without leaving a trace. Or even if you live long, the enemy that you have been avoiding becomes your friend and you have to live with him. When the servants that you once scorned and bullied become high officials, you have no choice but to bow before them and respect them. When the clothes and ornaments that you once disliked become fashionable, now you need them. When you think about all these things and analyse your way of thinking over the years, don't you feel embarrassed? It is your mind that fabricates all this

INVESTIGATE THE ORIGIN OF HAPPINESS

If we understand that whatever feelings of good or bad, and emotional fixation of good or bad, do not arise externally, but are the results of following the tendencies of good or bad created by the mind, it will be helpful in your daily life, no matter whether you have faith in and knowledge of Buddhism or not. We try to seek mental happiness through external objects such as a beautiful body, melodious sounds, sweet fragrances, *etc.*, and this is one of the basic reasons we remain unsatisfied. Due to our failure to seek mental happiness through the mind, we suffer from a lack of mental happiness. The little happiness one gets from seeing and touching a beautiful body, or hearing melodious songs and music, or consuming alcohol and drugs is momentary, and not only does the happiness disappear after a few hours, but it then also becomes suffering. Beauty, sexual intercourse, melodious songs and music, alcohol and drugs may be treated as causal conditions of happiness, but it would be wrong to recognize them as the origin of happiness. Because of our dependence on this wrong notion, we have been running after sensuous pleasures, which is insatiable. Like drinking salty water, it will never quench your thirst. In such a situation, one does not have the tendency to care for one's family members, let alone rendering religious, cultural and social service, and in desperation one is willing to sell one's own body.

The addiction to sensuous pleasure makes one pawn one's belongings or even resort to stealing. If one is able to realize that the happiness experienced from seeing a beautiful body, hearing melodious songs, smelling sweet fragrances or sexual intercourse *etc.*, does not arise from the object concerned but by the mind at that very moment, then one will understand it as momentary happiness or the suffering of change. So even if it is not an everlasting happiness, this will certainly help you gain a new understanding of the mind, and this experience itself becomes a teacher giving you instructions. Although this happiness, endowed with wisdom, is contaminated with affliction, it certainly helps one stop running after beauty, melodious sounds, scent *etc.* to the extent of risking one's life.

Today people spend a lot of time and effort preparing plans to go hunting or fishing, to go on a picnic or to discotheques and bars on the weekends, and with whom to go, but when you actually go as planned then there is nothing much to do. So when you think about the source of all these thoughts and acts, it comes down to selfishness, your desire for happiness. Not just this, but as mentioned earlier, our failure to understand the source of happiness makes us believe that happiness comes from external factors such as a boyfriend or girlfriend, sensuous pleasures of food and drink, fame, power and wealth. So, if one has the right mental bearing in the face of sorrows arising out of unfulfilled desires, caused by a wrong view, then whenever one goes somewhere or befriends somebody or does anything, all the joy and sorrow one experiences become teachings, and these teachers help the state of thought.

If at the moment of sorrow, one knows that it is a change in the state of thought, then one would not feel futile anger or be disheartened or depressed, and one would not think of engaging in meaningless acts like suicide, fratricide or any evil deed. Therefore, I think if one understands the salient point, it is not so difficult to lead a meaningful life.

> To the Lord of Compassion, Avalokiteshvara,
> To the sole protector, Mahaguru,
> To Glorious Naropa and Tsangpa Gyare,
> And to the continually incarnating teachers of the past,
> I pay homage.

As explained earlier, one has to understand that all external phenomena are the manifestations of the mind, and one should engage in the practice of checking the nature of mind. Since the law of karma is infallible, practising meditation to tame the mind, recitations to accomplish a deity, ethics to protect modesty, or generosity to gain wealth will certainly result in various worldly happiness or sorrows. However, without maintaining an altruistic disposition to help others and seeing kind-heartedness as important, and without practising them, it is doubtful that all the individual practices will lead to the attainment of the union state of Vajradhara.

Without the method of great compassion there is no way to attain the Form Body, and without this there is no way to establish the union state of Vajradhara. Ultimately, even the definition of the base, path and fruit of the beings of the three capabilities, has to be established on the basis of the power of compassion. Therefore, the level of compassion is described as the main root cause differentiating Buddha, Bodhisattvas, Shravakas, Pratyekabuddhas and Arhats.

THE TWO MIND GENERATIONS

In Mahayana there are two types of mind-generation: ultimate and conventional. But for beginners, the conventional mind-generation is given primacy and it is of two types – the aspirational mind of enlightenment and the engaging mind of enlightenment – and for beginners like us, training in the aspirational mind of enlightenment is more important. The aspirational mind of enlightenment ultimately means a kind heart because, as it is said, "If the intention is good, all ground and path are good; if the intention is evil all ground and path are evil", it is regarded as the foundation of the five paths and the ten *Bhumis*, or grounds.

A kind heart or good intention has to be trained through the Four Immeasurable Thoughts,[35] because when ordinary beings like us engage in any activity, spiritual or worldly, a strong selfishness arises simultaneously, and so it is difficult to have a completely genuine kind-heartedness. This selfishness becomes the cause of downfall even for spiritual practitioners who believe in the law of karma, and an evil-minded person can bring unhappiness to the whole world before his ultimate downfall. History shows that many a king, many presidents, the rich and powerful and those famed for their looks, voice or influence finally ended up committing suicide or falling victim to guns or poison.

Even in today's society, many people lose their mental balance, become depressed or become alcoholics or drug addicts, and because of this they suffer from incurable diseases. Because of their accumulation of merit in past lives, they become powerful rulers, or are born with good looks, a melodious voice and fame. But in this life they are driven only by their selfish desire and all the merit they had accumulated in their past lives has already ripened, and is now exhausted. Since their selfish desire is too strong, they are unable to do good deeds for the future, and this leads to their downfall. If we have all the sense faculties, and we are intelligent and as educated as we think we are, we must understand that the next life lasts longer

---

35. The Four Immeasurable Thoughts: 1. Immeasurable love, which is the wish that living beings may have happiness and its causes, which is the wish that living beings may be free from suffering and its causes; 2. Immeasurable compassion; 3. Immeasurable joy, which is the wish that living beings may remain happy and their happiness may increase further; 4. Immeasurable equanimity, which is the wish that beings may be free from the attitude of attachment to some and aversion to others.

than this life. Even if you do not believe in life after death, one should treat yesterday's experience as a lesson for today and what you learn today as the basis for progress tomorrow.

In brief, if one is not able to plan for ultimate happiness or lasting happiness in the future, then one's all intelligence and education is wasted. Even small insects work to fulfill their minor desires for happiness that lasts about an hour or so, and if you do the same thing then you are not using your human intelligence and smartness. Since the law of karma is infallible, major sufferings will certainly be lined up for you to experience in the future. If one is not able to take this into consideration, then one is bound to have a hard time. I often feel that even for a non-believer it is important to end one's life in happiness. Therefore, the path that eliminates selfishness and generates the altruistic mind is called the right path. Selfishness and kind-heartedness are like light and darkness. Just as there cannot be darkness where there is sunlight, there will be no selfishness where there is good intention and where there is selfishness there cannot be good intention. Knowing that the two cannot coexist, one must always check oneself. The wish to learn the good path is known as the two-fold or two-sided wish. The instruction manuals clearly describe them as: one side that concentrates on sentient beings out of compassion, and the other side that concentrates on enlightenment with complete wisdom. Therefore, it is clearly stated that a firm foundation should first be laid with pure love and compassion aimed at innumerable beings.

OTHER BEINGS, LIKE ONESELF, EQUALLY SEEK HAPPINESS AND DO NOT WANT SUFFERING

Before concentrating on innumerable beings, first concentrate on yourself, then your parents, then your relatives and friends and ultimately one will be able to concentrate on innumerable beings. As the Sutra says, "Look at your body, and do not harm others", it is important to see that just as you seek love, happiness, peace, good health and warmth – so all beings seek the same thing. When you ponder on this, don't you think you need to base this on the thought of taking care of yourself? If there is no mind that cares for yourself, then the example of "your body" in the above quotation "Look at your body" would be meaningless. Pondering on this, makes you realize that both you and others equally seek happiness and do not want suffering. All beings of different shapes and sizes, high and low, have an equal right to happiness.

UNDERSTANDING THE MEANING OF EQUAL RIGHTS

"Equal rights" means that since all beings seek happiness equally and do not seek suffering, they have equal rights to follow the path of negating suffering and generating happiness. This is not what people are doing today by fighting for rights to simply fulfill their petty selfish ends. If you understand this you will not want to be involved in violence, plundering, beating and verbal abuse. In brief, the mind that sees how sad and unhappy you feel when someone hurts you, will understand how others will feel if you hurt them. This will naturally decrease the thought of hurting others and increase the good intention of helping others. Otherwise, if your focus remains only on pursuing your own happiness and acting as though it is your right to achieve it by any way, you will never be able to help others. In fact you will destroy others' happiness. If you kill living beings and eat them, loot the rich and make them poor, and deceive others through fraud and enticement, who would consider this as a good deed? Think hard and you will understand it.

WE ARE LIVING GHOULS WHO DARE TO KILL AND EAT ANIMALS THAT LOVE US

While we seem so concerned over a minor toothache or headache and immediately take medicines, it is not fair and right to kill domestic animals, like goats, sheep, horses, cows and oxen that give us milk, wool, butter and cheese, carry loads or plough the fields. We even kill the harmless wild birds and skin them, eat their meat, chew their bones and drink their blood. If you think about it properly, it is not right to kill innocent animals to meet our petty desires. This is a true sign of our ignorance. Daring to do so also proves that we are living ghouls. We always think that ghouls are a different fearsome species that drink blood and eat flesh, but it seems that they are not worse than us. In today's world, we are increasingly scared of one another, because the number of such ghouls is growing. Dharma practitioners do not think about this, and so their practice of the Four

Immeasurable Thoughts remains unsuccessful. Some of us think that the view of emptiness, Mahamudra or Dzogchen is more important, and many prefer to stay alone on the pretext of doing meditation, without paying attention to mind training. Of course there may be excellent yogis among them who have attained firm compassion and Bodhicitta and nothing can be said about them. Otherwise, I see it as waste of time.

Sakya Pandita said, "The fool meditating on Mahamudra, will mostly become the cause of rebirth in the animal realm", meaning that unless one attains a certain firmness of devotion, and immeasurable loving kindness and compassion as the foundation of meditation, any pretension of meditating on emptiness, Mahamudra or Dzogchen will not yield results. Otherwise, meditating on Mahamudra according to the text could not be the cause of rebirth in the animal realm. He said, "Emptiness is meditated upon by Shravakas; its result is cessation." Novices like us need to first complete mind training to generate good intention and then use this good intention to aid meditation on emptiness. Without loving kindness and compassion, the view alone is of no use.

ANY ACT OF VIRTUE MUST HAVE THE TOUCH OF SINCERE GOOD INTENTION

There is no doubt that the ultimate fruit of complete enlightenment, accomplishing the dual purpose of self and others, will be attained within a short time if formal Bodhisattva practices like generosity and moral conduct are done with genuine loving kindness and compassion. Generosity and moral conduct by themselves may bring worldly happiness, or rebirth as beings of small or middling capacity.

In essence, the prayer, "May those who have not generated the precious sublime Bodhicitta, generate it. And may the one generated remain undefiled and grow from strength to strength". This should not remain just a prayer, but its meaning should be practised to train one's mind. If possible, one should try to practise the teachings given in the texts on Mind Training.

It is said that for people like us who lack diligence and intelligence, the Four Immeasurable Thoughts encompasses the entire teaching. Immeasurable loving kindness, compassion, joy and equanimity aimed at innumerable beings are known as the Four Immeasurable

Thoughts. This can be further summarized as loving kindness and compassion. Wishing happiness for others is loving kindness and the wish to free other beings from suffering is compassion. The compassionate mind that seeks freedom from suffering summarizes everything, according to many texts. Therefore, it is essential to practise compassion and to give it importance. My view is that we should first try to gain some understanding about equanimity, treating all beings as the children of the same mother, without prejudice, attachment or aversion. Train the conceptual mind to treat oneself, others, samsara and nirvana, good and bad, friends and foes, with equanimity. Then we can put into practise impartial and immeasurable compassion derived from joy, and loving kindness induced by compassion, as taught in the Mahayana scriptures.

As I said, most of us ignore the need to generate the compassionate mind and do not treat it as a quality, and instead pay attention to other fields of learning and study with diligence to achieve progress. We ignore the fact that compassion is the foundation of all physical well-being and peace of mind, power and wealth, fame and all qualities, and instead, we sweat to achieve something else; this is like hoping to build a grand building without thinking about the firmness of the foundation. This is really sad. It is because of this that even though those of us in the garb of Dharma practitioners engage in prayers, virtuous deeds, generosity and moral conduct, two-stage yoga, study Sutra and Tantra scriptures, the science of medicine and astrology *etc.*, we hardly see any progress in our minds. On the contrary, it seems to degenerate year by year.

Asanga meditated on Maitreya for almost thirteen years and he didn't get even a single auspicious sign. But then, he came across a dog whose lower body was covered with festering wounds and he felt great compassion, and so he attempted to clean the wounds with his tongue. As he closed his eyes preparing to lick the wounds, the dog disappeared, as in fact it was an emanation of Maitreya, and Maitreya then appeared directly before him. He embraced Maitreya and cried, saying "You were so unkind not to grace me with your appearance until today." Maitreya replied, "You and I have been inseparably together all along, but you did not see me because your compassion was limited. If you don't believe me, then carry me on your shoulders and walk through the market. Unless there is someone there with compassion, no one will see me." Asanga then carried

Maitreya, the future Buddha, on his shoulders through the market, and only one kind-hearted, compassionate old woman saw Asanga carrying a dog whose lower body was covered with wounds. Other people saw nothing. Asanga then believed it, and received teachings from Maitreya.

Taking into account such authentic historic tales, it can be said that we too may have accumulated merit and purified defilements to a small extent from time immemorial, but it is clear that due to the negative power of selfishness and the lack of the positive strength of Bodhicitta and compassion, we have not been able to nourish these positive qualities, and remain in a state of slumber. Compassion is the key to opening the path to happiness for disciples training in the path. It is an indispensable skill required for the yogis who have entered the path. Even after purifying all defilements, and nurturing all virtues, and achieving the ultimate goal of enlightenment, it is compassion that enables the enlightened ones to spontaneously tame beings through appropriate methods, and benefit them with great kindness. This is the key vow of Bodhisattva practice.

COMPASSION SUSTAINS US IN THIS WORLD

We must understand that we are only able to walk on our feet, speak, hear or see because of compassion. When we are first born – whether high or low, rich or poor – we are just an unclean lump of a body, and the mother with great love takes it into her arms, cleans it and feeds it, giving it the most nutritious diet and best clothes and necessary medicine to bring it up. She teaches us how to sit, walk and speak and to make us fit in to human society. Even if the mother passes away after childbirth, the father, an uncle or aunt takes care of the child and brings it up out of love. It must be understood that we have not been brought up out of ulterior motives or bad intentions. Not just human beings, but even fearful wild animals like tigers or leopards take care of their cubs with love and compassion, and train them in the skills they need as they grow up and enable them to stand on their own feet. I always feel it is important to understand this.

Most of us think we are self-reliant because of our own ability. Some feel that it is just good fortune and don't understand anything. This is what we call the ignorance that we talk about so much. Other than this, ignorance isn't something that stinks like a rotten blanket or appears black like smoke. Without great compassion as the base, all good things in samsara, like a cool breeze during the hot season, a warming fire or the sun during the cold season, a bridge to cross a river, a railway for long distance journeys or anything that makes us happy and healthy would not be there. There is no doubt that the compassion of a kind-hearted mother gives us happiness and not suffering – whether we be high or low, strong or weak.

From the philosophical point of view, since the subtle phenomena remain hidden, opinions remain divided and vary among the different religions. We blindly follow selfishness without thinking about compassion. If we use our intelligence we can certainly appreciate the importance and value of compassion and, except for the mentally ill or mentally disabled, any normal person in society should definitely accept this. It is really sad to notice the lack of a common stance regarding compassion.

As it is said, "What is known as Avalokiteshvara, is the Great Compassion", the compassion of all the Buddhas appears in the form of Avalokiteshvara for the benefit of all sentient beings. Possessing the wisdom that has arisen from hearing such logic and having devotion, thanks to my gurus, I have full faith that the root and lineage gurus, spiritual masters of different lineages and all the big and small, positive and negative things, that create the conditions, including my joy to practise Dharma with compassion as the base, are the blessings of Avalokiteshvara, the embodiment of compassion of all the Buddhas. Although I do not possess any political or spiritual wisdom, I am happy that I have no doubt that Avalokiteshvara will take care of me in this life, the intermediate stage and in the next life.

WE PRACTISE ALL THE THREE VEHICLES

Therefore, Avalokiteshvara followed by Guru Padmasambhava, are the main objects of homage in the second line of the invocation stanza. Guru Padmasambhava lit the Dharma torch in India, China, Nepal, Tibet, and Bhutan and throughout the Himalayan region. His kindness in leading so many countless beings to temporary and ultimate happiness cannot be measured, just as the extent of space cannot be measured. Texts and logic show that all of us who practise the higher and lower vehicles, and Mantrayana or Vajrayana Buddhism, and have faith in them, must remember the kindness of Guru Rinpoche.

The Buddhism we follow has the special feature of combining all the three vehicles. Externally peaceful conduct, similar to that of the Hinayana, forms the foundation; internally, the main focus is on training in the path of loving kindness, compassion and Bodhicitta; and secretly the view of seeing the duality of samsara and nirvana, cause and effect, good and bad and happiness and sorrow as the primordially complete state of union of bliss.

The process of the path can be practised without deviating from the vows, even for a moment, by an individual, gradually or simultaneously. If this path, leading to higher and higher realms is followed, not just in words but practically, one can complete purification within one lifetime and realize through experience the true nature of all appearance and existence. This may be called Buddhahood or enlightenment or liberation from cyclic existence. Then one need not take rebirth in samsaric suffering without freedom. Instead, one has the ability to happily and willingly manifest in various forms for the temporary and ultimate benefit of other beings. Knowing that we are able to practise such a Dharma, like an outer defence wall and inner jewel, indispensable pure gold-like teaching, is thanks to Guru Padmasambhava, and I pay homage to him with joy.

GRATEFUL TO BE SPIRITUALLY UNBIASED

If one is able to do genuine practice without engaging in acts of renunciation of Dharma, like stubbornly following only a particular teaching of the Buddha, categorizing the Buddhas and Bodhisattvas and saying I follow this Buddha or that Bodhisattva, discriminating between the higher and lower vehicles and praising one and criticizing the other, creating sectarianism amongst followers through factionalism among monasteries and gurus, one can be proud that the Buddha Dharma is special with many features. By their kindness, the Abbot, Master and Spiritual King[36] and the great translators introduced the pure undiluted view and conduct of the Nalanda tradition. I feel that it is our good fortune to possess this jewel-like precious teaching, to practise without internal contradiction and to

---

36. Abbot Shantarakshita, Master Padmasambhava and Spiritual King Trisong Deutsan.

have firm faith in this marvellous tradition. Those who have studied the scriptures would know this. Some of you might think I am praising our own tradition. I don't blame you. If some time in the future you get the opportunity to receive teachings from an impartial master, guru or abbot who possesses the qualities described in the text, and study and contemplate by focussing on the teachings and not the person, you will understand the characteristics of Buddhism in general, and in particular the distinctive features of the Lineage you are following. At that point you will personally know for sure what I am saying today. The teachings are flawless and there were many undisputedly great holy beings among us in the past. There have also been sad experiences in history as well. In his prophesy Guru Rinpoche said, "A ghost possesses the heart of every Tibetan" and "At that time the people will have neither fortune nor fame" and "The time of happiness will be like the shadow of the dome." Unwanted mishaps took place for many generations, finally leading to the present situation. I just mention this in passing.

The other object of invocation is the great Naropa, manifestation of Avalokiteshvara prophesied by the Buddha. A great scholar of the five major and five minor sciences, he mastered all the objects of knowledge and served Nalanda immensely well as a great Pandita, or scholar. A great yogi, who following the instructions of his Guru Tilopa, cleared all the doubts about the true nature of all phenomena, through internal experience without relying on words, he stood out like the moon amongst the galaxy of scholars and siddhas. We can neither completely narrate nor imagine the unfathomable biography of the three secrets of such a scholar and realized being. It is difficult for ordinary beings like us, however intelligent and eloquent, to give a complete narration of his activities in this human world.

However, to give a brief account, as given in the biography and relevant to the topic here, as you know he was born in Kashmir.

His father's name was Shiwai Gocha and mothers' name was Palgyi Lodo. He was a Brahmin by caste. He was born in 1016, over 1500 years after the Buddha's Mahaparinirvana, according to the biography. He learned grammar and logic at a young age. Later he became a monk and studied the meaning of the *Tripitakas* and the *Four Tantras* completely and became a great scholar. He also took on the responsibility of the scholar guardian of the northern gate of Nalanda.

While holding the spiritual responsibilities of listening and teaching, he felt, "Though I am a scholar I cannot hold my mind even for the duration of the time it takes to milk a cow. I am uncertain where to go and I have to find a way to control the mind", and he thought of going in search of a guru. He received a prophesy to go east in search of Guru Tilopa, and he suddenly left all his teaching responsibilities and went east in search of his guru. He asked around for the whereabouts of Tilopa, but no one had any information and he wandered around for a long time without finding the guru.

During his search, Naropa came across a man who had killed another man and eaten his intestines, and another time he came across a hunter. He did not realize that these were the manifestations of the guru appearing in order to tame him, and even after facing many hardships on his search he did not find the guru.

One day, Naropa saw a thin man inside the ruins of a temple, burning live fish and eating them. When Naropa said, "Don't do it", the man blew over the fish and put them back in the water and the fish were restored to life. As soon as Naropa wondered if this person of such power could be Tilopa, the person replied, "I am." Naropa realized that he possessed prophetic knowledge and immediately placed Tilopa's feet on his own head, and requested him to take care of him. Tilopa just kicked Naropa and walked away without saying anything. But Naropa just kept following Tilopa.

They reached the top of a multi-storeyed building and Tilopa asked, "Could there be anyone brave enough to jump off from here?" Naropa thought the question was meant for him and jumped off without hesitation. His body broke into pieces and he experienced unbearable pain. Tilopa came and asked, "Are you in pain?" To which he replied, "It is not just pain. I am as good as dead." Anyway with the blessings of the guru, he recovered.

One day they came to a river filled with poisonous insects and crocodiles. Tilopa asked Naropa to serve as a bridge for the guru to cross over. He did so but fell into the river and was bitten by insects. Again, by the blessings of his guru he recovered. Naropa underwent twelve such major trials. These are all mentioned in the biography and I don't need to go into details here. It is said that the twelve major trials symbolized cessation of the twelve dependent originations.

Then Naropa asked for teachings and Tilopa said, "Son, you have faced many hardships, braving the sufferings of heat and cold. Now offer a mandala and I will give you teachings." Naropa looked around for water but could not find any. So he cut his own veins and sprinkled the blood on the floor to cleanse the ground. He cut his ears and made the symbolic structure representing the universe, offered mandala and requested teaching. Tilopa then struck Naropa's face with his slippers and he fainted. When he regained consciousness he immediately realized the nature of wisdom of the innate Mahamudra. Tilopa said, "*Kye Ho!* This is self-cognizant wisdom. It is beyond speech and beyond the scope of the mind. I, Tilopa, have nothing to show. Understand it as symbol of self-cognizance", and with that, the secret link was established. Tilopa advised Naropa to give up his status as a scholar and to concentrate on meditation, and he prophesied that if he did so he would attain the supreme accomplishment within this life.

While Naropa was in one-pointed meditation, Jain scholars came to debate with Buddhists, and the Buddhists were on the verge of losing. The Buddhists in the neighbourhood requested Naropa to come to their aid and join the debate. Worried that the Dharma taught by the Buddhists would suffer if he did not, he accepted their request. During the debate Naropa faced great difficulty in countering the non-Buddhists, unlike in the past. He wondered why he, a great scholar, was experiencing such difficulty in debating against the non-Buddhists. He realized that he had broken the guru's advice not to engage in teachings and debates as a scholar. He prostrated and confessed, and then Tilopa appeared to him in a vision and said, "You have gone against my words. So you will not gain supreme accomplishment in this life. You will attain supreme accomplishment in the intermediate state of existence. Now work for the benefit of exposition and practice of the teachings. Your disciple's disciple will be greater than the disciple and the pupil's pupil will be better than the pupil. This way there will be more progress." So Naropa followed his guru's command and benefitted innumerable sentient beings. You all know this. His lineage holders Marpa, Mila and Gampopa and the equally accomplished root and branch gurus of different cultures, traditions and customs in India, Nepal and Tibet are all emanations of Avalokiteshvara, who out of compassion have come in the form of spiritual masters to tame the beings.

ONLY TEACHINGS TO GENERATE DEVOTION AMONG NOVICES SHOULD BE GIVEN

Some pretentious scholars, who themselves have not understood the Buddha's thoughts, attempt to analyse the state of other spiritual masters and categorize them as good or bad. They do not leave the biography of past masters alone and insert selfish distortions, spreading falsehood as genuine teachings, deceiving others and holding wrong views of others on the basis of regionalism and sectarianism. Buddha has said that such acts are more heinous than killing all the beings in the three realms. They are an object of embarrassment and a joke to the objective scholars. Except for exposing the writer's own pent-up faults, these writings serve no useful purpose.

Today, we not only eagerly engage in incidental acts of renunciation of the Dharma, but also teach them to followers and admirers as well as innocent foreign novices and people who have blind faith in their community. It is really sad. Maybe they have no option but to indulge in sectarianism since they have to spread their own tradition. However, I often wish that such gurus would, for a moment, stop using attachment and aversion to spread their own tradition and instead sow the seed of Dharma among the devotees who spend time and effort to meet the guru, with the hope of getting a teaching that would help them in this and the next life and undistractedly gaze at the guru's face with folded hands. I wish they would give some advice that would help them to develop their minds, and understand that sectarianism is the cause of rebirth in hell. I wish they would teach them to be devoted to their root guru and yet practise pure vision of all traditions and to remain humble.

As the saying goes, "Express if you feel uneasy, stretch your body if it feels unwieldy." This is just an expression of my feelings.

CHAPTER 3

Blessings of the Lineage
The Origin of the Drukpa Lineage

Tsangpa Gyare Yeshe Dorje, whose name is mentioned in the root text here, holder of both the Kadampa and Mahamudra Lineages and founder of the Drukpa Lineage, was born in 1161, the Iron Snake year of the third sixty-year cycle, according to his biography. He studied reading and writing at the age of four or five years and learned them without difficulty. He received the lay ordination vows at the age of twelve years and from that point on he upheld the three precepts without any violation.

From around the age of fifteen he studied the *Middle Way*, the *Seven Treatises on Valid Cognition*, *Paramita*, *Bodhisattvacharyavatara* and other scriptures for eleven years and completed the practice of listening and contemplation. At the age of twenty-two years he gave extensive teachings on the Middle Way, Logic, Paramita, Vinaya and Abhidharma in the presence of many scholars and spiritual teachers. He excelled as a scholar through extensive listening and contemplation. He then felt he should take up the practice of meditative stabilization and stayed at Ralung hermitage in his native land. The moment he heard that Lingre Pema Dorje was visiting the land, he felt an immense sense of devotion and went to see him and established a spiritual connection. The ripening of the karmic connection gladdened both the guru and disciple. At the age of twenty-three years, he heard that Lingre was at Naphu Monastery and went there, and he received teachings on the *Six Yogas of Naropa*, complete transmission, empowerment, teachings and instructions of all the Tantras of Marpa's tradition.

At the age of twenty-eight, when he was about to go for a life-long retreat, his root Guru Lingre told him, "There's not much purpose for you to go into retreat. You take care of my monastery of Naphu" and prophesied that later he would have to hold Druk and Ralung monasteries. At the age of twenty-nine, he retrieved the treasure text on *Six Equal Tastes* that was hidden by Rechungpa. According to the biography, he also received many teachings from Drikung Kyobpa Jigten Sumgon and Shang Drowei Gonpo.

In 1193 at the age of thirty-three, he received the ordination vows with Shang as his abbot. He stayed in closed retreat at the seats of past masters and in solitary places on many occasions. When he was forty-three years old, he founded the Nam Druk Monastery, which today comes under the Chushur district near Lhasa, and presided over large gatherings of disciples. Before founding the monastery, he went in search of suitable land and when he and his entourage reached the top of Tsewo La, he saw nine dragons at the site of the present monastery, and as they got closer the dragons flew away with three thunderous roars, according to religious history books. I heard from the khenpos that according to the oral tradition there were nine thunderous roars. Anyway, for the sake of auspicious interdependence, Choje Tsangpa Gyare named the monastery Druk (dragon) and he said that this is an auspicious omen that his lineage and lineage holders would spread to wherever there is the sound of thunder.

The spiritual lineage of Tsangpa Gyare and all the realized masters holding the Lineage came to be known as *Drukpa*. This is how the Drukpa Lineage originated. Some uninformed people today say, incorrectly, that the Lineage is called *Drukpa* because it originated in Bhutan (Druk-yul). However, it is the other way around – the country got its name, *Druk-yul*, because the spiritual Lineage of Drukpa spread across the country.

Tsangpa Gyare had innumerable disciples and wherever he went tens of thousands of disciples gathered and it became the talk of the town. All of the disciples genuinely practised the teachings. According to authentic history books, he dispersed his disciples thrice: the first group of excellent disciples had all attained rainbow body and were sent to the realm of gods, Nagas and other worlds, the second group of middling disciples were sent to Oddiyana, Shambhala, Sri Lanka, Suvarnadvipa, Tamradvipa *etc.* and the third group of disciples spread the Lineage from Jalandhara to the borders of China.

At the holy Palace of Yutso in Tsari, Vajrayogini prophesied to Tsangpa Gyare that the Drukpa Lineage would spread to cover the distance of eighteen days flight of a vulture, and it seems to have happened like that because, as the popular saying at that time stated, "Half the population is Drukpa, half the Drukpa are begging mendicants and half the begging mendicants are Siddhas." Even at this critical stage of Buddhism today, the Drukpa Lineage is spread across the Himalayan regions of Ladakh, Zanskar, Lahaul, Kinnaur, Nepal, Bhutan, and Sikkim and even in many foreign countries. So I think it's not just a saying but a reality.

At the age of forty-seven years, Tsangpa Gyare gave frequent advice to his disciples to meditate in the twenty-four lands and thirty-two sacred places, and he himself stayed in unwavering retreat on one mat for years. He said to his disciples, "We the followers of Milarepa do not bother about pleasure and sorrow, but persevere in our meditation and achieve enlightenment", and he encouraged his disciples to go into meditation.

Tsangpa Gyare had innumerable disciples but the two most outstanding disciples in the beginning were Pariwa Yeshe Gonpo and Kyangmo Khapa, the two outstanding disciples in the middle stage were Gyayagpa and Dremowa Sangay Bum, and the two outstanding disciples in the later stage were Lorepa Drakpa Wangchuk (1199–1265) and Gotsangpa Gonpo Dorje (1189–1258). Then there were the three yogis,[37] the four Zhigpos,[38] the three Repas[39] and the three Dampas.[40]

From Gyalwa Lorepa Drakpa Wangchuk originated the Lower Drukpa Lineage. His activities flourished and he attracted so many followers that the popular saying at that time was, "Lower Drukpa followers are as numerous as specs of dust on the ground." Some people ignorantly say that the Drukpa Lineage holders and monasteries in the Kham region of Tibet are called Lower Drukpa.

The lineage from Gyalwa Gotsangpa is known as the Upper Drukpa Lineage. His activities flourished so much that it was said that "Upper Drukpa followers are as numerous as stars in the sky." Again, some people mistakenly say that the Drukpa Lineage in Ngari area, Ladakh and Lahaul is known as Upper Drukpa. It is not right to distort or rewrite history and biographies. Speaking from the geographical point of view, what they say may seem convenient, but the point here is about the lineage of teachings and practices and not geographical locations.

The Central Drukpa Lineage of seat holders had 2,800 key disciples honoured with parasols. The Drukpa Lineage that exists today from Ladakh to Kham, Bhutan, Nepal and foreign countries mostly comes under the Central Drukpa Lineage. These details are provided as supplementary comments.

At the age of fifty-one, Tsangpa Gyare told his disciples gathered at Ralung Monastery that nine masters with the name Sengye will be

---

37. Jo Ye, Ga Ye and De Ye.
38. Re Zhig, Shang Zhig, Zhigpo Konchok Sengye.
39. Yak Re, Li Re and Dren Re.
40. Dampa Terkhungwa, Dampa Pagowa and Dampa Kodrakpa.

followed by three reincarnations of the three Buddha families, and then he will come back again. All this is mentioned in the biography, *Marvellous Wave of Devotion*, by Kunkhyen Pema Karpo. Then Tsangpa Gyare left for Nam Druk and gave teachings and advice and the remainder of empowerment and transmission to tens of thousands of disciples. He passed away at the age of fifty-one years in 1211, on the night of the 25th day of the 9th month of the Iron Sheep year.

You might wonder why the name of Naropa and Tsangpa Gyare are specially mentioned in this stanza. This is because I have been recognized as their reincarnation and the lineage I follow originated from them. So I felt it would be appropriate to do so. Notably, Drogon Tsangpa Gyare never gave importance to the dry spoken words, but regarded holding the internal thought of ultimate union without distraction as the supreme path. This does not mean evading and avoiding one's family and mundane responsibilities. The glorious Drukpa Lineage that teaches compassion in practice and loving kindness for the benefit of other sentient beings, emerged from his spacious thought of Dharmakaya.

In appreciation of Tsangpa Gyare's founding of the Drukpa Lineage, and his Dharma activities that benefitted innumerable beings, almost like a second Buddha, and out of my devotion gained through logical knowledge, I have paid homage to the reincarnations and lineage holders. The lineage can be of different types such as spiritual, reincarnation or hereditary lineage. Here, it is the perspective of the reincarnation lineage that is more appropriate.

As an emanation of Avalokiteshvara he took many forms in this world for the benefit of beings. To briefly name the well-known ones, as mentioned in the life story supplication, he took birth as Arhat Sonam Nyingpo (Punyagarbha) during the time of Buddha Shakyamuni, then as Bodhisattva Dawai Woi, Dechoe Zangpo, Rigden Pema Karpo of Shambala, King Songtsen Gampo of Tibet, Shantarakshita in India, the Tibetan translator Chokro Luyi Gyaltshen, the Indian Mahasiddha Naropa, Duzhabpa Ashadhana, Gampopa, the 1st Gyalwang Drukpa Drogon Tsangpa Gyare, the 2nd Gyalwang Drukpa Kunga Paljor, the 3rd Gyalwang Drukpa Jamyang Chodrak, the 4th Gyalwang Drukpa Kunkhyen Pema Karpo and so on until the 11th Gyalwang Drukpa. Their vast activities are mentioned in their biographies. I can only give a cursory account here. I am counted as the 12th reincarnation.

> To the great teachers of the snowy realms
> And emanations of former times,
> To their play of knowledge and compassion,
> Like the dancing reflection of the moon in water,
> I pay homage.

The previous stanza mentions the reincarnations born in India and other countries. This stanza is in reference to those who took birth in Tibet. "Snowy realm" means Tibet. The Tibetan national flag has a mountain. It is symbolic. Tibet is surrounded by mountains and so it is called the snowy realm. It is also called the land of activity of Avalokiteshvara and it seems so. If you go through the biographies of undisputedly great spiritual masters, most of them accept that they are emanations of Avalokiteshvara.

The popular form of Avalokiteshvara is white in colour and it is said that his pure land is also white in colour. The white colour of snow and mountains perhaps form an auspicious symbolic connection.

King Trisong Deutsan was the emanation of Manjushri. Shantarakshita was, as mentioned earlier, an emanation of Avalokiteshvara, and Guru Padmasambhava was the holder of power undifferentiated from the two. The holder of secret treasure, Dakini Yeshe Tsogyal, was the human form of the unborn Dharmakaya.

Here I want to make special mention of the great translator Vairochana, equal to Guru Rinpoche and his consort in spiritual realization, deliberately taking birth as master of the entire Dharma and to the Tibetan Buddhist followers, more gracious than the Buddha and Guru Rinpoche. The galaxy of his emanations, blessed by the three secrets and manifestations of wisdom and loving kindness, like reflections of the moon in water in various vessels, have benefitted the different teachings and innumerable beings. In recollection of former abodes, I too stand at the end of the row, engaged in the hustle and bustle of the affairs of the Dharma and of the monastery. Remembering the kindness of past spiritual masters, I pay homage to them.

> They are the world's eyes,
> And I take shelter in the blessings

Of their three secret dimensions (of body, speech and mind).
This, my humble tale, was composed
At the request of my friend Kunzang Tenzin.

As mentioned earlier, I seek refuge in Vairochana and all his emanations that are like the eyes of the world. Just as we depend on our eyes to see the material world and its inhabitants, the great translator Vairochana is like the eyes that cause us to accept virtue and reject non-virtue in our life, and ultimately to see and understand the nature and extent of phenomena in an unstained way.

All the texts and instructions that we have today in written form, available for study, contemplation and meditation, are the result of the hard work done by Vairochana and other translators of the past. They travelled to distant India, risking their lives and offering gold as a mandala in order to receive teachings. Then they condensed the essence of the three turnings of the Dharma wheel and meditated with diligence. As a result of their dedicated work, today everyone acknowledges that we have a unique tradition of practice and need not envy other Buddhist traditions in the world.

It is important to remember who left us these scriptural commentaries, that the eloquent speakers talk about and the profound methods of taming one's mind that the devoted practise today. I feel today most people do not know this and claim it as their own achievement or even if they know, they remain indifferent. Very few remember this kindness.

When I say, "I take shelter in the blessings of their three secret dimensions (of body, speech and mind)", it sounds a bit arrogant. But as the saying goes, "The dog barks because he sees the shadow of a thief", all the experiences, illusory visions and conceptual thoughts have been written down without fabrication as relevant speech and a timely rain. Or you may say that my humble self was unable to control the joy felt at attaining immutable faith, by the blessings of past gurus and some memory of past lives, innate wisdom, and by settling in the mind the understanding gained through impartial study, reflection and meditational training, of the many teachings and instructions of past spiritual masters. Or, maybe the joy felt by a crazy person like me on getting such a rare opportunity was indeed controllable and I expressed it in words.

THE MEANING OF "EXPRESSION OF REALIZATION"

The term realization means realizing, or understanding, the distinct true external and internal nature, and expression means an honest commentary on such a realization. However, since I do not have any profound realization, everything that arises in the mind will be treated as realization and honestly expressed. I don't think it would be a contradiction to call this "Expression of Realization".

From a young age, as my hobby, I liked to compose verses and prose – some good and some not so good – to express my crazy thoughts. I also liked to draw deities, ghosts and landscapes, humans, horses, donkeys, birds *etc.*, whatever came to my mind on paper and on walls. Keeping the drawings for a couple of days to observe, I would then burn or erase them. I never kept them as a collection nor showed them to other people. If I had kept them, by now I would have piles of garbage. I liked to write down whatever thoughts that arose in my mind with regard to spiritual teachings. However, I did not keep them or show them to others but rather burned them instead. The gracious Buddha had given us such a huge body of teachings and what is available on paper in this world is beyond imagination. An abundant number of commentaries, explaining the meaning of the scriptures, exist for us to study and reflect on. So I felt that without studying and practising the teachings it would be meaningless to keep and show to others my writings which were like the speech of a parrot, since I do not have even a literal understanding of the texts, let alone the confidence of realization of the view of the Middle Path, Mahamudra or Dzogchen.

I COULD DRAW WITHOUT HINDRANCE WHATEVER CAME TO MIND

Sometime later, I saw a painting of Guru Nangsi Zilnon that I painted at the age of twelve years, a painting of Amitabha that I painted at the age of fourteen years, and a plain drawing of Vajrapani, Vajrakumara and Tara *etc.* Recently while receiving *Rinchen Terdzö*[41] and other teachings and empowerments from my

---

41. *The Treasury of Precious Termas*, one of the Five Great Treasures of Jamgön Kongtrul the Great. It is a compilation drawn from all the termas that had been discovered up to his time, including Chogyur Lingpa's treasures.

Guru Kyabje Trulshik Rinpoche, my attendant monk came to me and said, "Kyabje Rinpoche has advised me to do the recitation practice of *Drakpo Jungwa Dul Bye*. But I have no idea how to visualize the deity. So please guide me." I thought for a while and the image came to mind clearly and I thought it would be better to draw than to explain it. So I asked him to get a pen and paper. He came back with paper and an old pen. I drew the image that came to my mind and gave it to him. The monk then said he was going to get it blessed by Kyabje Rinpoche. I told him it would be embarrassing to show this drawing to Kyabje Rinpoche and asked him not to go, but he went to get it blessed anyway. The next day he smiled and asked me if I could draw the same image again. I asked him why and he replied that Rinpoche had praised how the deity drawn on the paper had all the required qualities and seemed fully endowed with wisdom, and he wanted it for himself saying that, since you are an attendant you can get many more. So he had no option but to offer it.

Although I tried my best to draw a similar one, I could never do it. Most of my drawings are like this. I can immediately draw what appears to me but never do it again later. It is funny. I think this is because I have had no training in painting. Even my textual knowledge is like that. I don't get it when it is required but sometimes I can clearly recite and meditate.

A person who has complete knowledge of what he studied would have no problem because he will be able to recall it whenever it is needed and it will be there like the sunshine. It is important for ordinary beings like us to study with joyful effort. This is my experience.

Today people take interest only in a few subjects. If you are old, then there is nothing you can do. The young ones must not waste their time, except to have tea, food, a nap or short breaks. You must show interest in all major and minor subjects, both spiritual and mundane, and study them diligently. It is our habit to make the excuse of not having time. This is lying and deceiving yourself. Most of us waste our time gossiping, taking afternoon naps and doing meaningless things covertly or overtly. If you think earnestly, it is not as though we don't have time.

Why was this text written? There is no big purpose for writing this. I wrote this at the repeated request of my American friend

Kunzang Tenzin, popularly known as Surya Das today, whom I have known since I was about ten years old.

> These crazy ideas of mine
> Are not important to recount,
> But I jot them down anyway
> As a joke, just to ruin your eyes.

As said earlier, I didn't see much purpose in writing down these crazy thoughts of someone like me, who is intoxicated by the three poisons of afflictive emotion, and I held back from writing it down for a long time. Later in 1992, while in retreat at Maratika on the instructions of my guru, I wrote this tale during breaks, as a joke, to express my view and thoughts on the external and internal state of this dream-like world. It was also to express my happiness at being born in India, spiritually called Aryabhumi, which is held in high esteem by various religious traditions. One may even call it the capital of all religions.

From the worldly point of view, India is a vast country with liberal policies. One can live in peace without being harassed so long as one conducts oneself properly. One can live amidst song, dance and music. People in general are kind-hearted. It has rocky mountains and snow-capped mountains. It has desert and meadows. In terms of climate, it also has hot regions and cold regions to choose from. You can get almost every kind of food and beverages.

At the same time, I missed my kind mother who gave birth to me. I also remembered the three secrets of my root and branch gurus.

Thinking about all this, my mind, like that of a crazy man, had no conceptions and felt an inexpressible sense of joy, devotion and enthusiasm. To boost this sense and in order to ruin the eyes of the person who exhorted me to write it, as well as the eyes of the general readers, I wrote this. So there was no motivation of serving a greater purpose in writing this text.

At the same time it was also aimed at answering the inquisitive meddling people, who would always ask me where I was born, at what age was I recognized, when did I start my education, how difficult was it *etc.*, as well as for the devoted, so that I wouldn't have to keep repeating myself.

THIS BOOK IS A PART OF MY HEART THAT I GIFT TO YOU

At this moment I feel that I am giving a part of my non-fabricated pure love as my gift to all the readers in the form of this book, *My Crazy Tale*. I offer it to my parents, the most gracious and kind persons in this world, my dear friends and relatives. Similarly, I offer it as prostration to the gurus, the supreme saviours of this life and the next, who tame beings through peaceful, wrathful and powerful activities, completely holding them from the abyss of samsara, and to the teachers, abbots and Dharma brothers and sisters. I strongly feel that with this book I am sharing part of my kind heart with my disciples – male and female – who are close to my heart. I wish that even those readers who do not have any close connection with me, will be able to find loving kindness after reading this book and lead a non-harming peaceful life. As I said earlier, other than this, I do not expect this to serve any great purpose. In this world there is nothing more powerful than loving kindness. So, whether it helps other people or not I am happy and satisfied. An authentic sense of joy and happiness can be felt when you think about pure intention and loving kindness and practise them. I hope you all understood what I am saying.

INDIA IS THE LAND OF FREEDOM

> The Lotus Lake in India
> Was my birth place,
> The great sacred spot of the Mahaguru
> And the dance floor of the dakinis.

India, which has an abundance of everything, is a country rich in spirituality, culture and history. The people have freedom and one can engage in any religious or worldly activity and travel anywhere as one wishes. While describing the qualities of the Sukhavati[42] pure-land in the Sutras, the Buddha says one can travel from one pure-land to another, meet the Buddhas and receive teachings and then return

---

42. The blissful Buddha field of Amitabha. One of the Buddha fields of the five families, said to be located in the western direction.

back in the evening. One cannot help but feel that India has such qualities. Whether you do business, spiritual practice or train disciples, one can do so without being harassed either by the authorities or ordinary people. For example, if you play loud music, even if others don't like it, they don't make a big fuss about it. Personally, I do feel somewhat irritated when my neighbours play loud music. Generally in India, people don't make a big fuss about such things and when I think about it, I feel it is a true sign of freedom. I truly believe that this is why India is called a true democracy.

In the past, some high gurus and monastery heads received invitations from outside Tibet, but the then Government and authorities did not give permission to travel abroad on the silly grounds that the guru had a consort. The diary of the previous Taktsang Rinpoche of Ladakh mentions that he invited the 10th Gyalwang Drukpa to go on a pilgrimage to India, with the hope that he would be able to visit Drukpa monasteries and meet the patrons and followers in Ladakh, and the latter accepted the invitation. He even built the present Pema Woeling residence in Hemis Monastery, modelling it on the residence of Gyalwang Drukpa in Sangag Choling, Tibet. Taktsang Rinpoche himself spent a couple of years in Darjeeling, Kalimpong and Kolkata *etc.* to receive His Holiness the Gyalwang Drukpa. Ultimately however, His Holiness the Gyalwang Drukpa could not visit India. The 10th Gyalwang Drukpa had a consort and he was not permitted to leave Tibet on the grounds that he had a consort, so says the diary. Pel Drikungpa and many other gurus had also faced similar problems. Ordinary people too had to face major problems if they were to go on a pilgrimage, because there was always the fear of highway robbers and bandits. If they were to go on a long pilgrimage they could not be sure if they would return alive, according to the tales told by the elderly. This is all about the past.

Even in today's world there are a few countries which refuse to issue passports for foreign travel or they revoke them later. I have not seen the kind of freedom in any other country that you have here in India. Politically, I have no comments to make because I am apolitical and have no interest in politics, but you can understand that these comments are from personal observations.

For example, a friend of mine went to the United States on holiday. One night he lost his way while driving to his hotel and reached a dead-end. While trying to reverse his car, the tyres of his car got stuck in mud in the garden of a family. He said the father came out and he thought he was coming to help him and felt relieved. However, he beat him up and took out a gun and said he was going to shoot him. He shouted that he was going to call the police and send him to prison. After a lot of pleading the man let my friend off. He was shocked and said that we don't have to face such threats in India. This is really true.

For example when we were on Pad Yatra in India, whenever there was a problem with power or water, the local people would come with generators to provide us with light, give us vegetables, water and even lent us mattresses for the night. People of every caste and creed would come to our assistance. Their intention was to help us and not harm us. Those of you who have been on Pad Yatra know this. Abroad, while driving, if you park the car on the roadside for a moment the police will come immediately. A slightly kind and uncorrupted policeman will let you go with a warning, or else you will end up paying a fine of at least $100. Even if you want to make slight modifications to your house or refurbish it, getting official permission is a big headache.

So I often feel that Himalayan region of India that we live in, such as Ladakh, Lahaul, Kinnaur or countries like Bhutan and Nepal are like heaven on earth. However, I don't think this situation will last very long because with material progress people become more self-centred, arrogant, and harmful, jealousy, competitiveness and pride grow and these make things worse. Therefore, I feel those of us who are born in India and the Himalayan regions today are fortunate. One cannot say that there should not be material development for a better future, but it is important to improve our way of thinking and be broad minded simultaneously with material development. We should train our minds and practise with our experiences. The parents of today must advise their children to be well behaved and kind-hearted.

Anyway, I feel I was born in the right place. Looking at history and recollecting memories, I see that I have wasted many years without any specific objective in many lifetime, except studying the scriptures. From the spiritual point of view it is very fortunate to have studied the scriptures, because it helps your mind immensely. Some of my previous reincarnations were unrivalled scholars and helped many beings in various ways. But if you look at the bigger picture, one has been doing the same thing, life after life. I have been told by some of the elder members of the previous generation that some of our renowned scholars had no knowledge of world religion and culture, the rotation of the planets around the sun and the moon around the earth, of materialism and scientific views, of psychology and the functioning of the brain. They even had problems signing their names when they first came to India. Similarly, my previous incarnations just remained involved with the affairs of a few thousand monks, over a hundred monasteries and the local people, and as a result they couldn't do any great work.

Generally speaking, people like us cannot fathom the activities of the Buddhas and Bodhisattvas. The work they do, directly and indirectly, for all beings is immeasurable and unimaginable. But from the perspective of the ordinary beings their work is negligible. Except for giving teachings and empowerments once in a while, in the name of the welfare of beings, they haven't done much for the physical well-being of people, or environmental protection, or helping the needy with medical aid and food. In brief, they failed to do enough to connect with the people for mutually beneficial work.

As a result of such failure, after the Chinese invasion, many high gurus, khenpos, scholars and spiritual masters, faced great hardship. At the instigation of the Chinese, the people urinated on their faces and beat them in the name of "class struggle". It was mostly the local people who did such unthinkable deeds. I asked one of my older monks, "Who did such negative deeds?" He wept and said it was the local people. He said our big monastery was razed to the ground within a week. He wept and said that since the Chinese were powerful and the local people eagerly took part in razing the monastery, there was nothing they could do.

This is the consequence of the pompous and vain attitude that the gurus, rulers and masters held. They failed to maintain the close connection that is required between a guru and his followers, the ruler and ruled, master and servant, humans and animals. If they had helped the poor and taken care of the needy, it would not have been so easy for the Chinese to manipulate the people. I am not speaking only about our monastery. Exploitation had been going on for generations in most places and that is why the monasteries and khenpos, high gurus and managers, monks and storekeepers, the rich and the bureaucrats faced such difficult times. I just mentioned this in passing.

LOTUS LAKE

Lotus Lake, locally called Rewalsar, is near Mandi, the capital of the ancient kingdom of Zahor. When Guru Padmasambhava came to tame the king of Zahor, the king attempted to burn Guru Padmasambhava alive on a pyre at Rewalsar but Guru Rinpoche turned the pyre into a lake and appeared unharmed on a lotus bud. The history of how Guru Rinpoche brought peace and happiness to the kingdom is clearly mentioned in *Pema Kathang*[43] and other texts. There is no need to go into the details, but for those who don't have the propensity to read the texts I will give a brief account here.

The daughter of the king of Zahor, Princess Mandarava, was the epitome of beauty and grace. Indeed, her beauty and grace was the topic of discussion in the kingdom. Kings and princes from far and wide sought her hand in marriage. But the princess had no wish to marry and be involved in the meaningless hustle and bustle of worldly affairs as a queen of some king, and refused the proposals. The king advised her on many occasions to marry but to no avail. He became angry and scolded her for being disobedient and behaving irrationally but she remained resolute. After some time she thought it was the fault of her beauty that didn't leave her alone to engage in spiritual practice and so she scratched her beautiful face with sticks and stones and wept. Sometimes she thought that it was the fault of her body, which attracted all the male attention that would not allow her to follow the spiritual path, and she thought of committing suicide with prayers for a better future life. The king, queen and the royal retinue were concerned that she would commit suicide and kept her guarded.

Once the king, helpless in the face of the princess' refusal to get married, told her that since she was so determined to pursue spiritual practice she was free to go and do so. Fearing that she might come across a man, he sent her to pursue spiritual path with guards outside her quarters, to stop any male entering, and kept girls inside to keep

---

43. Treasure Text revealed by Ogyen Lingpa contains the life story of Guru Padmasambhava.

her company. The princess, surrounded by a female retinue of several hundreds, was quite happy to be able to follow the spiritual path that was beneficial for this life as well as the next. One day, Guru Rinpoche suddenly appeared in her residence on the rays of the sun and he taught the path of practice to the princess and her retinue. The guru and his disciples made Ganachakra offerings and had a great time.

A cow-herd, wandering around near the princess' residence, heard the pleasant voice of Guru Padmasambhava and he had mischievous thoughts. On returning to town, he told people that he had heard a male voice in the princess' residence. Eventually, the king heard this and in great anger he went to the princess' residence with a large army and walked into her quarters. Everyone appealed to him but he would not listen. He took off the princess' dress and bound her, and he ordered the minister and guards to throw her into a dungeon of thorns. They could not disobey the king's order and they threw her into the dungeon.

The dungeon can be seen even today in the town of Mandi. Today it has been turned into a Hindu temple. I visited it when I was small and it appeared as described in the chronicle. It made me shiver and cry in sadness, as I recalled the secret chronicles of Guru Rinpoche and his consort. It was a place that induced an authentic logical devotion, though not long-lasting, in one's mind.

The present day lake is the place where Guru Rinpoche, bound by jute ropes, was put on a pyre and burnt alive as punishment. Normally, when criminals were burnt alive the smoke from the fire would last only for a couple of days. But everyone observed that the cloud of smoke from the fire lit to burn Guru Rinpoche alive lasted for more than a week. Surprised, the king and the queen went to take a look. The dreadful ground had turned into a beautiful lake with lotus stems.

On closer observation, the king and his retinue saw Guru Rinpoche on a lotus bud, smiling and looking even more majestic. The king prostrated in regret for his actions and requested him to come to the palace. Guru Rinpoche told the king that he had committed all these negative actions due to his untamed mind and that the four elements[44] could not harm the guru, who has realized

---

44. Earth, wind, fire and water.

that the phenomenal world does not truly exist as it appears.

Considering the welfare of the kingdom of Zahor, Guru Rinpoche accepted the king's request. The king personally pulled the chariot and took Guru Rinpoche to the palace. He opened his treasury and offered a complete set of precious garments – a bejewelled hat, cloak, boots and ornaments – to Guru Rinpoche. The costume of Guru Nangsi Zilnon or Padmasambhava in that we see today, is the one offered by the king.

The king then ordered his guards to bring the princess from the dungeon immediately. The ministers and guards went and opened the dungeon door and asked her to come out, but she refused to do so, saying that she was following her father's orders. Even the queen failed to bring her out. The king then wept and saying he was responsible for all this, he went to the dungeon. Kneeling on the floor he called out to her repeatedly and when she looked up with a sad, wounded look the king almost fainted. Then he said, "You are innocent. I am to be blamed. The great guru is unharmed and is in the palace. You must come now," and he wept.

The king helped her out of the dungeon and they returned to the palace together. The king then offered his daughter, the kingdom and all his wealth to the guru and requested him to compassionately take care of them all. Guru Rinpoche accepted the king's offer and ruled the kingdom, bringing peace and happiness to all. The holy lake and lotus stem, symbolic of Guru Rinpoche's vast activities, can be seen even today. Since the lake has lotus stems in the centre, the devout Buddhists call it the Lotus Lake. Even other religions regard it as a holy place. This exalted place where humans and non-humans from everywhere gather is the place where I was born.

> Who was present when I was born?
> Padmasambhava's regent Dudjom Rinpoche was there
> Surrounded by many male and female wisdom holders
> Turning the wheel of the profound Dharma.

Who was present at the Lotus Lake at the time of my birth and what was the occasion? His Holiness Dudjom Rinpoche, the heart emanation and regent of Guru Padmasambhava, the master of all scholar-saints, was turning the Dharma wheel, giving oral transmission of *Nyingma Gyubum*[45] and other teachings to a gathering of over ten thousand devotees. His Holiness said that since going into exile, a proper Tsechu puja of Guru Rinpoche complete with ritual dance and Ganachakra offering had not been organized. He said that this was the perfectly auspicious occasion where hundreds of realized masters were gathered at this holy place for teachings on Dzogpa Chenpo, the pinnacle of the nine vehicles of the Nyingma tradition, to hold Tsechu sadhana practice complete with ritual dances and Ganachakra offerings.

Led by His Holiness, hundreds of yogis and yoginis, gurus and tulkus, khenpos and spiritual teachers held a grand Ganachakra offering. The lay people, young and old, men and women, danced and sang in celebration. The Lotus Lake resonated with the sound of song and dance, I was told. In the morning as the sacred dance of eight manifestations of Padmasambhava began, the sky was filled with rays and rainbows as a result of the pure devotion and *Samaya* of the people gathered there, and because of the blessings of His Holiness Dudjom Rinpoche. As his blessings entered their hearts, faith and devotion grew among the people. As a sign that they will all ultimately enjoy the essence of Guru Rinpoche's mind, rays and rainbows accompanied by the sound of thunder filled the sky; beautiful birds, unseen before, appeared on trees and sang melodiously.

At this time, I was born, in this body of flesh contaminated by afflictions and the womb, by the force of my past karma and aspirations.

> Due to favourable karma
> I emerged onto the lap
> Of Zhichen Bairo, my father,
> And so met the Dharma at the moment of birth,
> And was blessed by a sign from Dudjom Rinpoche.

Due to the strength of positive karma accumulated in past lives, I came out onto the lap of my father Zhichen Bairo Rinpoche. Prior to the Tsechu, His Holiness Dudjom Rinpoche was assessing the

---

45. "The Hundred Thousand Tantras of the Old School"; a collection of scriptures belonging to the Three Inner Tantras, gathered by Ratna Lingpa and re-edited by Jigmey Lingpa.

ritual dance among the spiritual masters gathered there and he told Bairo Rinpoche, "You can do any part of the eight manifestations[46] of Padmasambhava as you wish."

My father later told me that he requested His Holiness to allow him to do the part of Guru Tsokye Dorje, the Guru Lake-born Vajra. So he was performing the ritual dance at the time of my birth. Either he did not know that I was going to be born then, or he must have known and danced as Guru Lake-born Vajra in celebration of my birth! Jokes aside, he would playfully tell me, "While I was dancing as Guru Tsokye Dorje you were born in a corner of the lake." That is why I sometimes use the name Lake-born Vajra.

The distance between the venue of the mask dance and the place where I was born was about a hundred steps. So my father came back immediately after the performance and took me in his arms and said prayers. From that point on he held me in his arms during the day and had me sleep in his bed at night. He would say, "Even though you were an infant, you knew how to cling to me."

In brief, the prayer "May I meet the Dharma at birth" was fulfilled and I met the Dharma and the spiritual teacher. His Holiness Dudjom Rinpoche, my guru from past lives, gave me a highly blessed six-inch image of Guru Rinpoche, a white scarf and he gave me my name with his blessings that I may benefit the Dharma and beings. So when I think about all these things, I see that this is the meaning of being propelled by positive karma – just as we say, "Look at your present form to know your deeds in the past."

JUDGING BY MY BODY, MIND AND PARENTS I AM REALLY FORTUNATE

Judging by the moderate state of my body and mind, I am certain that positive karma accumulated in past lives brought forth the positive connection. Innumerable children are born into the world but only a couple in a hundred have the good fortune to be born in the Aryabhumi of India, to meet the spiritual master at birth, to be embraced by realized masters, and hear the teachings on non-

---

46. Eight manifestations of Guru Padmasambhava: Guru Shakya Sengye, Guru Padmasambhava, Guru Nima Odzer, Guru Sengye Dradok, Guru Dorje Drolo, Guru Tsokye Dorje, Guru Padma Gyalpo, and Guru Loden Chokse.

harming, to be in a family that doesn't harm any being, big or small, and to see their faces reflecting Bodhicitta and compassion. Over 95 per cent of the children born do not have the conditions for leading a life according to the path of non-harming and peace.

ONLY BAD ADVICE AND BAD EXAMPLES LET ONE DOWN

If from the moment you open your eyes, you have to live with parents and relatives who only indulge in killing and harming others, you will be taught how to kill innocent animals and deceive others through tricks and by lying, and it will be very difficult to find someone to show you the path of non-harming. Even if one follows a religious tradition, it will treat humans as special and different from animals, like dogs, pigs, horses, and cattle *etc.* who have the same feelings of happiness and sorrow that we do. Such religions teach that these animals, who are more kind to us than humans and whose love and affection is more steadfast than one's family members and relatives, are given by God to us to exploit. Some even kill hundreds of people as a service to God.

These days, some people teach that killing innocent people by bombing their houses or blowing up vehicles is a service to God. Some others teach animal sacrifice as a way of pleasing the gods to gain their blessings, and as a result hundreds of thousands of innocent animals are killed as sacrifice. Hundreds of years ago even human sacrifice was practised. It is thus difficult to find the right opportunity to follow the path of non-harming.

Therefore, even if one has accumulated positive karma in some past life, it could not ripen due to the absence of good conditions. Otherwise, it is not possible that these beings have not accumulated positive karma at all. Harming others in this life, one unknowingly adds more negative karma and one is bound to suffer the consequences in this life and the next. No one ever came across a result that they had not caused and causes sown do not become barren. We eagerly accumulate negative karma and suffer accordingly. This is how we remain in the cyclic existence of samsara.

If a person vows to do no harm and sincerely practises helping others, then gradually their major sufferings reduce until they reach a stage where there is no more suffering. This is known as the emancipation from samsara. It is said that after this one can return to samsara intentionally rather than without choice or freedom. Therefore, it is important not only to accumulate good karma but also to meet favourable circumstances.

Any good deed has to be done with an altruistic motivation, and especially at the time of death one should not fall under the influence of afflictive emotions such as selfishness and anger, but concentrate on practice and the instructions on loving kindness, compassion and Bodhicitta. When you have all the right conditions, it is important to use these conditions for a better condition in the next life and for the altruistic cause. This is called creating the connection. This is why I always stress that we should make our life meaningful right now.

We must work to make our mind accustomed to altruism. If you accept life after death, it is good because it will be easier to do things. One will be able to develop a good habit with far-sightedness. For someone who does not believe in life after death but perseveres to develop good intention and diligently works for the welfare of others, after waking up in the morning until going to bed at night, they will definitely have a different perspective and gain a particular sense of joy in this life by recognizing happiness. Everyone in your life, friends and family, will love you and appreciate you and this love and affection alone will make you happy.

It is like our saying, "One is good at what one is trained in; a cow-herd's child is good at using a sling", and as Shantarakshita said, "If one familiarizes oneself, there is nothing that does not become easy." Whether one believes in life after death or not, we have to face the consequences of our action. A good deed has to be inspired by good intention and it has to be done practically, not just said or thought. One has to familiarize oneself or get accustomed to it, and a person accustomed to good deeds becomes a good human being. And a person accustomed to negative deeds becomes wicked. This is how it is and we all know this.

RESPECTING BOTH PAST KARMA AND PRESENT CIRCUMSTANCES IS THE BUDDHIST WAY

Today in the Buddhist community, there are some people who indulge in careless activity, saying that it is their karma and do not make any effort to ward off negative circumstances to rectify the conditions. They say it is the Buddhist view or Dzogchen practice. I often feel that such an attitude stems from limited knowledge. Guru Padmasambhava said, "Even if the realization is higher than the sky, cause and effect is finer than flour." Whatever good or bad karma we may have accumulated, it is our responsibility to diligently prolong familiarization with efforts to create the positive circumstances. The good circumstances ripen the past good karma, encouraging one to follow the path of non-harming and gradually freeing oneself of even harmful thoughts. Today's thought becomes better tomorrow, and next year it becomes better than this year. In the case of a believer in life after death, the next life becomes better than this.

Practising generosity, giving up the smallest act of selfishness for the well-being of others, abstaining from non-virtuous deeds and upholding ethics is like building a dike before the flood – the way to counter the negative karmas accumulated in past lives before its fruition. Making such efforts to prevent fruition of results of negative activity is the sign of a moral person, moving forward to higher realms. This is the purpose of Dharma practice. As one gets accustomed to such thought and behaviour for months and years, the good habit becomes steadfast and one is able to recognize and counter all negative actions and circumstances, and to use them as a means to practise the path. So while you are in good health, it is important to develop this positive behaviour in your mind. Otherwise, when you are physically unwell or mentally unhappy, or as death approaches and all your family members and near and dear ones gather around and advise you to relax, not to worry and think of good thoughts, I think it will be very difficult for you to suddenly generate an altruistic mind.

As I think about myself, I feel I have all the good conditions in terms of my parents, my gurus and my friends. As the saying goes, "Look at your action today to know where you will be born next", your thoughts and actions in this life will prophesy your next life without having to consult any guru, a fortune-teller or an astrologer.

I was born on the morning of the 10th day of the 1st lunar month of the Water Hare year (5th March 1963). It is said that my mother did not experience any pain or difficulty at the time of my birth. My mother is kind-hearted, compassionate, very devout in her spiritual practice and has deep-seated devotion to Buddha Amitabha. She has done one hundred million recitations of the Amitabha mantra, complete with generation and completion process. From the age of thirteen years she renounced the world, did the preliminary practices and mind training, clearing the doubts through listening and contemplating the meaning. Having done meditation and applied it properly to the mental continuum, she experienced external and inner signs and heats as described in the texts, and also had visions of practice deities. She also has a pure vision of all the traditions and gurus.

Much later, she secretly told me that when I was in her womb she dreamt of young girls dancing and showing their thumbs which had the syllable *Hri* in a red colour and congratulated her, saying, "you will have a son". She also said that she sometimes heard the sound of recitation of the Amitabha mantra in her womb. Many Dharma friends, khenpos and writers had asked her about the dreams or auspicious signs she had had, saying they would use the information to write my biography, but she never told them anything. "No one will believe it anyway. So there's no point in telling them. It will only add to gossip. Telling the truth or lying will serve no purpose", she said.

Just as the saying goes, "Thirty people will have thirty thoughts. Their way of thinking is different. Thirty *Dzos*[47] have sixty horns and their way of growth is dissimilar." Some parents, whatever their intention, talk about signs and dreams they have had, even to passersby. If they are illiterate, they ask others to write them down and they show them to the gurus and khenpos, persistently asking them to recognize the child. Some have funny things to say that when the child was born he said, "*'Ah! Ah!'* and stared at the father without paying much attention to the mother. It is a unique child."

My parents on the other hand would never speak of signs and dreams. In fact they were so worried that I would be recognized as a reincarnate guru so they never stayed long in one place. So apprehensive were they of my being recognized as a reincarnation, that they dressed me in grey or dark-coloured clothes and never allowed me to wear any red or yellow. But funnily enough, I was fond of red and yellow clothes then. I say "funnily" because today red and yellow are part of the dress code and I have to wear them. Otherwise I am not that fond of red and yellow. When Bairo Rinpoche went out, I would bully the other family members and wrap myself in

---

47. A *Dzo* is a male hybrid between the yak and domestic cattle.

Rinpoche's Zen or wrapper. There were many things in the table drawer and I would take them out and shake them the whole day. As soon as I heard that Bairo Rinpoche was back, I would take off the Zen, quickly put everything back and pretend that I had done nothing. This was because of my deep love for Rinpoche and not out of fear. Forget about thrashing, he would never even scold me or show irritation. One day I had a great wish to wear red shoes and I threw away my new black shoes. I said that the pair of black shoes was lost and a new pair of shoes should be bought. They knew I had thrown away the shoes hence my wish was not fulfilled. I have many such anecdotes to tell.

My parents were able to carry on these evasive acts for over three years. But as the saying goes, "A vessel can hold water but no vessel can hold gossip", so many people came to meet my parents saying, "Your son is the reincarnation of the guru of our lineage" or "He is the reincarnation of my root guru". It seems that I too didn't stay quiet or idle. For example, I remember that wherever there was a table, I liked to climb up on it and sit cross-legged on top of it. A saying goes, "Goats and gurus like high places." At that time I didn't have the title of a guru, but it seems I had the mind of a guru. I also liked to place my hand on the head of people and pretend to bless them. Some humble people would act like they were receiving a blessing and when others did not do so I would wonder why they didn't take the blessing.

When I think back, it seems I had an inborn faith in something called blessing. I also remember having a small inherent thought of wanting to help others. When I was three or four years old, the previous incarnation of His Holiness Taklung Rinpoche was living in the same building with us. Our windows were connected. I loved going to his residence and climbing up onto his lap. Whenever my mother saw this, she would scold me for daring to sit in the lap of such a high guru and she would immediately pull me away. This made me feel very sad. One day when my mother came to fetch me, Rinpoche said, "Leave him. He is not filthy. A child is like Buddha". And he let me stay in his lap for a long time. The tip of Rinpoche's nose was red and rough. I remember rubbing it and pretending to say mantras blew over it. Rinpoche was happy and said that other children would not have such a naturally kind heart to help others. Sometimes he would say, "This is what you call Buddha. One must have such a pure heart. It is so nice to see the children have such a pure uncontaminated mind, unlike us elderly people."

As a consequence of my doing such things, my parents began to receive letters from many high gurus, putting them in a difficult situation. My mother told me that in one of the letters it was written: "His Holiness the Dalai Lama said that if the child is not recognized as a reincarnation there may be obstacles to your life. At that time your health wasn't good and seemed to be deteriorating. Thinking that if you were some reincarnation, giving you away may restore your health and remove obstacles, so we gave you away."

SUSTAINED BY KINDNESS AND ASPIRATION IN THE FACE OF SICKNESS

Around this time both my mother and I became paralysed after being hit by a heat stroke, as a result of coming into contact with some guru and deity with contaminated Samaya in Dalhousie. I still remember a red fire ball hit me and my mother on the head. Both of us fell down and started frothing and couldn't get up. A few days earlier, Bairo Rinpoche had warned us that "Samaya contamination is a serious matter and to be careful." But many unavoidable circumstances led to this calamity. I don't want to go into details.

Modern medicine says that blood veins burst due to high blood pressure, causing partial damage to the brain. Anyway, for many months I could not use my hands. Even today my health isn't that good. A doctor of an American aid group was consulted at that time. He hit all my joints with a small rubber hammer and said there was nothing wrong with me. "The boy was pretending," he said. I remember being given some painful injections.

At this time, His Holiness Dudjom Rinpoche revealed the mind treasure of *Hungkara*[48] practice and gave it to Bairo Rinpoche with instructions to do its practice, with the assurance that there would be no relapse after the practice is completed. Bairo Rinpoche and his disciples stayed in a year-long retreat and performed the cleansing ritual.

---

48. One of the Eight Vidyadharas; receiver of the tantras of Vishuddha Mind including Heruka Galpo. His lineage was transmitted to Padmasambhava and Namkhai Nyingpo who spread his teachings in India.

Gradually I was able to move my hands and legs. I am in good physical form today thanks to them. I became left-hander after this illness. Traditionally, being left-hander is regarded as bad and I remember that my family members sewed up the left sleeve of my clothing so that I would not be able to take it out. I remember trying to bite the sleeve to take out my hand. Sometimes I would be able to make a hole big enough to take out the tip of my finger and I would feel very happy. I felt quite uncomfortable using my right hand.

I had many similar health issues. Then, as advised by His Holiness Dudjom Rinpoche and as wished by my father Bairo Rinpoche, I was taken to Nepal on a pilgrimage. With purification of defilements and by the blessing of the holy places I took my first steps, without crawling, in front of Swayambhunath Stupa. Since then I became hyper-active and gave my mother and family members a hard time.

I also began speaking in front of Boudhanath Stupa. And again, since then I began to talk endlessly and asked a lot of questions irritating everyone. At that time Bairo Rinpoche had advised that when a child asks, the elder must reply properly. He used to say that a child coming into this world will certainly have a lot questions.

It is because of this that today, now I am in better health. I use my body to work for others' welfare, go on pilgrimages and do Pad Yatra and diligently practise offerings and worship to please my gurus.

Lama Pezin, a member of our family, went to see His Holiness Dudjom Rinpoche, to seek his blessing for my health. His Holiness told him that now there will be no danger to the boy's life since he is being protected by the Dharma protector Genyen Jagpa Melen. He jokingly said, "Won't it be better to hand him over under the care of guardian Genyen himself?"

All guardian deities subjugated by Guru Rinpoche are respected in general. However, Genyen Jagpa Melen is a guardian deity who was commanded by the 3rd Gyalwang Drukpa Jamyang Chodrak, Yongdzin Ngawang Zangpo, Thuchen Choekyi Gonpo and other masters of the Drukpa Lineage to be the special guardian of the lineage and is not commonly known to other traditions. So they did not understand what His Holiness meant and were confused. Later, when many high gurus unanimously recognized me as the reincarnation of Drukpa they seemed surprised that His Holiness had foreknowledge of this.

I feel happy that my mother is an uncommon woman who is being guided on the path by Buddha Amitabha. She was born in Mu village of the Lhodrak district, Tibet. She is a descendent of Terton Nyima Odser (1136–1204). An image of the deity *Dur-throe Lhamo*, produced miraculously by the Terton, remained the main deity of the family home till the time of political upheaval. The deity was so full of blessing and power that it became the object of refuge and worship for the local people. Thus, her family came to be called *Yul-lha* (house of the local deity) and was highly respected. There were many treasure-revealers and realized masters among her ancestors. Treasures revealed by them, such as a gong, a horse-head of Hayagriva *etc.* are still there. Later, some members of my mothers' family took to business, others served as district officers. Her family was respected as a spiritual family.

CHAPTER 4

Innate Loving Kindness and Compassion

LOOKING AT MY CONDITION AND FEELING VERY HAPPY

There are many species of beings in this world, and looking at the animals who are powerless to do anything but tremble in fear when they are about to be butchered, we should feel happy to be born as human beings. It need not be said that even among human beings, the poor, the uneducated and the powerless face suffering. But considering those who have experienced all these sufferings, as a result of the failure to fulfill their desires or prevent what they do not want, their inability to increase their wealth because they lack contentment or have jealousy for others' wealth and success – looking at all these beings, one has to appreciate one's own life. As we say, "Keep yourself happy, others will bring suffering". Even if you own the world there is only suffering, and it is important to have a sense of happiness in your mind. This is one of my main practices in life.

I often feel I am fortunate to have such parents and remain content with whatever material luxuries I have. It must be understood that I am not trying to make myself mentally content and happy that I have my parents, house and car, wealth, friends and acquaintances, *etc*. When I look at other people and beings in this world whose conditions are worse than mine, a true sense of contentment grows in my mind.

Without understanding this crucial point many people say they are practising contentment but deep in their minds, be they rich or poor, high or lowly, they feel a sense of dissatisfaction. It need not be said that to have such a feeling is a great fault for a spiritual practitioner, and even for a lay person this sense of dissatisfaction is the biggest enemy, bringing suffering. Even the millionaires and businessmen or industrialists are plagued by envy and competition. Some of my rich friends have told me that when their stock crashed in the market they didn't want to go home because they couldn't sleep. So they would stay late in the office and then go to bars around midnight and drink to numb their senses. This was all they could do. I think for them alcohol was useful. During the day they would smile at their competitors, but their mind was filled with fear, hope and doubt and there was no peace of mind, they told me. I think everyone in the higher echelons had to face the same feelings, whether they expressed it or not.

> Due to past good karma ripening at this time,
> I was quite happy as a child and,
> Without instruction, I naturally had
> A little kindness and compassion.

Generally there are two types of qualities: inherent quality and quality gained through learning or training. Even faults can be of inherent and cultivated types. Generally innate qualities are rare because we rarely do good deeds and even if we do positive deeds, very few of us are able to get accustomed to them and establish a stable familiarization. So the power of negative karma overshadows good karma, making it powerless like a glow-worm in daylight.

Both good and bad actions come naturally depending on what one is more accustomed to doing. For example, some people and animals such as tigers or lions, easily take to killing or taking lives without any training. Similarly, some people are naturally generous and do not like killing or lying.

GOOD IN THOUGHT AND DEED FROM AN EARLY AGE

From an early age I had this natural tendency to show love and kindness to all beings, especially the weak, without being taught by my parents or near and dear ones. Similarly, when I saw animals suffering I used to have this compassionate thought of wishing to alleviate their sufferings myself.

I remember when I was a child, if someone came while I was eating, I couldn't eat the food without sharing it with whoever was in front of me. My late Uncle Lodoe used to tell me later that my family members would say that no one should be allowed to come in when Wangchen was having his meals.

As mentioned earlier, when I was around three years old, to evade the many requests for me to be recognized as a reincarnation of this or that guru, my father Bairo Rinpoche took us all to Nepal for a holiday. I have a faint memory of visiting Boudhanath stupa and other holy places and making prayers and offerings. Unlike today, the road around Swayambhunath in those days was full of insects and I kept clearing them from the road.

The steward who was leading me would not let me clear the insects and carried me on his back, saying, "It is not possible to complete circumambulation of the stupa taking Wangchen. It is better to carry him." I remember I cried a lot when he did this. When I saw people trampling over the insects I felt pain and sadness as if they were trampling over me. From this experience I learned that if you genuinely think about the suffering of others you can actually empathize with them.

I remember that most of the time I could do nothing except keep my eyes closed, but since I liked watching the monkeys around, I had to open my eyes. Looking at the faces of people walking straight, holding rosaries in their hands and reciting mantras and prayers, not bothered about the insects they were killing under their feet, I used to wonder if they had poor eyesight.

Once a monkey snatched a paper bag from the hands of a person and ran away, and shared what was inside with the other monkeys; I felt happy that the contents of the paper bag was useful to many monkeys. Today even the monkeys, and not just the humans, have changed and they eat alone in a corner, not sharing even with their young ones.

Generally, whenever I had something delicious to eat, I would wish that everyone would have the same, or whenever I experienced anything unpleasant, I would pray that no one else should have such an experience; I had such genuine thoughts inherently.

I had a playmate who was a little older than me. He liked cutting off the head of earthworms and other insects. If he cut the head of an insect, while I was playing with him, then I would cry and run back home. To tease me, he would kill some more and all I could do was cry. It must be my karma because I did like going out and playing with him.

Every day that we went to play, he would kill insects and I would cry and that would be the end of our play time. I used to wonder, if I let him cut off my finger, would he spare these insects? Of course I didn't dare give him my finger, but I used to have such empty thoughts. Some years later someone cut off the head of my friend and left his body by the road side. I felt sad and my faith in the infallibility of the law of karma became even stronger.

In those days, I also used to find bathing miserable and every time I was given a bath I used to cry and pray that no one else suffered such misery! These are just silly anecdotes. Such were my thoughts when I was around three or four years old.

When I look back I find it amazing. I had great love for my parents and I treated all beings equally with love. I liked playing like many other children but never cared about material pleasures. I never made careless utterances or had any careless thoughts like today. Even while playing I thought about helping other beings. I had a natural liking for plucking fruits and flowers. The afflictive emotions were less present. So the accumulation of negative karma was less and my mind was more relaxed and peaceful. I often wish I could go back in time and relive those moments.

PROPHESY AND PREDICTIONS

Due to the clarity of perception at that time, I remember, whatever I said came true and some people took my words for clairvoyance or prediction. Two or three months before my recognition I kept saying, "A bearded person is coming to invite me." And putting ceremonial scarves around my parents, would say, "It is time to go. Goodbye!"

Some of the ordinary people didn't like it and saw it as an ill omen of the family's separation. They chided me and unable to stop me, they hid all the ceremonial scarves. Even then, when others were not looking, I used to cut all the old window curtains into strips and keep putting them around my parent's necks. I don't know why, but at that time I kept doing that.

Not long after that people came for my recognition and amongst them was Kyabje Drukpa Thuksey Rinpoche. He had heard people around me talking and started to see the reason why, for months, I had kept saying that a bearded man will come to fetch me. People said that I recognized some of the people who came with Rinpoche, but I don't remember that. Shortly afterwards, as I had told my parents earlier, I had to leave them and go to the monastery.

If I had remained quiet and humble, not saying or doing too many things, perhaps I could be leading a peaceful life without the responsibility of a lineage and its many monasteries. I may have even become the father of a few children! I would anyway have become a good and helpful spiritual practitioner.

Funnily enough, when I left for the monastery, I didn't feel sad or cry and until this day I have no regrets, though sometimes I do feel that if I didn't have the responsibility of looking after the monasteries and lineage I would have become an authentic practitioner. All this happened when I was three or four years old.

A year later, when there was incessant heavy rainfall in Darjeeling and the threat of floods loomed large, someone jokingly asked me when the rain would stop. I also jokingly told him the day and time when the rain would stop and it came true.

Again, when I was in a retreat in Hemis Monastery, Ladakh Chogyal (the King of Ladakh), who was the manager of the monastery, was coming to Hemis from Leh with some important guests. They took a long time coming, and those waiting for them wondered whether they were coming at all. At that time there were no mobile phones. Some of my attendant monks came to see me and asked if I knew whether the guests were coming or not. I told them what I saw: "They have reached Kharu and are having tea at Igu Hor's stall and are about to leave now." I had simply expressed my casual vision without any hope or fear. When the guests finally arrived, about half an hour later, the people asked if they'd had tea at Igu Hor's shop and they replied that they were indeed given tea by Igu Hor. I remember that everyone was surprised.

Relating such anecdotes is pointless, but I am telling you some of these in reply to your questions, just like the saying, "You are forced to answer a friend's insistent questioning; the dog had to bark on seeing the thief's shadow." Other people have a lot of these kinds of stories to tell about me, but I don't remember most of these things. Some could be true, some could be false and some could be true but exaggerated. I don't remember and don't care.

CHAPTER 5

Entering the Path of Dharma

> I have met many great teachers and studied many texts,
> Easily getting the conventional meanings,
> But I still do not get many of the ultimate meanings.
> Maybe that is why it's said there is no end to what can be known.
> Anyhow, I am glad to study and learn about everything,
> But especially about my own practice.

As mentioned earlier, by the power of good karma accumulated in past lives, I had the opportunity to follow many great teachers and study the scriptures, as well as other fields of knowledge. It was my father, Bairo Rinpoche, and my mother who first taught me the alphabet. They told me, "Even when you couldn't speak, when we gave you the texts placed upside down, you would place them in the right order and pretend to read." Even today, my mother sometimes chides me and says sarcastically, "Considering the fact that even as a child who couldn't speak, you recognized the top and bottom, and the front and back of a text, you should have become a great scholar by now."

I remember learning the Manjushri prayer and the *Seven Line Prayer* from Kyabje Soktse Rinpoche[49] and this was the first lesson I took in my life and by his blessings, I was able to learn them after repeating them a couple of times. Two years after being named as the reincarnation of the previous Gyalwang Drukpa, private tutors were appointed in the 6th lunar month, when I was six years old. I remember learning to read and memorizing texts. By the age of twelve, I had completed the memorization of the five major texts,[50] *The Ornament on the Three Disciplines* by Kunkhyen Pema Karpo, other miscellaneous texts and all the prayers of the Drukpa Lineage.

It is funny that, though all these are scriptural texts, some are easier to memorize than others. For example, I had difficulty in memorizing the texts on logic, such as *Commentary on Valid Cognition*, *Sutra on Individual Liberation* and other Vinaya texts, and even the Abhidharma. These texts I could only memorize only one page a day. I memorized the entire *Commentary on Valid Cognition*

---

49. One of the oldest living disciples of His Holiness Dudjom Rinpoche and the only surviving disciple of the 8th Drukpa Yongdzin Rinpoche Togden Pagsam Wangpo.
50. Prajnaparamita, Madhyamaka, Pramana, Abhidharma and Vinaya.

through sheer persistence. I had difficulty in memorizing just three lines each morning. Much later on, His Holiness the Dalai Lama told me that only a few amongst the great scholars know the complete *Commentary on Valid Cognition* by heart. However, I didn't have much difficulty in memorizing texts on Madhyamaka and *A Guide to the Bodhisattva's Way of Life*. I could memorize one and a half to two pages (the length of an arrow) of most of the *Five Works of Maitreya*[51] each morning.

I memorized the entire text on Dharmakaya in *Ornament of Clear Realization* in two mornings. Some stanzas were missing in the old hand-written text I was using and, as I read to memorize, the missing stanzas just came into my mind. When I went to take the test to the tutor, I recited these stanzas from heart. He said that these are not in the text and almost scolded me. After some time he said that the words sounded well composed and he stood up suddenly, saying he would go and check with another text. Later, he came with a small yellow book printed in Kalimpong. He smiled and asked, "How did Your Holiness know this?" All I could say was that they just came to my mind. My teacher and the elder ones had not known the missing stanzas and they all seemed surprised, and I was given six days holiday. I'll never forget this, because I was very happy to get a break. I remember similar incidents, but I don't remember which texts or which stanzas were involved.

Each year in the monastery, we had two to three days holiday during Losar (Tibetan New Year), and a couple of days holiday at the end of the monsoon retreat. Besides these days off, there were hardly any other free days. Not getting holidays and the failure to pass my morning tests were two of my biggest sorrows. I think this was the problem for all the pupils, not just me. But the other pupils had more holidays and playtime, because there was one teacher for twenty to thirty students. They got many breaks when the teacher was absent, or was sleeping, or when they went to get their food, or were sent on errands.

My education was slightly different as I had one private tutor and six or seven teachers, and I was the object of their focus. I was

---

51. 1. Ornament of Mahayana Discourse; 2. Ornament of Clear Realization; 3. Clear Distinction between the Middle Way and Extremes; 4. Clear Distinction between Phenomena and their Reality; and 5. Uttaratantra.

under their watch round the clock. If I turned around while reading the text, or did not read correctly, one of them would observe this and hit me on the face or head. I remember that although I wasn't mischievous as a child I just couldn't keep my hands still. Unintentionally, I would keep moving my hands, either under my shawl or under the table, and this caused me many beatings and also irritated my tutor and teachers.

FROM CHILDHOOD I BELIEVED THAT HAPPINESS AND SORROW WERE CAUSED BY VIRTUE AND NON-VIRTUE

When I saw other children running around in the courtyard from the window of my residence, I used to wonder what good fortune they must have accumulated. Even at the age of six or seven, I knew and deeply believed that happiness and sorrow were the results of virtuous and non-virtuous deeds.

Every day during the expiation and confession ritual of Mahakala, I used to reflect on the meaning of the words as I said the prayers and I remember crying and making confessions from the depth of my heart, with folded hands and respectful gestures. During confession I used to think about the cause of the beatings that I got, the bees in the hive outside, the cattle that were driven to the slaughter house for meat every morning and all the beings that had no one to protect them, and I remember feeling an unbearable sense of compassion. As I thought about cause and effect, and the beings that were the object of compassion, I didn't feel much hardship, despite the thrashings and scoldings by my teachers and the oppressive discipline of my education.

LAW OF KARMA

Even though I sometimes felt angry with my teachers, I never resented them. So today, when I see some of my friends and acquaintances feeling disturbed to the point of becoming suicidal by petty problems in their lives, (like being jilted by their lover, or suffering physical and mental pain caused by others), or when I see some people causing social chaos, I understand that this is all because of their lack of faith in, or understanding of, the law of karma or their failure to show compassion and concern for beings that are less fortunate than themselves.

I believe that even the realized Bodhisattvas do not have a complete knowledge of the law of karma, but we see differences even among children of the same parents; for example, some are good looking, prosperous and have a positive way of thinking, whilst others are ugly, more sickly and have a negative attitude. Similarly, even amongst people of the same country some are more prosperous and forward-thinking. Even among spiritual teachers some become scholars under strict tutors and teachers, and some excel in knowledge and meditative accomplishment without any private tutors or teachers. Some accomplish their education in a happy atmosphere where tutors and teachers are like friends.

I have heard the saying, "Tough times have to be faced to become a scholar", but it is not necessary that everyone has to face strict teachers. His Holiness Dudjom Rinpoche used to say, "It is not good to beat children when they are growing up. It will cause physical harm and mentally too they will lose interest in pursuing a spiritual education. I have never been subjected to harsh treatment." Kyabje Dilgo Khyentse Rinpoche said the same thing when the parents and attendants of his grandson Shechen Rabjam Rinpoche spoke of the need of a teacher for Rabjam Rinpoche. He said, "Just keep quiet. There's no need for a teacher. I never had anyone hit me even with a flick of the finger and I have done okay. If my grandson is a reincarnation of a guru he will do okay." Today, we can see that Shechen Rabjam Rinpoche has grown into a great spiritual master.

My root guru, the late Ontrul Rinpoche, was unrivalled in his knowledge of both Sutra and Tantra, of the old and new traditions. He had about four teachers when he was small and they never even scowled at him, let alone thrash him. He recalled, "When I felt sleepy or distracted while reading the texts, they would give me sweets, fruit or tea and send me outside to play or relax. Sometimes they would teach me ritual tantric dances, astrology, drama, *etc*. Then after some time I would return to read the texts." He would tell me that the teacher and the student must have a bond of love and devotion. He used to tell me stories and say that even if the teacher is not highly qualified, if he has genuine love and affection it makes a big difference in bringing up a pupil. He used to weep and say, "Why do the harsh teachers in the big monasteries treat the small children, who have no one to protect them, so badly?"

Similarly, my Sutra and Tantra teacher Khenpo Drimed Dazer,

popularly known as Khenpo Noryang, was a great scholar of the five sciences, and a hidden yogi. He used to tell me that while in Zigar Monastery he received thrashings on disciplinary grounds, but never received any beatings or even a rebuke while studying the scriptures. He used to say, "It is better to reflect on the meaning of the teachings received than to study in a suppressive manner. It is important to contemplate day and night with an open mind. I have not studied the texts in a suppressive way for many years. But while studying, after the teaching break, I used to go outside, cover my head with the shawl, and reflect and I used to be able to pass the tests."

Anyway, leaving aside the Buddhas and Bodhisattvas of the high ground, if one examines the cause of happiness and sorrow among Bodhisattvas who have come in the form of spiritual teachers and ordinary beings like us, it is clear that it is neither out of choice nor competence, but due to the law of karma. I believe even the realized Bodhisattvas do not have a complete knowledge of the law of karma.

One hears funny tales of some pupils putting lice in the bedding of the teacher, or filling the teacher's chamber-pot with nettles, but I had never thought of doing any such thing. Even when I was subjected to continual whacking and chastisement around the age of seven or eight, I always used to think it must be my karma to go through all this. Sometimes thinking with a firm belief, "If I confess all my mistakes in this life and past lives tonight, I will receive less whacking tomorrow." I used to say my prayers with full concentration. Funnily enough, the next day my teachers would either have to go out for some work, or have guests to entertain, and they would be more relaxed and I would get less thrashing and I used to think that my confession helped. Unlike now, I did not understand the object of confession or the antidote and there was no logical or textual support. But, if your mind is pure, prayers do help in some way. Perhaps this could be a delusion created by my mind. All phenomena in this world are either an illusion or a delusion created by the mind, and no exclusive reality exists. So I think even my childish thoughts were not wrong because they served my purpose. It is similar to the rituals we perform for success. Sometimes the other person changes their mind and your work gets done, or the person harming your interest gets transferred. So things change for the better after the ritual and you must believe that the performance of the ritual has helped.

Similarly, I think my believing that I got less thrashing as a result of my confession is not wrong. Some of you might think, why care about a child's thoughts. As I said earlier, if it helps practically then it is fine. Generally speaking, some people think that the various religions in the world are a source of conflict and feel there is no need for them. But on the other hand, the various religions do a great service to the society. For instance, by causing rainfall or curing the sick through rituals may seem childish to some. Because of this, the relationship between human society and religion has remained unbroken for centuries. That is why, even in today's time of material development, religion is needed. So it is important to keep the door of faith open.

USEFULNESS OF TEACHERS

Although my guru said one should have devotion to one's teachers, I could not develop much devotion to my teachers. This could be because they were too strict, even though they had love for me, and perhaps, like the Khampa saying, "He is sharp-tongued but his mind is clean." Did I like my teachers? Well since they did not show me any affection, but subjected me to thrashings and rebukes from sunrise to sunset every day, I did not like them very much then. But today when I think back, I feel that I am able to face any situation in life because of the way they brought me up. Today, I have the capacity to handle heat or cold, highs or lows, because of their strictness when I was young.

If I had been spoiled when I was young I would not have been able to handle problems as I grew up, and I would have become a problem, not only to myself but also to my family members, never being satisfied with anything. Sometimes I see people who have material comfort and friends but are never satisfied, and are perpetually in search of happiness, they eat and drink different things, wear all sorts of clothing and ornaments but behave like mad people. And after living like this for years they lose their mental balance, suffer from various illnesses and become social outcasts, unable to live on their own. Then, instead of appreciating others' good health and wealth they become angry and attack, kill or rob them, thus becoming a disgrace not only to their family but to society at large. When I see such people I remember the graciousness of my teachers.

IF YOU ARE HAPPY YOU DO NOT HARM OTHERS

A few years ago, I heard that it was risky to drive new cars to the market. A friend of mine had bought a brand new car and parked it at the market. Later he found that it had been scratched with a metallic object and badly defaced. When I heard this I was shocked and also felt sorry for the person who did this. It is so pitiable that due to a lack of accumulation of merit in past lives the person was in such a poor state and was indulging in such negative acts, instead of endeavouring to improve his or her future.

It is certain that people who engage in destructive activities have some problem in their mind, and they do such things in search of happiness. They feel unhappy when they see other people happy. Therefore, if you want happiness you must find it in your mind. Having less craving for material wealth and being content with what you have as a result of merits accumulated through past karma is the foundation of happiness. So you should never let your mind indulge in bad habits, because such indulgence becomes a cause of social disturbance.

CORPORAL PUNISHMENT OF SMALL CHILDREN BY TEACHERS IS POINTLESS

I did not get the opportunity to seriously study the scriptures uninterrupted, until the age of fifteen. Zigar Khenpo Sonam Dargay, who was appointed my tutor, fell ill when I was thirteen years old, which is considered the unlucky year astrologically, and so he could not teach me. Then I was invited to Ladakh, and it became an unintended holiday for me. There I never studied the texts or revised the scriptures that I had memorized earlier. Though I wasn't daring and mischievous, I think I lacked the capacity to encourage myself to pay attention to my education. I felt so happy about not having to learn texts that the mere sight of the texts and the room I used for memorizing them made me feel uncomfortable. When I think about this, I believe it was because of the strictness imposed while I was learning the scriptures. Like a prisoner escaping from prison, or a bird escaping from the snare, I did not wish to read the texts for months and I often wonder why.

Generally, I do not care much about the unlucky years described in astrology, but I do feel that my thirteenth year was seriously unlucky for me. My scripture teacher became seriously ill and my mother had a gall bladder problem and almost died. Uncle Lodoe, who had looked after me more affectionately than my parents since I was born, passed away in the same year. He was not a blood relation but I called him uncle. I don't know by what name he was called in Tibet, but he was called *Dolmai Gelong* (literally *Tara Bhikshu*) in Bhutan, because reciting the praises of Tara was his main practice. He was a monk of Ba Lithang Monastery. When I think about all this, the biggest disaster for me was my tutor falling sick and the start of my travels, because my distractions began at a time which was crucial for the study of the scriptures. A teacher who was needed to control and guide an adolescent and see that he did not get spoilt, was not there. I remained like this for a long time.

Usually, most of the pupils were so controlled that they lived in an atmosphere of fear until they grew up. Once they became adults, the teachers treated them with respect, even though they were not well educated, and would turn a blind eye to all their mischievous conduct. It was a funny situation.

My mother couldn't bear this and with great affection she sat with me and helped me to revise both the root text and the commentaries on the Middle Way, Pramana, Vinaya, Abhidharma and Logic, that I had earlier memorized. She made me memorize whatever I had forgotten. Later, when I received instructions on the scriptural texts and other fields of study from the Khenpo, she would join me and receive instructions as well. She did this to help me. She had already received instructions on all the major texts, *A Guide to the Bodhisattva's Way of Life*, *Words of My Precious Teacher* etc. In fact she had studied *A Guide to the Bodhisattva's Way of Life* and *Words of My Precious Teacher* over a dozen times. She told me this while advising me on the importance of studying the scriptures before starting Mahamudra and Dzogchen practice, and the importance of the practice of the foundation.

A pure loving mind has a lot of influence, and as I began reading with my mother, I had no difficulty and made much progress. Many people used to advise me to study hard and not waste my time, and that they would volunteer to be my teacher. Even some scholars of other traditions and Geshes of the Gelugpa tradition also offered their services. But I wasn't keen to accept their offers because I wasn't sure of their motivation; I felt that some of them just wanted the title of being my tutor. I am very stubborn in this way and I don't listen to what others say easily, even when I was young. I liked my freedom.

STARTING STUDY UNDER VAJRADHARA KHENCHEN NORYANG

When I was fifteen years old my father Bairo Rinpoche requested Khen Rinpoche Drimei Dazer, popularly known as Zigar Khenpo Noryang, to become my private tutor. He was an undisputed scholar in all fields of knowledge, and many unbiased spiritual masters of all traditions (including His Holiness Dudjom Rinpoche), recognized him as the reincarnation of Indian Mahasiddha Saraha. He humbly replied, "An ordinary monk with limited knowledge like me can never assume the post of private tutor and I have no wish to do so. For an ordinary being to assume such a post will be the cause of rebirth in hell. As an old man nearing death, it would be pointless for me to take the title of private tutor and disturb the mind of my root guru. It is like seeking hell. So I cannot accept this. But I can happily pass on whatever Sutra and Tantra teachings I have." He must have sincerely said what he felt, but I thought perhaps he knew my wild nature and felt it would be difficult and useless to be my private tutor.

Thanks to Bairo Rinpoche, under Khen Rinpoche I was able to study the fundamental scriptures gradually. I was able to slowly study the *Thirteen Fundamental Scriptures* compiled by Khenchen Shenga.[52] I also received individual and common instructions in religious history, the Three Vows, Individual Liberation, and *A Guide to the Bodhisattva Way of Life*, etc., according to the tradition of our own lineage. In Tantrayana I received teachings over many years on the various Tantras, starting with the Hevajra Tantra, and the *Profound Inner Topics*. But like the saying, "golden body with a dead mind", I wasted a lot of time as I was distracted.

---

52. Shenphen Chökyi Nangwa (1871–1927), an important figure in the non-sectarian movement who revitalized study in much of Eastern Tibet by founding shedras (monastic educational institutes) and by revising the scholastic curriculum with an emphasis on the classical treatises of India.

A MONASTERY'S CHARTER SHOULD BE IN ACCORDANCE WITH PEOPLE'S VIEWS

Unlike some of my friends, I did not like roaming around or going to watch shows at night. For some unknown reason, I did not have the inclination to do so. Some of my friends wanted me to go with them to watch films at night, but I never went. I don't know whether they sincerely thought that I needed a break or if they wanted to damage my reputation for being well disciplined. In those days, going to any entertainment, and especially watching films, was considered a serious breach of discipline. Playing football, learning martial arts, playing games and roaming around were considered bad behaviour. On reflection, all these things are not necessarily bad behaviour, but at that time this was how the people thought, and the monastery's charter was prepared accordingly. As Buddha said, monastic discipline should be in accordance with the customs of the country, so the charter of conduct was prepared according to the social attitude.

I have said many times the objective of a spiritual practitioner is to meet the immediate and ultimate welfare of all beings. This is the reason why, even if we can't do much, at least we should do no harm. That is why we have to be careful not to do what others don't like. Doing things they don't like will impair their faith and they lose faith in the Dharma and Sangha. In this way great harm is caused and therefore a charter of conduct is needed as a preventive measure and it is also beneficial for oneself. There is no need to go into details here.

MIND BECOMES HABITUATED TO DISTRACTION

I liked going out with close friends and I became habituated to this, since there was no one to control me; perhaps this is a common teenage problem. I got used to going out every second or third day. There were not many places to go, so I would climb to the top of the hill, or walk around the middle or the foot of the hill. I did not like going to the town, restaurants or market because people would come and seek blessings, or invite me to tea or lunch and not let me go where I wanted. But other than that, I went to every place.

ATTRACTED TO YOUNG GIRLS

Darjeeling is a beautiful place with a few houses and many parks and forests. It was built by the British, and the roads were narrow and the houses small. It was like a painting wherever one looked. One could observe young boys and girls walking through flowers and trees and sometimes they would sit on the grass whispering sweet nothings or playfully teasing one another. Darjeeling is also a popular tourist spot. Watching the young couples walking around made me envy them, and I used to think it would be a pleasure if I too could go around with a girl. Perhaps the innate gross affliction which had been kept hidden was now showing its true colour. The main practice for all spiritual followers is to keep their mental afflictions in check. Otherwise they would be out of human society and considered to be a part of the animal society.

I think the differences of the various religions can be ascribed to different methods of keeping the afflictions in check. As one gets used to keeping one's emotions under control, I think the afflictions become almost invisible, making things easier, and the mind becomes peaceful and relaxed. According to the instruction manuals on the intermediate stage, getting attracted to an object that generates affliction can be risky and a big blunder. Generally speaking, attraction has both risks and benefits: the benefit is the immediate samsaric bliss – which even insects like an ant can feel. It is a temporary benefit and this is also one of the main topics in the Tantric teachings, "using afflictions as the path of practice". For this one needs the quintessential instructions and if one can link the afflictions with the quintessential instructions, the resulting gain will be far greater.

Anyway, it was desire that did not leave me alone. At that time I had Jigme Dorje, the present Khenpo of our monastery, for company. I walked so much and such long distances, that the heels of his shoes, which he got from abroad, wore out!

DIFFICULTY IN UNDERSTANDING THE SCRIPTURES DUE TO STRICTNESS

My understanding of the scripture and my intelligence was not bad. I also had the desire to learn. But after having been influenced by distractions for so long my studying was like a bear trying to catch a marmot: what I learned in the morning was forgotten by the evening and what I learned today was forgotten by tomorrow. It was as though I had some knowledge in every field of study, but nothing was complete. I faced great difficulty. Although I had the opportunity to study under such a hidden yogi and great scholar, who like the past scholars of India and Tibet had complete knowledge of all the old and new school scriptures, I did not have a complete understanding. I used to feel sad thinking about my situation.

Looking back now, I see two reasons for my failure to understand the teachings: one was that I was controlled too strictly in my childhood that I had lost interest in studying scriptures. Although I wanted to study, the keenness was not there and time passed in a blur.

DISTRACTION DOES NOT DEVELOP DILIGENCE

Secondly, as I said earlier, I had become accustomed to distractions. Since I spent many years being distracted and without a teacher, I lacked the opportunity to develop diligence. By experience, I learned that the saying, "Intelligence and capability to understand are not much use without diligence", is certainly true. At that time there were at least sixty people studying under Khenpo, but I don't think there was anyone outstanding enough to be appreciated by him. Looking disheartened, one day Khen Rinpoche said, "None of you seem interested in learning the scriptures. Even if some of you have a little interest, I don't think any of you revise or even reflect on the meaning of the instructions once you go back to your rooms. Amongst you, Mayumla (my mother) and Tashi Namgyal have the best intellectual understanding. It makes me feel sad when I think about the future of the Dharma." Today, when I look back I think it was true. Amongst the gurus, tulkus and young monks were two lay persons: Tashi Namgyal la, the son of Kungo Lama la, the manager of the previous Gyalwang Drukpa, and my mother. I can't blame Khen Rinpoche for feeling sad.

GAINING THE FIRST CORE UNDERSTANDING OF THE SCRIPTURES

Later I received subtle instructions from Khen Rinpoche on the commentary on *Perfection* by Mipham as well as the Hevajra Tantra, and detailed instructions on *The Ornament on the Three Disciplines* by Kunkhyen Pema Karpo, and I gained a new understanding of the teachings I had received earlier. After that, whatever questions I asked for clarification of doubt, he would reply, "Yes. You have understood." Or sometimes he would ask, "How did you know this?" and would seem surprised. There was nothing profound to be surprised about, but I think he was surprised to find that I understood suddenly what I had not understood earlier. After that he never scolded nor showed any kind of dissatisfaction with me. As a person lacking enthusiasm for extensive study, and lacking the wisdom and confidence to analyse every word of the entire scripture, I felt I had completed the common learning after receiving detailed instructions from such a qualified Khenpo on *The Ornament on Three Disciplines*, *A Guide to the Bodhisattva way of Life* and *Madhyamakavara*.

Many years later I had the opportunity to receive the direct introduction to intrinsic awareness from the late His Holiness Dudjom Rinpoche, and he told me that a thorough study of the texts would lead to an experience like seeing sunlight in every field. This made me feel very confident. In brief, I had difficulty in learning the scriptures of interpretable meanings, and conventional learnings, and I still haven't understood them completely. On the other hand, I remain content knowing that knowledge is endless. After some years my way of thinking changed and as the saying goes, "Learn knowledge even if you will die tomorrow", I had a strong wish to learn everything, without being content with what I knew.

> If I do not become certain about it through listening and reflection,
> It is like having no hands and trying to scale a rock –
> If I cannot grasp hold of the meaning, I cannot properly practise.

As mentioned earlier, a time came when I wanted to read all the scriptures and study all fields of knowledge – games, art, songs, drama, painting, languages, the use of new machinery, driving, and using typewriters and computers. At that time, among my contemporaries I was the only one who knew painting, typing, driving, the use of different types of cameras and many other things. I was the first among my contemporaries to use a computer. In sports I had no wish to learn anything to do with fighting or violence.

SIGNS OF ATTACHMENT AND AVERSION

When I thought about the ideas behind violent sports, I found them shocking: hurting others, getting hurt oneself, hunting and killing animals that were living in peace. I had no wish to do sports that brought both physical and mental pain to oneself and others, or sports that had anything to do with fighting and violence, but paradoxically I liked watching fights, as entertainment. Perhaps this could be because of the hidden emotion of attachment and aversion within me.

WANTING TO LEARN DOES NOT MEAN WANTING TO DO

Wanting to learn everything does not necessarily mean wanting to do everything. The desire to learn and the desire to do are both desires, but I wasn't too inclined to do everything. Perhaps this is good, because being involved in doing too many things can lead to complications later on.

KNOWLEDGE IS BLISS, IGNORANCE IS SUFFERING

From the spiritual point of view, having more desire is not considered good. In my opinion, watching sports, dance, drama, songs and music is a source of temporary worldly happiness, like the joy you feel in a dream on meeting an old friend or sadness on losing him. However, if you have some knowledge of these sports and arts you will enjoy them, otherwise you will be bored.

For example, in the past I never liked the traditional Tibetan operas and whenever my teachers listened to them on the radio I felt irritated. But as I learned their meaning I found them meaningful and valuable.

Some of my foreign friends say that Tibetan music has just one style, and it is boring to listen to it for too long. Similarly, our elderly persons scold and say, "What is there to listen to in Western music or to watch in their dances? Noise that sounds like goats and pigs crying fills the air, and jumping around in the air with no rhyme or rhythm. This is the dance of a crazy person."

People enjoy watching a certain sport they know about, and the joy they get from watching it is temporary. For someone who has no wish for temporary happiness it is good enough not to know about it. Otherwise, I think it is important to have knowledge. A limited knowledge brings limited joy; moderate knowledge brings moderate joy and complete knowledge brings an immutable joy, almost like the state of Buddhahood. Omniscience, I think, is a state of complete knowledge because without knowledge, what is there to complete?

We must examine the narrow-minded restrictions on learning only what is in the text, and studying only a few fundamental scriptures. We must check whether the reasons given are reasonable and logical. In the current day and age we must be broad minded and widen our vision and understanding. We cannot force anyone to accept what they have learned as the truth. Whether a Buddhist says so or a non-Buddhist says so, it will not be acceptable.

I realized the importance of learning and understanding the Sutras and Tantras, Mahamudra or Dzogchen, or whatever one practised thoroughly, and I had a great urge to learn them. I felt the need to learn about compassion, renunciation, the Four Noble Truths[53] and the Two Truths, *etc.*, and the meaning of the generation and completion processes, doing retreat and the application of activities. I thought that unless I understood the purpose of the use of the musical instruments, the symbolism of the ritual dance steps, the arrangement of the offerings, which are all part of the monastic discipline, it would be meaningless – like an animal imitating the actions of a human being.

Without prior learning and contemplation of the methods of meditation and visualization, the Buddhist rituals of smoke offerings, sacrificial cake offerings, and of the wrathful Tantric activities, one would not be able to achieve results, and one would also lose immediate interest and genuine enthusiasm to learn them. Many unbiased scholars of the new and old schools have said that doing retreat or meditation without prior learning is like a person without hands attempting to scale a rock, and I believe it is true.

---

53. The first teaching of Buddha Shakyamuni after he attained enlightenment: 1. the truth of suffering, which is to be understood; 2. the truth of the origin of suffering, which is to be abandoned; 3. the truth of cessation, which is to be actualized; 4. the truth of the path, which is to be relied upon.

CHAPTER 6

Retreat and Meditation

DOING RETREAT WITH ONLY LOVE AND NO WISDOM WILL NOT LEAD TO ENLIGHTENMENT

So if you do not first listen and reflect
But just stay in retreat to meditate,
You are like a lost helpless prisoner,
Knowing neither what to meditate on nor how.
Not knowing even the meaning of the word faith,
The chance of insight arising from practice
Is as rare as seeing a star in daylight.
These defects I have experienced myself,
So I am quite motivated to listen well and reflect.

Even when I was small I liked to stay alone in retreat, reciting the Mani mantra and dedication prayers. With my innate compassion as the foundation of my practice, I used to think about helpless and saviourless animals that have been killed, that will be killed, and that are being killed for their meat and blood, such as buffalos, cows and oxen, goats and sheep, birds, fish and pigs *etc.* which were visible to me. It would appear as though they were standing in front of me, trembling in fear and with tears in their eyes, looking at me for protection and refuge. I felt great compassion for them but there was nothing I could do except pray. I would say all the prayers I knew, especially the Avalokiteshvara mantra, with a deep sense of anguish, and cry many times in a day.

Since I had not done any extensive listening and contemplation, the rituals I performed were perfunctory. I did not know the definition of refuge and mind generation, the three-fold concentration, the generation of the three-fold diamond-hard conviction, meditative equipoise and the difference between subsequent conceptuality and non-conceptuality, and the devotion needed for developing exalted wisdom through meditation.

It is said, "People without devotion cannot develop positive qualities, just as a burnt seed cannot yield a green sprout." Without understanding the true definition of devotion – expecting wisdom to arise from meditation – having a vision of deities or the guru is as rare as seeing stars in daylight. Being in retreat was like being under house arrest and I felt happy physically and mentally, but I had nothing to show as an accomplishment, and I never had any expectations either. I still remember hoping and wishing mainly to benefit the helpless beings indirectly, if not directly. Learning from my own experience the shortcomings explained above, and seeing that some others too seemed to have the same problem, I developed the urge and enthusiasm to learn and to contemplate on the Sutra and Tantra texts without prejudice.

PRIDE IS THE ENEMY OF VIRTUE

From experience I can say that if one is able to accomplish unbiased listening and contemplation under an objective spiritual teacher, one will be able to suppress the pride which makes one pretend to know or see things. This gives rise to the misconception that you are the only person full of qualities and without any fault, or it gives rise to the negative thought that you are better than others, even if you are a person without wealth, good looks and inherent or acquired qualities, like me.

Today it seems that pride is regarded as a good quality. In school a child is told by the teacher that he or she is different, even when the child does not possess any qualities, and this boosts their pride. Even at home, all conversation with family members and friends centres on topics that increase pride. As a result, the youth of today does not listen to advice, whether given affectionately or harshly. Like the saying, "The water of positive quality will not hold atop the peak of pride", when you have pride you have no respect or reverence for others with good qualities, and because of pride, you will never be able to develop positive qualities yourself. When you hear about someone highly qualified, instead of showing appreciation and respect or reverence for others with good qualities, you immediately criticize the person, thus accumulating negative karma and damaging your prospects in this life and the next. Most of us have such faults that embarrass the qualified person. Many of the teachings say that if one is able to control this pride, all positive qualities will grow naturally. One can understand this if one thinks thoroughly.

PRIDE IS WEAKNESS

Those of us who have no qualities are more arrogant and more concerned with the eight worldly Dharmas. The scholars and realized masters are humble, modest and without any pride. Bodhisattva Shantideva was an unrivalled scholar and siddha but he too was modest enough to say, "I have nothing to say that has not been said, nor am I accomplished at composition" and "How can an inferior being like me say anything?"

One can understand this from the activities, biographies and instructions of our past spiritual masters and other impartial scholars and realized masters. The body, speech and mind activities of our present excellent spiritual teachers and root gurus, the way they walk sit and talk are all lessons in humility. They walk with their body slightly bent forward as a gesture of humility, unlike us who can't seem to bend our bodies or turn them around, as though steel rods have been inserted in our necks and backbones. Even when they sit down, they do so with a smile and look around with great love, and when you see their face, tears well up in your eyes and the hair of your body stand on end, out of devotion. Unlike them, when we sit in a crowd, we fail to acknowledge their presence with a smile and compassion, but sit unmoving like a statue, staring into space, pretending to be in meditative concentration. I have never seen my gurus or spiritual teachers that I have come into contact with behave in such a brazen manner.

PRIDE AS A QUALITY

I have been advised that today if you are humble, show humility and dress in rags, not only will you be looked down upon, but all your friends and followers will be too. Perhaps it is like the saying, "A malicious dog is hostile to an evil person; a bad knife is hostile to the hand wielding it." A bad dog is unable to distinguish between friend and foe and will wag its tail when it sees a well-dressed person, even if that person has murdered his father, whereas even the mother of the house has to be careful if she is poorly dressed.

As Guru Rinpoche's prophesy says, "Times have not changed; people have changed", the way of people's thinking has changed and their ability to judge a person's inner quality and state has vanished. Instead, more importance is given to a person's external appearance and attire, than to what is being said. Under such conditions, even if one has to adopt various steps to achieve one's immediate objective, I don't think we should allow pride to rear its head. Once you allow pride to influence your mind, there is the risk of bringing unhappiness, not only to yourself but to everyone around you.

In the past I visited some Buddhist centres in the West and gave teachings at their request. Once, my translator Lama Chodrak, a humble scholar of the Sakya tradition, said to me, "During teachings you often say you don't know, you are not competent and that you are not qualified. This is our fine tradition. But today people will believe that you are not qualified, saying; 'he himself acknowledges he is not qualified,' and will treat you as a mediocre. They do not have the tradition of checking a person's inner qualities. Therefore, it is better not to say such things." But by habit I kept saying so, either at the beginning or end of the talks, for many years. Today I don't say it often because I feel there is no need to talk about my qualifications during teachings. I have been giving teachings for so many years and I know I owe no explanation to anyone about my qualities and shortcomings. All one has to do is check thoroughly without deceiving oneself, and never allow pride to arise in one's mind.

> At the time of hearing and reflecting,
> Many a scholar has been misled
> By fickle-mindedness towards meditation.
> I am happy to treat meditation as the life line.

Quotations from the Sutras and Tantras and the teachings of spiritual masters stress that we should meditate in order to root out pride and other afflictive emotions. Listening can only control the afflictions but it cannot root them out. It is said, "Calm and peaceful is the sign of listening; free of afflictions is the sign of meditation."

A CHILD WITH A PURE MIND CAN ACHIEVE RESULTS FROM MEDITATION

From the age of eight or nine years, my kind guru, the late Kyabje Drukpa Thuksey Rinpoche, taught me calm-abiding meditation and other methods or processes for controlling the mind. Although I did not possess any profound knowledge, I used to sit upright and look straight for a long time. Childish thought is funny. I received formal instructions on meditation when I was eight years old. There was a statue of Guru Rinpoche in our shrine and looking at it I used to think, "He has been staying so still with one-pointed concentration for so long. How wonderful! I seek refuge! I must try and see if I can also remain so." I remember staying like that unhindered by conceptual thought. I was not joking or play-acting.

Since it was done with full faith I had various experiences, like fainting with bliss. With good intention I told some of my Dharma friends about this, but they just laughed and paid no attention. I thought there was no point in telling them repeatedly and stopped talking to them about this.

One day my guru suddenly asked me, "Does your mind remain one-pointed?" I replied in the affirmative. Then he asked me how long could I stay? I said that if I meditated after the exhalation of air I could stay one-pointed, unhindered by conceptual thoughts, for about an hour. He said that such a long time is risky and I must be careful. Then he asked me how long I could control the breathing cycle of inhaling, retention and exhalation, and I replied that I didn't know. He said, "Try it and you will know." So, I held my breath in front of him and he said, "How good could the ability to retain air for so long be, at such a young age?" and then he discussed it with Khen Rinpoche.

TEACHINGS OF MY GURU

Sometimes, with great affection, my Guru Kyabje Drukpa Thuksey Rinpoche used to take me to watch artistic, sports and circus shows. Once while watching such a show he suddenly asked, "Is it entertaining?" I replied that it was, and he advised me, "You must know it is your mind." At that time, since my mind-stream was not ripe, I did not fully understand what he meant, but later I realized the profoundness of his words and this laid the foundations for confident faith.

Whether travelling or sitting I used to try and check the stability of the mind and one day, while we were travelling in a car, he looked at me and asked, "What is manifesting in your mind?" and I couldn't say anything. He just smiled and said, "We are on the path of Perfection of Wisdom. Do you understand?" Such teaching! Years later, after I had received all the quintessential instructions of our tradition he said, "I have to give you instructions on *Madhyamakavatra*."

I should have just thanked him and received the instructions, but my attendant said I had already received instructions from Khen Rinpoche. To this Rinpoche replied, "Khenpo's Madhyamaka of words and my Madhyamaka of meaning are not the same." Anyway I could not receive the teachings. Perhaps I did not have the karma to receive them.

IF THE ESSENCE IS NOT UNDERSTOOD, MEDITATION MAY BE HARMFUL

Around the age of fifteen, due to a combination of my youth and the attractions of earthly pleasures and worldly activities, and many other factors, I could not carry on the practice with diligence for some years, as I had when I was younger. As I became more interested in studying the scriptures, my interest in meditation waned.

Although it is said that interest in scriptures will harm meditation, I do not believe this at all. I had the opportunity to study the fundamental scriptures, other sciences, the *Wish-fulfilling Treasure* and its abridged practice, and many other major treatises, under Ontrul Rinpoche, my spiritual teacher of successive lifetimes, and he would sometimes jokingly say, "You seem like a good meditator. I mean it." Sometimes he would ask, "Is our studying the texts using the three modes of reasoning harming your meditation? Even if this doesn't help, it should not harm your meditation." So, judging by his words it seems that the wrong way of studying the texts could harm the practice of meditation.

IT IS IMPORTANT TO COMBINE CLEARING DOUBTS THROUGH DIALECTICAL DEBATE WITH THE GURU'S INSTRUCTION

Once Ontrul Rinpoche narrated, "Young Terton Sogyal, leading a yak on which an aged Dza Patrul Ugyen Jigme Chokyi Wangpo was riding, requested him to give him the teaching of *Guhyagarba Tantra*. The latter replied, 'Audacious son of a nomad! *Guhyagarba* cannot be understood by people like you and me. To learn *Guhyagarba* you must first be able to use the three modes of reasoning.' Terton said, 'I know a bit about the three modes of reasoning,' to which Dza Patrul replied, 'Then show me.' Terton explained the three modes of reasoning and their attributes, *etc.* Patrul said, 'It is amazing that this boy with knotted hair knows the use of the three modes of reasoning. If I don't teach *Guhyagarba* to you, then whom shall I teach?' Patrul immediately got off the yak and they sat down on the grass and he started teaching the young Terton. I heard this from my elders when I was young. So you must understand that the scriptures in general, and reasoning, are helpful tools for meditation." He would often ask me how my meditational experience was and I would reply, "I don't know, I can only explain in literal terms."

MEDITATION SHOULD BE STARTED FROM A YOUNG AGE

Ontrul Rinpoche advised me that meditation should be practised from a young age, otherwise it would not work. He said, "If our studying the scriptures hinders your meditation then it will be a disaster. The very purpose of studying the texts is meant to create the conditions for meditation. There is no reason for the texts to demolish meditation. I thought I would study the scriptures well when I was young, and after completing those studies I would do meditation, but there is no end to scriptural studies. I have been studying the scriptures ever since I was seventeen years old, until now, and I am in my seventies now. There is no end and, instead of clearing my doubts, more and more uncertainties have been added." He gave me such enlightening advice on many occasions. I try to identify all external phenomena that I see or hear with the nature of the mind, and diligently develop analytical meditation and stabilizing meditation as the life line and root of all practice.

FOR ORDINARY PEOPLE WISHING TO FOLLOW THE PATH, IT IS IMPORTANT TO STUDY THE TEXTS

Using self-cognisant wisdom to apply the pithy meaning of the Sutras and Tantras to one's mind, or even taking into consideration the joys and sorrows of daily life, and checking one's mind to see if any lessons can be learned to improve the mind, or reflecting on the words and meanings of conventional treatises to understand the state and nature of the mind, can be treated as meditation.

During a conversation, my guru once said to me, "For a monk who does not understand the profound essence of Dzogchen, it is better for him to spend his life studying the texts in a monastery where there is discipline. Reflecting on the meaning of the texts – maybe one could call it analytical meditation – will help prevent the mind going astray, under the influence of attachment and aversion, and serve as a means of familiarization. Since he will be busy with the texts, his mind will not be influenced by gross afflictions. From getting up in the morning until going to bed at night, except to read the texts, he will not have time for idle thought or idle conversations of attachment and aversion. Otherwise, he will be too busy visiting homes to perform rituals or guiding the spirits of the dead. It is such a pity. He, who has not found the way, pretends to guide the dead and the living, happy with petty offerings. These people are lured by petty offerings, day and night, their conversations centre on attachment and aversion and their thoughts centre on attachment and aversion. Even in their sleep they have attachment and aversion. They waste their life with attachment and aversion. They clasp their teeth so hard at the time of death that one can see scratch marks on their chests. They lose control of their bowel movements in bed. They have such a hard time," and he wept out of compassion on many occasions.

AUTHENTIC LISTENING NEEDED

When I reflected on this advice again and again, I understood that listening, to some extent, is a pre-requisite and the little understanding of the meaning one gains through contemplative wisdom, touched by the blessing of the guru's instruction, can lead to spontaneous realization, without having to persist with the verbal meaning – like a vulture soaring into the sky. One of the instructions talked of, "Dead body of an ordinary being in the bed of a scholar," which means that due to partial listening, one's entire life is spent in listening, unable to apply them to meditation and making the practice useless. In spite of having a huge following or fame as a great scholar, at the crucial time of death, such a person dies just like an ordinary being.

> Whatever virtuous actions I have done
> Are for the benefit of others and the next life.
> So I avoid actions of self-interest and the eight worldly motivations
> And I am glad that I am strong enough to resist such obsessions

All religions, Buddhist or non-Buddhist, teach that whatever we do must be for the benefit of oneself and others. The focal point of Buddha Shakyamuni's teachings is "the altruistic mind of enlightenment, if possible" meaning practical work for the welfare of others, and if not possible, "don't harm others", meaning you should not entertain even the slightest harmful thought. Doing spiritual practice for selfish interests, or the welfare of one's family or community, or to kill one's enemy or cause them suffering, doing refuge practice, or propitiating the guardian deities, only for the well-being of one's near and dear ones is against Buddhist teachings. It is not proper from the Buddhist perspective.

Many of the Mahayana scriptures teach that, not only during spiritual practice, but also during every activity such as walking, sitting, eating, talking or even while spitting or answering nature's call, one must think of benefitting other beings. Buddhism is called the sublime doctrine of peace and although I have not been able to practice it completely, I have a deep logical faith in it as an authentic doctrine befitting its name. Peace is something that everyone needs and seeks.

SELFISHNESS, THE ROOT OF FAULTS

All of us follow different methods to find peace. Many countries in the world hold peace talks and sign peace agreements. This is all very good, but I doubt if the results are as expected. It must be understood that peace is the result of an altruistic mind and the absence of peace is the result of giving prominence to selfish interests. Just as all the bacteria and pus needs to be removed from a wound for it to heal completely, peace can only be achieved if one is able to eliminate selfishness. Even controlling or reducing selfishness can make a big difference. Personally speaking, although I had the opportunity to study under Buddha-like spiritual teachers, I have not been able to understand Buddha's thought due to my strong selfishness. When I think and analyse the ups and downs in life, the lack of peace of mind, the desire for unnecessary articles, not feeling elated when one gets them, discontentment with worldly pleasures, not wanting to stay at a given place or not wanting to go where one is supposed to go – I realize that these are all illusions caused by selfishness in one's mind-stream. How did I know this?

CHECKING WHETHER ONE HAS DEGENERATED IS HELPFUL

Having had the great opportunity to drink the nectar-like teachings of my gurus on many occasions, I began investigating the various things I had done over many past years: what activity constituted spiritual activity and what constituted non-spiritual activity? What results have I achieved? How happy was I while doing those things? And, if I was happy, was it enough or do I need more? One can be certain to wish for more. Then, for how long do you need to go on doing this? For how long do I intend to run after objects of desire? Will it be alright to lead a more relaxed life? If not, then for what reason? Is it the body or the mind that feels it is not enough? The mind finds it is not enough because the body is an inanimate object like earth and rock. The mind is filled with competitiveness, the desire for superiority, happiness and prosperity and is never content and cannot give anything up. The body is the slave of the mind. Until the body and mind are separated at the time of death, it has to run along with the mind.

I used to investigate in this way while in bed, or while travelling or when I was alone. Sometimes, I wondered if I had gone crazy. I don't know how much such investigations help spiritually, but it certainly bring peace and happiness in one's mind and are very useful.

DEMON OF HOPE AND FEAR

Whatever one may say, it is selfishness that causes sorrow. When Buddha said, "Give up your life," I think it was one way of saying, "Do not be selfish." Selfishness gives growth to attachment and aversion, and these two are the cause of the demon of hope and fear, the main cause of suffering. This 'hope and fear' creates many problems, not only for lay people but also for old practitioners. Even when they pledge to stay in retreat, hope and fear doesn't let them stay; even if they wish to uphold their commitment it doesn't let them do so. They are unable to control anger at not getting petty selfish things done. Hope and fear doesn't let you practise the path of the Six Perfections, and even if you start practicing, the desire for high status, riches, honour and fame comes attached with the practice. Like erasing the footprint with the hand, spiritual practice is replaced by demonic practice. Thus it becomes the cause of rebirth in the lower realms. Gampopa and many past spiritual masters have commented on this. As Milarepa said that the Dharma was taught to subjugate the demon of hope and fear, of worldly concerns, but practitioners like us face a lot of difficulty overcoming this demon of hope and fear.

SPIRITUAL ACTIVITY MUST NOT BE STAINED BY SELFISHNESS

Therefore, all selfishness related to this life has to be abandoned. But people like me lack the mental strength and good conditions to do so. However, I do have the determination not to let selfishness, especially the eight worldly concerns, stain any spiritual activity that is aimed towards the next life or the welfare of other beings. Even when I wish to get teachings from a spiritual master, I only ask for teachings after first checking whether I have the wrong motivation of hoping to gain honour in the future. These days I hear some people say, "This guru is old. So we must receive all the initiations and transmissions he has so we can give them in the future when people ask for them." Some have even advised me to do so.

I don't know what the motivation was for the advice, but I didn't like what I heard. My ear certainly lacks accumulation of merit: I hear what I don't want to hear or what I shouldn't hear. It is better not to hear such things. If one is able to develop pure perception, hearing such things will not bother you. But being unable to develop pure perception, hearing people say such things makes me uncomfortable and uneasy.

Even when I give teachings, I check my own motivation. Sometimes I am able to generate an altruistic mind and at such times I rejoice. Most of the time, even though I am unable to generate an extensive altruistic mind, I never let the expectations of offerings or praise from my disciples enter into my mind. Sometimes, due to the strong propensity of afflictions and the distraction of carelessness, such thoughts try to arise, but immediately I remind myself that treating Dharma as a commodity is a serious act of abandoning the Dharma. It is not such a difficult thing to do. I don't know if worldly thoughts arise unconsciously as an undercurrent of thought. Anyway by doing so, at the end of spiritual practice I feel good. My guru often told me that teaching with pure motivation will have positive effect on those receiving the teachings.

SELLING THE HOLY DHARMA

Building monasteries, making reliquaries of the body, speech and mind of the Buddha, founding a Sangha and a community of followers are acts of spirituality. But if the real motivation is to gain respect and fame, then in reality one is leading one's life by selling the Dharma.

While receiving teachings on Abhidharma from my guru, Ontrul Rinpoche, I asked him if there was any non-virtuous act greater than killing. He told me that it is usually said that killing is the most serious non-virtuous act, but from the point of taking refuge, using the three reliquaries as commodities is a more serious sin, and he gave many quotations from the Sutras and Tantras. I felt everything we did was non-virtuous. I thought, teaching Dharma and displaying images in the hope of material gain and honour, and opening a shop to sell the three reliquaries for profit are the same, and the degree of sin should also be the same. Turning the Dharma into a commodity out of worldly concerns, and building three reliquaries for selfish ends, by people in the garb of spiritual practitioners like me, is like drinking poison knowingly, and a more serious act of non-virtue. Since then I pledged not to use the Dharma for my selfish ends. I thought, when the past masters in their instructions said that it was better to earn one's livelihood by using swords and guns than to use the Dharma robes as a means of livelihood, they must have meant this. The mind training *Parting Away From Four Clingings* of the Sakya tradition says, "One clinging to this life is not a spiritual practitioner", and it means one using the profound Dharma for comfort in one's life is not a spiritual practitioner, although he may appear as a practitioner. Even at a young age, I used to think about this a lot and sometimes expressed my thoughts in public.

A PURE MIND CANNOT BE CONTAMINATED BY NON-VIRTUE

Many people did not appreciate what I said, and sometimes people from within our circle used to advise me, saying, "What you say is hurting the sentiments of people, including our patrons. You are someone involved in building monasteries, reliquaries and giving teachings and if you say all this, then it is like pouring water over your own head, it serves no purpose." I did not blame them for their advice. Later, thanks to the explanations given by my gurus on many occasions and pondering on the meaning of the stanza, "Everything depends on the mind", I understood that building monasteries as centres for listening, contemplation and meditation, schools and hospitals solely for the Dharma and welfare of others, and as service to one's guru without self-interest, is not contaminated by the eight worldly concerns.

By my karma, I was born to take care of the old and new buildings called monasteries, and assemblies of people known as Sangha. Gyalwa Longchen Rabjam said, "The lay family has to look after a small house and those of us supposed to be seeking enlightenment through the path of renunciation build huge buildings, a hundred times bigger than the layman's house, called monasteries. An average family of a layman would have twenty members at the most. We are surrounded by hundreds of people called followers. gurus and tulkus are under the illusion that it would not be proper, spiritually and mundanely, not to look after these people. Not only you but your retinue, friends, parents and patrons would face difficulties and worries. You would achieve nothing spiritually, and from the worldly point of view, you would not be able to spend one relaxed and happy day. Months and years pass swiftly without realizing and when you think about how distraction has deceived you, it is pitiable. So, reflect again and again on the teachings of the spiritual teachers and the words of your root guru, and change your way of thinking. Build reliquaries according to your capacity, without any self-interest or worldly concerns, thinking only of service to your guru, the Dharma, and the welfare of beings and of the next life. In this way, all positive activities like giving or receiving teachings, will give you mental satisfaction. All the material contributions, big or small, made by friends and patrons will not be wasted and will bring peace and happiness in this life and the next. If someone does more than you have done, don't be jealous, but rejoice and applaud instead. Thus all activity will be virtuous and pure from the beginning, in the middle and at the end." So when I look back at my activity, I feel I have done well enough.

THE HARMFUL THOUGHT OF THE EIGHT WORLDLY MOTIVATIONS

In brief, "the eight worldly motivations are the worst enemy of a spiritual practitioner". In a piece of advice my Guru Ontrul Rinpoche gave me, he quoted Tsangpa Gyare's words, "Unguarded birth of meditation practice is like a rich man blown away by wind, a lion in the company of dogs, a jewel sunk in mud. So guard against aversion." In his last letter of advice from Tibet, he quoted Milarepa's instruction, "The jewel of human beings in the past, gave teachings to overcome the eight worldly motivations; have not the eight worldly motivations grown among today's practitioners?" as well as the above quotation from Tsangpa Gyare and said, "The key practice of all past spiritual masters was to abandon the eight worldly motivations. With folded hands, I request Your Holiness to work for the well-being of the Dharma and sentient beings, without falling under the influence of the eight worldly motivations. You are intelligent and being close to me, I thought you would not mind my saying this. Although I do not have any qualities, as an elder I offer this advice with sincerity."

With great humility and kindness, he sent me this advice as his last testament. This advice is the gist of the instructions of all my past spiritual teachers, and had a great effect on my mind. I carry his last letter in my daily prayer book.

As advised by my guru, when I study the way Milarepa, Gyalwa Gotsangpa, Gyalwa Lorepa and all the spiritual masters of the past carried out activities for the Dharma and sentient beings, I realize that they have cut off all attachment and aversion, and hope and fear. Like the saying, "Freedom is happiness; dependence unhappiness", they did not give in to others' influences and, like the old saying of "treating wherever you are happy as one's native land, and whoever shows you kindness as your parents", they roamed the country and practised non-attachment. They cut off the shackles of the eight worldly motivations and, following the word of the guru, some led an ascetic life, living in high hills with mist as their clothing, giving up all attachment to food, clothing and fame; some built monasteries and turned the wheel of activity, built the three reliquaries extensively and gathered followers; and some concentrated mainly on giving teachings. In essence, they kept the words of the authentic guru as their witness and spent their entire lives working for the welfare of others. This is known as equating life and practice. This is a great accomplishment for the Dharma and for beings.

NEVER GIVE YOUR FREEDOM TO OTHERS

We let attachment and aversion take control of us and become slaves of delusion. Because of that, we have no freedom and whatever few possessions we own are taken away by friends and relatives. You don't have the freedom to do spiritual practice, or go on holiday to a scenic spot as you wish to. Even if you do go, you have to explain everything to your partner and other family members, and rarely will they appreciate your explanation. Or you worry about your partner and children and want to return home. Those in the garb of monks, who have no family to worry about, are not left alone by the desire for wealth. They do not have enough time to acquire wealth, and those who have sufficient wealth worry about losing it, or they are tormented by the sight of their wealth being exhausted. Seeing the wealth of others, jealousy arises and doesn't leave your mind in peace. There is no history of anyone, who, shackled by hope and fear, and motivated by selfishness, has been able to do real great work for the Dharma and for sentient beings. The lay person faces a lot of problems that ultimately leads to their own downfall, as well as that of others.

As someone in the last ranks of these past great spiritual masters, I always give importance to checking my mind to see if any worldly motivation arises or not. It is difficult for a person like me to have such a strong mindful awareness, but whenever I engage in spiritual activity with full concentration, I do not let such evil thoughts arise in my mind, and I cultivate the antidotes to prevent them. As a result, I am sometimes able to control the eight worldly motivations and resist the evil thoughts of clinging to riches, honour and fame. Like the great translator Vairochana said, "Even if others don't like it, I am happy", and at such times I feel a sense of satisfaction.

> Whoever bestows teachings and empowerments
> Should be cherished as your very own eyes.
> If you insult the teacher's consort or attendants,
> It is obvious your realization is far away.

As mentioned above you should lead your life happily, without being influenced by the eight worldly motivations. You have to live your life. Even from a very young age I used to think: I have to live my life, but wondered how I should lead it.

THREE TYPES OF LIFE

One way of living is that of a person, who, with sufficient accumulation of merit, seeks worldly fame through lies and deception. Such a person may live long, and may even have the illusion of happiness in their old age, due to the accumulation of merit in their past lives.

Another way of living is to leave the world behind, dedicate one's life to spiritual practice, and meditate in the mountains.

The third type is somewhat like my way of living, which Drukpa Kunga Legpa, commonly known as Drukpa Kunleg, described as "Jo Drapa" or "gentleman monk", which is neither completely spiritual nor completely worldly. It is a funny lifestyle, and hard to describe.

One has to choose which way one wants to lead one's life. Like the old Tibetan saying, "It is good that you have a choice, but the wrong choice will lead to suffering"– it is nice to have a choice, but it is difficult to make the right choice.

When I was young I would compare the lifestyles people had chosen and seeing their choices, I would feel compassion for them. Wherever I went or whoever I was with, I had the habit of saying, "What a pity". Once, when I said, "What a pity", one of my teachers scolded me and said, "Why does a small child speak like an old mother? Stop saying this in future."

The object of compassion need not necessarily be a poor way of life. When you look at the way people, rich or poor, high or low, lead their lives in this world, it certainly is an object of compassion. When I see marriage ceremonies, I immediately think that person has chosen the samsaric world of suffering. It is funny because personally, I have a strong love for sensuous pleasure, but when I see the situation of other people I feel strong compassion. I remember when I felt such compassion, it was helpful for my practice, but these days, I don't get that feeling so much. I get a vague feeling of compassion sometimes. I am telling you this because I think you might see some point in it. Think well and you will understand what I mean.

CAN SPIRITUAL LIFE AND WORLDLY LIFE BE CONCORDANT?

Generally speaking, all past spiritual teachers from Longchen Rabjam, Dza Patrul to my own gurus, are unanimous in saying that spiritual life and a worldly life cannot be led simultaneously. In a teaching Dza Patrul said, "If someone says that a person is leading a spiritual life and a worldly life simultaneously, then it can decisively be said that he may be leading a worldly life, but not a spiritual life." All treatises and commentaries agree that a spiritual life and a worldly life cannot be led simultaneously. However, as the Khampa saying goes, "Scriptural quotations and the skin of a deer can be stretched in any way", it can be interpreted in many ways. Yet, when it comes to interpreting the intention of the Buddha and gurus, like stretching the deer skin, it will be too confusing for people like me. Those who have realized the mind of the Buddha can see the interpretational definitions clearly, like holding an olive in the palm of one's hand. So, however they interpret the meaning, it will not go beyond the boundaries of "the four insignias of the view". There may also be special cases among spiritual practitioners.

As I said earlier, I have not understood this well. If you reflect on the hustle and bustle of worldly life and understand your own condition thoroughly, it certainly helps in the generation of compassion. Personally speaking, I am in the form of a spiritual practitioner, but my actions do not always go the spiritual way. But looking at the mundane world leads to progress in my thoughts. For a person like me, the foundation of Dharma depends on the profound teachings and advice of the spiritual teachers. Hence, a qualified spiritual teacher has to be found first.

Cleansing the defilements of self-interest you should then serve the spiritual teacher who is showing you the path of progress – with the three kinds of satisfaction; then receive empowerment to ripen your mind-stream; instructions to liberate the ripened mind-stream;

and teachings to weigh the essence of all phenomenal existence of this world.

FULFILLING THE WISHES OF THE AUTHENTIC GURU

Until such a relationship is established one is free, but once the guru-disciple relationship is established, you have surrendered everything to the guru. The teachings of all the traditions clearly state that you cannot bully or scorn your spiritual teacher, and even common vehicle teachings and non-Buddhist teachings say the same thing. One must care for the spiritual teacher as one cares for one's own eyes and follow him or her with utmost care, and carry out his or her wishes.

Some of our acquaintances say, "I seek refuge in my root guru," and prostrate and make offerings to him with great respect, but look down upon his consort, children or attendant monks as the epitome of fault, calling them "demons", "devils" and a disgrace to the guru. Such behaviour is the basis of accumulating bad karma. I committed such transgressions when I was small. I did not know better, because no one had taught me. Receiving teachings later on the *Fifty Stanzas of Guru Devotion*, was like waking up, though a little late. In remembrance of the kindness of my gurus, and especially Ontrul Rinpoche, who opened my eyes, I offer the mandala of practice to them. Some people, I think, fail to wake up for their entire lives.

The text says, "Treat even your teacher's beloved family with the same respect as you show towards him." Beloved means anything or anyone that is especially dear to him. For example, if the guru is in the form of a lay person then it is his consort, a Dakini in human form, and his sons and daughters, who are heroes and heroines, who should be shown the same respect as the guru. If the guru is in the form of an ordained monk, then the same respect should be shown to the managers and attendants who are close to him, and to the Vajra brothers and sisters, since the guru is regarded as the father, the mandala as the mother, and all the disciples who ripen under the same guru and mandala are called Vajra brothers and sisters. The respect as you would show to the guru should also be shown to his pet dogs, the guru's robes and even to the guru's shadow.

One should diligently refrain from using or keeping the guru's belongings without his permission, or showing disrespect or abusing them. Otherwise the achievement of even the ordinary actual attainments, not to mention the supreme actual attainment of Buddhahood will be delayed by months, years and even lifetimes. This was explained by my Guru Ontrul Rinpoche, with quotations from many texts. After reflecting on the meaning of what I heard, I made an effort to practise it and gained some experience, thereby boosting my confidence.

CHAPTER 7

Faith in Ultimate Reality

WITHOUT FAITH IN ULTIMATE REALITY, COMPASSION FOR THE PHENOMENAL WORLD IS DIFFICULT

Although I remember possessing inherent compassion, my standard of devotion was low. I think if I had had firm confidence in devotion when I was young, then I would not have had to struggle for so many years. I received completely, like pouring from vase to vase, all the ripening instructions of the glorious Drukpa Lineage, and the secret instructions of attaining Buddhahood within a lifetime from my late guru, the three-fold Vajra holder Kyabje Drukpa Thuksey Rinpoche, son of the 10th Gyalwang Drukpa. His kindness in looking after me both spiritually and mundanely cannot be repaid. There is no need to go into details.

Since I was eight or nine years old he gave me instructions every day. Even before I went to bed he would come over and explain the nature of the mind, the way to establish it, the meaning of the Four Empowerments and the teaching on dreams, *etc*. His kindness can never be repaid. On my part I diligently practiced, watching the essence of mind over many years. However, I did not make any progress over and above whatever experience and understanding I had achieved during the time of my late guru. In retrospect, I think the reason for this was that I regarded the Guru Vajradhara in human form as a human and a friend. I did not know that one should not tread on his shadow, use his cushion or other articles.

For example, the text teaches that when the Guru Vajradhara is seated on the throne, one should sit on a lower seat, showing respect to the three doors, but I sat on a high throne and my guru sat on a lower throne and gave me the instructions. All the Tantras and treatises say that the disciple should prostrate with respect to the three doors of his teacher, but instead of my prostrating to my guru, he prostrated to me thrice. I heard that this is a tradition in Kham. When I received teachings from Pawo Rinpoche, he told me that in Kham this was done, when high gurus like the Karmapa were receiving teachings. I asked if it was alright for me to do so and he simply replied that it may be alright in special cases and circumstances, but he did not seem very pleased.

Even though I was young and did not have extensive knowledge, I knew that only special cases deserved such treatment and it was not appropriate in the case of someone like me. I used to feel uneasy and uncomfortable, but I was a small boy and the attendants were authoritative, and I didn't have the courage to tell them how I felt. There was no option and it was I who suffered the consequences, because there is no bigger loss in the world than accumulating negative karma. But then as Kunkhyen Pema Karpo said, "What is unknown and unseen can be forgiven". I hoped it wouldn't be too bad since I had no desire for superiority or any sense of competition. I asked the late Ontrul Rinpoche what should I do to rectify this and he advised me to confess from the depth of my heart and said, "Since you did not sit on the throne out of competitiveness or desire for elevation, against the advice of your guru, this is not a serious transgression that you should worry about."

THE NEED TO BE CAREFUL IN BOTH SPIRITUAL AND MUNDANE ACTIVITY

Generally in our society we commit serious transgressions out of ignorance and lethargy, and when we realize this it is too late. Whatever we do, spiritual or mundane, we must not blindly follow our greed. We must first check by asking the elders, or studying biographies or history, and use our intellect to make a final decision. During the investigation, if irrelevant questions and doubts are raised, then one will be unable to take a decision and irreversible mistakes will be made. Sometimes you can't think, or even if you do think you are too distracted to take a decision, or even if you have mentally reached a decision, you fail to take a committed decision, and by then it is too late. You can only regret, but then there is no point in regretting what is done. So I think if you have a set of rules, even though you face difficulties initially, it will be useful. Nagarjuna said, "Rules are like the animate and inanimate ground, the foundation of all qualities." This includes mundane qualities too.

One has to create the conditions for following the rules without having to depend on too many people. There are many instances of spiritual practitioners facing obstacles after asking for advice from their parents instead of the guru. I understood this later from my root gurus. This does not mean that one should disrespect one's parents, or show no love and affection for them, or deride and bully them. Most parents, friends, religious teachers and spiritual friends, who have not abandoned the eight worldly motivations, do not have adequate experience in the skillful methods of ultimate happiness, even if they are knowledgeable about worldly affairs. Milarepa said, "When you yourself have fallen into the abyss of samsara, boasting that you can guide others on the positive path will be meaningless, since both of you are in samsara. If two men have fallen into the river, they won't be able to save each other even if they want to, unless the right conditions are there." This means that asking others for advice is like one blind man leading the other blind man. It also means that decisions should be taken on the basis of the guru's advice, because the qualified guru has completed the path and gone beyond samsara and yet, with great kindness, deliberately comes in human form to lead us on the path of liberation. So following his instructions and advice will not let you down.

When I was young I found the texts and teachings that said, "Don't ask your father for an opinion; don't seek your mothers' counsel. Completely trust the guru." I used to wonder about the basis and reason for this and felt very uncomfortable with doubt. But today I see that this doubt was a great obstacle to the progress of my education. Later, when Ontrul Rinpoche gave the explanations, it was like facing the mistakes of my thoughts in the past, and it was thought provoking and helpful. I think some of my friends are also facing the same problem, but no one has openly asked me about it. Perhaps they think I will be resentful.

UNDERSTANDING WHOM YOU CALL A GURU

It is important for Buddhists in general, those interested in learning about Tantrayana in particular, and especially those pretending to be doing Mahamudra and Dzogchen practice, to understand this: one must understand who it is that you call a guru or spiritual teacher. Basically, our attitude is a problem because we have a strong natural materialistic view. For example, when we talk about a friend, we talk about his external behaviour, his house, wealth and looks because we have nothing deeper to discuss. Even if we have, very few will be interested to learn or listen. All conversations veer towards what the eye can see, such as mountains, countries, buildings, gatherings of men and women, the weather or what we hear, like good or bad news and a little about happiness or sadness. Other than that there is nothing profound to discuss.

Whatever you talk about, see or think every day, it is only about the things we can see, hear or think about, but there is nothing new. In today's society, people of different castes and creed, male or female, young or old, almost all think alike – what is invisible does not exist and what is visible must exist. Therefore, we repeatedly talk about things in this world that our two eyes can see or that our two little ears can hear. If we like something we praise it and run after it; if we don't like something we criticize it and avoid it. Even a spiritual practitioner leads his life this way. In a way it is good enough, because this is how it has been until now, and this is how it will be. So there is no reason why someone should question this way of life. But if you reflect deeply, then the way people, rich or poor, high or low, lead their daily lives is very uninspiring and dull.

NEVER INSIST ON ANYTHING

Our way of thinking is very amazing: you can neither laugh nor cry. We are obstinate about whatever is good or bad that comes to our mind. The scholars are obstinate about what is convenient to talk about, or what appeals to their thought, and they are attached to their view. The foolish believe what they see to be the truth and are attached to the colourful, worldly phenomena. Even small children and insects have such attachment. This is what is called "innate delusion" in the scriptures. This irreversible clinging makes us insist that what we see as good is good, and what we see as bad is bad, and if someone disagrees then we get irritated and argue without trying to find out why the other person has a different opinion. Nagarjuna said, "In the process of pulling back and forth it gets torn. Since I do not accept anything I am the only one without fault." This alone should suffice, but we are not satisfied and we bind ourselves with the net of pretentious scholarship and knowledge, and everybody is confused. Since we are never broad-minded enough to accept others' points of view, and instead remain hard-headed, this becomes the cause of unhappiness in the lives of ordinary people.

INSISTENCE ON RELIGIOUS THOUGHT

Buddhist and non-Buddhist scholars are having a hard time. Hundreds of non-Buddhist scholars have used rock solid reasoning to defeat Buddhists in debates in the past. One cannot say how much this has harmed Buddhism. Similarly, thousands of Buddhist scholars have used logic as extensive as the sky, and as deep as the ocean, to defeat non-Buddhists. But today it is just history and we can all see how much their teachings have flourished. It would be futile and problematic to insist that one's spiritual path is right and faultless, out of attachment to one's spiritual tradition. It is better to understand the essence of the spiritual tradition one has chosen to follow, to clear the doubts by studying the scriptures and logic, to serve your tradition by practising it silently and with a broadmind, and accepting that the other traditions too may have some truth. Being rigid and narrow minded can only make you deride and criticize other traditions, and not see the positive quality of other traditions, or refuse to acknowledge them simply because you want to hear what pleases your ears, see what pleases your eyes and believe what pleases your mind.

> Watching the actions of your teacher
> And hoping they will coincide with your wishes –
> This will be the source of every misfortune.
> So regard every action of the teacher as perfect.

As explained earlier, being stubborn and rigid you will never be able to like others and genuinely see the qualities in their mind-stream objectively. You lose respect and reverence for all the qualified people in the world, and you lose any opportunity to gain even a part of their good quality. Your mind-stream degenerates day by day, with hardly any chance for progress. I learned this from my experience. It is a big loss and you gain nothing.

DO NOT BELIEVE YOUR EYES AND EARS

It is said that all of us ordinary beings have positive qualities as well as shortcomings. This can be proved through proper investigation, but we have never given ourselves any chance to investigate. If we see something pleasing then we immediately follow our feelings and we insist that it is good. Likewise, if we see something unpleasant, we simply follow our thoughts. But something that looks bad may actually be good, and what appears good may in reality be bad. So you can understand that you cannot always believe what you see, hear or think. It's like the saying, "Don't believe everything being said as the truth; don't treat everyone you hate as the enemy." This is similar to the meaning of the stanza in the Sutra, "The eyes, ears and nose are valid; the tongue, body and mind are not valid. If all the organs are valid, what use will the path of the Noble One be to anyone?" Similar comments can also be found in the commentaries on the Six Ornaments and the Two Excellent Ones. I strongly believe that the interpretational texts by Indian scholars are precise, less verbose and very helpful for meditation and practice, even though I couldn't understand them completely, due to my lack of intelligence.

My root guru, Lopon Kunsang Dorje, a jewel among siddhas, popularly known as Lopon Gangri, named after the place where he meditated, attained yogic achievements at Drira Phug, the meditation cave of Gyalwa Gotsangpa. He was a hidden yogi, respected and praised by a galaxy of accomplished spiritual masters of all traditions, such as His Holiness Dudjom Rinpoche, Dilgo Khyentse Rinpoche, the 16th Karmapa, Apho Rinpoche Yeshe Rangdol and my Guru, Drukpa Thuksey Rinpoche. I received the complete instructions of the Drukpa Lineage from him. The late Lopon taught directly from the heart and never used instruction manuals. He would sometimes quote from Milarepa, Gyalwa Gotsangpa, Longchenpa and Barawa, but his teachings were based mostly on the Buddha's words and commentaries on the Six Ornaments and the Two Excellent Ones, and treatises by Indian scholars.

Once, during the teaching Lopon Gangri jokingly said, "Since you are well versed in the scriptures, you must easily understand the commentaries by the Tibetan scholars. Since I have not done much listening and reflection, I find the works of the Tibetan scholars too verbose and difficult to comprehend. The commentaries are meant to be the explanations of the Buddha's words and so they should be easier to understand. The Tibetan scholars have written many treatises explaining the essence and crucial points of commentaries composed by Indian scholars. Hence, they should be easier to understand than the Indian texts. The extensive, medium and short texts on the *Perfection of Wisdom* are very simple, precise and easy to understand when you go through them, but the commentaries on them by Indian scholars are a little harder to comprehend and the treatises by Tibetan scholars are even more confusing and difficult to understand. I always keep in mind the instructions of my guru and nurture them. I could not do much study and contemplation when I was young, and now at this old age I can't read the small fonts of the mechanically printed texts. Sometimes I bring the *Perfection of Wisdom* Sutra from the monastery of my hermitage and read it. When I get hold of biographies of past spiritual masters I read them. Lately I had the good fortune to read the *Seven Treasures* by Kunkhyen Longchen, and the collected works of Jigme Lingpa. They explained the view and practice of Dzogchen so clearly. No wonder he was called Omniscient. He really was a holy person, whose view was as high as the Buddha." Lopon folded his hands and held them on his crown and remained in that pose for a long time. Then he said that he had great devotion to Kunkhyen Longchen and his spiritual son.

Lopon Gangri then said, "Later someone presented *Nyingma Gyubum* to the monastery and I read them all. They contain texts expounding the ultimate meaning of Dzogchen. I read them again and again. Some of the volumes are about conventional rituals and the four holistic actions. I read them once quickly."

My guru was a Buddha in human form and had realized both wisdom and loving kindness. It was not possible that he did not understand the texts due to their verbosity. He was simply being humble. In fact, knowing my faults and nature as an ordinary being, he was giving me advice, by virtue of clairvoyance. At that time I was studying the scriptures and wanted to know everything, without having a clear motivation. Knowing this, he was advising me not to waste my short life on conventional knowledge, but to concentrate on the ultimate knowledge. Much later I asked my late Guru Ontrul Rinpoche and he explained all the crucial points in detail and I gained a new confidence.

LESS TALK, MORE BROAD-MINDEDNESS

What I am trying to say here is that everything that appears as good or bad to your sensory perceptions is just a temporary shifting display, without any profound trustworthy foundation. Therefore, spiritually and mundanely, one should not be stubbornly attached to what appears to you as the truth. From the worldly point of view this is called being foolhardy. However eloquent you may be, your speech will show arrogance and self-importance, embarrassing the wise ones. After some time, even your spouse, children and relatives will disagree with you. You won't be able to spend a relaxed, open and pleasant time with your few friends, since they too will be tired of your insistence that they should do what appeals to you as the right thing.

DO NOT REBUKE OTHERS

Talking endlessly and pretending to be giving advice are the same. After some time everyone, including your children, will get irritated. Longchenpa has said that such behaviour will only bring you problems and this is also true. We have a saying, "If you don't control your long tongue, it will cause a problem to your round head." When you see fault in everything and everyone, and start criticizing everyone, without looking at your own faults, no one will like you. You may be gradually ostracized.

When I was young, without checking my own shortcomings, I interfered with all the people around me, laymen and monks, especially the older monks, as a show of concern for monastic discipline. For a long time I tried to rectify their faults by every means, pointing them out directly and indirectly or by showing my displeasure. We had a monk who did not like dogs and he used to hit the dogs whenever he passed by them. I remember thrashing him once. Other than him, I have never beaten anyone. I have scolded or made critical remarks on many occasions, with the hope that this would help them. But the result was contrary – it only made them angry and unhappy. For example, many left the monastery, and they were not able to continue spiritual practice after leaving the monastery. If they had at least been able to lead a proper worldly life, then it would have been good enough for them. But sadly, they had neither a good spiritual life, nor a good worldly life.

On the other hand, if those within the monastery had seen the hardship faced by those who left the community as a lesson, and studied hard to make their life meaningful, then that too would have been good. But such things hardly happen. After some time I felt frustrated, not knowing what to do or not do. The monks and lay persons who were close to me also felt scared to come and see me, and they hid themselves when they saw me. Some said that it was out of respect for me and not out of dislike. Of course, in the Tibetan tradition, as a sign of respect, you remain out of sight or don't look at the face of the teacher or speak directly. But I could guess whether it was out of respect or dislike. All this saddened me.

DO NOT SPEAK TOO MUCH IF YOU HAVE SELFISHNESS

I think it is better to keep quiet until you are able to cleanse the affliction of selfishness. Buddha has said that, except for a Buddha, who has uprooted the two obscurations and their innate propensities, and attained the state of omniscience, ordinary beings cannot pass judgements on one another. Similarly, he has said, "Speech is the root of all faults; control it at all times and in every manner." So, instead of talking too much it is better to check, day and night, what qualities and faults you have, what are your actions, whether you behave as well in private as in public and whether you practice what you preach to others.

ONLY SPEAK AFTER CHECKING YOUR OWN BEHAVIOUR

Parents giving advice to their children, a teacher guiding his students and a leader giving orders according to the rules and regulations of the human community, are normal social traditions. But there is no need for anger, or for too much hope and fear, while giving advice and guidance. If you remember how you were as a child, what your thoughts were, what mischievous activities you did, and how you are now as an adult, what bad behaviour you indulge in, directly or indirectly, you will understand that there is no need to show anger, give beatings or use abusive language. It is like the saying, "Look at your own body as an example, and don't harm others." If we can think in this way, then all of us can become good and understanding human beings. Otherwise, we will become thoughtless, evil human beings.

DHARMA CANNOT BE PRACTISED BY TRUSTING YOUR SENSES AND SENSORY PERCEPTIONS

From the spiritual point of view, if you believe and follow what you perceive as the truth, then things will get out of control. There is nothing worse than this. All efforts to achieve enlightenment following any path – starting with devotion, compassion and renunciation – be it Mahamudra, Dzogchen or the Middle Way – will not be successful. You will not be able to enter the path, and even if you have entered the path there is not much hope for progress. Some of us have faith in Vajrayana, but judging by our way of thinking, we cannot be considered as followers of Vajrayana or Mahayana or even the Sravakayana (the vehicle of the listeners). Therefore, without rising above the class of ordinary beings, there is no point in pretending to be a follower of the high vehicle just by one's external appearance, or in claiming to possess the higher view.

If you reflect on the Buddha's words, "Neither by matted hair nor by staff", it becomes clear that any pretension of good external behaviour, diligence, meditation, scholarship or compassion is of no use. As for those practicing the path, the Tantra says, "He who has devotion, diligence, wisdom and compassion is a disciple." Devotion, which is indispensable and the most precious of possessions, must be one of the qualities of a disciple. There are many types of devotion, or faith, but going by the biographies and instructions of past Indian and Tibetan masters, what we need practically is an immutable faith in the three secrets of the qualified spiritual teacher. If you have a rigid view of trusting or believing your sensory perceptions, it will be difficult to have an immutable faith in one's spiritual teacher, as described in the texts.

According to the texts, a firm conviction of seeing your spiritual teacher as Buddha is required, but our eyes see him as a human being, and the mind too believes and treats him as a human being. One may come across sentences like, "Considering the guru, who is Buddha, as human" or "The glorious Guru Vajradhara" in many texts and teachings, and you might even show reverence in your mind once in a while, but we will never be able to develop in our mind-stream the genuine devotion of seeing the spiritual teacher as Buddha. The Tantra says, "Having faith in the inconceivable", but we have not even moved towards the inconceivable, and it is difficult for us not to have any mistaken views and ordinary perceptions with regard to the activities of the spiritual teacher in human form. Personally speaking, the repeated advice of my gurus and especially the teachings, with examples, given by Ontrul Rinpoche, reawakened my accumulated potentialities, and I was able to overcome most of the problems.

Saying that all sins and downfalls committed out of ignorance or carelessness can be purified through confession, I was advised to confess, and I devoted myself to confession and purification every day. As a result I was able to clear a lot of confusion.

The moment you feel happy when the guru acts or speaks as you want, or unhappy when he doesn't, praising the guru as kind and wise when his action, speech or manner conforms to your expectations, and criticizing him on seeing him act, speak or behave in a different way one day; you have lost the devotion you need. The moment you start talking about the good and bad things about your guru, you have started believing your sensory perceptions and thoughts. When you talk about the qualities of the guru's genealogy you are simply repeating the history that your ears have heard. Since you have deep trust in your ears, you start talking about the history for justification.

I have heard people say that if the guru is Buddha then he must have a crown protrusion like Buddha Shakyamuni, or if he is a manifestation of four-armed Avalokiteshvara, or thousand-armed Avalokiteshvara, then he should appear like that; or a Vajravarahi emanation should appear naked with bone ornaments. The moment you hear that there is a woman who claims to be the emanation of Vajravarahi, for no reason you start saying, "The way she lies and deceives people! How can she be Vajravarahi? Maybe she claims to be Vajravarahi because she has a red face. Or maybe she is crazy." Or if you are told that such and such a guru recognized her, then you say, "He who recognized the crazy woman must be crazy himself. Maybe he wants to keep her as his consort." In this way you accumulate the karma of abandoning the Dharma. If the guru who recognized her is reputable and is someone you like, then immediately you say, "The guru's manager must have tricked him", or "It is the doing of his demon-like consort." Thus you pass so many judgmental comments and accumulate a lot of negative karma. Once, I too used to think like that. Like the saying, "If one follows the golden hill, even the birds turn golden", your way of thinking and attitude changes according to the company you keep.

BELIEVING EVERYTHING ONE HEARS

Since I was earlier surrounded by people who praised their own guru and lineage and reviled most other spiritual teachers, and especially those performing pacifying and enriching, subjugating and wrathful activities, I too sometimes viewed their appearance, activities and speech with doubt and discomfort. My intellectual investigation was of no use because it created more doubt and suspicion. In such situations it is difficult to have pure vision, even when you hear about the presence of a realized being, and then you feel "I am like Rudra, who said, 'I have no faith even if the Buddha flies in the sky'," and you lose faith in yourself. It is important to be careful.

Showing devotion to your guru with folded hands when he does something impressive, and losing faith the day his actions go against your view means that you have lost everything, despite your external pretension of devotion. It is said that such persons will not receive the blessings. Without the blessings, it is not possible to make progress to a higher level. We fail to make progress because we all have this fault in our mind-stream. Some people may think that even if this guru is not good enough, then I can follow other gurus and practise different meditational deities. But I don't think it is like divorcing your spouse legally, following marital incompatibility, and paying alimony.

Once the blessings are no longer received due to breaking of the auspicious connection with a guru, then unless and until the defiled commitment is purified, following any other guru, or practising different kinds of meditational deities will be like looking for water in a dry pond. The texts, the general advice, the Tantras and the scriptures all say that doing so is meaningless. Therefore, however eloquent the scholar may be, or however powerful such a person may be, he has no choice but to face the sufferings of samsara. It is like the saying, "Ordinary dead body in the bed of a scholar."

The reason for this problem is that we do not believe, or have faith in what is beyond our conceptual mind or beyond our understanding. Our lack of faith stems from our over reliance on, or trust in, the sense organs: eyes, ears, nose, body and mind. The stanza: "What use will the path of the Noble One be to anyone?" means that if we trust only our sense organs, and believe what our senses see or feel as existing, and what they don't see or sense as non-existent, then the practitioner loses his path and returns to the cyclic existence of samsara. It also means that even if ordinary people like us, who believe sensory perceptions to be the truth, pretend to practice the higher paths like Mahamudra, Dzogchen or the Middle Way, are exercises in futility.

As Shantideva said, "The ultimate truth is beyond the scope of the conceptual mind." Open-mindedly trying to open the door of one's wisdom, and having faith in the truth that is beyond the conceptual mind, is a quintessential precept necessary not only for Vajrayana, but also for the causal Perfection Vehicle. The most important point that those of us who have faith in the essence of Mahamudra and Dzogchen must have, even if we have not realized the truth, is an understanding that external phenomena such as hills, rocks, houses, men and women *etc.* do not exist in reality, as they appear to be.

As a result of meditating on the ultimate truth taught by the Buddha (according to the guru's advice, with faith in the root guru as the personification of the four bodies of Buddha), and the Bodhicitta generated by an overwhelming compassion for beings shackled by attachment, the illusion of dualistic grasping (such as: this size and that size; big and small; back and front; hot and cold; good and bad *etc.*) transforms into the non-dual state of Vajradhara of great bliss, and the hazy perception of the eight aggregated consciousness, turns into something totally different – so said my root Guru Lopon Gangriwa Kunsang Dorje in the course of the many teachings I received from him. By this I think he meant that before seeing the guru as Buddha, and contemplating and meditating on the view, one must have faith that there is something beyond what is perceived by the sensory organs. By the kindness and blessings of my late guru, the teachings on the profound scriptures that I received from him made a big difference to the practice and meditation I do in my life.

During conversations he would talk about spiritual as well as mundane topics, giving examples that were easy to understand, beneficial to the mind and effective while practising. I often felt that the experience would be the same if I was to meet Milarepa, and got the sensation that the joints of my body had disintegrated. Once when we were together, a visitor came. The visitor spoke about the female leader of his community and said that many years ago a guru had predicted that she was the emanation of White Tara. Immediately my guru folded his hands in a gesture of respect and said, "It must be true. Many Sutras and scriptures say that, in this age, a thousand times more emanations of Buddhas and Bodhisattvas will come, than during the aeon of good fortune," and he cited a few quotations.

Then he quoted from the life stories of Tara, and said that emanations of the Buddha will come in various female forms – rich and poor, high and low, and with various characters – thus germinating seeds of devotion in both the visitor and me. The qualities of the three secrets of my guru, the Buddha, cannot be told by someone like me. Even while joking or playing with friends, his speech always inspired faith, joy, compassion and rejoicing. He would never say anything that would cause a loss of devotion or provoke anger in others. He would inspire joy, devotion, peace and happiness in the course of conversations, games and jokes, or in his daily activities. It was a lesson in daily life.

GOOD FRIENDS ARE NEEDED

In my view vulnerable people like me, who are like wet white clothes that can be coloured by any hue, must have good friends from the beginning. Spiritually speaking, one has to depend on a good friend to accomplish all the qualities, from the nine excellent qualities such as scholarship, diligence and kindness, to the qualities of Buddha. Therefore, the spiritual teacher, who with great kindness shows you the right path is called the "Spiritual Community Jewel", and is the most supreme of all friends. So, if you reflect on this, you can understand why the spiritual teacher is called the embodiment of Buddha, Dharma and Sangha.

There are different ways of defining the crucial points, but for people like us who do not have extensive knowledge, we should define them on the basis of how beneficial they are for us. When you get a different physical and mental experience, immediate and ultimate, filling the mind with calmness and peace, like sunshine, you realize that the spiritual teacher is a good friend, and that his benevolent teachings have brought changes to your mind, endowing you with the authentic Dharma.

The teacher gives teachings in response to a stirring of the mind. If you wonder what type of mind shows the path, you will know that only the wisdom that understands the suchness, or the nature of mind can show the path, and that an ordinary mind, that knows only the conventional truth, cannot show the path of vast and profound benefit. As you reflect this way, even if you do not have extensive knowledge of the scriptures, you get an understanding of the meaning.

By the kindness of my kind gurus I was able to recognize my faults, and pay less attention to the flaws of others. I tell myself that the qualities or faults I see in the body, speech and mind of my gurus are merely reflections of my mind. And that the three secrets of the guru are beyond imagination and beyond the scope of my mind. Trying to analyse and assess the positive and negative qualities of the guru's body, speech and mind is like trying to measure the sky, and I would not engage in such an exercise. However, since my mind lacks firm confidence, sometimes doubts arise in my mind but unlike the past I am able to correct my thoughts. You can really train yourself.

How do I train myself? When I see the flaws of ordinary friends or neighbours, I ask myself if these flaws are a reflection of my own flaws, and sometimes I try to think that the person cannot be blamed. Most of the time I try to reduce the habit of finding fault in others by keeping quiet, not bothering about others' faults unless the issues are serious. I think you too should try to do so. The results can be amazing.

> This "perfect view" sounds great,
> But it is rare to find anybody correctly practicing it.
> That is why the "Practice Lineage" is degenerating,
> And just adding numbers to the ranks of the vow breakers.

I am trying to develop the perfect view by the attitude explained above. Otherwise, people like us, who are covered by a thick layer, a tendency to believe what the deluded cognition sees as truth, cannot easily develop the pure vision explained in the texts. This is why we are facing much difficulty today. Very few practise "perfect view" and "carrying out every word" according to the scriptures. Most people don't bother about this. The lower vehicles do not accept this. However, it is important that those who acknowledge the interpretive and definitive meanings, and especially people like us, who show faith in Vajrayana, no matter whether we have a thorough knowledge or not, must reflect on the perfect view. Some of us, with egos inflated by our knowledge of dialectics, try to use logic for justification. But it is difficult. Most are attached to the co-emergent ignorance of believing what is visible as truth and have no other profound reason for their belief.

The phrases "perfect view" and "carrying out every word" concern the fundamental point of "beyond imagination" and so, if neglected, they cause great damage. If you don't pay attention to this then the Practice Lineage will degenerate. Even if you have some thought of renunciation and the wish to practice, you still withdraw when it comes to this crucial point and thus your path is closed. It would seem that when it comes to practicing the "perfect view", many substantial conditions seem to be lacking, making things difficult. Looking back on my personal experience, I think social traditions make things difficult. But as practitioners of the ultimate path of Vajrayana we just cannot ignore it.

Most spiritual practitioners – young and old, high and low, rich and poor – know this popular stanza:

> Without holding wrong views of the glorious Guru, even for a moment,
> By the faith of the Perfect View,
> May the blessings of the Guru enter my mind.

Most of us recite this in the morning. But as Tsangpa Gyare said, "You are in the form of a spiritual practitioner, when the belly is full and the body warmed by the sun; but in the form of an ordinary being when faced with disaster," I think there are many who show devotion when things are going well, but the day the guru scolds them they immediately lose faith, and begin to deride the guru. Like a prisoner freed from prison, they just leave the monastery and the guru, without looking back. Even if they have to come back for some work, they come slyly when the guru is not around. If the guru is there, they make every effort to avoid seeing him, or hearing his speech, as if wishing never to see the guru again, in this life or the next. Such behaviour is despicable from both the spiritual and the worldly point of view.

Some people show respect externally, hoping to gain the knowledge and skills of the guru and spiritual friends, to be used later to lead a comfortable life. This is what the texts describe as the four distorted concepts: the concept of the guru as a musk deer; the concept of Dharma as the musk; the concept of oneself as the hunter; and the concept of receiving teachings and practicing, as seeking musk. There is a category of people who patiently receive teachings, practice and remain humble with such an intention. Today most of us belong to this category.

SUPERFICIAL PRACTICE OF VAJRAYANA WILL NOT WORK

Such a person would make a good pupil in a normal school, but as a follower of the Practice Lineage, if one lacks the foundation of the Practice Lineage then learning and contemplation of the scriptures, reading and reciting of the texts, the practice of meditational deities, the playing of musical instruments and performing of ritual dances, the showing of respect and devotion, calmness and self-discipline, *etc.* will remain superficial acts, and will not reap any practical results. When I observe all this I see that this is how the Practice Lineage degenerates.

As Kunkhyen Jigme Lingpa said, today most Vajrayana practitioners like me are satisfied with external glitter and tuneful tones during sadhanas and do not know the other salient points, or are not very interested in reflecting upon them. In every sadhana one's root guru has to be seen as the master of the Mandala, but most do not know this. It is doubtful whether they see him as a good person because of their wrong view and their doubt. If you call out at the gate of a huge empty house whose owner is not there, you will not get any response. Similarly, it is said that it is difficult to achieve the resultant common and supreme attainments of performing sadhanas, and this can be seen from experience also.

When you read the biographies of the siddhas and realized beings, you see that when they practiced they did not need any glittering arrangements, clothes, cushions and headgear, *etc.*, as we need today. Whatever little they had was enough, and they had no difficulty in achieving the complete supreme and common attainments in their mind-stream. When you read about their pacifying, enriching, subjugating and wrathful activities for the welfare of the Dharma and beings, you understand that the difference between them and us lies in the presence or absence of devotion with the Perfect View, resolute faith in the guru's words as authentic, and the pure vision of seeing worldly phenomena as a manifestation of the three bodies of the guru. Otherwise there is no reason why they were able to achieve everything they practiced, where we hardly achieve anything.

AN ORDINARY BEING CAN ACCOMPLISH ANYTHING

Some of us might think that they were able to achieve everything because they were extraordinary beings, and we cannot expect to achieve anything. But this is not true. All those who attained realization were not extraordinary from the beginning. Take the example of Milarepa. He acknowledges that initially he was an ordinary person, and a sinful one at that. He said, "I went to meditate in the mountain from fear of death" and "Now I am liberated from the fear of death." All these biographies show that the thought of renunciation made them learn the path and improve their mind-streams and they gradually became extraordinary.

Some people reason that those were good times, suitable for practice, and it was easier to achieve the attainments. They say these are degenerate times, symbolic times, and we cannot hope to achieve such attainments today. But if you check these statements you may understand that such people say these things because they are unable to, and incapable of practicing. If they truly believed what they say, it would be a big mistake.

When you reflect on the words, "Times will not change, people will change," it becomes clear that our attitudes change and our devotion and sense of renunciation degenerates, and consequently the outcome of our practice also diminishes. Due to our failure to check and tame our minds, we let our emotions run wild. This leads to confused behaviour, and we indulge in negative actions like killing, lying, stealing and deception. As such behaviour spreads from communities to villages and from country to country around the world, we unanimously say, "Times are bad," and never think about improving our minds. This is really sad. It is my belief that if one is able to improve one's mind-stream then there is no difference between today and the olden times.

TIMES ARE BETTER TODAY THAN IN THE PAST

In my view the times are better today from the material point of view. For centuries the human brain was used to improve the standard of life, and in a short span of time great technological progress has been achieved. This has made life more comfortable. For example, one can comfortably reach a destination within a few hours which in the past would have taken months or years on foot. In the past, letters, however urgent, would take a long time to reach their destination, but today you can send mail with the click of a mouse. If you put all this into perspective, then times have become better. You must have the wisdom to see the good as good.

Many of us have the tendency of looking at the past as good and the future as bad. Such a perspective is wrong and will make you unhappy. From past history and tales told by the elders, you learn that businessmen and pilgrims in those days feared robbers and wild animals on their way, and there was always the possibility of not returning home safely. Today, people don't face such problems and return home safely. All this has been made possible by material development.

SELF IMPROVEMENT NEEDED

Leave aside lamenting about the degenerate times and instead work to improve your mind. Sitting idly without making any effort and engaging in empty talk, will not bring any result. Both Buddhists and non-Buddhists, instead of doing authentic practice, blame everything on the bad times, or God, or the government or the people, and waste their lives. As a result one's mind-stream becomes rigid, like the saying, "Practitioner untamed by religion and 'butterskin' unsoftened by butter." As a practitioner your mind-stream becomes more gross, and you lose devotion towards and admiration of the Buddha and the spiritual teachers, as in the saying, "Feeling no devotion, even if the Buddha flies in the sky, feeling no compassion, even at the sight of animals with torn intestines."

Even when you transgress the commitment of the body, speech and mind, you have no sense of shame or guilt. In fact, you stay with your head held high as though you have done something heroic but you have also become a bad influence to your friends. Gradually the practice of breaking vows spreads far and wide. As a result, society faces unwanted situations like sickness, starvation and wars. If you look at history you see that the difficult times experienced by India, China, Tibet, Mongolia; and the east, west and central countries were the result of not upholding the commitment of the guru-shishya relationship properly. The commitment had been broken by wearing the mask of religion, deceiving the gods, competing with Vajra brothers and causing obstacles to the guru's life, under the influence of the eight worldly motivations.

In his prophesy Guru Rinpoche said many things like,

"Misbehaving yourself, you blame it on bad times." In public advice, His Holiness the Dalai Lama has said, "The upheaval in Tibet and consequent sufferings can be attributed to the ripening of the collective negative karma accumulated by the Tibetan people over many generations."

THE HERO WHO DOES NOT CARE ABOUT THE NEXT LIFE

What I have just said is about the sufferings in this life and not what may be suffered in future lifetimes. But this stanza in the Tantra, "Going against the words of the guru makes you fall into Vajra hell." This alone makes one understand how risky it is. But when you reach the stage of having no faith in the doctrine, I think you do not even fear hell. It means you don't believe in hell. Similarly, you don't believe in anything that cannot be seen. You have no belief in the state of Omniscience.

YOU SUFFER WHEN BAD KARMA RIPENS

In this way you gradually stop efforts to attain liberation from samsara. Diligent effort for positive action and altruistic work gets corrupted. Good intentions and actions degenerate. The power of latent tendencies make you happily take to actions, such as lying, stealing and killing. When you suffer the consequences of negative karma you don't know what to do, or where to turn for succour. You may possess wealth, power, good looks and a good family, but when your karma ripens nothing will be of use, and you have to suffer the consequences of natural disasters or wars, sickness and hunger on your own. This is there for everyone to see and yet we fail to develop the mind of renunciation even after seeing all this. Even if you have the mind of renunciation, I think you lose it after a few years.

The instruction manuals say that without this mind of renunciation one cannot generate devotion, which is the foundation of all qualities. When I was young I could not comprehend its meaning and used to be confused. Later, I understood the meaning by reflecting repeatedly on the advice of the gurus.

IF YOU REFLECT, CAUSE AND EFFECT CAN BE UNDERSTOOD

If you don't leave this understanding as it is, but sharpen it with daily life experiences, you gain a wider understanding, and even if the understanding is not profound, you achieve the wisdom of partial knowledge. To use a pompous term, it can be called "opening the potency of wisdom" or "entering of the guru's blessings in the mind" or "spontaneous bursting of realization". A non-fabricated wisdom of seeing that "the phenomena do not exist as they appear" emerges.

Like the saying, "If the intention is good, the ground and path are good. If the intention is bad, the ground and path are bad." Everything – from a good human being, good deeds, and Buddhahood and Buddha activities – to afflictions, bad intentions, negative actions and their consequent suffering – has to be explained on the basis of positive or negative changes in the mind. This can be understood from these words from *A Guide to the Bodhisattva Way of Life*: "Who will smelt the iron in hell? From where did the ball of fire come?" Without improving your mind there is no point in blaming bad times or bad people. Unless and until change is brought in the mind, these problems will remain unsolved. Sending people to prison or executing them may bring only temporary relief.

CHAPTER 8

The Essence of Guru's Kindness

> It is essential to grasp a vital point –
> What is it?
> In the Pure Realm, Buddhas appear in perfect form
> To train pure beings.
> But impure beings like us
> Have no chance to see a perfect Buddha,
> Nor to hear his voice.
> For beings like us could not be tamed
> By Buddhas of the past.
> That is why our present teacher was reborn
> In ordinary human form –
> To help tame us.
> That is why our teacher's kindness
> Is far greater than that of other Buddhas –
> A kindness beyond reason and logic.

Generally it is our tradition to use the term "kind teacher". This term is used even in mundane songs. But most of us do not understand why the teacher is kind or how to identify their kindness; I too did not understand this for a long time. In this regard a vital point has to be understood. To say the teacher is kind because he or she gives you food and clothing is too simplistic. When I was young many people used to say this while speaking about my late Guru Kyabje Drukpa Thuksey Rinpoche: "We survive because of the kindness of the teacher. He is what is known as the kind teacher."

One day a fight broke out among some of the young monks and this disturbed my guru. He thrashed some of the monks. After that they did not praise our guru so much. I wanted to check what was in their minds, so during a break I spoke to some of them and said, "People here say that our guru is very kind. But since I am just a child I don't know what they mean." Immediately some of them said, "What kindness? He should be grateful to us. We are feeding him and not the other way around. When patrons and foreign visitors come, he tells them that he has to feed all these monks and asks for help. With the funds he gets he is able to lead a comfortable life. We are the source of income for the guru and not the cause of expenditure." They said such incredible things. I did not believe that the guru would not have had anything to eat without these monks, but I could not give them an explanation. Today, when I think about this, I see that their confusion was caused by their failure to identify the kindness of the guru.

DISCIPLES NURTURED WITH FOOD

I share a close relation with Je Kunleg, the great scholar and realized master and the ex-Je Khenpo of Bhutan. One day he said jokingly, "You must change the practice of nurturing pupils with food, to nurturing them spiritually. The disciples who gather for food and clothing, like stray dogs, will not be of any service to the Dharma and other sentient beings. In fact they will be burnt by the 'black offerings' and become worse than laymen. If you nurture them spiritually, however big or small their number, they will have devotion to the doctrine. This is the way the spiritual masters of the past adopted." It is true, as we say "the kindness of giving food, clothing and Dharma." But today we will be burnt by the charity of the guru before our mind-stream is ripened by his teachings. I learned this clearly.

From a very young age I lived off the food, water, clothing and accommodation offered to the guru, without making any effort to confess or purify. As a result, all the qualities like devotion and compassion remained dormant and the confidence in the generation and completion processes was lacking. I was unable to practice the Bodhisattva teachings. When I look at others it seems that many are surviving on the offerings made to the guru. Most of the monks living in the monasteries, those engaged in learning and contemplation, as well as male and female yogis in meditation today, discuss their monthly allowance, the quality of food and the condition of their residential quarters. Hoping to go to some centre with the title of guru after completing their scheduled retreat, they learn the English language while in retreat. I heard that many know English very well when they come out of retreat. Thus, most plan to collect money in offerings and very few have the intention of equating life with accomplishment. So, like the saying, "Accomplishing *mara* (the demon) before accomplishing Dharma," the practitioner faces a lot of obstacles. As regards the guru, his giving of food and beverages to the practitioners with good intention makes his action meaningful. As the text on confession says, "The merit of giving one mouthful of food to those born in the animal realm"; even giving one spoonful of food and drink is an act of virtue. But I learned from experience that as disciples we must not have the wrong view.

DO NOT CRAVE FOR BLACK OFFERING BUT FEAR IT

My Guru Vajradhara Gangriwa Kunsang Dorje visited our monastery on many occasions during the recitation of 100 million mantras of Avalokiteshvara, but he returned to his hermitage as soon as the recitations were complete, without spending even one extra day at the monastery. Once, after receiving teachings from him I requested him to spend a few days at the monastery. He said, "I will stay for an extra day to fulfill your request," and he spent one night at the monastery. The next day he said he was returning to his retreat hut and added, "By your kindness I had the comfort of sitting on a fine carpet and eating a lot. It was like being in heaven. But this is all black offering to the guru. To be placed in front of the guru, either an uncountable merit must ripen or one must have the misfortune of being driven from lower to lower realms by the force of black offering. There is hardly any third option. When this old man dies I should have the provisions of spiritual practice to carry with me. It will be very hard for me if I have to drag the burden of black offering." He then returned to his hermitage. My Buddha-like guru certainly would not have had any such problem, but he was advising us to be careful.

THE GURU-DISCIPLE RELATION IS A SPIRITUAL RELATION

Whether he gives you food and clothes or not, the relationship between the guru and disciple has to be a spiritual relationship. The physical relationship, material relationship, food and clothing relationship or fraternal relationship that you share with the guru is an illusory, temporary, conventional relationship though it may seem appealing. One must be resolute in deciding that for spiritual practice and attainment of enlightenment and the state of omniscience, a spiritual relationship with the guru is imperative, and no other relationship is of any use. On the foundation of such awareness, if one can practice daily with diligence, then one would be offering the mandala of accomplishment from afar to the guru, without having to defile oneself with the black offering to the guru.

The purpose of meeting the guru should be to do spiritual practice. After receiving the teaching one should go back to one's home and practise the teachings. Accompanying the guru and indulging in mundane gossip about how close you are to the guru, what you said and what the guru said – half truth and half lies – will serve no spiritual purpose. In fact, it is very dangerous for you to do so. Because then the devotion of seeing the guru as Buddha gradually diminishes, blocking every opportunity for progress in the development of view, realization, loving kindness and compassion. From the very beginning one must make sure that the notion of seeing the guru as Buddha is not distorted. One must reflect on the meaning of the teachings and meditate to apply them to one's own mind-stream.

LEARN THE FOUR NOBLE TRUTHS AFTER IDENTIFYING SUFFERING

As Buddha said, "I have shown you the path of liberation; liberation is in your hands." Samsara is the nature of suffering and suffering is what no one wants. So we have to first identify what suffering is, and then find the cause of suffering. Cause and effect is the backbone of Buddhist doctrine. For example, to cure an illness one has to identify the disease and find its cause. Once you get all the information you will then be interested in taking medicines and getting yourself cured. Since such cause and effect of suffering is inseparably with us in samsara we should all know this.

Due to our ignorance most of us have a problem in recognizing suffering *as* suffering. Take the case of "the suffering of pervasive conditioning" for example. When you see something good you become attached to the desire to have it and you will go to any lengths to get it. Or if you see something bad, then your aversion to it unnecessarily causes a lot of pain in the mind. The cause of this attachment and aversion is the ignorant clinging to the existence of phenomena as true. Suffering is identified as being influenced by the affliction of ignorance twenty-four hours a day, without giving us any freedom. But very few care about this. As long as our mind-stream remains under the control of afflictions, we will have only illusory happiness and not genuine happiness, according to the texts.

The definition of happiness and suffering can be understood from this saying: "Independence is happiness, dependence is suffering." It is very rare to find an ordinary being who is independent and not under the influence of afflictions. During any action like eating, drinking, sleeping, standing or sitting, there is not one moment that is not controlled by the ignorant conception of self. Because of this, all samsaric beings in the three realms face suffering and the nature of suffering unwillingly. The obscuration of conception of the self is the root cause of samsara and the aggregate conceptualization originating from this is dragging us up and down in samsara. All beings – form or formless, foes and demons *etc.* – that cause you physical and mental pain are illusions created by your afflicted mind.

Even if you cannot understand the true situation experientially, you can understand it if you use your brain and reflect. Like the moth is attracted to the flame, we are attached to illusory happiness and we do not wish to give it up – or we don't know how to give it up. When the fruits of karma suddenly ripen, it is a bit too late to regret wasting so many years and lifetimes – and to wish you had a few lifetimes or a few years to prevent the sufferings – so say the texts.

Abiding by the guru's instructions and the words and advice of authentic spiritual friends, and if you reflect on the happy and sad experiences in life and the substantiality of afflictive actions, you will realize that it is affliction that is causing all the suffering. If we cannot cultivate the antidote to affliction from the beginning, the fruitional suffering will ripen in the form we have always experienced it for years and lifetimes – until it is exhausted. This is called purification through suffering. This is the worst form of purifying fruitional obscuration. What is needed is purification through skillful means.

If urgent refuge is not taken in skillful means, then as we suffer the fruitional suffering of past lives, we keep on accumulating new negative karma under the influence of afflictions. Thus, like a fly caught in a vase we remain caught in cyclic existence, not knowing how to get out of the web of suffering. How can we find the method? We find it by relying on the teachings of a qualified spiritual teacher. Listening to and contemplating on 'the basket of teachings' given by the qualified spiritual teacher, the understanding of the path of three trainings grows until finally you achieve the state of peace. Even if you do not achieve such a state within this life, you are bound to achieve it soon. None of us want any type of suffering, not even a headache, and we want happiness even if just for a minute. Who then is it that correctly teaches you the Four Noble Truths and the way of discipline to fulfill all your immediate and ultimate aspirations? It is the spiritual teacher who gives you the instructions and that is why he or she is called the kind spiritual teacher.

QUALIFIED SPIRITUAL TEACHERS IN HUMAN FORM ARE MORE GRACIOUS THAN BUDDHA

I think some people feel that Buddha Shakyamuni and Guru Padmasambhava, who are in Nirmanakaya form, or Vajrasattva, who is in Sambhogakaya form, are more kind and gracious than the spiritual teacher in human form. In a way this is true, but you have to think from the perspective of your own practice. Exalted disciples like Bodhisattvas, who have reached the attainment ground and are in the pure lands, like the Manifest Joy Pureland, see and hear the Buddhas in Sambhogakaya form. Those who have followed the path, purified the defilements and possess the 'four causes' – like the precious mind of aspiration – have the good fortune of seeing and hearing Buddha Amitabha in the Western Pure Land. Many also had the good fortune of meeting Buddha Shakyamuni and Guru Padmasambhava, and receiving his teachings as disciples and they attained perfection. But people like us, whose visions are clouded by the obscurations of karma and afflictions, do not have the good fortune of seeing or hearing the Buddhas.

The spiritual teacher in human form, behaving like a human, guides the beings in whatever is an appropriate way through pacifying, enriching, subjugating and by wrathful activities. Beings like us, who could not be tamed by other Buddhas and Bodhisattvas of a high level, are like chickens left on the ground, or blind men not knowing which way to follow, or being unable to walk, like a man without legs. Many Sutras and Tantras clearly say that for crazy beings like us, the spiritual teacher who teaches us discipline is more gracious than anyone else. One does not need to be a scholar to know this: even a fool like me can understand this, if one thinks properly.

MANY WAYS TO DEVELOP FAITH

Our eyes being covered by the cataracts of ignorance, all that we see is impure vision. Even the wish fulfilling, jewel-like spiritual teacher is seen as an aggregate of faults. As we learn the path, the darkness of ignorance gradually becomes lighter and the sun of pure vision slowly shines through. Therefore, as a means of purifying defilements, like the ignorance of conceptual self, you have to diligently follow the path of accumulating merit, prostrations, offerings, pilgrimage, the practice of generosity, guarding your conduct and tolerance. As pure vision grows, faith and devotion also grows. After that, it doesn't seem very difficult to see the face of the inherent Dharmakaya.

The scriptural quotation, "Other than the imprint of accumulating merit and purifying defilements, and the blessing of the glorious spiritual teacher, relying on any other method is sheer ignorance," and the common saying, "All these branches (of the path) were taught by Buddha for acquiring wisdom" explains that the sun of the spiritual teacher's blessing will shine after accumulating merit and purifying defilements. Only by relying on this can all sufferings be subdued and permanent happiness achieved.

When the text says that: depending on any other method is foolishness and will be useless in the end; it means that faith in the spiritual teacher as the manifestation of the four Buddha bodies is the essence of the path. Gyalwa Gotsangpa said, "No teaching can guarantee Buddhahood within a lifetime. Only devotion to the guru can." From this, one can conclude that devotion to the spiritual teacher alone, aided by training in the path of perfection – such as good intention, doing virtuous deeds and abandoning non-virtuous deeds, circumambulation, making offerings, giving alms, *etc.*, is enough to attain enlightenment.

There is no doubt that those who lack diligent effort due to the distraction of the mind by sensual objects; lack wisdom and intelligence due to severe karmic obscurations or face the paucity of food, drink and conditions for spiritual practice due to a lack of accumulated merit, should make offerings to the spiritual teacher and give alms as much as he or she can, prostrate at, and circumambulate holy places, render service to the spiritual teacher and spiritual friends, care for the sick and destitute, save life and do other virtuous deeds to cleanse obscurations and accumulate merit. The Sutra describes the way of accumulating merits thus: "The Seven Merits arise from: making gardens and sanctuaries; continually providing cushions and livelihood; taking care of those who fall sick suddenly; and giving alms to the destitute."

Although it is important to practise meditation, it is said, "You cannot attain *siddhis* (accomplishments) without accumulating merit, just as butter cannot be made by pressing sand." It is said that an intelligent person will accumulate merit first by making offerings to the spiritual teacher and the Triple Gem, especially through altruistic work, before starting spiritual practice. Some people consider accumulating merit and training mind as a practice of the lower vehicle and of no importance. Such people straight jump to the main practice of Mahamudra or Dzogchen. Doing so is useless unless you have met a spiritual teacher in a past life and accumulated merit by serving him or her.

RELYING ON THE ROOT GURU ACCUMULATES GREATER MERIT

Although there are many ways of accumulating merit as explained earlier, it is said that prostrating and making offerings, circumambulating and serving a qualified spiritual teacher – even sweeping and cleaning the area around his residence – is a way of accumulating great merit. I gained confidence in this from personal experience. From the spiritual point of view, adhering to the spiritual teacher in the right way aids the attainment of enlightenment, and from the worldly point of view one will have good health, be free from sickness, and all one's wishes will be fulfilled. Making offerings to the spiritual teacher, who is the embodiment of all Buddhas, will not only eradicate the suffering of poverty but also bring prosperity. Prosperity thus gained is not like prosperity from propitiating spirits and demons that later torment you physically and mentally. I have seen that the prosperity gained by the blessings of the spiritual teacher aid you in spiritual practice and altruistic efforts. When I was young, some people advised me to practise 'the god of wealth' since I had to look after many monastic and spiritual projects. Some said that I would need the support of the guardian deities.

FUNNY INSTRUCTIONS – LIKE MEDITATING ON MY MOTHER

I have received funny advice like "Visualize your mother in front of you during public teachings, public talks and questions and answer sessions and you will not be scared." I used to think such advice should be checked. I have never been very keen to do the practice of 'the gods of wealth' for material wealth or to propitiate the guardian deities for support and power and I am still not very interested in this. Even as a small child I knew that deities of long life, gods of wealth, guardian deities and deities of the enemy are all meant to be used for the welfare of other beings. I used to feel that there was no need to beat drums, ring bells, blow trumpets and the bone trumpet and disturb the guardian deities for one's own longevity and prosperity or to beat the competition. I did not appreciate those who practised the longevity deities, or the wealth gods, with a selfish motive. Maybe I was being rigid or childishly foolhardy.

I sometimes used to wonder, "When everybody was doing these practices, what special reason did I have for not doing so? Am I crazy?" Later when I analysed this, using the blessings of speech of my root gurus and wisdom acquired through meditation I realized that I had made no mistake. Ever since I first gave a long life initiation and teachings to a gathering of thousands of people and I had to give public teachings every year, I used to feel scared and tense, and then my teachers advised me to meditate on my mother to overcome my fear. I used to visualize my mother and it worked sometimes. It is maybe because of the mothers' love for her child.

Later when I was about twenty years old I had to give teachings on the *Seven Point Mind Training* to an assembly of thousands of people. My kind Guru Ontrul Rinpoche was with me and I asked him not to come to my teaching venue. Although he did not come, it seems he could hear me in his room by means of the public address system. He later said to me, "It sounds like you are a little scared in public. Are you?" I replied, "Yes. I have felt like that since I was small. I was told to visualize my mother and I sometimes do that." He laughed for a long time and then said, "I don't blame you. Children will do whatever they are taught. Your root guru and Avalokiteshvara are the same. From today on, visualize their inseparable smiling face clearly in the space in front of you. Without fear, pray from the depth of your heart that the teaching may benefit all beings listening to your teaching. Discard the thought of the eight worldly motivations and teach with loving kindness and compassion for the listeners. Then you will have no fear and the listeners will also benefit. This fear is a sign of the presence of the thought of the eight worldly motivations." He repeated, "From today, do not think of the eight worldly motivations."

GRACIOUSNESS OF THE GURU IN THIS LIFE

Since that time I have followed my guru's advice and by his blessings I have felt no fear. The words and quotations flowed from my mouth without error and I felt relieved. From that time I followed his advice and I pray to my root gurus before giving teachings or public talks, however large or small the crowd may be.

Even for gaining wealth, I did not find anyone more gracious than the gurus. For some time now I have been undertaking worldly activities, called the wheel of activities in spiritual terms, like building statues, schools, hospitals, and big halls called monasteries. I do not have any wealth as such but I experienced that by the blessings and prayers of my root gurus everything could be accomplished without any difficulty.

For example, we never had any thought of building the huge new temple of our monastery in Darjeeling. One day, my root guru, the late Drukpa Thuksey Rinpoche, suddenly called me and from the roof of the old temple he pointed his walking stick and said, "This hill has a strong foundation. A new temple that can accommodate about three hundred monks has to be built."

Behaving like a friend I said, "We have just over a hundred monks. Is it necessary? Won't there be financial problems?" He said, "Don't say such a thing. It is said that except for oaths and sins, everything should be big. Money will not be a problem. It will work out. I don't think this old man has the time to build it. You have to build it. Understood?" He was in fine health at that time and although he was sending the message that he would not live long, that thought did not strike me then, but he passed away after two or three years.

I am not competent or wealthy. I did not have any rich patrons, but with the blessings of my wish-fulfilling jewel-like guru, his wishes were accomplished without any difficulty. Similarly, when I look back, I think I was able to carry out his instructions and build the few reliquaries and the monastery in Nepal almost effortlessly, solely because of his blessings and prayers. I did not have to work hard like others, as all the construction work was completed like a dream.

Nepal has many holy places, including the three stupas,[54] but personally I did not have any special liking for Nepal. But as I said earlier, my late guru had a keen interest in Nepal. He repeatedly spoke about the need for spiritual activity such as building a monastery in Nepal.

On many occasions he said, "It would be great if I could visit the three stupas before I close my eyes." My father Bairo Rinpoche told him, "I will arrange the travel expenses whenever you are ready to go," and he was very pleased. But he did not have much freedom about his travels and he could not visit Nepal. For example, when I was small he wanted to take me out for entertainment. He would say, "Tomorrow I will take you to the market" or "We will go to see the mountains", but when it came to actually going out some of the elder monks would object and not let us go. Kyabje Rinpoche would be angry and I would feel sad and tears would fill my eyes but there was nothing we could do. I remember many such occasions. Sometimes, when Rinpoche was invited to the market, he would bring back sweets and *momos* (dumplings) hidden in the pocket of his shirt and give them to me secretly without being seen by the attendants. On a few occasions the attendants found out and both of us had a tough time.

He was kind to everyone, not just me. He would take out money hidden under his mattress and give whatever came in his hand and say, "Take this and go. Don't show it to anyone." The amount depended on your luck. Some would get a hundred rupee note, some would get a ten rupee note and some would get a five rupee note. Having attained the state of equanimity it did not make much difference to the guru but, from the point of view of an ordinary being, from a young age I used to think that even the Buddha-like guru needs some level of authority to carry out his activities. Whenever I talk about this, the history of Buddha and Ananda comes to mind. All this is my gossip.

In brief, the kindness and blessings of the spiritual teacher is not limited to our next lifetimes. Even in this life, it helps with the accomplishment of many things. While receiving initiations, teachings and instructions on treasure teachings and pure vision from the late Kyabje Trulshik Rinpoche, I went to his residence to receive 'hand

---

54. Swayambhu, Boudha and Namo Buddha.

blessings' during a break. I said to him, "I am undertaking a lot of projects on many fronts that seem meaningless but they have to be done. These works are so extensive I don't get time for spiritual practice. Please give me your blessing for this life and the next so that spiritual practice can he completed." He smiled and said, "Do not worry. Carry on with your work. With joy I will pray that your wishes are fulfilled according to the Dharma, without any obstacles." On many occasions later I also received similar assurances. Since that time, I have experienced that all my activities have been completed successfully without any obstacle. I think there is no end to the graciousness of the root gurus.

SPONTANEOUS GROWTH OF DEVOTION BY THINKING OF THE ROOT GURU

The gurus' kindness, protecting and caring for us in this life alone, like a mother cares for her only child, not to mention life after life until enlightenment, is beyond imagination and expression. On quite a few occasions I felt faint as the conflicting perceptions disappeared, or tears welled up in my eyes making me feel like crying when I thought about the special kindness, blessings and power of the qualities of the guru's body, speech and mind or during prayers or while chanting the prayer of *Calling the Guru from Afar*. I try not to display such feelings in public because it is embarrassing and uncomfortable, as I sit on a throne with the microphone in front of me. On such occasions, some people think I have a common cold or a sore throat, and the tissue papers, cough syrup or other medicines they give me fill the top of the table in front of me. Since they are given out of kindness I accept everything without saying anything. During discussions amongst themselves some disciples say that I cried, feeling sad that the disciples were not practising properly. Since such scenes are not common in today's society people do not understand what is happening. It is said that the "symbolic period" is approaching now and I feel that from the point of view of spiritual and meditational practice it is true. To accomplish success in practice, faith in the qualities of spiritual teachers and the unimaginable state of reality is necessary, and practitioners like us lack this. Thus we become "symbolic" practitioners.

THE REALITY STATE OF ALL PHENOMENA IS UNIMAGINABLE

The point is this:
Buddha activity is beyond conception.
The import of this vital point really astounds me!

Since this state is beyond the imagination of our delusional mind it is called "the unimaginable state" and cannot be understood by the ordinary mind. But those of us practising Vajrayana should practise the fruitional path at the start of the path, and do precise Mahamudra practice of the generation of the unimaginable state of the secret form-body of the Buddha-like guru, completion of the unimaginable state of the secret truth-body of the Buddha-like guru and the state of great bliss of primordial union of the two. This is called the ultimate accomplishment of the guru.

In order to get accustomed to this, from now on we must practise according to the instructions given in the Tantras and other instructions without any worldly motivations; without seeing the non-existent as existing, and meditating, treating the existing as non-existent, and reciting mantras, mistaking delusion as bliss, and viewing the existent as void. We have to purify the conceptual mind that sees perception as the truth. During recitation of mantras, we have to practise the three modes: taking all appearances as the body of a Buddha, taking all sounds as the speech of a Buddha and taking all thought as the mind of a Buddha. This has to be done during every ritual. The reason for this is so that one does not trust the delusion of the conceptual mind as the truth: you cannot call it appearance because its way of being present is empty and you cannot say it is empty because its appearance is bright and illuminated. Its mode of being cannot be described. In this way the practice of the three modes of concentration on mantra becomes easier. If you can do this, it is a big progress on the path. Some people practise for months and years without understanding this crucial point and then, instead of developing faith in the unimaginable state, they lose faith. As a result they do not realize afflictions as wisdom and fall under the influence of afflictions, leading to the growth of non-virtue and defilement and loss of stability in practice, and are born again in samsara.

Even if you cannot actually realize appearance as Buddha's Body, sound as Buddha's speech and thought as Buddha's mind, without an intellectual understanding of this you will only have a superficial and not a true faith in the unimaginable secrets of your root guru. It would be difficult to explain from the point of immediate practice, why the guru in human form has to be considered as Buddha and beyond imagination and stands out like a white crow, while the other humans, dogs, hills, plains, trees, flowers, houses, buildings and all sensuous objects can be seen as they appear. I learned the essence of this practice from the activities of my root gurus, the biographies of Lineage Gurus like Gyalwa Gotsangpa and Gyalwa Yangonpa and other realized masters of the past, especially while receiving instructions and teachings from Lopon Gangri Kunsang Dorje. Experience from my little practice and explanation of the refined essence of dialectics, mind-training, *Teachings of Maitreya*, *Middle Way*, *A Guide to the Boddhisattva's Way of Life* and many other scriptures, in conjunction with the profound Tantra that I received from my Guru Ontrul Rinpoche, opened the door of my awareness.

As mentioned earlier, from an early age I had no interest in the wealth gods or guardian deities aside from the guru and it is the same even now, in my old age. By the grace of the teachings of my Buddha-like gurus, I understood that the sense organs, thoughts, elements, sensual pleasures and all impure perceptions are primordially 'the hundred families of Buddha', which can be further grouped into the 'five families of Buddha', and that the nature of one's mind is primordially the fundamental nature of the truth body, the glorious guru. Due to our contaminated mind-stream we do not understand the ultimate reality and perceive different appearances leading to unstoppable sights of phenomena. Such appearances are called deceptive appearances and we regard them as bad. But there is nothing bad about them.

If, as practitioners, we are able to meditate on this, then there is not even a grain of difference between the pure appearance of the Buddhas and Bodhisattvas and the impure appearance of horses, cows and donkeys. As the text says, "Whatever appearance the beings may perceive, its nature is the emanation of the guru's wisdom." Glass has no colour of its own but it reflects the colour of the object on which it is placed. There is one moon but it is reflected in water in different shapes and sizes depending on the container. Similarly, the Tantras and scriptures say that the unimaginable activities of the body, speech, mind and wisdom of the guru appear in the form of one, five or a hundred supreme deities appropriate to each being. A little conviction in this truth will lead to the growth of a genuine faith. I do not know if someone with deep faith in Vajrayana can identify a wisdom deity as being separate from the guru, the personification of the four bodies of Buddha, unless the person is practising a haughty deity. Perhaps I am wrong. Forgive me. Otherwise it is a big mistake. Only someone who has realized the nature of truth can explain the distinctions in detail. Someone like me cannot. However, we must all be very careful.

> Lord of Great Kindness,
> Sole Protector dwelling in my heart:

The personification of kindness who opened my eyes to what to accept and what to discard was Zhichen Kyabgon,[55] popularly called Ontrul Rinpoche and also known as Alag Ontrul. I have held in my heart his blessings of body, speech and mind and especially his nectar-like advice, and tried to practise as well as I could. As advised by him, I discarded the thought of worldly motivations and gave teachings whenever necessary to inspire positive action. Day and night, whenever I am aware, I remind myself of his instructions and advice and have the confidence that he inseparably dwells in my heart.

Generally, once you have established a relationship with a qualified spiritual teacher it is important that you follow his advice and try to improve your mind and your life. To improve your mind does not mean to make your mind better. It means to reflect on the various conceptions that come to the mind. As a result of reflection you will gain a new understanding that these conceptions are illusions and dreams. Dreams fill our mind day and night alternately: a cycle of dreams. So it is important to know that life is a dream. The positive effect of this understanding is that clinging to something as real becomes less. Without the backing of affliction, the untamed wild elephant-like mind becomes more peaceful. From the point of

---

55. *skyabs mgon*; a mark of respect for reincarnations of great masters who are lineage holders, meaning supreme protector, supreme refuge.

view of developing positive qualities you become less selfish and your character becomes better. As a result of this you become happier in this life, physically and mentally. If you believe in life after death then your next life will also be better.

LIFE IS A DREAM

Many people have heard that life is a dream. When I was about ten years old, I went to a stationery shop to buy a letter pad. I saw a set of letter pads and envelopes with the message "life is a dream". I thought, we the Buddhists and spiritual practitioners do not understand this very well and it is so nice that a foreigner knows this and I bought it. I used this letter pad to write to friends and after a few years a motherly figure, after getting my letter, wrote back to say that this type of letter pad is used by lovers and asked whether using this to write to her was appropriate – with a question mark and a smiley. I realized that I had written to many people using the same letter pad but no one had made any comment until then. I asked people about this and everyone said it was used to write love letters. Either the people I wrote to didn't dare to tell me or they assumed I was their lover! I am just joking.

TODAY IS TOMORROW'S FOUNDATION

What I mean is that we are all dreaming. Everything – whether it is love between a man and a woman, devotion to a spiritual teacher, compassion for beings, wishes of generosity, maintaining of ethics, all good, middling and bad actions – are all dreams, although one may discuss the extent, profoundness, and good or bad nature of the action. We wish for a better, happier tomorrow. This can be called a dream. In reality yesterday's tomorrow has become today and so we chase tomorrow again. We keep running after the future.

WITHOUT TOMORROW TODAY IS USELESS

When we think about today we are never satisfied. This is the meaning of the saying, "Desire is like salty water" and "Life is like ripples of water". The dream of tomorrow is very powerful and I think it becomes like the backbone of life. In one way it saddens me but in another way I find it funny – like a child's game. We live for tomorrow and remain alive. If there is no tomorrow and no future, then today and the present are dead. There is nothing. The only thing left is the useless confused memory of yesterday.

As practitioners we must remember this is harmful and not beneficial. It takes away the opportunity of seeing the present with awareness. It is like the saying, "The past is a ghost, the present is a God and the future is a human." For a yogic practitioner, past memories are like thieves and robbers. It seems the meaning of non-dualistic co-emergence manifests between the past and the future, but it is clouded by confusing past memories. Otherwise, experientially it can also be called the Great Middle Way. That is why the present is called "God" because it surpasses human intelligence. The thought of the future that occupies the mind is like the backbone of life and that is why the future is called "human". Among the many methods of longevity described in the instructions, the method suggested for ordinary people like us is to have a longer future plan.

Recently I met a good doctor of medical science. Narrating my health history, I told him that in the course of my practice I had slept for only thirty minutes a day for six years and I felt very healthy at that time. Then later doctors advised me to sleep for at least six to seven hours and my family members also insisted I do so and how difficult I felt then to even lie down. If I lay down on the right side I felt pain in my neck, shoulders, ribs and knees on the right side and it remained the same for many days, when I tried to lie down on the left side, but gradually it became easier and now I can sleep for two to three hours; but if I sleep more than that I don't feel good the next day. I explained all my experiences to him.

The doctor told me that generally six hours of sleep is advised for good health but that scientific research has shown that dreaming while asleep is better for health. At that time I didn't feel like telling this to others, but I suddenly remembered my experience of many years ago. If I fell into a deep sleep without dreams for more than three to four hours I certainly did not feel good the next day. Later when I practised the teachings on dream yoga for one hour, I could revive my health and even the mind became clear. I think it is even better to recognize a dream as a dream. It may be related to longevity and to curing sickness. When you reach the stage of "path of no more learning" it is said that you will have no dreams. That means one has attained the yogic state of endless primordially pure time which has no past, present or future; at this stage you don't have to chase the future like we do today. At that stage you realize the nature of both day dreams and night dreams and so you don't dream at night.

Samsara is called the city of dreams and illusions and truly there is nothing but dreams. It is important to analyse your thoughts with such understanding, to study and reflect on the teachings of the spiritual teachers and bring positive changes in your life. Otherwise, even if you say that you are inseparable from your guru and that you have meditated in a sealed room, it will remain just a tale without achieving anything.

Similarly if you speak of the scholarship, diligence and kindness of a Khenpo, it remains just a narration without much purpose. Even if you talk about having studied the scriptures under a spiritual teacher for decades, all you have gained is the benefit of seeing the scriptures. It will not be of much use at the time of death, since pride and jealousy would have ruined your mind-stream.

The sentence, "The glorious guru dwells in my heart", appears repeatedly in Guru Yoga. It may be difficult to understand the hidden meaning. But a simpler meaning of this is that if you practise the teachings and instructions of your spiritual teacher without arrogance or jealousy and, as Vairochana said, "Even if no one likes it I am satisfied," you have nothing to regret or feel guilty about in the present, future and the intermediate state. Then the sentence "The glorious guru dwells in my heart" becomes real and not just a poetic composition. My guru repeatedly advised me that the essence of Guru Yoga is to cut off all doubts connected with grasping the self.

> For a mind free from doubt, blessings come,
> But for one plagued with doubts, there is no chance.
> On this it is said, "The Tantras and Updesas both agree."
> That is the counsel of Choje Ongpo,
> And I have complete trust in it.

The presence or absence of doubt can be decided by the presence or absence of faith. Buddha said, "It is possible for the sun and moon to fall down to the ground, it is possible to catch the air element with a lasso." As Nagarjuna said, "The view of nothingness leads to birth in the lower realms and the view of the existence of everything leads to birth in the higher realms." This is simply based on the belief that what can be seen exists and what is not visible is non-existent.

The wise and the foolish both have a lot to say about what is not possible. If you use your wisdom to investigate, then there is nothing impossible in the world we live in. That is why it is called "the three realms of possibilities or existences". The mind with faith in such a notion is what we need. If you develop such a mind, then the belief driven by monkey-like selfish notions will diminish and your vision and knowledge will expand gradually. Then you will have a view of everything you see, have a closer relation with whomever you befriend, and your confidence in whatever you do will be greater.

As you investigate the root and peak of all phenomena, you will understand that there are no phenomena that do not have a cause, just as Buddha said, "All phenomena occur from a cause." You further find that the cause is not a result of the thought of a permanent natural being, and that the various types of beings are born as a result of one's karma; just as Buddha said, "The various types of transient worlds emerge from karma." So one has to keep a check on all negative actions of body and speech; as Buddha said, "Do no sin," and diligently engage in positive action; just as Buddha said, "Engage in completely virtuous action." Thus you develop faith in the fact that you must be aware of cultivating virtue and discarding negative action, which is the root cause of all happiness and sorrow in life. This respect for the law of cause and effect should not be as some children behave: they behave well in front of their parents out of fear, or how people are well mannered in the presence of a spiritual teacher or the fearsome guardian deities but indulge in all sorts of things behind their backs. Rather, this respect should be based on the knowledge that any negative action, done in public or private, will leave an imprint of non-virtuous action in your mind and as a result you will face unwanted sufferings in life on the other hand the seed of virtuous action will result in happiness.

Ultimately, you realize that your mind is the king of activities, and since your thoughts are not hidden from you, you understand that hypocritical activities are of no use in the long run, and thus hypocritical actions diminish. And then you discard all activities of harming others and cultivate the altruistic mind. Thereby, you develop a special keenness to tame your mind and pay attention to it: just as Buddha said, "Tame your mind completely", because the mind is the real door of all phenomena. It is very important to understand this.

If you believe that the Triple Gem is a fearsome person monitoring all your activities, when you are told not to deceive the Triple Gem it is a big problem. At best, such fear can be useful for the time being to handle tough people who cannot otherwise be brought under control. Based on such fear, good and bad behaviour and many traditions have been founded over thousands of years and human society has survived. But as explained earlier, even if a harmful action is committed against someone else, the mind of the doer degenerates so much that the person would not have any hesitation in taking his own life. He or she becomes a social outcast. Knowing this, if you are able to discipline your mind, you become a good person who neither fears someone higher up nor does anything deceptive in public or private.

Any practice done with such a motivation will have no clinging to the pleasures of higher realms, such as the God and human realms. Gradually, the path will be followed with a genuine longing to renounce the cause and effect of samsara and strive for the cause and effect of enlightenment. In this way, once you gain firm faith in cause and effect, you will feel a sense of joy and peace at merely hearing the name of the Buddha-like spiritual teacher in human form who can explain the meanings clearly. This feeling is called the "devoted mind". There is no doubt that practice done with joyful effort without any complacency will yield results very quickly.

If you practise with a mind free of doubt about the law of karma and the manifest and hidden qualities of the Buddha-like spiritual teacher, all your wishes for this and the next life will be accomplished. Otherwise, as the saying goes, "You cannot sew with a double-pointed needle; and you cannot achieve your purpose with a hesitant mind." If you keep on doubting and hesitating then you will never be able to practise it at all. This is what my guru used to advise me.

As I told you on many occasions, every religion has the tradition of seeking blessings, but blessings in Buddhism, and especially in Mahayana and Vajrayana, are directly related to the mind. As a result of setting your heart on observing moral conduct as the foundation, the practice of meditational stability as the path and developing wisdom as the fruit, your view of life will gradually change and simultaneously all your immediate and ultimate wishes will be fulfilled. "This is called blessing," Ontrul Rinpoche had said on many occasions. Such a mind, free of doubt and hesitation, is called devotion or faith. Like the saying, "A person without devotion cannot attain positive qualities, as a burnt seed cannot sprout." If you have devotion or faith, the fruitional blessings come naturally, but if you lack faith, then just as a burnt seed cannot sprout, all your practice will not yield any fruit. All scriptural texts agree on this point.

Though devotion is important, many of us neglect it and some even disparage it. It is important to pay attention and investigate this. Since this is an important issue it does not matter even if it takes years to understand this. It is important to have a complete understanding of this by comparing the Buddhist and non-Buddhist doctrines with an open mind, using your intelligence, checking your own experience and reflecting on the teachings of the spiritual teacher. From my own experience I learned that one cannot make any progress in one's mind-stream by being careless about devotion. This is also the main point of instruction given by past spiritual masters and many Sutras, Tantras and instructions.

Today's neo-Buddhists of the east and west immediately interpret devotion as oppression the moment they hear about it. They say, "Every religion has something rigid in it, but we had heard that there is nothing rigid about Buddhism. Now, when you tell us this we don't know what to do," and they look disheartened. Some adopt a distorted view. Some remain indifferent, saying all religions talk about faith and devotion. They have misunderstood the whole point due to insufficient learning and contemplation.

From the Buddhist point of view, devotion or faith is a skillful method of cutting off the shackles of what is and what is not, and what exists and what is non-existent. To say, with strong grasping, what can and cannot be proved, to debate and say you have to believe in a creator, or that all phenomena have no cause and that you cannot dispute the texts and writings, is like binding oneself with a new religious shackle. Such a faith is faith only in name, and is totally different from the faith according to Mahayana and Vajrayana. When Buddha said, "As gold is melted, cut and rubbed, test my words," he meant that one has to investigate the appearance and the real nature of phenomena minutely until the ultimate meaning is found – by using valid yogic awareness or by contemplating the instructions of the spiritual teacher or by studying the authentic scriptures.

This word of the Buddha is called the "Fearless Lion's Roar". It is unique and magnificent. In this sense, faith according to Buddhism is a jewel found within oneself through experiential realization, by contemplating the fundamental nature of external and internal phenomena. Faith, according to other traditions, is based on decisions made by the Vedas and teachers. But looking at so-called Buddhists today, I wish they had at least a faith similar to the followers of other religions. It is such a pity just to pretend to have faith or to show modesty, as if forced by tradition, showing faith unwillingly in this life and doing things that have no meaning for the next life. I lament the condition of faithless arrogant beings like me who waste their life, roaming samsara aimlessly, neither benefitting the self or others, nor making this life or the next life meaningful.

SPIRITUAL LEADERS HAVE A GREAT RESPONSIBILITY

Today all the religions are degenerating. Especially those of us claiming to be Mahayana followers, as I just said, lack the strength of faith and as a result our practice remains ineffective. Take the Muslims for example. They religiously abstain from eating pork or consuming alcohol, some of them don't take meat not slaughtered by them and they do *namaz* five times a day without fail. I feel it is really nice to have faith in and dedication to whatever religion one follows. Similarly, followers of Hinduism do not consume meat or alcohol; they follow the Vedas and don't eat beef. Whether it is out of compassion or not, having faith in the scriptures and following them with dedication is a matter of pride.

Now look at us Buddhists. We say, "Muslims don't eat pork and Hindus don't eat beef, but we proudly eat both pork and beef. You don't drink but we can drink." Although not said openly it is implied that we can engage in all immoral activities. It is really sad.

The Buddha said, "Do no sin. Engage in completely virtuous action. Tame your mind completely. This is the Buddha's teaching." So as Buddhists, young or old, men or women, whatever your caste or birth, we have to respect and follow this. Out of respect for the teachings some say, "The spiritual teachers, monks and nuns cannot consume meat and alcohol. They have to be calm, peaceful and modest in their behaviour. But lay people can eat and drink anything." Such utterances, I believe, betray their lack of faith in the Buddha's words and the teachings of the spiritual teacher. It is clear that such people lack faith in the law of karma and the Buddha's teachings.

Under the influence of afflictions we may do wrong things. If possible we should confess and take a pledge, as explained in the scriptures. Instead of confessing, if you proudly proclaim in front of others that we can eat and drink anything then, I think, you are causing a lot of damage to Buddhaism, especially Mahayana and Vajrayana practitioners. All this is due to the lack of education. If possible, all of us, lay people, monks and nuns, should study, reflect and contemplate the scriptures thoroughly or at least have some knowledge. Our general attitude is that only monks and nuns should study, contemplate and meditate thoroughly or that it should suffice for nuns to do a little meditation; that lay people do not need spiritual education, but should have a worldly education, and that neither spiritual nor worldly education is necessary for lay women.

This is backward thinking. This attitude may have worked for a few centuries, but it will not work in the twenty-first century. To remain rigid in this attitude will keep oneself and one's spiritual tradition backward and lead to its degeneration. Therefore, we must see our flaws and accept them. If we remain humble, without losing sight of studying, reflecting and meditation, we will be rendering service to the spiritual teachings.

BEING HUMBLE

> It is as if I have been given the wish-fulfilling jewel
> By the saviour of beings,
> Kyabgon Ontrul of Zhichen
> Who is inseparable from my heart,
> Filled with the three forms of faith.
> This is my understanding.

Spiritual teachers of all traditions unanimously say that whether you are a spiritual practitioner or not, if you want the best for yourself, then being humble is the best way. This really seems the best way from both the spiritual and the worldly points of view. From the spiritual point of view, we keep saying that grasping the self is the main force that is making us do all the wrong things and yet we don't know that our mind-stream is bloated with arrogance. Judging by this, I think we have not served the purpose of being humans. However learned and accomplished ordinary beings like me may think we are, since our minds are not hidden from us, we know what we are.

As I said earlier, we should know that life is a dream. So long as we don't have such a notion, it is what is called, "dog excrement wrapped in brocade": looking good externally, trained in eloquence, with a clean face and being superficially appealing. But so long as we do not uproot afflictions and their tendencies, everything will be ever-changing, like the divination of a fake fortune-teller or the autumn weather. We know that nothing is stable or free of mistakes and whatever we do or say cannot be trusted fully.

For example, it seems that when one starts meditating with concentration, all obtrusive thought is blocked and one encounters the subtle strings of mental cognition, which is the dwelling place of innate propensities, and one sees past and future lives, or gods and demons that others cannot see and even talk to them. But as soon as the meditation session ends, these visions wane and you become an ordinary human. When we experience this we do not realize that this is just a superficial experience and remain humble. Instead we let our ego become bloated, scorn other practitioners and spiritual teachers and brag about our experiences to anyone who listens. This is poor behaviour. It is "showing off", one of the four causes of degeneration of one's character, consequently whatever little quality one has gets wasted.

Past masters have repeatedly said that one must think there is nothing beneath you except for the water flowing on the ground. I believe this means one should discard pride and arrogance. But today, arrogance is regarded as a quality and even taught from childhood in the name of one's right or service to one's religion and nation. All this is bound to bring unhappiness to the entire society. This is the basis of all the intolerance between two people, two neighbours and even between countries.

It is amazing to see that children are taught arrogance – because arrogance is inherently present in the character of all beings, including humans. Making the inherently present disease worse, instead of trying to cure it is neither a wise act nor the way of a wise person. We all lament the fact that times have degenerated today and there is less trust, more incidences of violence and theft, discordance among family members, children have no respect for their parents, the elders and the learned; the elders are selfish and show no love and affection to the children. It is good to show such concern about these things, but it is more important to know that we ourselves are the cause of all this.

One should be able to control one's mind and know that we are all beings, living in this cyclic existence of possibilities, and all of us will have flaws. If we can teach this to children at a young age then it will make us not react immediately with violence over small disagreements, like negative and positive electric wires touching. I, for example, may think that all I do or say is out of a good intention, but the residual notion of "I" and "my" is subconsciously present due to grasping the self, and because of that I will not like what others do or say and remain unhappy. If I do something harmful and atrocious I will feel proud instead of feeling guilty. If someone questions me I will be angry and unhappy mentally and physically, like the saying goes, "A horse with a sore back will jump, a person with guilt will show aggression." Not knowing this in the past due to my ignorance, all I could do was face suffering for months and years. But later, thanks to the opportunity to meet my spiritual teachers, I began to realize my faults just by looking at my teachers, even if they did not utter a word of teaching, and I knew how I should behave in future.

It was the late Zhichen Ontrul Rinpoche who first introduced me to the wish-fulfilling jewel-like awareness of the faults and gave me hands-on instructions. May you always regard me with kindness! Remembering the kindness of my gurus and knowing the reasons, I hold them in my heart and vow to practise the instructions. I always pray for their blessings so that I never have the thought of harming others, and that all my activities – sitting, walking, talking, building reliquaries or giving teachings in this life and future lives, similar to their activities – may be for the benefit of others, and devoid of the eight worldly motivations.

> These things are just a sketch of what I know,
> Today's crazy ideas.
> So please do not be bored by all this
> And listen some more:

All this is a narration of my ideas, or rather my confused thoughts. It is normal practice that the majority looks down on the minority as wrong or crazy. For example, western culture and the western way of dressing are popular and so one has no problem fitting in, whatever part of the world one goes to and with whomsoever you meet.

On the contrary, if you are dressed in the costume of an eastern minority community you will be treated like an alien and those who have cameras will flock to take your picture, dogs will bark at you and even the monkeys on tree-tops will follow you. Some might even run away from you and call the police. It is clear that such discrimination is based on a majority and minority view point. It is normal to treat something that is against your perception as wrong and invalid. So, considering the views and opinions of the majority, I think I may be called crazy.

According to a tale, thousands of years ago an astrologer informed the king that it was going to rain for a week and warned that anyone who drinks the rain water will go crazy. The king covered all the wells of the palace but the general public had no way to take any preventive measures. So all the people except the king became crazy and then they started calling the king crazy. The king could not convince them that he was not crazy. Finally the king drank the rain water and began to think and behave like his people.

I still have crazy ravings to tell. Listen without being bored and you may find some lessons in these ravings. Even if you do not find any lessons, just listen out of curiosity.

> Toward the Great Lord Guru – my father and mother –
> And toward his spiritual descendants and lineage holders
> I naturally had single-minded faith, even as a child.

I remember, even as a child, I had general respect for all Buddhist and non-Buddhist deities, gurus, meditational deities, Dakinis, the guardian deities and gods, except those who harmed and took the life of others. When I was around five or six years old, being ignorant and not having studied, I used to have doubts when I saw the Buddhist Dharma protectors with their tongues rolled up, stains of blood drops and human corpses held in their mouths. I asked my guru, the late Drukpa Thuksey Rinpoche, about this and he explained a lot of things but I don't remember them all.

Once he pointed to a scroll painting of the protectress Palden Lhamo and said to me, "The human corpse in her mouth is our mind." Being very young, I did not think about it much at that time but I understood that the objective of the guardian deities with gazing eyes and wide open mouths was to eat and destroy our vicious minds to help us and not harm us. This changed my view of the guardian deities. Being small though, I did not have a profound understanding, but the blessing of just one word from the root guru helped clear so many doubts.

If one reflects on the instructions on inseparability of appearance and the mind, the pure vision has to be understood as the inseparability of good and bad, and of gods that help others and demons that harm others. But due to my ignorance of the view and obscurations of negative karmic imprints, it was difficult for me to have a pure vision of the deities and spirits, called guardians and wisdom holders, to whom one makes offerings of blood and meat. Due to a lack of this pure vision, I could not develop natural faith and consequently I could not make any progress in my mind. Even if I had some understanding, realization could not be achieved. This must be the reason why I am still lingering in samsara. When I was young, I thought all Buddhist and non-Buddhist deities and gods were just different forms and it was I who had the pure vision.

When the elders praised their own tradition and its followers and criticized other traditions, I did not find them soothing to the ear, even though I could not argue with them. Even when I heard terms of attachment and aversion, like Buddhists and non-Buddhist, I did not feel comfortable. They even made distinctions within Buddhists; such as the New School being better than the Old School; or the Old School being better than the New School; Mahayana was better than Hinayana, or the Middle Way was better than the Mind Only School. I used to be very disturbed for days when I heard such things. Even today I cannot accept such biased opinions.

As an argument from a dialectical point of view, they may have a lot of things to say to justify their opinions. Even a person like me may have a lot of rhetorical things to say. But like the saying, "Woman standing up to urinate when there is no man around, langurs dancing when monkeys are not around," such people can say anything when scholars of other religions are not around.

One sees in history that sometimes the scholars of Nalanda

faced great difficulties while debating with non-Buddhist scholars. It is like the Old School followers back-biting when scholars of the New School are not around and vice-versa. Every tradition has its own supporting logic.

I don't think people like us can face up to Buddhist philosophers or even to non-Buddhist philosophers like the Jains. Some of the teachers criticize Guru Padmasambhava and praise their own spiritual teachers. I used to feel sad when I heard such things in my childhood, because even at that young age I knew that we were able to say our prayers thanks to Guru Padmasambhava. I remember having deep faith in Guru Padmasambhava and his consort from a very early age and this faith is unshakable.

A SLIGHTLY DIFFERENT APPEARANCE OF GURU RINPOCHE

> As a child, whenever I had good food and nice clothes
> I thought they were bestowed on me
> By my Great Father Padmasambhava.

As a child I had a firm belief that Guru Padmasambhava was taking care of me, providing me with every comfort, although I did not know the reason why I thought so. Whenever I got new clothes or some delicious food I always thought it was given to me by Guru Rinpoche. It was a natural, pleasant feeling. At that time, whenever I thought of Guru Rinpoche I saw him in the form of a child-like me, smiling and handsome, wearing a loin cloth made of tiger-skin and bone ornaments, with different mudras and holding various emblems, sitting on a rock. I do not remember seeing him in the attire offered by the king of Zahor, sitting on the seat of the lotus and moon discs, as in the statues we have.

Once I saw him looking stout without any ornaments, wearing a white cloth as an upper shawl, holding a staff in his right hand. I don't remember what he was holding in his left hand. I remember he appeared as a cotton-clad yogi in my deluded vision. Like the saying, "Anything can appear in a yogi's mind," a yogi should have varied experiences and deluded visions.

Based on my experiences and blind faith, I can say that even from a young age I had some karmic connection with Guru Rinpoche. Even today, I seek the blessings of the wish-fulfilling jewel-like Guru Rinpoche and his consort, and also from Tara, who is inseparable from them, for the next life as well for every activity in this life, without any hesitation.

SPOILED BY IMITATING OTHERS

For a time, instead of doing necessary spiritual practice sincerely and remaining humble, I listened to others and mistook the body of a guru and the desire for a name as happiness. I distanced my mindstream from the doctrine and, bloated with ego and pride, I engaged in superficial religious performances and did not do anything genuine. The pure mind of faith and respect that I had as a child seemed suppressed in my adolescence, as I lived off the black offerings made by the lay people, impressed by my good behaviour and eloquence.

Generally, with age, we all go through hormonal changes. For example, as a child you play in the dust, then as a teenager you seek romantic pleasure; in adulthood you think of business and making money, and as you age you start meddling in others' affairs and in your old age you behave like a child. This is a process of life that we all know. My way of thinking too may have changed similarly. I believe that friends and especially karmic obscurations make a big difference to the study of Buddhist philosophy.

I remember that even before I could say, "Papa or Mama," I had a genuine sense of faith, remorse and compassion, and because of that I had a clear, fearless feeling – like looking from the top of a mountain peak. After coming to the monastery, if I had cultivated devotion and compassion continuously along with my common studies, I would not have degenerated, even if I had not progressed.

Like the saying, the mind of a child moves as an oar on water moves with the wind, my mind was driven by the wind of afflictions. On top of that, I did not find the awareness to respect and follow the spiritual teachers and friends, and I lived off the offerings made to the monastery. Until I was seventeen years old everything was superficial. Seemingly I was studying the common sciences, but my character worsened day by day.

Once I came to my senses, devotion had faded away and the sense of compassion was like the sun setting on the western peak. Because of this, I had lost interest in the supreme doctrine and although I heard teachings or did meditation once in a while, I felt sleepy under the influence of dullness. There were times when a session of teaching by the Khenpo would end without my having heard a single word.

Sometimes, under the influence of desire I would peek from my window and look at the girls passing by and waste my time comparing their looks in my mind. Whatever I did was superficial, selfish and contaminated by the eight worldly motivations. When I realized this I found that I was in a pathetic situation, without even the qualities of a good lay man, let alone the qualities of a spiritual practitioner. I felt depressed, considering I was in the form of a spiritual practitioner.

Generally speaking: projection, withdrawal of thought, dreams, distractions – which are aspects of desire, loving music, dance and sports, attractions between men and women, *etc.* are present in varying degrees amongst us all as a characteristic of being born in the realm of desire.

But my situation was a little different. Like the saying, "Thinking about reflection at the time of listening is Mara's obstacle; thinking about listening at the time of meditation is Mara's obstacle," and "Poor meditation leading to sleep, and clear perceptive function when not in meditation, can be regarded as the function of obscuration," and "Where the rain of Dharma falls, there is the whirlwind of Mara". The moment I started a session of hearing, reflection and meditation, projection and absorption of sleep and dreams would begin, or some object of desire would distract me and would not let mindfulness settle. The moment the session ended, sleep would vanish and even the objects of desire did not hold any attraction.

For example, I liked the practice of fasting, but during practice I would start feeling hungry from the second half of the fasting day. I couldn't sleep at night and would have a headache or my body would tremble the next day, giving me a hard time. I know some people feel unbearably hungry if they don't get food on time, but I normally don't feel hungry and am not very keen on food. If sometimes, due to a busy schedule I don't get to eat, I don't feel hungry and even forget that I have not eaten. Sometimes when my kind friends brought food in the evening I would ask why they were serving me food when they knew I did not take dinner.

Similarly, when I relaxed in my room and said my prayers, I

would get sudden urge to go out, or insects would die under my feet or I would have to tell lies. The whole day would pass away in distraction. I would even feel very distressed when I came across people who irritated me. Mostly, such incidents always happened on the holy days of the Buddha. When I think about these things, I feel certain that obscuration of negative actions had remained unexpiated.

CHAPTER 9

Defilement of Black Offering

> These days, due to hindrances of *Kor*
> My devotion is not as pure as when I was a child.
> Repeatedly receiving this poison *Kor* is bad,
> And I will have more to say about this presently.

Such obscurations are divided into many types in the texts, like: "the obscuration of karma," "the obscuration to liberation" and "the obscuration to omniscience". For the lay person's understanding, the obscurations may be defined as "the external obscuration of karma," "the internal delusive obscuration" and "the secret obscuration to knowledge". For novices like us who do not recognize the gross external delusive obscurations, it is important not to be contaminated by external causes, like the obscurations related to actions of body, speech and mind, such as the obscurations of black offerings. For example, for a lay person, immoral actions like drinking, killing animals and eating their meat, smoking, taking snuff or extra marital affairs; for spiritual teachers and monks the worst is being attached to black offerings, roaming around the town and in foreign lands where there is no spiritual discipline, indulging mainly in sleep and meaningless talk are obscurations. It is important to prevent one's mind from becoming habituated to the attachment of such actions and thus wasting time.

LACKING FRIENDLY SUPPORT

For many years I remained ignorant of the reasons. I don't remember any of the elders advising and guiding me. There are a few factors that can change your way of thinking and behaviour, such as the power of a friend, the power of wealth and the power of foundation. For people like us who have not achieved stability, the power of friendship is very important. For many years the people who accompanied me, instead of engaging in conversations that inspired faith and compassion, kept talking about things that impaired faith in the guru and Buddha and created doubts about the activities of the spiritual teachers. As a result, faith, which is the foundation of developing qualities, disappeared behind a cloud. For example, I remember some of the elders would say, "There cannot be two gurus for one doctrine. It is inappropriate to call Guru Rinpoche the second guru", and speak impiously about Guru Rinpoche directly or indirectly. I used to hear many such things. They would treat a spiritual teacher with a consort like an ordinary lay man and say that monks should not seek a hand-blessing from such teacher.

About thirty years ago, His Holiness Dudjom Rinpoche visited our monastery and they said I should be seated ahead of His Holiness, on the grounds that, although he was a good spiritual teacher, he had a consort and was like any lay man. A couple of years later, His Holiness Sakya Trizin Rinpoche of Phuntsok Phodrang visited our monastery and they said similar things. Some advised me against receiving a hand-blessing or an initiation. I was young then, about thirteen years old. Although I did not have the authority to talk back, I felt such talk was malicious. Today when I look back I feel they may have said all those things with a good intention. Today I try to develop pure vision by thinking that they must have feared that if they had not said such things, then young monks like me might get disrobed.

Some, who pretended to be the scholars of scriptures, said that one could not take ordination vows from rulers and kings, and made sarcastic remarks against His Holiness the Dalai Lama. Some said that someone with delusions of attachment and aversion could not be a spiritual teacher. When the topic of conversation came to compassion they would say, "These spiritual teachers talk about compassion but they eat meat. Even if they don't eat meat they take all sorts of dietary supplements made from precious ingredients. They mistreat the attendants and monks." Like adorning the *torma*[56] with butter sculptures, they had something to say about all the spiritual teachers. They would say, "Buddha said, 'As beings die due to their karma, there is no point in mourning.' Everyone has to face one's karma. What is the big deal?" For years I heard such things.

To be honest, this habit of judging the external behaviour of the Buddha-like spiritual teachers, and considering them good if it conformed to one's culture and liking, or bad if it did not conform, perverted my own attitude. This was one of the causes of the degeneration of my view and meditation. Later, thanks to the

---

56. *gtor ma*; Skt. *balimta*; a ritual cake, usually hand-moulded from butter and tsampa (roasted barley flour) and coloured with dyes, which can symbolize a deity, a mandala, an offering, or even a weapon.

kindness of my gurus, I acquired some understanding, but remained confused for a few years, not knowing what to do.

Now when I look back, I think I was saved by the kindness of my gurus and the improvement of my karma and I was fortunate to recognize my own faults and make progress gradually. Although a decrease in the manifestation of affliction was not visible, since that time, afflictive emotions became less important and I did not have the arrogance to speak impiously about other spiritual teachers nor had the intention to do superficial religious performances to deceive others, as in the past. I felt calm and humble. It was like pouring cold water over boiling water.

As mentioned earlier, the external defiled action by body and speech may be influenced by friends, causes and circumstances but for novice spiritual practitioners, the basic harmful cause is the black offering. This is the main cause of a gradual waning of faith and compassion. I have heard this saying, "Don't use black magic. Use black offerings." But living off black offerings is worse than suffering under the spell of black magic and witchcraft; it destroys both your spiritual and your worldly life.

It leaves no opportunity for those of us aspiring to improve our mind-stream and follow the path of non-harming to achieve our goal. Living off this destroys the foundation, damages the path and spoils the fruit, leaving us empty handed at the end. The instructions say, "This poison of black offering, if consumed excessively, will cut off the life-vein of liberation," and describes it as something to fear. And from personal experience I learned its meaning.

> In my own life I have met no enemy
> Worse than such *Kor*;
> I have been with this enemy a long time
> And I know his faults.
> So it is appropriate for me to remark on these faults.
> I will explain how I got caught up with such *Kor*.

I have no external enemy, human or non-human to show. But I recognized that black offering is the main support that aids the grasping of the self which destroys the mind. Just as, the greater number of supporters the more powerful the king becomes, consumption of more and more black offering boosts grasping at the self, leading to the growth of pride and other defilements and wasting of the mindstream. It seems that realized beings who have attained the two levels of understanding are not affected by black offering because the text says, "To eat the iron hammer of black offering, you need the bronze jaws of the two levels (of understanding)." Otherwise, for people with no meditational experience and understanding, and especially for someone like me, who has eaten and drunk black offering since childhood, living off black offering is like eating burning embers or drinking boiling water. It is really sad. But, even though you do not have much meditational experience and understanding, if with age, you recognize your mind and follow corrective steps like confession, then the damage would not be so great. But for people like me who have fallen into the pit of black offering since childhood, it was a difficult situation.

CHAPTER 10

Recognition as a Reincarnation of Drukpa

> Though starting with a store of good karma,
> I ended up with bad results.
> But somehow prior karma and prayer
> Created this guru form of mine.

As a result of adequately adhering to moral discipline in my past life and accumulation of sufficient merit I was born as a devout human being. But due to a prior karma playing out along with prior aspiration I unintentionally took the form of a 'guru collecting black offerings, like insects drawn to the fire'. Today when I think about this and feel sad, I ask my parents, "Why couldn't you take care of your only child? Why did you give me away to be turned into someone living off black offerings?" In reply they say, "Don't blame us. As soon as you learned to speak you said you had a monastery and that you will be leaving. You couldn't keep quiet. We tried many ways to avoid the situation. But in our absence you kept saying you are a guru and, sitting on the table, you openly pretended to give teachings and hand-blessings. Naturally, many people hoped you were the reincarnation of their guru and many people came to us. We received letters from His Holiness the Dalai Lama and other high Lamas. In particular, His Holiness the late Dudjom Rinpoche also told us not to worry about your health and said that Jagpa Melen, guardian deity of the Drukpa Lineage, will take care of you. So there was nothing we could do."

> At the age of three and four I had some memories:
> The messenger of demon deceit entered me,
> Going straight into my infant heart.
> Thus before I could talk,
> I began to give blessings with my hands,
> And was thrilled when I was put on a high seat;
> Even though my father struck me, trying to stop such action,
> I continued to do it behind his back.

Today some parents feel very happy when their child is recognized as the reincarnation of a guru, and if my parents were like them I certainly would have fought and sued them! But since they were not guilty, all I could do was keep quiet. Past masters have said that every seemingly good action which causes non-virtue and suffering is, out of the four evil forces, the work of "the evil son of god" (lust). So inspired by this, I kept acting like a guru, saying and doing a lot of things that impressed people, despite my father Bairo Rinpoche's rebuke.

My mother later told me: "Some of the monks and nuns who were part of our family suggested that you should be dressed in yellow and maroon clothes since you seemed to be fond of them, but Bairo Rinpoche scolded them and said, 'What do you mean? If this child has pure karma he will naturally do what helps others, with a spiritual mind, as he grows up. There is no hurry to dress him like someone living off *Kor* (black offerings) right now. Don't any of you think of changing the physical appearance of my son!' Since then, only black and white clothes, shoes and caps were put on you. But when Rinpoche was not around, you would wrap yourself in Rinpoche's upper shawl, or any yellow or maroon cloth around, and sat cross-legged, pretending to be meditating. As soon as you heard Rinpoche was coming, you would take them off and pretend you didn't do anything. Do you remember?"

I don't remember all this, but I do remember that when I was around three years old, just able to walk around, I had a pair of good quality white shoes with a black lining. I never liked the colour and was hoping to get a brown pair of shoes, so I hid the shoes in a dug-up hole about thirty steps away.

A couple of hours later everyone was looking for my shoes and they asked me where I had put them, but I didn't say anything. But looking at my face they must have seen my guilt. After some time, Akhu Lodo, a monk who was very fond of me, took me aside and said, "Tell me where the shoes are and I will buy you a mango." I held Akhu's hand and took him to where I had hidden the shoes. Everyone praised me saying I was so smart. The instructions say that all such acts are the work of the "evil son of god" and I believe this is so.

> When I was able to speak, I proclaimed that
> I had a monastery and a Guru's residence,
> And I spoke many pointless silly things.
> Right before my actual recognition (as an incarnation),
> I blurted out it was now time to depart for my monastery,

> Saying farewell to my family and offering scarves.
> Through such behaviour this "Guru" form was created without true Dharma.

Since people today are impressed only by external behaviour, they just looked at my apparent good behaviour, without checking whether I possessed any spiritual qualities, and put me on a throne. A spiritual throne is used by great spiritual masters who have realized the nature of truth, whilst they turn the wheel of Dharma in order to uphold the greatness of the teachings of what is heard and realized and to sow seeds of devotion in the disciples. For example, before giving *Perfection of Wisdom* teachings Buddha made his own throne. This is how it should be.

The thrones we use today, lacking substance and built out of competition and envy, can be called thrones of the eight worldly motivations. I was put on such a high wooden throne. In the past, realized masters, such as Gampopa and other Tibetan and Indian Siddhas who, having completed their own welfare, had started working for the welfare of others, drew gatherings of people spontaneously. But today we publicize teaching events, using the term "Religious Circular" and feel happy when a big crowd comes. If we don't call this worldly then what is it?

I remember thousands of people: lay men, monks, school children and cultural performers, lining the road to receive me. My relative Lobsang told me he was part of the group. In the midst of such a huge crowd I was taken on the back of a white horse, covered in brocade and adorned with precious ornaments, with a parasol over my head and supported on either side by two huge men wearing traditional cloaks of yellow brocade and wearing red hats with tassels. I felt good. All the beautiful precious ornaments belonged to the monastery of my late root Guru Vajradhara Pawo Rinpoche, and were arranged by him in consideration of the auspicious connections between the previous incarnations of Pawo and Drukpa. May my saviour Pawo Rinpoche regard me with care and affection!

In the midst of all the hustle and bustle I saw a toy car in a shop and said I wanted it. But no one cared to listen and I remember feeling sad. As I was carried off the horse towards the throne, people started pulling at my leg and putting it on their head, and my shoes fell off. Everyone was holding sticks of incense and flowers and I remember crying out of fear when the incense sticks burned my bare feet.

Sometime after, when I was seated on the throne, Bairo Rinpoche brought me a plastic deer. I think he heard me asking for the toy car on the way. But I could only keep the plastic deer on the table and had no time to play with it, because I had to acknowledge the offerings of mandalas by representatives of all the schools of Tibetan Buddhism, the Tibetan Government in exile, and various monasteries. To some I had to give hand-blessings and to some I had to touch head-to-head. There were many such worldly traditions that I didn't understand much then and even now I don't understand. It was difficult for a four-year-old child to do everything, but I did all that I could.

After meeting the representatives of various monasteries, I had fallen asleep on the throne out of exhaustion, and I don't remember much about what happened during the public audience. I don't remember, but I was told that to the embarrassment of everyone, I refused to do head-to-head touch with Ratoe Chuwar Rinpoche, a senior guru and representative of the Religious Affairs Department of the Tibetan Government in exile.,

Later my root Guru Ontrul Rinpoche told me all about this in detail. He said, "I don't know why but you refused to do it even when Drukpa Thuksey Rinpoche held your neck and pressed your head forward." I asked, "How did I behave with you?" and he replied, "You affectionately touched my cheeks with your small hands." I asked him why he came to my enthronement ceremony. He smiled and kept quiet for some time and then said, "Since coming into exile in India the only person from the same monastery and with the same commitment was Bairo Rinpoche. Since you are the son of Bairo Rinpoche it would have been wrong not to come." Despite his show of such humility and modesty, I believe from the depth of my heart that he had come to form the auspicious connection to take care of me from my childhood.

CHAPTER 11

Grave Consequences of Black Offerings

> Set on the throne of the eight worldly dharmas,
> These hands of mine collected offerings and bestowed blessings.
> At the age of eight I gave a public empowerment
> Without having the proper qualities of a teacher.

Since even before I was recognized as a reincarnation I liked putting my hand in the gesture of blessing on people's heads, I must have felt very happy to have the opportunity of putting my hand on the heads of people during the enthronement ceremony. I don't remember how I felt then. I remember I liked giving blessings with my hand and did not like touching people's heads with the *Dar-pom*, a long ceremonial stick covered with silver and gold, with a protection wheel attached at the top, or touching their heads with images of Buddha. I don't know what I had in my mind then as a child. Qualified spiritual teachers and realized beings were able to establish a meaningful connection simply by touching people with their bare hands.

Though for people like me, I think, blessing people using the *Dar-pom* is preferable. I do not know if, as a symbol of grandeur, using the statues and the *Dar-pom* decorated with gold and silver for giving blessings is spiritually correct. Generally speaking, today I feel it is better to bless people by putting holy objects like the statues and scriptures on their heads, instead of touching their heads with the sinful hand used for collecting *Kor,* because the purpose of giving hand blessings is to bless the mind-stream of the recipient. When your own mind-stream lacks blessing, putting your hand on others' heads is merely like a broom for gathering the dust of *Kor*.

I may have been endowed with some qualities of blessing from past lives, but at the age of eight years I had neither the power of purification nor the power of accomplishment, and yet I gave teachings and empowerments to a gathering of thousands of people. I don't know if I had even a single qualification of a Vajracharya, and yet I performed rituals of wrathful direct action, fire-offerings and consecration, *etc.*, without hesitation. With such external pretensions I went to many places, as a guru appropriating sacred offerings.

> At sixteen I gave a teaching on Hevajra, the king of Tantras.
> I gave teachings before knowing the meaning of the words,
> Before doing any practice I gave empowerments:

> Doing these things was like a child's game for me
> And I am not interested in recounting everything.
> This is how I got involved with *Kor*,
> The poison *Kor* which gradually burned my mind.

There are two types of *Kor-La* or *Kor* collecting gurus; those who have complete inner realization to digest the *Kor*, whose activities are purely altruistic, unstained by selfishness at any stage, either directly or indirectly, and who nurture disciples and accept offerings for their completion of accumulation of merit. Such behaviour should be recognized as the sublime activity of a Bodhisattva and such a qualified spiritual teacher can also be called *Kor-La*. A person in the form of a guru, without any inner realization, who tries to impress others with external behaviour, who deceives others with pretensions of nobility and wastes others' mind-streams with pretensions of scholarship with the selfish motivation of gaining social recognition, and who collects followers for the benefit of their family, retinue and attendants – such a person is also called *Kor-La*.

I DON'T LIKE PRAISE BY OTHERS

From a very young age I was praised as a good guru because, except for petty childish distractions, I was not a hyperactive mischievous child. In order to enable other pupils to get a break, I used to insist on going for walks with other children or playing badminton with them. When I got a break I would let the other children play and then I would search for an older person and sit with him and ask him about old stories. As I grew older the other monks liked to go out with people of their own age, and within the monastery they did not show much respect for the elders, and indulged in acts of indiscipline. In violation of the rules, they escaped from the monastery at night to watch movies and even if they were punished, they did not show any remorse. I did not like doing all this; perhaps I did not have the courage. There were some elders who tried to oppress us when we showed them respect and I did not like them much. Apart from them, I preferred the company of elders to the people of my own age.

The elders, having had many experiences in life, had lots of interesting things to relate. People of my age knew what I knew, and I knew what they knew, and so talking with them was a mere waste of time. On top of that, being with the elders saved me from being blamed for others' misbehaviour and being punished along with them. I remember I sometimes wished to join the younger lot and do mischievous things, but I didn't actually do anything. This was why people praised me, and not because they saw any sublime quality in me, as I possessed none. Their praise for me was not based on any genuine qualities I possessed.

A CHILD SHOULD BE LEFT ALONE AS A NORMAL BEING

I didn't like being praised by others when I was young because their praise did not improve my mind-stream. On the contrary, firstly, I had to keep up the pretension of nobility and discipline every day, and secondly, when someone praises you, your ego gets boosted and then you become disheartened when they stop praising you. Those around me too had great expectations and looked up to me and relied on me. So I lost my freedom and became like a street juggler's monkey. Both from the spiritual and worldly point of view I had no prospects. Once you start clinging to praise, you immediately expect praise from your teachers or attendants as soon as you do something good. I think this is really an abuse for the child. When a monkey or a sea animal makes a good jump, something is fed to the animal. It is similar. You lose your human dignity and become similar to an animal, and it becomes difficult to develop good intentions or positive actions. I think we are all running after fame, sacrificing happiness in this life and the next and trying to overcome a lot of obstacles. For many such reasons, since the age of eight or nine I realized that praise was something that I did not need.

Generally, I think there is hardly anyone who does not like praise, and especially if a child is given sweets and praised he or she would feel happy and forget everything else, and would not dare to say what he really wants to say. The elders would thus achieve their objective of keeping the child quiet. I remember a similar experience. When I was around five years old I could not keep my hands still, and some of my teachers said, "You are such a holy reincarnate. It is amazing that you can sit still with your hands in meditative equipoise." Immediately I thought I should sit still and kept my hands still for a long time. Being attached to praise I sat still, giving up whatever I wanted.

If you call animals, such as dogs, pigs, monkeys and dolphins by their name and pat their heads, they will jump in the air, play in the water or sing and dance. They will listen to every command you give. Seeing all this, and considering my own experience, I understood from a young age that being attached to praise without having any quality within you caused unnecessary problems.

I think there are many kinds of praise: sincere praise, superficial praise and sincere praise (but for the wrong reasons). The object of praise also must check whether he or she is worthy of it and if so, then well and good. If you have no quality worthy of praise, then you become doubtful about the praise. Then check that are you unnecessarily becoming proud. This is where most of us lose the plot. Some may say it is your good fortune and that may be right. But like the saying, "Merit of past life and burden of the next life," those of us who believe in life after death should not be too fond of praise and honour without possessing any inherent and acquired wisdom, for this could make a big difference in the formation of your character.

FAME IS THE MOST DIFFICULT TO RESIST

It is for this reason that many of the scriptures and instructions stress that fame should be abandoned. But in reality it is difficult to remain joined to the mother earth, and if one is able to remain humble a genuine happiness can be felt within. Most of the physical and mental dissatisfaction we find today is mostly related to the desire for a name. The inability to meet the desire for a name and the fear of being criticized by others makes us wear clothes, ornaments, eat things, show off or use make up. It makes you lie, steal or even kill. You worry about it even on your death bed. If you get a little fame you are not satisfied with what you have.

Seeing the rich you are worried about for not being able to catch up with them. The more you struggle for worldly gains, the more suffering you get. If you are able to give up the desire for fame, whatever wealth and name you have will only be a source of happiness and not suffering. Even a pauper with no wealth can live with a peaceful mind, happy and smiling. If one thinks well, then this is a big gain. All these things I learned later, thanks to my spiritual teachers. I did not know all this when I was young.

As I said earlier, I did not like praise much when I was young but, as a human, I may not have liked those who maligned or humiliated me. I would be happy to be left alone without praise or derision. I still remember that I didn't like people who praised me and carried me, or embraced or kissed my hand, or patted my cheeks affectionately. I used to think that if they really loved me then there was no need to praise me, hold me or kiss me. As *A Guide to the Bodhisattva's Way of Life* clearly says, there is no need to be happy and egoistic when you find a few people praising you, while many are humiliating you, and since there are people who do praise you, there is no need to feel hurt, angry or depressed when some people abuse you. I thought like this even before I studied *A Guide to the Bodhisattva's Way of Life*. Many texts stress that the eight worldly motivations should be suppressed, and I understand the reason why. I believe it is due to *Kor* that I have not made any progress, if not worsened, even at this old age.

KOR LINKED TO DESIRE FOR FAME IS BLACK *KOR*

It is clear that if one has desire for fame and praise they drag you down and give you no happiness in the present, the intermediate state or in the next life. If you have no desire for fame, then whatever praise and offerings you get are a result of merit accumulated in your past life. This makes a favourable condition for working for the welfare of others, and is great. Since the contamination of selfishness is absent there is no cause for faults. If you do not give up the desire for fame, it is like salty water or alcohol, and the thirst for it cannot be satisfied. This desire can equally be the cause of suffering for the rich and poor, laymen, monks, men and women, young and old alike. But from experience I have learned that, for a spiritual practitioner, this desire for fame is like the sword that cuts the life-vein of liberation and omniscience.

The offerings collected with an egoistic desire for fame, either with perseverance by someone known as learned, noble, and good, or simply by relying on fame, are equally *Kor*, and this is called black *Kor*. It is said, "Consuming the Halahala poison of black *Kor* excessively cuts off the life-vein of liberation" and since, like the black Halahala poison it cuts off the life-vein of practice, it is called black *Kor*.

Some people who read *My Crazy Tale* asked me if there is white

Kor. Although I have not heard of white *Kor*, I see no reason why there can't be a term like white *Kor* when there is black *Kor*. The offerings received by a realized being with the qualities and the two levels of yogic attainments described in the scriptures, cannot be called black *Kor*, because such a being will not have the defilement of desire for fame in his inner thoughts. Hence, such a being is not contaminated by *Kor*. In my view, the differentiation of white and black *Kor* should be based on the intention of the person using the offerings, rather than the objects offered.

> Even though others said, "this guru is really good"
> They exaggerated:
> These days a "good" guru is anybody
> Skilled in the eight worldly dharmas.
> Whoever is known as "authentic" is just
> Skilled in deception.
> Whoever is known as "learned" is merely
> Expert in oratory.
> Learned, authentic, and good
> Are the three qualities of a sublime guru
> Which are so loudly praised.
>
> Thus the stream of poison *Kor* pours down like rain
> And the door to hell is wide open.

The nine supreme aspects are the common qualifications that a person using the *Kor* should possess. A number of qualifications are required, but being learned, noble and good are regarded as the foundations of all qualities.

DEFINITION OF LEARNED, NOBLE AND GOOD TO BENEFIT ALL

Either due to lack of education or lack of interest to investigate, like the rabbit running at the sound of a loud noise; today, humility, respect for the law of karma and good intention without the eight worldly motivations are not regarded as "good". Today most of us regard someone as good if they keep the eight worldly motivations and desire for fame hidden, and are superficially soft spoken and well mannered, but have a coarse intention, like the popular saying, "smooth outside and coarse inside like the donkey's dung". The more you are an expert at this superficiality, the more "good" you are regarded.

Even though, according to the scriptures, a noble person is one disciplined in speech and body without any hypocrisy and conceit, today the more hypocritical and conceited you are, and the more desire for the eight worldly concerns and fame you have, you are regarded as nobler.

A learned person is required to be an expert in accomplishing virtuous deeds and discarding non-virtuous deeds, according to Buddhist tenets. But today our speech and practice are contrary, and we believe those with oratory skills are learned and do not check the person's practice.

Milarepa said, "The Victorious jewel of mankind in the past, gave teachings to subjugate the eight worldly motivations. Haven't the practitioners of today become more concerned about the eight worldly motivations?" I believe he was speaking about people like me who lack the qualities of being learned, noble and good. So, loudly praising an unholy being for possessing the qualities of a realized being is not only meaningless but also dangerous, because it might be the cause of damaging oneself and others in this and the next life.

Pretending to be qualified even when you don't possess any qualities is like an ugly person wearing a beautiful mask in order to deceive others. For the time being, you may get showers of black *Kor* in the form of offerings from uninformed persons, and because of this your life will be wasted by the demon of distraction. You may feel that you can lead your life with superficially good manners, but in reality you waste your life running after wealth, leaving no time for spiritual practice. Wasting your entire life in this way, without finding the antidote for consuming black *Kor*, is really the key to the gate for rebirth in the three lower realms after death, and especially the realm of hungry ghosts.

You can learn this if you read the chronicles of Buddha's life and spiritual instructions. It is said that a single insect being eaten by hundreds of other insects is the reincarnation of an unqualified spiritual practitioner who lived off *Kor*. It is very difficult when you have to repay the debt of *Kor* with your own flesh and blood. It is said that some reincarnations are born inside rocks and remain there to suffer for millions of years. People who break rocks and boulders while constructing roads have seen such beings. I have not seen such beings, but I have seen fossils.

> So whoever lacks the three qualities
> Cannot be counted among the sublime gurus –
> "You are a bad person, have a bad temper, and are from a bad family."
> Thus, on and on, the mountain of abuse crashed down upon me
> And I gathered the bad karma of having rejected true Dharma.

The realized beings who do not have desire for fame, pretentious behaviour, selfishness or deceit in their mind-stream lack oratory skills, cunningness, and the skill of the eight worldly motivations to meet selfish ends – the requisite conditions for deceiving others. The thoughts and actions of such realized beings are different from our attitude of passionate attachment, and so we criticize them as crazy, foolish, hypocritical and fraudulent, and ostracize them. A liberal few might say, "He might be a realized being, but he is from a bad family and has a bad nature." Some say, "He may be a good spiritual practitioner, but lacks the worldly skills to achieve anything." We heap abuse and show disdain. The little merit one has is destroyed, leading to rebirth in hell in the next life.

Showing respect and faith in the inner qualities of the realized beings could have benefitted beings like us, but our thoughtless speech and actions obstruct the avenue of their activities, and the collective meritorious karma of beings is defiled. Like a dog finding meat, we run after the selfish and deceitful with pretentious religiosity, without any investigation. So, such superficial beings gain fame and followers. I thought this could be an indication of the time that Guru Rinpoche prophesied, but my gurus later advised me, on many occasions, that such thoughts should be used to check whether I have acquired any sublime qualities to improve myself, rather than expose others' faults. My mother too, used to give me the same advice. So I make an effort to control my mind and not utter words critical of others. Buddha has said that only an enlightened being like him, and not ignorant ordinary beings like us, can judge another being. So I remind myself of these words and their meaning to improve my mind.

> As the glorious Great Guru said:
> "The times do not change, people change."
> It is very sad that this is coming true.
> It is very sad that the power of evil forces is increasing.

As I reflect on our actions and behaviour, I feel that Guru Padmasambhava's prophesies on the impending future are coming true. I don't remember the whole stanza, but in one prophesy he had said, "The time when the genuine will fail, but the fake will succeed." For example, today people who follow the right procedures face a lot of problems in getting a passport or a visa, or at banks and hotels, or even while boarding an aircraft; while those who adopt the crooked path face no such problems. While no one checks or stops the consignment and transportation of a huge cache of weapons that destroy hotels, schools, hospitals and office buildings; innocent guests are stopped at the hotel gate and frisked or questioned. Similarly at some airports, money is extorted and baggage checked on the pretext of security checks, while real terrorists successfully enter and exit without any problem.

An acquaintance of mine, for example, had all the requisite documents and had no intention of staying in the United States for more than a month, and yet he was not given a visa. Another person who applied for a visa at the same time with a fake passport and invitation letters was given a visa for ten years.

Buddhism generally gives prominence to karma, and if you consider these things from a more profound view of karma, it may be the nature of things. But at that moment you are shocked and feel uncomfortable. We talk about truth and yet today we don't see truth prevailing and this makes us sad. If you don't think about all these things, then you feel cheerful and happy like the saying, "Leaving things unexamined and unanalysed keeps you cheerful." If you have some money then everything seems to work out, for the time being.

At the hotel, for example, the staff greets you and asks which services you need. If you analyse this, you know that such a show of respect is not in recognition of the inner qualities of the guest, but an artificial show of respect, more of a dramatic performance, based on the external appearance of the person -- such as being the guest of a five-star hotel, surrounded by a host of people. So unless we urgently find some way to improve the mind of the people, the situation will deteriorate and this world will become like a ghost town, where there will be no true love or genuine intention to help one another. The few that have genuine love and good intention will be disrespected, derided and abused. Divine and positive forces will diminish and the dark evil forces will become stronger. Civil manners will degenerate, mutual trust will be lost. No one will listen to good advice, and incurable diseases will break out.

Spiritual practitioners will not hesitate to accumulate non-virtue by misusing religion, and will damage the mind-streams of everyone. Lay people will not hesitate to kill goats, sheep, chicken, fish and small insects, and even their parents and brethren if necessary, for personal gain. Trees and forests will be cut and razed, air and water will be polluted, harming millions and millions of humans and other beings. Like live demons, we will be harming all the beings. Without considering what I have said or not said here, you can check yourself and you will understand a few things.

What is an impious action of our body and speech? All spiritual and worldly views agree that anything harmful is an impious or negative action. If you investigate the causal conditions of impious actions you will find that it is our mind. To become a good person you need good intentions or a kind heart. If you have bad intentions you cannot become a good person. With selfishness in your mind, you cannot become genuinely kind-hearted. So, if we make selfish motivation our life-long ambition, then the world will degenerate.

Instead of only being selfish in the short period we are alive in this world, we must pledge to do whatever we can for the well-being of the other sentient beings in this world, and not to harm them, even if we are unable to do anything beneficial. We should have no wish to do harm to others. In this way we can expect real happiness in this world. Otherwise if all spiritual followers and lay people remain self-centred and keep deceiving others, as we do today, then the collective mind-stream will degenerate and the situation of the world will worsen.

Perhaps this is what Guru Rinpoche meant when he said, "The times do not change, people change." As people degenerate, it appears as if the times have degenerated. It can be scientifically understood that if people don't degenerate, then the times will not degenerate. Scientists don't have anything special to say about changing times. Nothing but human beings can bring progress.

The happiness and sorrow of a nation, community or even a small family can be defined from the point of progress of the mind. Although we think happiness and suffering depend on wealth, the genuine mental happiness has to come from contentment with your prosperity. Or it should be achieved on the foundation of a kind heart, aided by wealth. But unfortunately, we are never content and happy with our wealth, fame or youthful body.

When we use the expression, "This family's joy and sorrow is good," we mean it is well-to-do. We think in terms of sufficient wealth and never think about the happy or sorrowful state of the mind. The state of the mind, in fact, has not improved. Instead, there is more anger and envy, and that keeps you busy day and night, leaving no time for spiritual practice or benevolence. This even leads to marital discord, increased lies and deception, and loss of mutual trust. I believe it is the lack of a foundation of goodness that makes you the slave of wealth, and therefore face suffering.

So "goodness" is a valuable quality that we all need. For someone in the form of a spiritual practitioner like me, this quality is indispensable and if you have it, then that will suffice. Since the quality of goodness is based on good intention or a kind heart, there is no bigger disgrace than a wicked spiritual follower. All religions, Buddhist and non-Buddhist alike, agree on this.

The instructions of the Buddha-like spiritual teachers of the past advise us to be kind-hearted, and stress that with a wicked mind, you will not achieve your own purpose, not to mention the welfare of others. I have gained confidence in this advice from personal experience, although it is not always easy to practise as one wishes. From a young age, I had some notion that the root of all this is the desire for fame. Later, my wish-fulfilling jewel-like gurus pointed this out to me, and especially after my kind guru, the late Ontrul Rinpoche, pointed out faults on many occasions and guided me purposely, I was determined not to commercialize Dharma for selfish gain.

> So I pray that I will not be praised and honoured with the
> Poisonous virtues of being falsely learned, authentic and good.
> For this praise and honour is the cause of being dragged into
> Samsara.

As I said earlier, if you get honour and all these things as a result of merit accumulated in your past life, without making any effort, and if you can remain indifferent without being attached to them, then they become an adornment. Otherwise it is clear that this hankering after worldly objects will bring forth all the other afflictions, such as attachment and aversion. So this wish to seek honour with a selfish motivation is the "wicked or impious mind".

After every virtuous deed I perform, I pray from the depth of my heart that I do not have any such impious thoughts, or that even if such thoughts do arise, I do not carry them out pretending to be learned and noble in order to deceive others. In my life I do not have much to pray for, and so this is my main prayer. Along with this prayer, I check myself frequently to replenish qualities, purify defilements, and if I am unable to purify – I confess.

> They cause pride to increase
> And disturb the development of true qualities.
> Without recognizing the smell of my own rotting head
> Yet pretending to help someone else
> Both of us are doomed.
> This is how I have gathered terrible karma.

You might wonder why so much importance is given to this. If you care for yourself and hope to benefit other beings in some way, you have to give it importance. Because hankering after this meaningless honour gives growth to unwanted pride, and completely destroys the opportunity to develop true qualities. As it is said, "The peak of pride will not hold the water of true quality." Pride boosts your ego and destroys whatever few qualities you have, and blocks any chance of developing new qualities. Like not recognizing the smell of your own rotting head: advising others; pretending to be a spiritual practitioner; giving refuge to others; gathering followers and collecting offerings, without realizing that selfishness has rotted your mind-stream, can drag yourself and those who have faith in you down to hell. It is the same with leaders: it is difficult to lead others without a kind heart. So, like building a dam before a flood, constantly checking yourself is helpful in making you less egoistic and arrogant.

In the absence of pride, sensuous pleasure does not become a fault but instead becomes a cause for helping others spiritually and mundanely. As the texts say, "Manifesting sensual objects as an enhancement is the characteristic of a yogi." But don't you see that having a little wealth and respect, or even wearing a good hat or a good pair of shoes, makes us feel proud? We should pay attention and be careful, because if we remain careless then our character degenerates and we risk causing suffering to other beings, and ultimately we have no chance of getting out of hell. My root guru, Lopon Gangri Kunsang Dorje used to often tell me this during our conversations.

My guru said that once, when he was in retreat, an old butcher living nearby who was devoted to him came to see him and Rinpoche asked the butcher about his background. He said he had been a monk when he was young and had studied and contemplated well enough to earn himself a name. But driven by the "evil son of god", he degenerated day by day until he met a female butcher and became a butcher himself.

Then Rinpoche wept, saying, "It is such a pity that he failed to use the spiritual education he received at the monastery to improve his mind, and had to live by taking lives in his old age." He further said, "One can live comfortably off the *Kor* of the monk community and especially the *Kor* of a qualified spiritual teacher, but it is difficult to digest without the support of authentic spiritual practice. Though many conditions are needed for authentic spiritual practice, the main thing is not to use the Dharma for selfish arrogance. Otherwise, Dharma will cause rebirth in the lower realms. As Gampopa said." When I reflect on the words of nectar that my kind gurus let fall during our conversations, I realize that they were words of advice for my benefit in this and the next life.

> There are many ways to gather poison *Kor*, but mainly two:
> Offerings from devotees and offerings for the deceased.
> When I received these, I laughed and enjoyed myself,
> But neglected my obligations both to the dead and to the devotees –
> And this is terribly sad.

If we spiritual practitioners maintain a nice external appearance, without any love and compassion in our minds for other beings, and instead think only of our own selfish desires, then there is no way of liberating oneself from suffering and non-virtue. This is because, pretending to be spiritually correct in order to deceive others, using offerings from devotees and for the deceased for your own comfort, without sincerely dedicating prayers for them, is like a business person living off his or her profit. This is the worst *Kor* of all the *Kor*. Since, by doing so you are giving up the guru, the Triple Gem and all the spiritual friends – this is the most terrible and shameful thing one can do. One's attitude and action deteriorates day by day until, unable to tame one's own mind, one becomes a demon in human form.

From conversations with my guru I learned that those who wish good for themselves, and especially those with little altruistic intention, must from the beginning, beware of *Kor* of the living and the dead. This is also clear from my own experience, as narrated earlier. It is my belief that, even if you don't have extensive knowledge, if you sincerely dedicate prayers, both before and after using the offerings, for the patron, and all beings with whom you have a connection, this will not only lessen the defilement from *Kor* but will also benefit others.

A person like me cannot fathom the profound activities of my Buddha-like gurus. But today, when I reflect on the activities which I saw of my late guru, Lopon Gangri Kunsang Dorje, and the words I heard from him while in front of him, I realize that they were teachings for liberation from samsara. For example, after having his meal, Rinpoche would close his eyes and recite mantras, sutras, confession and dedication prayers without missing a word.

When you consider that all the activities of the root gurus are meant to tame beings like us, it becomes clear that, however high our view and realization, we must not neglect the consequences of *Kor*, and dedicate prayers for other beings without selfishness. As Guru Rinpoche said, "Even though your realization is higher than the sky, karma is finer than flour."

> To block the development of the three kinds of wisdom;
> This is the worst, isn't it!
> To block the development of the three kinds of faith;
> This is the worst, isn't it!
> To block the development of the three kinds of contemplation;
> This is the worst, isn't it!

For a selfish person there is nothing worse than receiving *Kor*. As a number of superficially good activities are lined up, due to this offering of *Kor*, spiritual practices like listening, contemplation and meditation for the welfare of others – all suffer as a natural consequence. Even when you get some time for prayers, study or contemplation you don't feel like doing them, or the mind becomes dull and you fall asleep as soon as you attempt to practice. Or your mind becomes agitated and you don't feel like staying in and you want to go out. If you stubbornly stay at home, your inanimate body stays still, but your monkey-like consciousness sees your handsome friends, entertainments, such as dancing and music, public adulation and the wealth of others, and does not stay within your body.

At the time of learning the scriptures you become more interested in learning art, astrology and other sciences, and while studying art, astrology and other sciences, your intellect becomes dull and you can't learn anything. Then you feel that all this study is useless and it is better to meditate. You lose interest in conventional education and try to meditate, to contemplate the nature of the mind. Due to the influence of aversion you look at the activities of the spiritual teachers with the wrong view, you feel disgusted with the way of the tormented beings, and looking at your spiritual friends, you feel jealous. A mirage of thoughts blocks the path of your practice. If you reflect on this, there is much to understand. If you see a series of faults, rather than qualities, when you try to develop faith by appreciating the qualities of realized beings; or when you feel anger or no sense of compassion when you try to cultivate compassion for all sentient beings; then you can be certain that the defilement of *Kor* is actively at work. For many years I experienced great difficulty, not being able to complete any virtuous activity, like swimming in muddy water.

> I cannot explain it all, but
> In short, *Kor* is the real enemy and demon of practitioners.
> It will not give a moment's peace.
> It will torment the body with strange diseases,
> Ruining chances of practice.
> Yet when not practicing, the body and mind are fine,
> Being quite healthy while doing unwholesome things.

If a spiritual practitioner engages in altruistic activity, with compassion as a witness and uncontaminated by selfish motivation, then with each day of practice he or she becomes happier and more eager to learn, reflect and meditate, or do other virtuous deeds for the welfare of others. You become healthier physically and have no problem in accomplishing the welfare of oneself and others in this and the next life.

But these days, spiritual practitioners lose interest in spiritual practice and sometimes feel like crying for no reason. We have no peace of mind and get angry at everything and everyone, even becoming suicidal. Thoughts that come to mind which are against the Dharma, such as denouncing the spiritual teacher and the doctrine, are due to the defilement caused by living off the guru's *Kor*, the community *Kor* and the *Kor* of performing rituals.

ENFOLDED EQUALLY BY QUALITIES AND FAULTS

When you go through the biography of past masters, like Naropa, Marpa, Milarepa, Gampopa, Tsangpa Gyare and his spiritual sons, or Gyalwa Longchen Rabjam or Je Tsongkhapa and his spiritual sons, you don't find any account of them receiving the guru's *Kor* or living off community *Kor*, or visiting homes to perform rituals, or treating the Dharma as a commodity. As a result, they were able to realize the nature of truth within one lifetime, to cut off all the shackles and to soar into the space of enlightenment like a vulture. We remain in samsara, enfolded by obscurations. The good are enfolded by their goodness, the learned are enfolded by their knowledge, the ignorant are enfolded by their ignorance, and the noble ones are enfolded by their nobleness. Everything becomes a veil and a shackle that we are unable to break.

WITHOUT A KIND HEART YOUR HEALTH SUFFERS

It is difficult to make one's body and speech positively buoyant without a positive working mind. So, unconsciously, we commit numerous negative acts of body and speech. Your body is tormented by unknown diseases and, especially during spiritual practice you suffer from what is called "harm by the king spirit". In reality, the wind of attachment and aversion, aided by defilement of *Kor*, pushes the basic inherent ignorance into the heart channel, leading to stiffness and pain in the upper part of the body and deprivation of sleep. Thus you are not able to do spiritual practice. Similarly, when the fire of desire burns, the heat, aided by the powerful defilement of *Kor*, causes blood pressure and diseases of bile. The dark element of ignorance is manifest in all beings at all times, like water and moisture, conspicuously or inconspicuously.

When the potency of ignorance is combined with basic selfish motives, such as desire and the defilement of *Kor*, it becomes the cause of many unidentifiable diseases we see today and proves an obstruction to spiritual practice. Maintaining the balance of the three elements is important. When the elements are in balance, you become healthy and happy and you are able to do virtuous deeds. How does one know this? When you don't do spiritual practice or engage in non-spiritual activities, or activities that are against the doctrine, you don't feel sick, your mind is not agitated and you don't feel sleepy. Your mood becomes cheerful. If you have to stay up late to read or write, learn, reflect or meditate, you will hardly be able to stay awake. On the other hand, if you are engaged in non-spiritual activities or activities that are against the Dharma, such as gossiping, drinking or singing and dancing, you will not know how the night passed.

When I was young, in every village that I visited, the local people, young and old, used to sing and dance in celebration and I would happily accept their invitation to the entertainment and watched the show, however late it went on. Before the end of the performances I would give them some money to thank them for their performances, and they would continue the performance for another couple of hours. When the show ended I would wish it had continued for some more time.

On the other hand, when we had to perform expiatory rituals and prayers at night, sometimes I would fall asleep at the generation stage, and even though these sessions would last for just a couple of hours, I would feel the prayer session was too long and dreaded it. Judging from experience I understand that all this was the result of defilement of *Kor*.

Then there are some people who can play dice at night in a poor light but find it difficult to read the texts in daylight. These are all the results of the same cause. Whenever we try to do what is good for us it doesn't seem to succeed. We don't like to eat what is healthy but have a natural liking for unhealthy food. Except for some fortunate people, most of us either don't have the time or the willingness to exercise, swim or go for walk in the mornings and evenings.

Recently I had some health issues and went to consult my doctor. She said, "This is due to lack of exercise such as swimming. About eighteen years ago I advised you to do physical exercise and until now you have not done any exercise." I really felt it was lamentable that I was not able to take steps to keep myself healthy and fit. This is why many people die before their time, or suffer from various ailments. I think most of what we are keen on doing in this world is harmful to us.

> And not caring about the next life:
> So whether one receives poison *Kor* oneself,
> Or "benefits" from the poison *Kor* of someone else –
> Teachers say it is the same thing.

As our attitude and behaviour worsens, we are bound to be unhappy and suffer from ill health. My root guru, Vajradhara Lopon Gangri Kunsang Dorje, explained to me that the contaminating effect of black *Kor* is the same, regardless of whether it is acquired by yourself, by treating Dharma as a commodity, or by benefitting from the *Kor* collected by someone else, and it is similar to Halahala poison, which destroys your present life and the next life. After receiving complete teachings from him, I made a symbolic offering of a mandala and he looked at the offering and said, "Taking *Kor* from the Lord of Buddhist doctrines and a member of the Sangha – the foundation of Dharma – such as yourself, would not only be too heavy for a pauper like me, but I will also face defilements from all three at the same time. So I will not accept this offering."

After the teachings I requested him to stay for a few more days but, out of kindness, he agreed to stay for just one day and said, "A dead body like me cannot be of any service to the Dharma and beings like you. But the little practice I do, such as reciting mantras will be obstructed by distraction. I ate the food of *Kor* of Buddha-like guru, sat on the cushion of *Kor* and had a good time for the last few days. But this is temporary, the future consequences are serious and not good. So I will take your leave."

I asked him, "If there is *Kor* then it is the *Kor* of my possessions. Why should you bother so much?" He replied, "The saying is: 'The *Kor* heaped on *Kor* is the guru's *Kor*; the shit heaped on shit is dog's shit', and this means that it is difficult to digest the *Kor* of what you receive from a qualified spiritual master, who selflessly takes care of the Sangha community," and then he told me a lot of anecdotes related to *Kor*. Although it is not possible that someone like him, who has attained the state of Buddhahood, would be affected by the defilement of *Kor,* he was advising his students like me, to be mindful.

> So *Kor* heaped on top of *Kor*,
> A guru's *Kor* is multiplied over and over,
> Until even dogs start "honouring" you.

Reflecting on my guru's words of advice, along with examples and my own experiences, I later realized that my past lifestyle was wrong and I was filled with regret.

IDENTIFYING *KOR*

All material wealth and pleasure is not included in *Kor*. As explained above: money, clothes, houses, cars, *etc.*, offered to gurus and spiritual practitioners are black *Kor* because 90 per cent of the offerings to gurus and spiritual practitioners are made with the expectation of happiness, success, good health and long life. It is difficult to say whether all the gurus and spiritual practitioners can fulfill the wishes of those making the offerings; about 90 per cent cannot fulfill those wishes. Even if the wishes are fulfilled, the materials offered become the cause of ill health, mental disturbance and inauspicious incidents for the present and the future. Hence it is called black *Kor*.

Two ways were explained to me on how to have only white *Kor* and prevent black *Kor*. The first is that the person offering should make the offering with an altruistic mind, without expecting anything in return. The second is to fulfill all the wishes of the person making the offering, and not waste a single penny of the offering, "making the Gods believe and the ghosts give up hope", as the saying goes. But it is difficult that such a thing could happen those days, as it was in the past.

For example, Je Ngawang Chogyal (1465-1540), the brother of Drukpa Kunleg, was giving teachings to a crowd of people, and he had hung his religious robe on the rays of the sun. Drukpa Kunleg arrived there and, pretending to compete with Je, with his own magical powers, he hung his bow, arrow and everything he was carrying on the rays of the sun. The sun rays which Je Ngawang Chogyal had used was slightly bent, while the sun rays used by Drukpa Kunleg stayed straight. The gathering of disciples asked Je the reason for this and he replied that there was no difference between them in the level of view and realization, and said, "Since Drukpa Kunleg is a hidden yogi and not contaminated by *Kor*, his sun rays are straight. I have many disciples and because of *Kor* my sun rays are slightly bent."

Kor affects even Buddha-like gurus who have such high views and realization. When you use the material possessions of the guru, it becomes *Kor* on top of *Kor,* and the *Kor* of gurus and monks contain twice as many obscurations. I get extremely scared and stressed when I think of the karmic obscurations I might have to suffer, considering that I have been living off both the guru's *Kor* and the Sangha's *Kor* since I was a child.

You cannot help but be scared if you have to repay with your own blood and flesh, over many life times. We remain indifferent, deluded by distractions. This can be understood not only from the spiritual teacher's instructions but also from what you can see. Seeing one insect being attacked and eaten by hundreds of other insects, my guru used to say, with sadness, that most of such insects might be the rebirth of mediocre gurus. So when I come across people who are not scared of *Kor* I think they are either a supreme being, with the confidence of not being affected by defilement, or an extremely evil person who deceives everyone, with total disregard for karma. Apart from these two there cannot be a third category for a qualified spiritual practitioner.

If I really think hard about the meaning
Of this poison *Kor*, then I am doing
Neither real Dharma practice nor worldly work.
I am in between, wearing Dharma robes
Which cover this body of mine infested with poison *Kor*:
I am like a pretend lion, having no essential qualities.

A TSA MA!
O dear, this really upsets me!

THE BEST WAY OF LIVING

Out of the many ways of living in this world, the best is to use one's body, speech and knowledge and to work hard to earn your livelihood. There is *Kor* involved here but since you are earning through physical work, the *Kor* is considered clean.

Take the example of those who use their physical strength to pull rickshaws, or taxi drivers who work day and night to transport passengers. It is a difficult job and yet, from the karmic point of view, it is the best way of life. Living a comfortable life with wealth acquired by exploiting others, or through extortion, and even the wealth gained as inheritance are all burdens of debt. Depending on wealth not earned by oneself may give you a comfortable life for the time being, but in the long run it is a big problem. Therefore, earning your livelihood through sheer hard work, without causing any harm to other beings, is the best way of living. So it is important to check our actions constantly.

THE LIFESTYLE OF A SPIRITUAL PRACTITIONER

Those of us in the garb of spiritual practitioners should always perform virtuous deeds, learn, reflect and meditate with diligence, without breaking the words of the spiritual teacher; as Naropa did with Tilopa or Milarepa did with Marpa. Even if we are unable to do as they did, if we spend our life cultivating loving kindness, compassion and Bodhicitta, with a firm faith of equating the guru with Buddha, then this would be the proper lifestyle of a spiritual practitioner. In brief, both the lay person and the spiritual practitioner have to earn their livelihood through hard work. Some of us think that as a spiritual practitioner, it will suffice to live off the guru's *Kor* and the *Kor* of the Sangha, without any spiritual or mundane effort. This is wrong.

KOR AWAKENS PAST NEGATIVE KARMA

Having lived off the guru's *Kor* and the *Kor* of the Sangha for many years, doing a little bit of meditation but failing to make my mindstream spiritual, I now think that those in the form of spiritual practitioners, such as me, are going to face a lot of problems. Though

I did not possess much knowledge when I was young, I remember having a genuine impartial sense of compassion and faith in the deities, the guru and in life after death.

When I was about eight or nine years old, on many occasions, out of devotion and the thought of renunciation, I had tears in my eyes while saying supplication prayers to past masters, or the prayer of Calling the Guru from Afar, or the confession of non-virtue. Later, such feelings disappeared like a rainbow. I felt sad looking at myself. One may say it is karma, but I think that only a serious negative condition like black *Kor* can awaken such karma.

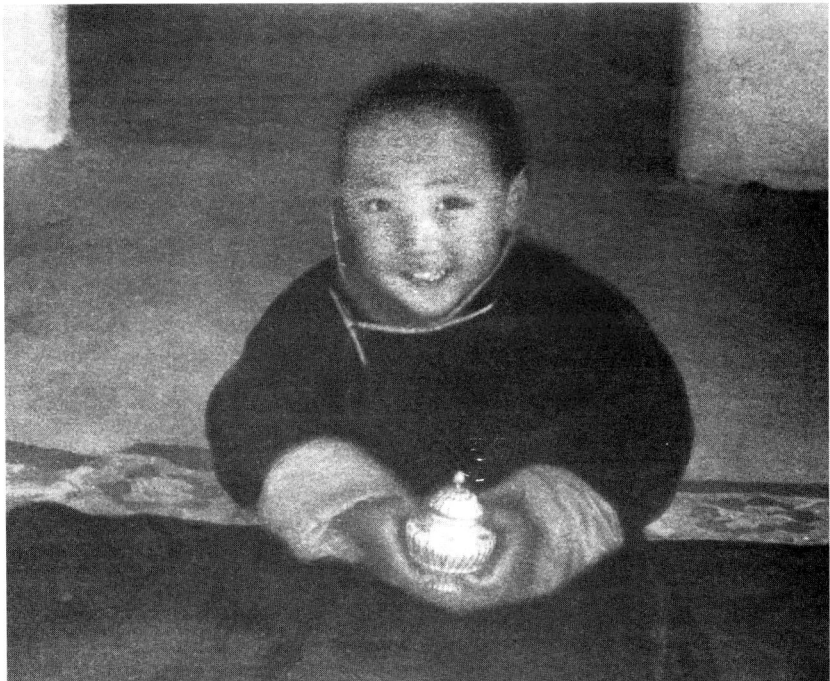

Above & Below: At the age of two before being recognized as a reincarnate (Dalhousie, 1965).

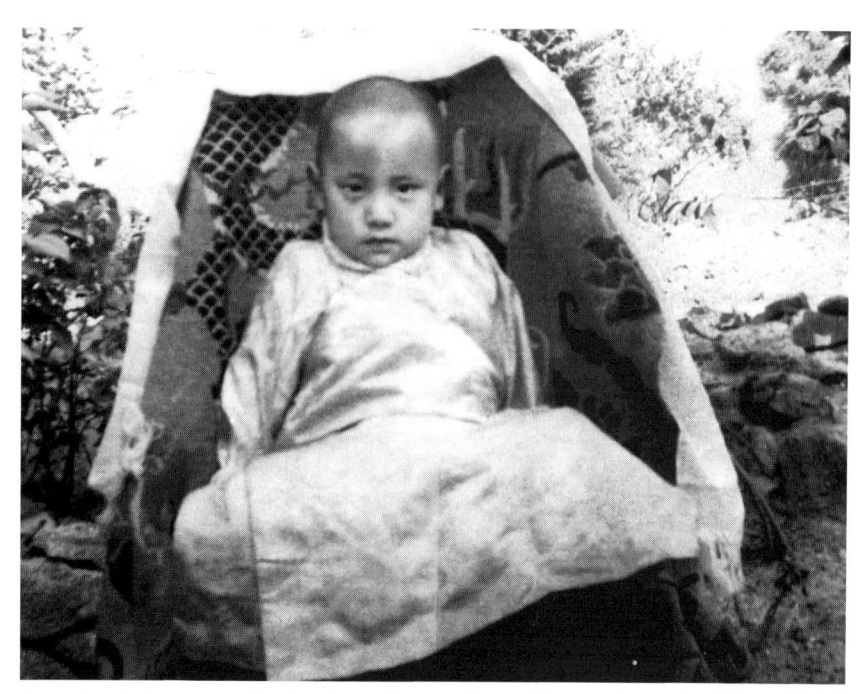

Just after being recognized as the reincarnation of the Gyalwang Drukpa (Dalhousie, 1966).

Four years old, with my father, Zhichen Bairo Rinpoche, in Darjeeling, after recognition and just before enthronement (1967).

Above & Below: After enthronement in Darjeeling (1967).

With (from left) Soktse Rinpoche, Akhu Woesel, Dorzong Rinpoche, and being carried by Akhu Lodo (right), while waiting for an audience with His Holiness the Dalai Lama, shortly after being recognized (Dharamsala, 1966).

Name-giving by His Holiness the Dalai Lama (Dharamsala, 1966).

At the age of four (1967).

At the age of five (Darjeeling).  At the age of six, with the First Drukpa Thuksey Rinpoche (Darjeeling).

At the age of seven.

At Druk Sangag Choling Monastery in Darjeeling with other reincarnate masters and abbots.

Aged eight, with my cousin Lodo Gyatso, my mother and pet dog Tashi.

At the age of twelve.

First visit to Ladakh in 1974.

In Ladakh at the age of twelve with Drukpa Thuksey Rinpoche.

At the age of thirteen.

With Drukpa Thuksey Rinpoche in Ladakh (1975).

With His Holiness the Dalai Lama (centre) and His Holiness the 16th Karmapa (left) in Darjeeling (1975).

With His Holiness Sakya Trizin (centre) and Drukpa Thuksey Rinpoche (right) at the age of thirteen.

With Drukpa Thuksey Rinpoche (left) and the 8th Gyalwa Dokhampa Dongyu Nyima (right) (1979).

With (from left) Sey Rinpoche, the 8th Kyabgon Drukpa Yongdzin Rinpoche and the 5th Sengdrak Rinpoche (right).

A painting based on a photo with His Holiness the Dalai Lama (left) and then West Bengal Chief Minister Siddharth Shankar Roy (right) (1975).

At the age of twenty-one, with His Holiness the Dalai Lama (centre) and my father, Zhichen Bairo Rinpoche (left).

Receiving empowerment from Pawo Rinpoche in Kathmandu, Nepal (1987).

Meeting my guru Zhichen Ontrul Rinpoche in New Delhi (1992).

With Trulshik Rinpoche (left) at Thupten Choling Monastery in Solokhumbu, Nepal (1993).

Receiving important empowerment of a precious *terma* from Trulshik Rinpoche at Thupten Choling Monastery in Solokhumbu, Nepal (1993).

A light moment with Trulshik Rinpoche in Kathmandu, Nepal (1993).

With Do Drubchen Rinpoche.

With my uncle Kathok Moktsa Rinpoche (left) and my father Zhichen Bairo Rinpoche (right) in Darjeeling.

Soktse Rinpoche, one of the oldest living disciples of His Holiness Dudjom Rinpoche and the only surviving disciple of the 8th Drukpa Yongdzin Rinpoche Togden Pagsam Wangpo.

His Holiness Dudjom Rinpoche.

Lopon Gangri Kunsang Dorje.

Gen Khyentse Gyatso, the great yogi.

Khenchen Noryang.

In two different retreats, at a monastery in Maratika, Khotang district, Nepal.

With my cousin Lodo Gyatso who was sending me to Maratika in Nepal for my retreat (1992).

Going to Maratika in Nepal for a six-month solitary retreat before granting the second public audience on "Six Ornaments of Naropa" (1992).

My parents and one of their attendants sending me off for the six-month solitary retreat in a cave in Maratika (1992).

Donning the Six Ornaments of Naropa in Ladakh (1992).

Relaxing in Ladakh.

With His Holiness Drikung Chetsang Rinpoche (left) and His Holiness Drikung Chungtsang Rinpoche (centre).

With His Holiness Taktsang Rinpoche (left) in Ladakh (1987).

A pilgrimage to Mount Kailash with my father Zhichen Bairo Rinpoche (1999).

With the present reincarnation of Drukpa Thuksey Rinpoche (left) and Gyalwa Dokhampa (right).

Receiving the United Nations Millennium Development Goals (MDG) Honour in New York (2010).

Named "Guardian of the Himalayas" and the "Founder of Himalayan Glacier Waterkeeper" by Waterkeeper Alliance, an NGO founded by Robert Kennedy Jr. (right).

With the Honourable President of India, Pranab Mukherjee, at Rashtrapati Bhavan (Presidential Residence), after the successful completion of the 7th Drukpa Eco Pad Yatra (2014).

With Auxiliary Bishop Dr Hans-Jochen Jaschke of Hamburg, Germany (September 2014).

With the present reincarnation of Drukpa Thuksey Rinpoche (left), at the historic release of a commemorative stamp on the Drukpa Lineage by Department of Posts, Ministry of Communication and IT, Government of India, as a part of Buddha Purnima celebrations in New Delhi (14 May 2014).

Receiving a recognition from the Legislative Assembly of Mexico (July 2014).

With the former President of Sri Lanka, Mahinda Rajapaksa, who joined the 6th Drukpa Eco Pad Yatra in Sri Lanka in the beginning and at the conclusion, sending more than 200 volunteers (March 2013).

Breaking two Guinness World Records for "Most Trees Planted" in Ladakh, as part of the Million-Tree Planting Initiative (October 2012).

At a reception hosted by His Excellency Nguyen Xuan Phuc, the current Prime Minister of Vietnam, in Hanoi (April 2014).

On the 3rd Eco Pad Yatra in the summer of 2009, passing the majestic Gongpo Rangjung, a sacred mountain in Zanskar, Ladakh, with 700 pilgrims.

Teaching on Shantideva's *A Guide to the Bodhisattva Way of Life* during the 7th Eco Pad Yatra in Uttar Pradesh and Bihar (November 2014).

Chief Minister of Uttar Pradesh, Akhilesh Yadav (right), joined in the 3rd Eco Cycle Yatra (November 2015).

Cycling from Kathmandu to Ladakh and covering 2500 km, with 250 of our Kung Fu nuns in support of eco-friendly way of living and gender equality (August 2016).

Blessing a child with visual impairment during the 3rd Eco Pad Yatra in Ladakh (summer 2009).

Helping out at the 6th Live to Love Eye Camp in Kathmandu, Nepal (March 2013).

CHAPTER 12

❖

Remember the Guru's Kindness

I have some idea how to avoid this poison *Kor*,
Which I have discovered through my precious Lord Guru's kindness.
This kind teacher is truly a Buddha,
His supreme qualities of the three secret aspects [of body, speech and mind]
I, his fortunate student, can remember,
And with great respect I can follow his way.

REMEMBERING THE QUALITIES OF MY GURU AND CONFESSING MY FAULTS

The kindness of my root gurus in general, and especially the immeasurable kindness of the ascetic Lopon Gangri Kunsang Dorje, the master of the ultimate teaching, gave me the opportunity to remain under the shade of their teachings and to open my eyes afresh to acceptance and rejection, I found a new determination not to be defiled by this black *Kor*. One can learn from the instructions of the Buddha-like gurus, the Sutras and the Tantras, that the only root cause of this black *Kor* is the poison of selfishness. Whilst replenishing the altruistic mind, I practised mind-training to purify the evil mind of selfishness, along with Guru Yoga and confession, keeping in mind the qualities of body, speech, mind and activities of Lopon Gangri Kunsang Dorje, although it was beyond my deluded mind to fully understand his profound qualities.

The quality of the defilement of non-virtue is that it can be purified, and authentic confession of non-virtue is a practical and transparent practice. Other people do not give much importance to confession of non-virtuous defilement and, instead, show diligence in reciting, chanting and practising deities. In a way, if you have the right attitude, all reciting and chanting can be and will be the antidote for non-virtuous defilement. So there is nothing wrong with it. But, according to the texts, lacking repentance for all negative things done in the past and lacking the vow not to do negative things in the future – simple recitation and chanting will not yield much result. Some of these people may be realized beings with the confidence of not needing purification of defilements. Otherwise, the teachings of Buddha say that the practice of compassion and the perfection of wisdom and emptiness should be practised on the foundation of the accumulation of merit and the purification of defilements.

So if we are able to do genuine spiritual practice, every practice, starting with refuge, can be a purification practice. For example, take meditating on the view of Mahamudra, Dzogchen or emptiness: a practitioner, who, after completing the accumulation and purification practices, and after receiving teachings from a Buddha-like teacher, is able to identify the view of emptiness by reflecting and meditating. Sustaining this identification of the view will shred samsara into tatters, and there is no better means of purifying defilement than this.

THE IMPORTANCE OF DILIGENT MIND TRAINING

Nowadays, most of us don't have the confidence of view, and many novices are keen to do meditation without doing any accumulation and purification practices. I think such meditation will not take you far. Then again, among senior disciples, some, after doing a bit of accumulation and purification, get attached to meditational deities and mainly recite their mantras and propitiate them. Reciting mantras and meditating on deities is not unique to Buddhists: even non-Buddhists meditate on gods and recite mantras.

Phenomena have two characteristics: visible phenomena and the state of intrinsic nature. The kind and skillful Buddha gave all his teachings based on the two truths – and that in itself is unique. The proper way to practice is to have an understanding of the two truths, and with this understanding the two minds of enlightenment should be generated, and both accumulation of merit and purification of defilement should be practised. Only then, can meditating on a deity correctly, according to the instructions of the Tantric texts, become a marvellous swift method to achieve progress on the path.

The texts say that chanting and propitiating, without knowing the correct method of meditating on a deity, will cause suffering and rebirth as attendants of the spirits in the next life. So it is your responsibility to make sure that your practice is correct and proper without meddling in others' affairs.

ALL FAULTS AND DOWNFALLS SHOUD BE DISCARDED AS POISON

Most people like me, who are in the form of spiritual practitioners, since time immemorial until now, and since birth until today, are not able to turn negative actions – such as taking life, stealing, sexual misconduct, lying and cheating, creating discord, craving for others' wealth, idle chatter, harmful thoughts, wrong views, acts of abandoning the Dharma such as denouncing the spiritual teachers and Bodhisattvas, using the Dharma and reliquaries as commodities, as well as the *Kor* from living off offerings made to the Sangha – all of which are causes of defilement – into conditions for purifying defilements. Seeing that very few are able to do this is scary. So it is important to hold the guru's instructions in your heart, reflect on karma, and practise purification of defilements immediately.

> Oh precious Lord Guru, I call on you
> To bestow your compassion!
> Please do not let me fall into the pit of poisonous *Kor*!
> May I be able to practise the Dharma like you!
> Grant me blessings to accomplish my Dharma practice!

Knowing that practising without understanding the proper way of practising, is like a parrot reciting mantras in imitation. I intend to train in the unimaginable qualities of body, speech, mind and activity of my root guru. With deep faith, I pray to him to regard me with kindness, and bless me so that I am able to meditate with diligence, according to his instructions, without being contaminated by the eight worldly motivations; to overcome all hardships, and not fall into the abyss of samsara, drunk with the poison of selfishness. As Atisha said, "To accomplish the sun and moon-like Bodhicitta, persevering for aeons would not be difficult." I practice according to my capability, with the prayer that I may be able to lead my life just like my gurus.

FOLLOWING THE GURU WITHOUT PROPER THOUGHT CAN BE RISKY

When people see the calm and chaste activities of a guru, they praise him or her as being different, touch their heads with his or her picture and display the photo on the altar, treating him or her like a precious golden statue. And yet, in the same house, they indulge in all sorts of misconduct, like eating meat or drinking alcohol, without any sense of fear. Most people remain indifferent to the altruistic activities of their root guru, and merely appreciate the unimaginable external and secret qualities of his body, speech and mind. Some people simply imitate the guru as if out of necessity, especially when the guru does something that suits their thinking. For example, if the guru has a consort, the disciple also becomes a lay man and imitates the guru's way of dressing, walking, sitting and even hair style, but they don't bother to pay attention to the guru's practice of loving kindness and compassion.

On the other hand, if the guru is an ordained Bhikshu with fine ethical conduct and yet is wealthy and famous out of necessity, then his disciples imitate the way he dresses, even matching the colour of his robes, and try to achieve wealth and fame like the guru, without paying attention to the guru's moral character and inner qualities. Such disciples waste their lives with superficial practice, trying to earn wealth and fame, which is like a fox attempting to leap like a tiger. So for ordinary beings like us, to imitate the realized beings, who have intentionally taken birth in this world to help beings through various activities, will not only be futile, but will become a cause for rebirth in hell.

ALL GOOD AND BAD CIRCUMSTANCES IN LIFE SHOULD ULTIMATELY BE FRIENDS

> I have been nourished by the kindness of my father Guru
> And many other teachers.
> I have found the wisdom eye to discern
> The difference between defects and qualities.
> This achievement I realized through the kindness of my teachers.

Since our birth in this world, we have had to rely on the direct or indirect guidance of a spiritual teacher, or any teacher, to learn to stand on our own two feet; to teach us the normal ethics; the pure altruistic disposition and the identity of the suchness of phenomena, to bring changes in our thought and to keep us on track. According to the chronicles, even the Buddha was depressed by the sight of birth, old age, sickness and death at the four gates of the city, and the sight of a renunciate monk inspired him to renounce the worldly life.

Similarly, a spiritual practitioner, or even someone without much interest in spirituality, may one day meet a spiritual teacher in human form, whose teachings may directly influence his or her mind towards spirituality; or some other incident may become your teacher. For example, illness, or being fed up with legal cases, or the death of a near and dear one, may make you turn towards spiritual practice. All such negative circumstances that make you renounce the world are messengers of the spiritual teachers. There can be both favourable and unfavourable circumstances in one's life, and it is important to see how one can adapt to these circumstances to improve one's mind.

The negative circumstances are the best circumstances for reshaping one's mind, and it is important to utilize them positively. Most of us simply wait for the teachings of the spiritual teacher, and don't bother about the use of good or bad circumstances. If we face good circumstances, we feel proud to have achieved something on our own, and if we are faced with bad circumstances then we get angry or sad, remain quiet or cry, and some even become suicidal, and never look at the circumstances as new opportunities, or teachings for mind-training.

THE ESSENCE OF BUDDHISM

The key content of the guru's teaching is to look at the joys and sorrows in life as teachers. The inability to make any changes to the mind, even after receiving many teachings and understanding many teachings, is the result of being dull and inattentive to the essence of the teachings. But if one sees external and inner changes, and good and bad circumstances, as the teacher, then there is no reason to let one's pride boost one's ego, or to look down on the weak and destitute, or have the desire to rob, bully or kill. This humble disciple, nurtured by the kindness of the late root Guru Lopon Gangri Kunsang Dorje, and many other teachers, was able to gain a new eye of wisdom to see my own faults, not to be arrogant about the few qualities that I may have, and not to envy the learned, but instead rejoice, seeing their conduct.

As Buddha said, "Just as the bee sucks the nectar from the flower without damaging its colour or fragrance and then flies away, so the sage passes through the town," I try to acquire their qualities with humility, and to remove my own faults. I have the faith of understanding in the kindness of my gurus, who gave me a new eye to see clearly the qualities and faults of the view, meditation, and conduct of Samsara and Nirvana, and especially the faults, defects, and the cause and effect arising from grasping at self.

I understood that seeing one's faults is the foundation on which all qualities grow. To improve one's mind-stream, the faults have to be cleared, but if one doesn't see the faults *as* faults, then it is difficult to do anything. Once you see your faults you make a diligent effort to clear them, by practicing merit accumulation and purification.

You rejoice and have pure vision, rather than envy, when you see the faultless and the learned. You feel compassion on seeing others with faults similar to your own, or even if you don't feel compassion, you don't look down on them or criticize them. Looking at them, you feel that they are also suffering beings, in the same boat as you are, and you wish to help them. In short, there is no doubt that your attitude and conduct will undergo a gradual change. There is no end to speaking about the flaws of not seeing one's own faults. Most of the shortcomings in our life are the result of not being able to see our own faults.

CHAPTER 13

Nirvana is Within Your Hands

However, regarding the path shown by the Buddha,
It is said: "Liberation depends totally on us."
So, accordingly, I understand that it is up to me
Whether I go for it or not.

PRACTICE OF THE THREE TYPES OF MORALITY

Realizing one's own faults is the foundation of all qualities, but it is not enough to learn this in the teaching arena or see it in one's mind-stream. As Buddha said, "I have shown you the path to liberation. Liberation depends totally on you." One has to practise moral conduct, the method of discarding faults and their causes, in your daily life. The moment the thought of misbehaving arises, one should consider that this thought is arising from the mind, which is under the influence of afflictions; that the mind itself is not independent, and that the afflictions arise from the delusion of ego-grasping. One should then know that by rooting out ego-grasping, the afflictions will become rootless and baseless. Even if one is not able to understand all this, the thought of misbehaving should be left alone, knowing that the thought is arising because the mind is being influenced by afflictions.

As one gets accustomed to moral conduct by abandoning immoral conduct – as the poison that causes physical and mental suffering – one should train in living up to the ethical standards of saving lives, generosity and honesty, *etc.*, as described in the Mahayana texts. In this way, gradually one will be able to develop genuine compassion for all beings that are visible to you; or that your mind can encompass all sentient beings as vast as space, cherishing them more than yourself; or at least treating them as your equal. This compassion will generate an immeasurable joy in working for the welfare of these beings.

This sense of joy will increase your mental power to work for the benefit of others, so much so, that you will only think of working for the purpose of helping others. Thus the foundation will be laid for "The morality of working for the welfare of other sentient beings". As a result of working for the welfare of other beings, all your own purposes will be achieved spontaneously. When the purpose of both yourself and others is thus achieved there is nothing more to strive for.

Maitreya Buddha said, "I pay homage to Bodhicitta, which blocks the road to the lower realms, shows the road to the higher realms, and leads to the path of the ageless and deathless state." By the kindness of my gurus, I understood that everything depends on the mind. As long as one is not able to watch and tame the mind, which is like a mad elephant, by every means and make it workable, simply listening to the teachings of the spiritual teachers without practising them, is not enough.

> Whoever does not take this path is no better than an ox.
> Whoever does take this path is the best among humans.
> I have the complete freedom to choose whatever I wish to do,
> This is an amazingly rare chance I have got.

Who has the conditions for improving the mind? Only we human beings have this condition, and because of this, the Buddha has often praised human birth. But the category known as "mere human form" does not have the necessary conditions. The characteristic of a human being is defined as "having the ability to speak and understand the meaning" and this category of "mere human form" does not meet this definition. They may possess the physical basis but lack the mental basis of a human. They have a strong attachment to "I" and "mine", and because of this attitude, they are bloated with selfishness and pride, and have no respect for the qualities of the spiritual teachers and friends, and have no wish to listen to their advice. If they listen, they don't understand the real meaning. They give importance to their own opinion and just follow that, and fail to practice mind-training. In this way, they cannot find faith in life after death, or karma, and thus shut the door to liberation. In fact, though they are in human form, they are not very different, if not worse than animals and other beings. Hence, they are known as beings, "mere human form". Some texts criticize such human beings as "bulls with upper teeth", meaning they are no better than cattle.

WHO IS THE WORST AMONG ALL BEINGS?

Looking at our way of thinking and behaviour I sometimes feel that we humans are the most daring and scary among all beings. Although all beings are selfish, there is no limit to our selfishness. The other fierce animals attack and eat the weaker animals only when they are hungry, and when their stomachs are full they don't harm others. They show ferocity when their life is endangered, or attack other animals to protect their young ones; they mostly attack in self-defence.

HUMANS ARE UNGRATEFUL AND GREEDY

We human beings kill animals when they become old; they give us milk, butter, cheese, carry our loads and plough our fields, and then we slaughter them in the autumn. But we exploit them when they are young; think of the unimaginable and unspeakable way we treat them and you will know what I mean. There is almost nothing that we don't want. Because of this selfishness we kill and eat everything and do anything to get what we want. Other animals don't behave in this way.

WHO IS MORE IGNORANT – HUMANS OR ANIMALS?

Normally we say animals are ignorant and humans are intelligent. However ignorant the animals may be, they know who is kind to them and who is not. They remain loyal to the person who is kind to them until death. If we humans cannot appreciate the kindness and affection of others, then our intelligence and smartness are of no use.

HUMANS WHO HARM THE INNOCENT AND FEEL PROUD

We humans hunt or kill other innocent and harmless animals, such as wild birds, wild animals, fish and sea animals, either for profit or as sport. I often feel that it is better not to be born as this kind of human being. Only human beings are capable of such evil and atrocity in this world.

REAL HUMAN INTELLIGENCE SHOULD UNDERSTAND KARMA

I feel I am fortunate in that after being born as a human being, the instructions of the spiritual teachers and the guidance of my parents and friends, gave me the freedom to decide whether I wanted to live without improving my intellect or not. Whether I wanted to improve my mind in order to make my ordinary human birth valuable, by sincerely training in altruistic activities with higher aspirations.

> The habit of noting others' faults is completely wrong
> And for many years I have had this terrible custom.
> For far too long I was plagued by this, the source of all wrong actions.

I was often advised on the importance of checking my own faults, and I followed this advice. After many years I was able to identify them one by one and made a sincere effort to discard these faults – although I was not always successful. This helped me become less proud of my material possessions, my name and my inner and outer attributes. It also helped me develop genuine devotion and respect for other learned spiritual teachers and my own root gurus.

FINDING FAULTS IN OTHERS

The ability to see my own faults was a kind of new freedom, like finding the key to enter a house. Just knowing the reason for doing, or not doing something, was like taking a heavy weight off my head. But being young, my mind was immature like a balloon, and for many years I did not realize that others' faults were a reflection of my own faults. Seeing others' faults made me unhappy and, although I don't remember saying any harsh or hurtful words directly, I remember criticizing them behind their back and accumulating negative karma by speech. Some say it is not good to criticize others behind their back, instead it is better to say things directly to their face. Well, they may be brave and be able to be up-front. I felt that I should criticize directly only if something seriously wrong was done, and so I never had the will for confrontation. Whether you criticize someone directly or behind their back, it is not good. If someone criticizes me, directly or indirectly, I feel angry and unhappy. So others might also feel the same way. Therefore, it is important not to make others unhappy by criticizing them, either directly or behind their back.

MY MOTHER'S PROFOUND ADVICE

> Until my kind mother showed me all the faults of others
> Are one's own faults: the more one has,
> The more one finds them in others –
> Like reflections in a mirror.
> So rejecting one's own faults is best.

With kindness and sincerity my mother said to me, "Finding fault in others is totally needless. Don't do it. It is said that the state of a Bodhisattva is like a fire-pit covered with dust and one should be very careful about this state. We cannot know in what form, guise, caste or birth a Bodhisattva may appear. It is hidden. You may not have the wrong view in your heart, and being young, you eagerly denigrate others, but the consequent suffering will make you cry."

Initially, I did not understand the importance of her advice. Later, on many occasions she told me anecdotes as examples and explained how denigrating others is the base of, and the door to, moral fallacy. One day, during a conversation, I said that the presidents and prime ministers were working for their own gain and fame, and not doing anything for the people. My mother replied, "However much we criticize them will not help them improve their conduct. No one will reward you for criticizing them. I don't think there is anyone who would not be happy to become the president or prime minister of a country, but you do not have the merit and good fortune to become one. To become the leader of millions of people, you must have an accumulation of merit. So criticizing a person with a huge accumulation of merit will diminish your merit. So it is better to keep quiet." Her advice made me think, and was helpful for my mind.

My mother rarely criticized others and always said that spiritual teachers and spiritual practitioners are different from others in that they never criticize anyone. Her fine example gradually made me see things in a correct perspective. The Buddha has said in the Sutras and in many teachings that denigrating a Bodhisattva is more heinous than killing all the beings in this world. When I read in the scriptures that Bodhisattvas can take any form, guise or manifestation, and can display any activity, beyond our comprehension, and that we should not underestimate and criticize others, I realized it was better to keep quiet.

ADVICE FROM MY GURU BAIRO RINPOCHE

Once, feeling distressed by the situation all around, I said to Bairo Rinpoche, "Whatever you look at – high or low, laymen or monks – it is disheartening," and he replied, "That means you are becoming like that." He said, "You must have heard the saying, 'It is not others' faults but your faults, like a reflection in the mirror.' When you get such feelings, it is a sign that you need to check your faults and work to improve your qualities. Otherwise there is the risk of wasting all the qualities within you." This made me conclude that finding fault in others was a serious fallacy that destroyed the seeds of merit and blocked the path of liberation. His advice was indeed greatly helpful.

As I said earlier, for many years, I analysed objectively the manner and way of thinking of the faultless learned spiritual teachers, my kind parents and impartial noble people, and made efforts to follow their example. Like the saying, "One is skilled in what one is accustomed to doing, like a cow-herder is skilled in using the sling," with every step I began to see an improvement in all that I had seen as faults in others in the past, and this made me realize that one's own attitude makes a big difference in how you look at things.

FAULT IN OTHERS IS BASED ON YOUR DELUSION AND HABIT

The condition of your eyes gives you different visions: the jaundiced eye gives a yellow tinge to everything; a difference in height in the left and right side shows two objects, and cataracts makes vision cloudy and darkish. Similarly, if your mind-stream is faulty, you see faults in everything, but as your mind improves, your vision also improves. If you reflect on this essential point then I think there is a lesson in everything we do, think, say and view in our day to day life.

Take the example of a fisherman. He will take a keen interest and pleasure in the method of fishing, fishing equipment and fishing skills. Whether they are a thief, butcher or an assassin, the person will remain interested and involved in their vision. Similarly, spiritual practitioners, politicians, scientists, engineers, doctors and astrologists, *etc.*, will speak highly about the subject they are skilled in, and show little interest in other fields of knowledge. Some even criticize other fields of knowledge. For example, men of religion criticize politicians and politicians criticize religion; religion criticizes science and science criticizes religion; doctors criticize astrology and astrologers criticize doctors.

Most spiritual practitioners criticize performing arts, or take little interest in them. However, all fields of science are knowledge and there is no reason to look at them as inferior. It is the characteristic of ordinary beings to look at what one is accustomed to as special and different. So, if you are able to use your intelligence and look at things from a different perspective, then it becomes clear that due to your faults you are not able to see the qualities of others, and the more faults you have, the more faults you see in others, and are eager to expose them.

As your own faults decrease, you begin to see the qualities of others and take more interest in them. Therefore, I don't like to mix with those who criticize others and I avoid them. For example, if you have a beautiful face, then you will see a beautiful face and not an ugly face in the mirror. If you have an ugly face with lots of shortcomings, then you see the same in the mirror. Taking this example – the moment the thought of exposing the fault of someone else arises, if you are able to think that the fault you see in others is a reflection of your own fault, you mind relaxes, and you will have the opportunity of developing qualities by seeing others' faults. For this reason, when you see faults in others, if you can abandon the thought of exposing them, then the qualities of wisdom, nobility and goodness, along with other spiritual and mundane qualities, will grow within you. My parents and spiritual teachers used to advise me thus.

CRITICIZING TOO MUCH EXPOSES YOU

> Fault finding is the cause of broken Samaya between Dharma friends.
> It creates terrible karma, resulting in the rejection of the Dharma.
> This and much similar advice I received from my mother.
> Her tender council was absorbed into my heart
> So that whenever I notice someone's faults,
> I have vowed not to mention them.

My kind teachers, and especially my mother, used to tell me, "If you keep criticizing others, then the wise lay men will think that you are criticizing others without realizing that you are full of faults, and ridicule you. So other than exposing yourself, finding faults in others is of no use. As Buddhists, and especially Vajrayana practitioners, we must guard against this habit. Your old mother doesn't know much, but Buddha has said that denigrating, not only other sects within Buddhism, but also other religions, is undesirable. Not only scholars, but even an old woman like me can understand that mutual criticism of followers of the same Buddha and the same spiritual teacher is a serious fallacy. Spiritual brothers and sisters are required to train in pure vision of one another. Criticizing them is tantamount to breaking the commitment (Samaya), and except for realized beings that criticize others for a special reason, one cannot hope for accomplishment after criticizing your spiritual brethren." She further said, "It is clearly mentioned in the longer version of the *Prayer of Sukhavati* that this is an act of abandoning the Dharma. I am giving you this advice hoping you will not be angry, because you love your mother dearly." I hold her kind advice in my heart and, though sometimes out of a bad habitual propensity I see faults in others, I have vowed not to speak about them.

This is my tale.
There are both good and bad stories,
And I should speak of them equally.
But I have far too many bad stories,
Some almost as bad as those of dogs and pigs –
So I do not want to elaborate on them.

This is a brief account of my thoughts and life. Narrations can be of different types: good, middling and bad. Here, only the middling understanding is mentioned, and faulty understanding and conduct have been mentioned. Isn't there faulty understanding and conduct? It is said that wherever beings like me exist there is defilement and where there is defilement you are bound to be deluded.

Wherever you look you see illusory visions and you follow them blindly, and as a result you are faced with different kinds of suffering. For example, a wild animal will fall into a trap due to its attachment to a melodious sound, or a moth gets burnt due to its attraction to light. The fox gets attracted by the smell of meat, jumps into the pit and gets trapped and dies at the hands of villagers. We human beings too, not realizing the illusive visions as illusion, commit a lot of negative actions due to our mistaken perceptions, and then we have to suffer the consequences.

When I look back at my wrong conduct caused by illusive vision, I see that it was not very different from the behaviour of dogs, pigs, monkeys and savages, but I see no need to go into details here. I will keep it as my secret. The difference between animals and human beings, from a negative point of view, is that we are very cunning. From a positive point of view, we do have a sense of shame. This is a unique characteristic. This veil of a sense of shame is conspicuous, but it saves us a lot of unwanted trouble in life, and the joy it gives is also tremendous. From the spiritual point of view, you avoid a lot of negative actions due to this sense of shame, and as a result you don't have to face new sufferings. It is also helpful in attaining the ultimate state of omniscience. So this characteristic can be interpreted from both negative and positive points of view.

From the general point of view, I think human beings are very cunning as I said earlier, because there are two layers, inner and outer, to everything we say and do. These layers can be called deceit. We pretend not to have what we possess; we pretend to be what we are not; the good pretends to be bad or the bad pretends to be good; and all such pretensions can be considered as lies. Any human being without this inner and outer layer will be shamed and reviled as an animal, and not even be allowed to enter the house. It will be the cause of a lot of trouble for the person himself or herself.

You can understand this if you observe other animals like dogs and monkeys. Since these animals do not have this veil of shame, they do whatever comes to their minds and fight and kill one another. Getting into meaningless fights, killing one another and living in fear all the time is the common way of life for most animals. The dogs of our monastery, for example, run out of the compound during the mating season, and then get into fights with huge stray dogs, and by the time everything is over they limp back into the compound with wounded necks and ears. Some come back almost dead.

Although we humans are not very different from the animals in our attitude, thanks to this layer of veil, we hesitate to openly carry out our delusions, and this saves us from a lot of trouble. Pretending not to like something that you like, not showing anger when you are angry, and pretending not to want what you want, is a unique way of living of a smart human being. Those more expert in living this two-layered lifestyle are respected as experts in civility, or as cultured people – smart in subduing foes and looking after near and dear ones, expert in business and accomplishing self-interest by deceiving others, skillful in speech and easily making friends. But if this smartness is not used properly then it can be risky. I feel today that people have lost trust in one another, because this smartness has been used excessively.

AREN'T WE HUMAN BEINGS LIVING DEMONS?

Of all the many sentient beings, I feel that human beings are the most scary – either extremely good or extremely bad. In this world, no being is more destructive than us humans. Who is responsible for polluting the air with poisonous emissions and toxic waste that causes diseases and deaths of mankind and other animals? We humans are responsible for this. All this environmental pollution is causing floods and tsunamis. Cutting down forests for business is causing landslides that cause suffering to many people and animals. Forest fires destroy many houses and burn birds, insects and other animals. Such disasters are brought about by humans. Only we human beings are capable of culling millions of animals on the pretext of preventing an epidemic.

We not only claim to be smart, we also claim to have a constitution and security systems, but we depend on laws and systems formulated with an idiotic idea, that has no sense of shame, love or kindness. How sad! If people who do such things and make others do them are not demons in human form then what are they? If such people fill the world, then I am really scared.

There are many people who suffer from infectious diseases and we have to give medical treatment to cure them. We can't just kill them all. I see no reason why the animals, who have no one to support them, should be subjected to such atrocities. We are able to carry out such atrocities because we humans are demons. Very few people oppose such actions. Being a human myself, I can't trust myself and I get scared of myself when I see all these human atrocities.

Generally, many things one has done, or the thoughts one has had in life since childhood, are not worth telling others, because they are embarrassing. So they have to be kept secret. Some people proudly say, "I have no secrets." I don't know if it is true. If it is true, then this is a quality.

Being able to lead a transparent life in today's society and achieve the welfare of self and others is indeed unique. It is said, "It is difficult to find a man without fault, but filled with qualities; it is difficult to find a tree growing straight, without warts," so such a person must be one of those full of qualities, without faults, or like the saying, "The persistence of a wicked person is like the tracks left behind by the furious flow of the river." Hence, such a claim must be the pure bragging of a fraud. Personally, some of my thoughts and conduct were like that of dogs and pigs, and not worth sharing with others.

> Talk about visions of deities and the like
> Are the business of worldly gurus.
> I keep silent about my experiences;
> If one leads a simple and happy existence,
> One can actually accomplish great things
> For this and future lifetimes.

Since it is difficult to find unbiased devoted disciples, there is no point in talking about clairvoyance, which is one of the positive insights, let alone claims of visions of deities, ghosts and miracles, which the worldly gurus indulge in, and there is no purpose in being truthful. The Tantras say that loose talk about the true experiences of worldly gurus, except for a definite purpose, is a moral downfall. I have realized that making fraudulent claims of having visions of Gods and ghosts saying, "I have befriended a God" or "I have exorcised the ghost"; or even prophesizing a life span or prophesizing the ups and downs in someone's life is a moral downfall, and is meaningless talk – unless requested by someone devoted.

My root gurus have attained enlightenment and their wisdom eye is unobstructed and yet, in front of disciples like us, who are unable to cut the web of doubt, and faithless people with wrong views, they pretend not to know, or not to see what they know and see. If you persistently request them to make a prediction they will say, "I cannot make predictions, but the Triple Gem is infallible and I will do a divination," and pretend to make a divination. They have the ability to speak spontaneously from foreknowledge, but today it is rare to find such genuine gurus doing so.

Looking at their activities, I find it strange that we young gurus make predictions to everyone we come across, whether they request one or not. Even if one has to make predictions, one has to reflect on oneself and know what is true and what is false. If it is a lie, then it is better to change the topic of discussion. If what you are going to say is true, then you have to check what effect it will have on the other person before you do anything.

NOTHING TO BE AMAZED ABOUT IN VISIONS OF GODS AND GHOSTS

Generally speaking, there is nothing surprising about seeing gods or ghosts, because if a human can see a human, why wouldn't they be able to see a god or a ghost? There is not much difference between humans, gods and ghosts. Since only a few among us see gods and ghosts we are amazed. Ghosts and spirits do not have solid physical bodies of flesh and blood like us; they have the ability to read others' minds and know many secrets, and those who see them have some sort of clairvoyance to make predictions. We can see distant landscapes clearly with binoculars but as soon as the binoculars are removed, the landscape becomes a blur. Similarly, such people are able to see and say things when these spirits enter their mental continuum, but they usually don't have this ability. We consider people with such ability as different and gifted, and if they use their ability for the welfare of other beings, then we should appreciate it, but it is nothing surprising.

Some communities don't believe in such things and the person with an ability to see spirits is treated as crazy and they are belittled which causes them a lot of worry. Not knowing that there is no difference between humans, gods and ghosts, and remaining indifferent, the person gets stressed and depressed and gradually goes crazy. In our society if such people are left alone there would be no reason for them to become crazy. We cling to the external appearances we see, like animals, birds, *etc.*, and accept them as the truth, and believe that there cannot be any other state. That is why we treat visions of gods and ghosts as surprising.

If you see a dark apparition with one eye and one leg, unlike a normal human, you will definitely be scared. And without any investigation, such an appearance is called a ghost. We say, "I saw a ghost" because we are not used to seeing such a being. We cling firmly to the deluded view that a human has two eyes, two hands and two legs, as we are used to seeing. Otherwise, there is no reason to call this other being a ghost and to be scared. If we are able to familiarize ourselves with the view that such visions do not truly exist as they appear, we will become truly fearless, having no fear or pride when we see visions of gods, ghosts, humans and non-humans, foes and friends, in this life, in the intermediate state, and in the next life. If one is able to achieve such fearlessness, then it is a big accomplishment, worthy of being born in this world. Although there are many kinds of qualities in our society, this state of fearlessness is the supreme quality.

Although I respect and admire the qualities of others, as well as those I have, as long as one does not reach the state of fearlessness, I find nothing surprising about these qualities. For this reason, I have not had the wish to talk to others about whatever little acquired and innate qualities I have, nor have I liked being praised by others, since my childhood. Like the popular sayings, "Keep quiet and there will be no legal hassle", "If you want happiness, keep your independence" and "Lead a carefree happy life" It is better to go to the beach with a close, virtuous friend and lie down and relax, instead of running after praise and getting entangled in the web of the eight worldly motivations.

MEDDLING IN OTHERS' AFFAIRS IS A HEADACHE

Generally, people who like to listen, gossip and watch, end up facing problems. Like the saying, "If you don't keep the long tongue under control, the round head will face problems," the habit of telling others everything that one sees, hears and thinks is the worst disease because, from the spiritual point of view, it creates discord between teachers and disciples, leading to the breaking of Samaya and other problems.

From the worldly point of view too it causes many problems. It is also the worst enemy of people like me who like to lead an open and relaxed life. When we check, we find that we say false things during our conversations. As a Khampa proverb goes, "The golden statue does not drink tea, the guru does not lie," but it seems that gurus like me say false things unintentionally during conversations; I hope they are not big lies.

On investigation, I find that most lies such as this are told for selfish purposes; trying to hide one's mountain of faults, and exaggerating the little quality one has, to impress others. Although the objective of lying is selfish gain – and at the most, one may gain social recognition – ultimately, one wastes the opportunity to live this short dream-like life in a happy relaxed way, according to one's standing. One becomes the slave of material wealth and fame and indulges in deception and conceit until death comes.

The result of such deception and deceit makes one the laughing stock of society and an embarrassment to the wise and learned. Even close friends become distant and gradually you lose respect in society, your wealth diminishes and ultimately you can't trust yourself, and losing mental balance, you take to drinking and smoking excessively and fall into a pathetic state.

KEEP QUIET AND DON'T REVEAL SECRETS

Telling others everything you hear, see or think not only exposes you, but it also hurts others and causes social disharmony. It is like the lyric of this song, "It was too early to confess to the mother of three children."

In today's time, it is difficult to trust each other from the heart, though people kiss, hug, invite each other to dinner, confide in each other, and lay bare their hearts at the first meeting, as though they have been best friends for decades. After a few days or months the same people dislike each other, back bite, expose each other's faults and become foes. Or if someone tells you a secret you immediately tell this to a friend saying, "It's secret. Don't tell anyone." This friend tells it to some more friends and gradually everyone comes to know about it, causing discord and unhappiness.

When you reflect on such funny behaviour, which causes physical, mental and material stress, you find that this is the result of one's inability to keep quiet. As I said earlier, there is no need to talk about your own or others' qualities and shortcomings until you have come to know the person well and closely. It is my experience that it is better to be thick-headed.

CHAPTER 14

Meeting a Qualified Guru

In brief, [a word about my teachers]:
The regent of the Lotus Born Lord,
His Holiness Dudjom Rinpoche;
And the lineage holder of the Drukpa Order,
The most kind teacher, Lord of Speech [Drukpa Thuksey];
And the Vajra Holder of the three vows, Trulshik Rinpoche;
Lords of the Mandala, actual Buddhas who eliminate all delusion

They introduced me to the nature of existence
Through the direct experience of the Base.
The kindness of these Vajra Masters was measureless.

His Holiness the Dalai Lama is sole refuge
And protector of our social and spiritual welfare.
From Guru Khyentse Gyatso,
I received the oral transmission of Mahamudra,
Opening the Eye of Wisdom,
Discerning the difference between Dharma and non-Dharma,
Through vast kindness bestowed on me,
Great holder of the three vows,
Lord [Zhichen] Ontrul, you are the eyes of the world.

The kind spiritual father Do-Drubchen
Passed on the droplets of authentic thoughts of Longchenpa
Into the heart of this devoted son.
May you always remain as the jewel of my heart!
The great translator (Vairochana) – the eye of the World –
Emanated as the father of this degenerate son
The Guru, whose kindness extends to this life and the next,
May Zhichen Bairocana remain victorious!
The emanation of Vajrapani and Chakzampa (Thangtong Gyalpo),
holding the life-line of the Oral and Treasure teachings
at the divine seat of Kathok,
May the truly fearless Moktsa excel in your activities!

I was fortunate to receive transmissions from these Buddhas,
These roots and branch teachers.
Though I have not achieved

> Confident realization of their teachings,
> I have not displeased them.
> And though I have not had prophecies induced by trance,
> I am sure that I have received the blessings of their compassion.

In my life, I have done a lot of things that may be considered good, rejected faults, and accepted qualities. When I reflect on the question of what was the most meaningful thing I have done that would benefit me and others in this life and the next, I find that it was getting and taking the opportunity to study under spiritual teachers. These Buddhas in human form, who showed me the essence of accepting and rejecting, of listening, reflecting and meditating; I feel happy about it. I often feel a great sense of devotion. I don't talk about this to others because I feel they will not understand. Before telling something to others, I should have some idea of it in my mind. It is difficult to give a special name to or conceive of the physical and mental sensations I get at the mere thought of the face, body, speech and mind qualities of my glorious Buddha-like gurus.

Perhaps it is like the proverbial saying: "A mute person eating jaggery (raw sugar)"; it would be very difficult to describe the experience. The devotion and faith that we normally talk about may be classified into different types. From the view point of intensity or power, devotion can be divided into three types: devotion that permeates the flesh, devotion that permeates down to the bones, and devotion that permeates down to the marrow. These terms mostly concern the different sensations, and such experiences are inexpressible. The experiences relating to the guru and spiritual teachings remind you of impermanence, the essencelessness of all apparent phenomena, and they make you realize that in the face of disasters of earth, water, fire and wind there is nothing but suffering. This further brings to mind flashes of memory of the teachings on compassion, Mahamudra, Dzogchen, wisdom and emptiness, given by the guru, as a means for cessation of all the physical and mental sufferings of all sentient beings.

In brief, all such experiences must serve as a reminder for the practice of loving kindness, compassion and Bodhicitta. If it makes no difference to your practice, then talking about this guru or that guru, carrying their photo in the car, displaying their photos in shops and bedrooms, and looking at the photo with raised eyelids isn't going to be of much use when it comes to the essential point. I don't know about the spiritual teacher of the common vehicles, but I think it is not appropriate to publicly display the photos and names of a Vajrayana teacher, unless it is for some great purpose.

According to authentic texts, when using the name of the kind spiritual teachers, the preface, "For the purpose of stating the name", has to be used before his name. Unless it is for some altruistic purpose, using the name or photo of the Vajrayana teacher in public, for selfish reasons or idle talk, is regarded as a gesture of disrespect and is inappropriate. As I said earlier, from every point of view, the most meaningful thing I have done in my life was being able to adhere to these gurus therefore, I don't think calling their name once would be a violation.

HIS HOLINESS DUDJOM RINPOCHE

From among my gurus, I have full confidence that I have a karmic connection with His Holiness Dudjom Rinpoche, the regent of Guru Padmasambhava. I had the good fortune of meeting him as well as being blessed and named by him, a few days after my birth, and leading me on to the spiritual path in this life. I received many pith instructions of the Nyingma tradition, including the *Treasure Texts*, from this great Vajracharya. I also received teachings from him in visions and dreams and have accomplished the firm faith of conviction.

From the age of twenty until His Holiness's passing away, I often saw His Holiness in dreams, together with his consort, and received instructions from Him. Mostly, I would see him in dreams on the night of the 9th day of the month (according to the lunar calendar). I don't see any reason to go into details here. Surprisingly, in my dreams, I would always see His Holiness and his consort together, and rarely saw him on his own. I had personally met his consort only two or three times, and so I did not know her very well, and I had hardly ever met them together. The instruction texts say that there is not much difference between the guru and his consort, and making a distinction between them and making pretentious comments is a serious fallacy, which will close the door not only to supreme higher attainments, but also to the common higher attainments. Always seeing them together in my dreams confirmed this in my mind.

One day, I dreamt that my guru, Ontrul Rinpoche, took me by

the hand, saying that we should go and see His Holiness today, and we arrived at the highway. Ontrul Rinpoche asked me if I had the ceremonial scarf ready to give to His Holiness, and I replied in the negative. Then Ontrul Rinpoche said to me, "Offer this scarf for the sake of auspicious connection. You can give me a similar scarf later," and he took a long special ceremonial scarf out of his pocket, and holding it, we waited there. A long car arrived, in which His Holiness and his consort were sort of sleeping, and at the urging of his consort, His Holiness touched my head with his hands, and my entire body felt an unbearable heat and then he said, "I am in a hurry. Bye bye!" And the long car swiftly passed over a high mountain peak. One week later, I heard the sad news that His Holiness has passed away. Since then I have neither had a vision of him nor seen him in my dreams. I don't have to narrate his activities in this world. You can read them in his biography.

KYABJE[57] DRUKPA THUKSEY RINPOCHE

My kind Guru Drukpa Dungsey Rinpoche Ngawang Gyurme Pel Zangpo took care of me ever since I was recognized, at the age of three, as the 12th reincarnation of the Gyalwang Drukpa. He had been most gracious in both worldly and spiritual ways. Since I was eight or nine years old, he instructed me every day, in the essential teachings of the ultimate lineage which can lead to enlightenment within one life time, and guided me on the ripening and liberation path according to my level of learning, understanding and experiential realization. Considering the kindness with which he passed on the instructions to me, like one vase filling another, I should have attained enlightenment years ago, or at least embraced the path and achieved freedom in death and birth, and the confidence not to fear samsara. But my lack of diligence and intelligence has left me in this present state. The qualities of his body, speech and mind are endless, immeasurable and beyond the imagination and expression of an ignorant person like me.

In order to speak clearly about the qualities of Buddha-like gurus completely, one has to attain the state of Buddhahood, in the

---

57. *skyabs rje* is a mark of respect reserved for the senior masters of a tradition, whose realization and powers are extraordinary.

same way that one has to first taste the fruit before describing the sweet or sour taste of it. One who has not even completed learning, contemplation and meditation, let alone attained enlightenment, cannot make random casual comments. However, in order to guide us on the path, the Buddha-like spiritual teachers carry out activities that ordinary beings like us can comprehend. These activities are in accordance with the Dharma and tradition, and suitable for our minds. We can narrate such activities.

My late guru was the son of the 10th Gyalwang Drukpa and his mother was Phurbu Lhamo, the daughter of the Drubwang Shakyashri. The 10th Gyalwang Drukpa told the 7th Zigar Rinpoche Ngawang Tenzin Palzang, "I am giving this son to you so that he is able to work extensively for the welfare of the Dharma and beings. You take care of his proper education." He studied in Zigar Monastery for many years and completed his education in Sutra and Tantra. He gave away all his belongings and introduced the initiation rites of four-armed Mahakala at the monastery. He invited Zurmang Khenpo Dhonden and started a new philosophical college with about fifteen students. He told me, "A few students worthy of becoming khenpos graduated after a few years." Even today, renowned khenpos are passing out of this college. He also opened a new meditation centre.

Because of his long association with Zigar Monastery, he is known as Zigar Thuksey, and being the son of Gyalwang Drukpa he is also known as Drukpa Dungsey. He is the first Kyabje Drukpa Thuksey Rinpoche and his activities are immeasurable. He started a new retreat centre for the Six Yogas of Naropa at Chitray, on the India-Nepal border, and it currently accommodates twenty practitioners doing the three-year retreat.

Prior to the political upheaval in Tibet, he had started a new philosophical college at Sangag Choling, the seat of the Drukpa Lineage, and rendered many services to the monastery. After the political upheaval in Tibet, when Buddhism was on the verge of extinction, with undaunted courage, he reignited the flame of Dharma for the benefit of not only the Drukpa Lineage but also the Drikung and Taklung traditions. His graciousness – from performing the funeral rites of the 11th Gyalwang Drukpa to guiding me, the supposed reincarnation of the 11th, on the spiritual path, and teaching me both spiritual and worldly manners – is inexpressible.

Although he possessed the eye of wisdom to see all objects of knowledge without obstruction, following tradition he consulted many learned and realized masters, including His Holiness the 14th Dalai Lama, His Holiness the 16th Karmapa Rigpe Dorje, Drukpa Choegon Rinpoche, Gyalwa Dokhampa Dongyu Nyima and Kyabje Apho Rinpoche Yeshe Rangdol, and invoked the oath-bound protectors and went to great lengths in search of the reincarnation of the 11th Gyalwang Drukpa. Following the identical conclusions of their respective investigations, I was recognized as the reincarnation. Otherwise I don't possess any acquired, inherent, inner or external qualities, as you all can see. Whatever I have is purely his kindness.

My guru, Drukpa Thuksey Rinpoche, constructed the present monastery in Darjeeling from the foundations, and built all the body, speech and mind reliquaries. He also turned the three wheels of activity at two retreat centres and monasteries in the region. He visited Ladakh at the invitation of the monasteries and the people of Ladakh. Although I don't remember the year, he gave teachings on the foundation and actual practice of Mahamudra, calm abiding, and special insight meditation according to the Drukpa Lineage, to all the devotees. He introduced the three basic practices at Hemis and other monasteries, and bestowed the novice and ordination vows to hundreds of monks, reviving the Vinaya teaching which is the foundation of Buddhism.

At that time, the region of Ladakh faced drought and the threat of famine loomed large, but by his miraculous powers he brought timely rain. In some areas the land was parched, and both humans and animals were suffering from extreme heat. We went to the upper part of the land to retrieve a water treasure and everyone witnessed that his return coincided with rainfall, and water, white like milk, flowed from the springs, filling all the drains. Until today, the local people talk about this wonderful sight. Even the non-Buddhists began to call him the "Water Guru", in appreciation of being saved from the threat of famine.

My guru built many new temples and reliquaries and renovated the old ones. He reintroduced the practice of the public recitation of a hundred million Avalokiteshvara mantras, which, although it had once existed generations ago, had since declined. He donated money to many causes, he encouraged spiritual practice, and this practice of reciting a hundred million mantras is now practised all over Ladakh by holders of all the traditions. He also introduced the hundred million recitation practice in Darjeeling and many other places too. He visited Bhutan and bestowed novice and ordination vows, and gave teachings to guide them on the path of enlightenment. I was fortunate to receive instructions, empowerment and essential instructions of the Drukpa Lineage from him, as well as the aural transmission practice of Drubwang Shakyashri, the transmission of the collected works of Phagchok Dorje, the son of Shakyashri, and I also received essential instructions on Dzogchen.

Although Rinpoche was invited abroad he did not show any interest in visiting the West. He would even discourage us, saying it was not good to go abroad. But one day he said, "I must go to the West once – like the saying, 'The ant flies before its death'." He said many such unusual things, indicating that he was going to leave us soon, but we were too ignorant to understand this. He visited France and some other countries in the West, and gave many common teachings to disciples and also founded a couple of centres as a foundation for Buddhism in the future; and the teachings are now flourishing in these centres.

When he fell ill, we asked him what medical treatment and prayers would be appropriate, and he replied, "Do a divination for me. Whatever you do is fine. Most of my work in this life is complete. This illness will be the cause of my death." Although he was not seriously ill at that time, he would say this often. I and all the other spiritual friends performed various prayers and rituals, and he lived for another three to four years. Then he became ill again and was brought to Delhi for treatment. Rinpoche was not keen on going, but out of concern for him we forcibly brought him to Delhi.

One day, while in the hospital, he secretly asked me, "How is your practice?" Taken by surprise, I did not know what to say for some time. He smiled and said, "It is good. It is surprising that you have understood the meanings I showed you. I am satisfied. There may still be doubts to be cleared. Approach Lopon Gangri Kunsang Dorje. A guru as learned and realized as him is rare to find in this Lineage today. He is a humble, hidden yogi and if someone like you requests teachings from him, he will refuse. If you say you want to discuss them, then he might accept your request." He said this with great emphasis. When I think back, I believe it was his oral testament. Shortly afterwards, Kyabje Rinpoche passed away on 8 March 1983 at the age of 67 years.

LOPON GANGRI KUNSANG DORJE

Following Kyabje Rinpoche's oral testament, I approached Lopon Gangri Kunsang Dorje and have been practising his instructions from that time until now. I think even the Buddha would not be able to give a complete account of his activities. But to give a brief account of his activities in human form: this sublime being has many names, but his popular name was Kunsang Dorje. He was born in Driji, a village that was the patron of Drira Phug Monastery and Jiwu Monastery, belonging to the Drukpa Lineage, located in the north behind Mount Kailash. And because of his birth place he later came to be known as "Gangri Rinpoche".

When he was nine years old his father passed away and he had to look after his family affairs until he was 25 years old. Gangri Rinpoche said, "From an early age I wanted to renounce the world and become a monk, but, I had to look after my family. Having seen the true nature of samsara, all I could think of was doing authentic spiritual practice. Being in samsara for some time turned adversity into a friend."

He then joined Drira Phug, a monastery of the Drukpa Lineage, and learned the monastery's ritual traditions for five years. One day he took a guide book to holy places and developed an infallible faith in the holy places of the past lineage masters. After going on pilgrimage for a few years, he returned to the monastery and met a guru from Kham who was on pilgrimage. He told Rinpoche, "If you want to do proper practice you must follow a qualified spiritual teacher. Pilgrimage and prostrations will purify your physical defilements, but you will not understand the nature of mind. It is better to approach a teacher who has realized the nature of mind." Rinpoche thanked him for his advice and asked, "Is it possible to find such a guru in this part of the country?" and he replied, "Haven't you heard that Tripon Pema Choegyal, disciple of Shakyashri and treasure house of all teachings of the Drukpa Lineage, is turning the Dharma wheel in Tsibri Neuteng?"

"Just hearing the name made me forget mundane thoughts for some time, and I could not say anything," Rinpoche told me. He was around 27 years old at that time. Seeing everything as meaningless, he was determined to do authentic spiritual practice and, without consulting his mother and relatives, he secretly went to Tsibri. There he met Kyabje Tripon Rinpoche who explained to him how all phenomena have to be brought to the mind, and how to do this in one's mind-stream, through the practice of Mahamudra, Dzogchen or the Middle Way. He advised him that spiritual practice has to be done, or else it was useless. He received the complete empowerment, oral transmission and instructions of the Drukpa Lineage from Tripon Rinpoche, and stayed in retreat for fourteen years at the Neurang retreat centre.

Following the 1959 upheaval, he came to India. His spiritual friend-cum-disciple Dromo Kagyu Tulku Rinpoche asked him if he had decided where he was going. He replied that he had no idea. Then Tulku Rinpoche said that there was a solitary retreat at a place called Rinak Arita in East Sikkim, and if he was interested he would make arrangements. Gangri Rinpoche replied that he would like to stay there if the place was desolate, with no people around. So Tulku Rinpoche found a house in the middle of the forest, with no neighbours around, owned by a Sikkimese couple, Ajo Tseten and his wife Ama Goleb. The couple happily agreed to offer the house for as long as Gangri Rinpoche wanted. So Rinpoche went there and meditated. As the place was extremely desolate, he sometimes remained there without food for months, in meditation. He said that sometimes the military barracks close by would give him their leftover food.

Later, the soldiers, knowing that he was a spiritual practitioner, would sometimes leave fresh vegetables outside the door of his retreat house. "They were very kind," he said. He stayed there in strict retreat for six years, taking a vow of silence and not meeting anyone. In 1965, he came out of his retreat and went on a pilgrimage all over India. Once, he went to see the 16th Karmapa, who kept him in his private residence and praised him, saying it was difficult to find a yogi like him. I heard that the Karmapa received Mahamudra teachings and transmissions from Lopon Gangri Kunsang Dorje. Lopon Rinpoche said, "The Karmapa asked me to give teachings on Mahamudra to the Karma Kagyu spiritual sons and tulkus. I could not refuse and had to give some teachings." I think he gave the teachings of *Moonlight of Mahamudra* at that time.

During his stay of 31 years in the Rinak hermitage, he never visited the village or houses to perform rituals, but stayed in meditation day and night without a break. He used to visit the monastery in Darjeeling, where I lived, to join the hundred million recitation of the Mani mantra, but he would only stay for a few days at a time. He was always humble, without any wish for a name or recognition, and most people did not even regard him as a standard monk, let alone as a guru.

Being a yogi content with pitiful clothes and food, I remember that even the dogs of the monastery were more hostile to him than to others. Needless to say, this is a sign of the inferior collective karma of beings. These days, both dogs and humans mostly look at outer appearances rather than inner qualities. Since Lopon Rinpoche was content with poor clothes, both humans and dogs looked at him in the same way. It is the character of people today to bully those with an inferior external appearance, without looking at the inner qualities of a person. Like the proverb says, "The wise look good among the wise," so Lopon Rinpoche used to meet often with Drukpa Thuksey Rinpoche and Khenpo Noryang and discuss teachings and enjoy each other's company.

During conversations, Khen Rinpoche often used to tell me, "It is rare today to find a follower of Milarepa's, a scholar in name and deed, a yogi who has attained understanding and experiential realization like Lopon Rinpoche." Drukpa Thuksey Rinpoche said to me, "It would be very nice if one day you could receive all the teachings from him again. You must receive the teachings. How do we go about it?"

As a result of Drukpa Thuksey Rinpoche's advice, I was able to receive all the teachings and instructions, including Mahamudra – both explanations and instructions from experience, from Lopon Rinpoche, like pouring from one vase to another. Being very strict, he rarely gave the profound instructional teachings. After my second request he said, "I will give you the instructions. It is important that Dharma holders like you do not leave the instructions as mere words, but minutely analyse them through meditational experience."

For a few days he gave advice on mind-training, intermixed with worldly anecdotes, and these were highly beneficial for my mind. Normally he would explain things even before we asked, and gave sermons to suit the mind of an individual disciple, and his foreknowledge developed faith in us. He would usually say he had no knowledge, or that he did not know the scriptures, or that he had forgotten the instructions. He always remained humble and praised the quality of the person he met, however small it was. But while he was teaching, he never looked at the texts, and taught flawlessly from experience. He always quoted the words of the Buddha and the instructions of past spiritual masters as the background of his teachings. Sometimes, he would relate funny mundane tales, to instill in us faith in karma and dependent origination. He was an amazing Vajracharya. He never showed partiality towards any religion, guru or spiritual practitioner – male or female, young or old, high or low – and praised everyone equally. His speech was devoid of any sense of attachment and aversion. He had the astonishing quality of seeing purity in everything.

On the 25th day of the 6th month of the Iron Horse year, 15 August 1990, he had a slight breathing problem and told some of his close disciples that he might pass away. Usually, he would go to hospital and take medicines whenever necessary, but this time he said he wanted to stay at the hermitage and not go to the hospital. But at the insistence of his disciples he went to the hospital, and his health seemed better for four or five days.

On the morning of the 30th day of the 6th Tibetan month, 20 August, he asked his disciple Sangay Palzang to give him a bath. I heard from his disciples that at 10am that morning he turned towards the east and passed away with the sound "*Ah Ah*" as a sign of his mind merging with the mandala of the three bodies of Buddha. At the urging of his disciples who had realized the mind, and devoted patrons, I went on the 3rd day of the 7th Tibetan month and performed the rites for two days, and also composed a prayer that I gave them, for the quick birth of his reincarnation. His body was cremated in Gangtok on the 9th and many relics were found in the ashes. I have many of these relics with me. Everyone present agreed to my advice to divide the relics and build two stupas – one in Gangtok and one in Rinak.

I feel that his turning towards the East and saying "*Ah Ah*" while passing away, and the fact that a white cloud descended on to the body during the cremation, were indications of his going to the pure land of Manifest Joy in the East, like Milarepa. The construction of the two stupas was also completed. Although, at the request of Dromo Kagyu Rinpoche, all of us disciples had been making Ganachakra offerings and prayers for his reincarnation, I still have not been able to find one. Perhaps he has not reincarnated. It is almost impossible that a Buddha and Bodhisattva like him would not take rebirth for the sake of other beings, but it is also possible he is performing activities for sentient beings in the pure land, or he is engaged in activities for beings in other spheres, and has not taken rebirth in this world.

KYABJE TRULSHIK RINPOCHE

A long time afterwards, I met Vajradhara Kyabje Trulshik Rinpoche. He was a guru that I adhered to on the advice and instructions of the great Treasure-Master, His Holiness Dudjom Rinpoche Jigdral Yeshe Dorje. I had heard that His Holiness had a great fondness and respect for Trulshik Rinpoche, even when he was young. The mind of the spiritual teacher and his disciple were inseparable. Moreover, the Treasure-Master had anointed him as the master of secret treasure teachings, and placed him on the high spiritual throne a long time prior to this.

Before His Holiness Dudjom Rinpoche passed away, I received two letters from His Holiness to come abroad to see him. At that time, all we disciples had hoped that His Holiness would come to India or Nepal and this hope delayed my departure. In the second letter, His Holiness set a deadline for me to come and visit him. At that time I did not have a passport. Since I was born in India I applied for an Indian passport urgently, and went via Italy and met the Pope in Rome. From Italy, I travelled via Germany to France in order to see His Holiness.

During the evening and the next morning of the appointed time, there was a sudden heavy snowfall and the railway track was blocked. His Holiness's consort telephoned to suggest postponing the audience. I thought about her suggestion and also asked other people about the weather. They seemed surprised, and said that normally they did not have rain or snowfall at that time of the year. Then I thought to myself that the wish-fulfilling gem-like guru had given the time for the audience and I had come this far. This sudden change in weather must be an obstacle, and I decided to go, even if I had to walk. We drove for a few kilometres and when it was not possible to drive, we got out of the car, not knowing what to do next. I said I had to go, come what may. And, carrying the few offerings we had on our back, and walking through knee-high snow after some time we reached the peak from where we could see the wooded hill, where His Holiness's residence was located. We prostrated three times in the direction of his residence and offered the seven branch prayer.

Then, all of us saw his residence clearly, through the clouds, and with a double rainbow. I felt an inexpressible sensation in my mind and my whole body became numb.

After walking for some more time, we reached our destination and I saw His Holiness and heard his speech. At the end, His Holiness said, "Now I have given you the complete teachings and transmissions," and after placing two or three volumes of text on my head, he prayed for a long time. He gave me his robe, his lower garment, spectacles, hat and blessed pills. I came out of the inner chamber with sadness, not wishing to leave.

I had tea and stayed in the outer chamber for some time and then thought to myself, "His Holiness is old and his residence is so far from India; I do not know if I will see him again. Although he said that he had given all the teachings and transmissions of the Nyingma tradition, this is not enough for a disciple like me who looks at the words and not the meanings, and has a low awareness of conventional signs. Should I dare to request him to guide me to a guru whose realization is equal to his?" As I was having tea, with these thoughts in my mind, His Holiness's consort came out, sat on the cushion, and had tea with me. She seemed delighted. After some time she said, "His Holiness is very fond of you and especially Bairo Rinpoche, and all your family members. Just now His Holiness said, 'I am old now and it may be difficult for him to come over here. Tell him to receive all the remainder of the teachings from Kyabje Trulshik Rinpoche. He has all my teachings and empowerments. There is no difference between him and me. I have anointed him the master of all my teachings. Tell him to relax his mind and go to see Rinpoche'." I felt great devotion thinking that His Holiness knew my thoughts by clairvoyance.

Later, both His Holiness and his consort wrote to Kyabje Trulshik Rinpoche to ask him to compassionately take care of me if I came to receive teachings from him. And later, while receiving teachings and empowerments from Trulshik Rinpoche, he happily showed me the letters saying, "I received these letters."

I think very few people know about the life of the late Kyabje Rinpoche, who was thus revealed to me as my guru. About a decade ago, I requested him to write his autobiography and he said, "I will not go against your words and I will do what I can." There are only brief biographies available; I have not seen a complete biography.

I had the opportunity to receive the complete teachings of the oral lineage, treasure and pure vision teachings of the Nyingma tradition, and especially all the treasure teachings, pointed instructions on channels and energy, and essential instructions on Dzogchen. His kindness is beyond imagination and expression.

GEN KHYENTSE GYATSO

From a young age, I had some understanding and experience of Mahamudra. By the blessings of instructions and teachings that I later received from Gen Khyentse Gyatso, I attained an infallible inner realization and gained firm faith in its practice and the lineage. He started his spiritual journey by joining Druk Sangag Choling Monastery in Tibet. His hair-cutting ceremony was performed by the 10th Gyalwang Drukpa. So, because of our past connection, I had the opportunity to see him again and again. His mind was undistracted and clear whenever I met him, and there was almost nothing that he did not know about Sutra, Tantra or Mahamudra. His knowledge was clear with authentic sources, and was not limited to spiritual practice.

On the worldly front, he knew a lot of games and I remember him playing many of them with me when I was young. He knew about twenty different types of games: some were related to mathematics, some were related to art and some were related to magic tricks. He would have become very popular in today's world but he never craved fame. He lived humbly, hiding his knowledge, without any pride or arrogance.

As mentioned earlier, his mind was never distracted and even while speaking, playing or eating his gaze was unwavering, and this, I believe, is the sign of an adept in the union of calm abiding and special insight. When such skill is attained in the state of union, one spontaneously trains in Bodhisattva activities, the method of infallible karma and dependent origination, and accumulates both merit and wisdom on a large scale. Due to this accumulation, it is not as difficult to attain enlightenment as described in the texts. Later, understanding that an auspicious connection can be established to attain enlightenment from within, I developed an uncommon devotion to him.

His Holiness the Dalai Lama also described him as a root member of the meditation lineage, and advised me to follow him as my guru. His Holiness said that he met Gen Khyentse a couple of times while going to the hot springs in Manali. He said that he was an extremely good guru, from whom His Holiness had received many explanations on the pith instructions of the ultimate lineage, experiential instructions and transmissions. His Holiness said that he immediately contemplated the meaning of the instructions as advised by the guru, and the results were not too bad.

HIS HOLINESS THE DALAI LAMA

His Holiness the Dalai Lama, who guided me to follow Gen Khyentse as my guru, had recognized me as the reincarnation of the 11th Gyalwang Drukpa when I was young. He bestowed the refuge vows, conducted my hair-cutting ceremony and gave me the name *Tenzin Jigdral Lodoe*, and has regarded me with kindness to this day. He has been extremely gracious in the outer disciplinary code, inner Bodhicitta, secret mantra and profound Dzogchen. He is the spiritual teacher endowed with the three kindnesses, not just for me, but for the entire world.

I received from His Holiness the Kalachakra Tantra, Hevajra Tantra – the king of Tantra – and Avalokiteshvara empowerments, the initiation of peaceful and wrathful Guru Padmasambhava, and in particular, the instructions on *Manjushri Namasamgiti* – the crown jewel of all Tantras – according to the commentary composed by Omniscient Gedun Gyatso. In general, there are commentaries on *Manjushri Namasamgiti* according to *Yoga Tantra* and *Annuttara Yoga* (I am not sure if there are any commentaries according to *Kriya Yoga*) and within the commentaries according to *Annuttara Yoga*, there are commentaries according to the general perspective, and some in accordance with Kalachakra. The commentary by Gedun Gyatso is a powerful commentary focusing on the *Three Cycles of Bodhisattva Commentaries – Chagdor Toedrel*; a commentary on Hevajra Tantra according to Kalachakra; *Dorje Nying-drel*, a commentary on Chakrasamvara according to Kalachakra; and *Drimed Woe*, a commentary by Rigden Pema Karpo. The subject was amazing and the instruction manual was amazing.

As for the teacher, I was certain His Holiness was the personification of Manjushri during the teaching. Being intellectually inferior, I cannot claim to have cleared all doubts about the expressions; but since that time I felt more open, and found it easier to relate the examples with the meaning while going through the texts, meditating or saying the prayers, unlike in the past. And because of this I was able to lead a more open life and have a better view. It was an amazing feeling. I don't believe that this newly acquired understanding of the meaning of the expressions was the result of my intellectual function, but it was due to the blessings of His Holiness.

From a young age, I had started reciting *Manjushri Namasamgiti*. Most probably one of my teachers must have told me to do it. I don't remember when I started or who advised me to recite it. It is commonly believed that reciting the *Namasamgiti* will improve one's intelligence. It is great to have such faith. But I feel that reciting the words of the Buddha with the hope of becoming more intelligent, wealthy or successful, and to have a long life, is not right. My understanding is that improvement of one's intelligence should be treated as a side effect of reciting the *Manjushri Namasamgiti,* and the main purpose should be to attain the analytical wisdom: to understand that there is no difference between the intrinsic empty nature of phenomena, and the dependently originated appearance of phenomena, and to apply this wisdom to reflect on the joy and sorrow, the good and bad, the hope and fear, *etc.*, that are experienced in life, and to understand that the meaning of dependent origination, as described by Nagarjuna in the six Middle Way treatises, is an aspect of our life.

This understanding should further make us put into practice the view of non-acceptance, non-grasping meditation and boundless activity that the Buddha-like spiritual teachers speak of all the time, and not to let them remain as words written on paper, or verbal sounds spoken by them. To achieve experiential feeling or understanding, and accomplish authentic experience, which, with nothing to be meditated upon, should further lead to the development of an impartial and overwhelming compassion, devoid of hope and fear, for all sentient beings. In my pinion achieving the wisdom born out of compassion that spontaneously causes the interdependence of working for the welfare of sentient beings should be the main purpose of reciting *Manjushri Namasamgiti*.

My Guru Ontrul Rinpoche once said to me, "The teaching on *Manjushri Namasamgiti* will help sharpen your wisdom, develop qualities of inner understanding and purify the two obscurations, including the defilement of *Kor* and karmic traces. You must request the teachings during His Holiness's visit." Hence, following the advice of my guru, I made the request when His Holiness visited our monastery, and he happily accepted my request and very kindly gave the teaching. The kindness of my root gurus is inconceivable and inexpressible. His Holiness said that I should give the teachings to others in the future and gave me the text. His Holiness said that this text was rare and that he would send a few more copies later through the Tibet Office in Delhi. His Holiness told me to inform him about whatever teachings and empowerment I needed, and that he would give them to me whenever time permitted.

About a decade ago, I had the good fortune to receive Bodhisattva vows from His Holiness, and at that time he gave me a text in praise of compassion with his blessings, and said, "As you had non-fabricated compassion since your childhood, practise the intrinsic meaning of this text and it will be of great benefit to others," and he gave me much advice. I was certain that my guru was advising me to diligently practise loving kindness, compassion and Bodhicitta. Since that time, I have been making a diligent effort to minimize selfishness, and to cultivate the thought and behaviour of working for the benefit of others. Although I am not doing any great work for the welfare of others, it is my belief that whatever little I am able to do is thanks to the blessings of His Holiness.

Although there is nothing to be amazed about with regard to my being a vegetarian, I heard that His Holiness had praised me during his teachings for being vegetarian and stopping animal sacrifice in some places. I don't deserve such praise from His Holiness for my little practice of acceptance and rejection and yet as the text says, "Love the miserly, love the deceitful, love the thieves and robbers, love the non-conscientious and love those influenced by others," and I believe that out of kindness, His Holiness might have hoped that a little praise may encourage me, and benefit the Dharma and beings, the general public and me individually. I am persevering to fulfill His Holiness's wishes in carrying out altruistic action according to the Dharma, without the contamination of politics and the desire for a name or recognition.

KYABJE PAWO RINPOCHE

I also had the opportunity to receive many general teachings, especially teachings of the Karma Kagyud tradition, and the *One Hundred Short*

Discourses in particular, from the late Kyabje Pawo Rinpoche Tsuglag Mawei Wangchuk (1912-1991). Later, I had the good fortune of receiving many instructions from him, including the empowerment of Palden Lhamo, which can lead to enlightenment within one lifetime. I had heard that he was very strict and normally did not give teachings easily. All the biographies mention that many of the previous Pawo Rinpoches had been the spiritual teachers of previous Gyalwang Drukpas and that they shared a profound bond of mutual affection and respect. I have firm faith and belief that this must be dependent co-origination. Also, he always had great love and respect for me.

The Gyalwang Drukpa institution had left behind everything when coming into exile and had nothing during my enthronement; in fact they did not even have a proper base at that time. As a sign of the spontaneous fulfillment of prayers of the previous Pawos and Gyalwang Drukpas, Pawo Rinpoche arranged everything that was traditionally needed, such as a golden saddle, a golden cushion, a mane-cover, a golden badge, all requisites of the throne and gave all the necessary guidance; I learned later that he oversaw the enthronement ceremony. At that time I was about three years old, turning four, and I don't remember much.

I remember riding a big white horse covered with brocade and having a good view as the big horse was taken through the crowd, and holding a plastic deer in my hand when I reached the throne. The enthronement ceremony was held at Do-tsuk Monastery where Rinpoche was staying. These are mundane things that I am mentioning. Auspicious omens are very important for the meditation lineage, and it is my belief that he had made all the worldly arrangements and gave full support for the enthronement, as a continuation of close relations of the past, and to set the auspicious omens for the guru-disciple relation in the future, because everybody knows that he usually did not appreciate the eight worldly concerns – fame, recognition, adulation and show of reverence. So it is certain that any activity that such a qualified guru like him performs has a special reason and purpose. Later, every time I received teachings and instructions from him, I always received wonderful omens, in the form of dreams, experiences or visions. As mentioned earlier, I received all the instructions of the Karma Kagyu tradition and Dzogchen teachings on the state of the mind. I am confident that he will compassionately take care of me in all my continuum of lives.

KYABJE DO DRUBCHEN RINPOCHE

The special faith that I had in Gyalwa Longchen Rabjampa since childhood grew stronger as I grew up, and I felt a great urge to practise his teachings, like a thirsty man wishing to find water. All the prayers and practices of my mother are the *Heart Essence of Dzogchen*. On many occasions, when I heard her in the morning, recite the *Quintessence of Guru*, I had tears in my eyes and the hairs on my body stood up out of devotion, but I never had the opportunity to practice it. One day, I asked my mother to give me instructions. She was shocked and said, "The day I give you instructions will be the sign of my death or the degeneration of Buddhism", and she never gave me any instructions. But I know she has the qualifications of a spiritual teacher.

I expressed my wish for the *Heart Essence* teachings, to my Guru Ontrul Rinpoche, and he folded his hands and said, "It will be great merit if you can receive the teachings from Do Drubchen Rinpoche (1927-). But he is a siddha and I do not know if he will give the teachings." After that, he repeatedly told me the biography of successive Do Drubchen Rinpoches and I also wished to meet him. He did not live very far away, but for a long time I did not get the opportunity to meet him.

Whenever Ontrul Rinpoche came to see me or wrote to me, he always asked if I had met Do Drubchen Rinpoche and said, "You should not delay, or else it will be too late." Therefore, one day I went as a wanderer to find out if I could get an audience with Do Drubchen Rinpoche and stayed at a hotel close by for the night. When I asked around, people said it was difficult to get an audience, but sometimes he gave a public audience for two hours. When I enquired further, I was happy to learn that he was giving a public audience for two hours the next day. So, the next day I went to the monastery and the sight of over a thousand people waiting for an audience made me think that it would be difficult to get a private audience. And even if I got an audience, I would not have the opportunity to request teachings and I felt discouraged.

I stood in the queue, and after some time an attendant came and asked me, "Are you the son of Bairo Rinpoche?" and I replied in the affirmative. He asked me to follow him and took me to the private quarters, gave me tea and biscuits and asked me to wait there. Since no one knew me, I wondered about this, and asked him why he was treating me as special. He said, "Since the morning, Rinpoche told us that Bairo Rinpoche's son will come and he will be humble. So watch out for him," and seemed surprised. I remembered Ontrul Rinpoche telling me that all the successive Do Drubchen Rinpoches were enlightened messengers of Guru Padmasambhava and I was not surprised that he would have foreknowledge.

After a break in the session, I was taken in for the audience. I made all my requests slowly, and pretending not to know, he asked me a lot of questions. Then he said, "If it will benefit you I will do whatever I can. But now I am old. I may not be able to fulfill all your wishes." I thought he was asking me why it took so long for me to come and see him, and I felt a great sense of regret. I still regret this when I think about it. I regretted having wasted so many years not meeting such a realized master, inseparable from the primordial benefactor and the regent of Gyalwa Longchen Rabjampa's teachings. I thought this was evidence of the degenerate times, and that this could only happen to a guru like me who lives off *Kor* offerings. Because of his advanced age, Do Drubchen is not able to give many teachings or initiations. Anyway, since that time, he kindly took care of me whenever he gave teachings.

During an elaborate empowerment of the *Four Branches of Heart Essence*[58] he opened the offerings on the table and some sort of vapour emanated and it smelt like the fragrance of ambrosia. I felt a great sense of devotion, and my body went numb – without any thoughts, good or bad, arising. I don't know how long I remained like that – it couldn't have been long. I also received detailed instructions of *Yeshe Lama* and when it came to clearing the doubts about literal explanations, one could not help but think that he was the personification of Longchen Rabjampa. His humility, always saying he did not know, this alone inspired devotion. Though there may be many biographies of him, I have only seen a brief autobiography.

---

58. Famous collection of Dzogchen scripture by Gyalwa Longchen Rabjam: Heart essence of Daka-Dakini, Quintessence of Daka-Dakini, Heart essence of Vimalamitra and the quintessence of Guru.

KYABJE ZHICHEN ONTRUL RINPOCHE

Kyabje Zhichen Ontrul Rinpoche (1922-1997), who advised me to seek the *Heart Essence* teachings, is popularly known as *Zhichen Kyabgon* in his native land. He was born in Amdo Mayul and his pet name was Rigpo. After being recognized as Zhichen Ontrul by both Dzogchen Thupten Choekyi Dorje and Jamyang Khyentse Choekyi Lodoe, he came to Zhichen Monastery. He learned the rituals, the use of ritual musical instruments, ritual melodies, mudras and common Nyingma practices from Akhu Gyarongwa Kalsang Gyatso, a disciple of the previous Ontrul Rinpoche. I heard that merely on being shown, he learned the practice known as *The Pure Vision of the 1st Zhichen Kyabgon*, which was different from the other Kathok traditions.

Rinpoche said that he received many teachings and initiations from Kathok Ngaga, also known as Kunkhyen Pema Ledrel Tsel, one of the many spiritual masters he studied under. Khenpo Ngaga told Rinpoche, "Now you have understood the profound view and if you go and meditate in a solitary place, you will definitely achieve the rainbow body. If you return to Kathok, you will become the life-vein of the doctrine." Rinpoche said, "During an initiation, he had a statue of the Buddha in his hand and he hit my head with it, as if giving me a hand blessing. I thought he was being playful and looked up, but saw that he had a very serious look. Today, when I look back I think it was an indication that he had foreknowledge that I would not be able to carry out his instructions."

I asked Rinpoche how one could explain this and he said, "It was a clear prediction that due to the upheaval in Tibet I was not able to do as he had advised, that I would study in a Gelug Monastery and that I would neither meditate to achieve the rainbow body, nor be of much benefit to the Kathok lineage."

Soon after, he returned to Zhichen Monastery and became the Vajracharya during *Drowa Kundol*, Vajrakilaya, *Tsechu,* and other sadhana sessions, and gave many initiations and teachings. When he was told to take the responsibility of looking after Zhichen and its branch monasteries, he felt that the monastery must have a proper system of training and learning of the Mahayana and Vajrayana doctrines, in order to restore the monastery to the state of glory it had been in during the times of Dza Patrul Rinpoche and Terton

Lerab Lingpa. So he told the management that simply being able to hold the bell and vajra, read and write and falling into the trap of *Kor* of monastic affairs and followers, would only be a waste of life and of no use to either the monastery or to others.

He requested the gurus, tulkus, the monastic community and lay followers to allow him to pursue learning and contemplation as he wished, but he had some difficulty in getting their support. Around that time he fell ill and almost died, "This adversity turned into an advantage, and I then did not have to take responsibility for the monastic affairs. I am certain that this was the blessings of the guru and the Triple Gem as, since that time, I had the opportunity to study the scriptures," he said.

It was certain that he had deliberately taken on the serious illness, because although all the medical check-ups and divinations were certain that he was in a critical condition, the day he was given permission to pursue his studies and not get involved in the monastic administration, his health improved without any medicine. His wish was fulfilled. As I said earlier, anyone with spiritual wisdom does not like to be contaminated by *Kor,* and this realized master must have felt that it would be better to take birth in another sphere, rather than be defiled by *Kor* of the monastery. Then he went to see Shugchung Tulku Tshullo, a disciple of Dodrub Tenpai Nima, Khenchen Damcho Lodoe and Terchen Sogyal, and, starting with teachings of the *Fifty Stanzas of Guru Devotion* and other mind-training instructions, he received the complete teachings on *Valid Cognition*, the Middle Path, the Perfection of Wisdom, Abhidharma, *Teachings of Maitreya* and many Tantras of the Old School, including *Guhyagabha Tantra*. He not only learned the literal meaning of the scriptures, but cleared doubts through inner experience. He remained with his guru, night and day, for almost two decades. He not only cleared his scholarly doubts, but also pointedly introduced the Dzogchen view. He thus completed his practice and pleased his guru with his accomplishments. He studied under Shugchung Tulku until he passed away, not like us today – rushing to receive teachings and initiations on the same day and then returning home to live carelessly.

Rinpoche used to tell me, "If you have the intention to receive teachings, initiations and instructions from a guru, you must have the non-fabricated thought of entrusting your body, speech and mind to that guru." If you stay with the guru and train in the path of preparation and other practices, it is certain that you can experience the signs of the path as described in the texts, even if you cannot attain enlightenment within one lifetime.

I know that Rinpoche possessed various signs of the path, but I cannot narrate them because I am bound by secrecy. Some people claim accomplishments but I don't believe them. Rinpoche was usually very prudent and did not like talking about these things and so I wouldn't dare to ask him. He received the transmission and initiation of *Rinchen Terdzö Chenmo*, and the Oral Lineage teachings of Nyingma, *The Seven Treasures, The Three Cycles of Relaxation* and collected works of Rongsom Pandita from His Holiness Dudjom Rinpoche. From a young age, Rinpoche had studied under many qualified spiritual teachers and completed learning and contemplation with intense and continuous application, and attained the state of omniscience. He would always advise us disciples, "Do not think you know enough about Dharma. When it comes to Dharma you should never think you know enough until you attain enlightenment.

"There are some people who claim to know all the scriptures and I feel amazed and think it is inconceivable. Until you know all the objects of knowledge, you can never know all the scriptures. So I am amazed by the claim of knowing all the scriptures," he used to say.

Although he was a great Yogi, who had realized Dzogchen thought, he remained humble and a hidden yogi, as explained in the Sutra. He later joined Gomang College of Drepung Monastery and studied there for many years and received the Geshe Lharampa degree of the Gelugpa tradition. About this, he said, "Since I was not studying the scriptures for a name or a degree, I felt the title of Geshe was needless, and for many years did not take the degree. Later my friends told me, 'If you stay quiet and don't take the exam for the Geshe degree, it will be seen as disrespectful to the Gelugpa School and as disregard for the monastery's discipline. So it would be better for you to take the Geshe exam at the earliest opportunity.' Moreover, His Holiness the Dalai Lama also asked me, on a few occasions, when I was taking the Geshe exams. So I thought it was a prestige issue and took the Lharam exam."

He had received teachings of the great and abridged *Graded Path to Enlightenment* from His Holiness the Dalai Lama and many other spiritual teachers. I have never heard him speak ill of any guru or monk. Although he was a practitioner of the Nyingma School, he always spoke of the qualities of the guru, the khenpo or the students of the Gelugpa School and never spoke with envy. Having been among Gelugpas he never spoke with prejudice against the Nyingma School.

How did Rinpoche come to be my tutor? When I was around twenty years old, I wanted to study the scriptures again, in order to master an understanding of the teachings that I had earlier received from Zigar Khen Rinpoche Noryang; and I asked Bairo Rinpoche for advice. He said, "Ontrul Rinpoche, a guru of my monastery, is at present living as a Geshe. If you are fortunate to have him as a teacher it would be wonderful. But no one has been able to request him and he has refused requests by many other gurus and chieftains to become their teacher. You make a request to him. The two of you have karmic connection. Moreover, he and I have a very strong and pure bond of Samaya. I will also write to him. He might agree."

During an audience with His Holiness the Dalai Lama, I sought His Holiness' advice on whether it would be better for me to study at an institution like the Buddhist School of Dialectics or the Gomang College. His Holiness said, "You will need a guru who has extensive knowledge of the tenets of both the Old and New Schools and is non-sectarian. Such a guru is rare to find these days. We might find one. I will check and inform you. You cannot join an institution such as the School of Dialectics because you have many monasteries and followers to look after. With the best of intentions, I brought the reincarnation of Dzogchen Rinpoche to study at the School of Dialectics, and now many people are accusing me of trying to put a yellow hat on Rinpoche."

I felt Dzogchen Rinpoche was very fortunate and wished I too had such good fortune and persisted with the idea of joining the Dialectics School. His Holiness rejected my idea and jokingly said, "If you join the Dialectics School, people might stone me. So, as I said earlier, we will try to find a non-sectarian guru who has extensive knowledge of both the Old and New School tenets."

During an audience a few months later I informed His Holiness about Ontrul Rinpoche, who was known as Alag Gyakpa in the Gelugpa monastic university, and asked His Holiness if it would be possible for His Holiness to write to him. His Holiness said, "This is good. I don't know if he will listen; on your part also, make a request to him." His Holiness wrote to him and I too made many requests. My father Bairo Rinpoche, who belonged to the same monastery and the same spiritual lineage as Ontrul Rinpoche and shared a pure bond of Samaya with him, also wrote to him. As a result of all this I was very fortunate to have Ontrul Rinpoche as my tutor.

Later, during conversations in the course of teachings, Rinpoche said that his root Guru Do Shungchung Tshullo told him, "In the later part of your life you may get requests to teach the scriptures. Do not refuse the request. It will be beneficial. So, it seems you are the one he predicted." I felt happy to hear this and at the same time it was like a heavy burden on my back. Even today, I get an indescribable feeling when I think about his words and feel it would be shameful if I cannot work for the welfare of others. Whenever any sense of selfishness arises within me, the words of my Guru Ontrul Rinpoche come to mind and I feel embarrassed.

Normally, I cannot avoid giving teachings to the best of my ability to those interested in listening. Ontrul Rinpoche once said to me, "There is no doubt that you can debate on the Sutra. We must go around monasteries for a proper debate on both Sutra and Tantra. Before that we must study the *Guhyagarba Tantra*. For example, Gyalwa Longchen is a Nyingma but he went to other monasteries, especially the major monasteries of the New School, to debate. You are intelligent. You must study the scriptures for another three years." But unfortunately for me, Rinpoche had to go to Tibet. He told me, "Come to Tibet in the summers. We have a lot to learn and discuss about Tantra." But because of the China-Tibet issue I could not go at all. Some people even advised me, "Just go with your eyes closed. There should not be any problem."

The Chinese side may not have a problem, but there will be a problem on the Tibetan side. Or the Tibetan side may not have problems, but the Chinese side will have problems. For example, if I went to Tibet to continue my studies, people here will not say I went to Tibet to study. They will publicize that I am pro-Chinese and went to Tibet for political reasons. In today's time, due to the influence of the spirit of broken Samaya, people will believe the disinformation propaganda that discredits the innocent, and very few people will use their intelligence to investigate the truth.

There are quite a few people waiting to find any opportunity that will make life difficult for me. Such rumours are spread out of envy and contempt for our spiritual lineage. I say contempt, because although the lineage has a large following, with monasteries spread all over the Himalayan region, for many years the monasteries and followers remained rudderless. The lineage holders could not work in cooperation and the lineage remained like an ember under ashes. So it was natural for them to show contempt. You cannot blame them for being envious either, because there are so many followers and monasteries, not only in central Tibet and the Kham region in eastern Tibet, but also in Bhutan, Nepal, Sikkim, Ladakh, Lahaul and Kinnaur in the Himalayan region of India. The Drukpa Lineage has now spread to North America, Europe and Southeast Asia. So it is natural to feel envious. Moreover we are now more active than ever on many fronts, and this is difficult for them to digest.

Activities of other spiritual leaders who have always been active would not have bothered them so much. But our history is different: there were internal differences, with bigger monasteries taking over the smaller ones, and each being critical of the other. We have never been supportive of one another – whether in dealing with external threats to our monasteries or communities, or regarding the education of monks or the welfare of lay followers – but we remained aloof and quiet. So when they suddenly saw our lineage coming alive within a couple of decades – restoring the monasteries, establishing communities of male and female practitioners, rebuilding connections with lay patrons and followers, and being involved in numerous social welfare projects and environmental campaigns – it becomes difficult for them to accept and digest the reality. Then some of them resort to spreading rumours and lies in our society, giving a bad name to me and my lineage. For example, some of them say I have no devotion to His Holiness the Dalai Lama or that we have contacts with the Chinese. Recently, an anonymous letter with similar contents was sent to most of the monasteries in India. However deplorable I may seem, people understand that I know the spiritual discipline and so hardly anyone would have believed the rumours.

I feel pity for the people who waste their time in such meaningless work. In Tibet, and especially to Chinese authorities and offices, a similar letter with the opposite content was sent. I think it is the same people writing the two contradictory letters. The letter sent to the Chinese states that I am an ardent supporter of His Holiness the

Dalai Lama, and engage in anti-Chinese political campaigns in the United States and many other countries. I had a project to install a huge statue of Amitabha Buddha in Nepal, but unfounded rumours were spread, saying that the project was the idea of His Holiness. This scared the Nepalese authorities about a Chinese reaction and created some controversy.

People ask what purpose such rumours will serve. I also ask the same question. But if one looks at the bigger picture, the people who write such letters or spread such rumours have a lot to gain. The negative motive is to give a political tinge to all projects to revive and restore the Drukpa Lineage in Tibet, thereby creating new doubts and suspicions in the minds of the Chinese authorities, and blocking the necessary official permission for the projects. Many years ago, I applied for a Chinese visa to visit Tibet with the hope of visiting my monasteries and followers. In those days, most of the gurus and spiritual teachers had no problem in getting Chinese permission to visit Tibet. But I was denied permission. I even contacted the late Panchen Rinpoche and other high-level personnel. I also phoned Ngabo Ngawang Jigme, who had close ties with the father of the previous Gyalwang Drukpa, for his help in getting permission. A few months later, Ngabo briefly told me about the above-mentioned information and said, "Your record in the Chinese official documents is not good and nothing can be done now. Please do not mind my inability to help you." Like the saying, "When the shepherd is away, it is a picnic for the wolf", my not getting permission was good news for them.

Since the upheaval in Tibet, the view, meditation and conduct, prayer tunes and music, ritual dances, mandala and the painting traditions of most of the Drukpa Lineage was lost. I have a list of Drukpa monasteries from Mount Kailash to the Kham region in Eastern Tibet, that had no choice but to follow gurus of other lineages, since I was refused permission by China to visit Tibet. It is really sad, because in the name of help, these gurus completely changed the lineage of the monasteries. I am telling you this, because this attitude of the gurus makes me uneasy. This is the concern of a few people like me and it may not be important to most of you.

Anyway, in brief, I was not able to follow the instructions of my guru and also lost interest in visiting other monasteries for dialectical debate. In a letter from Tibet, Rinpoche advised me to abandon the eight worldly motives and, quoting Milarepa and Tsangpa Gyare he said, "Renouncing the eight worldly motivations was the main practice of all past spiritual masters, including Gyare and his disciple Gyalwa Yangonpa. You too must carry out activities for the welfare of the Dharma and beings without falling under the influence of the eight worldly motivations. Always do whatever you have to do sincerely for the preservation and promotion of your lineage and monasteries without interfering in others' work, because meddling will give rise to attachment, aversion and disputes. Remember this."

Reflecting on his advice, I understood that by "sincerely" he meant not to seek selfish ends like a name and wealth and by "not interfering" he meant not to do any harm to others, even if I cannot do anything to help others. In his letter he said, "You have a lot to do for the Lineage and monasteries. Make the practice of Bodhicitta your main practice and your activities will flourish. Today's use of eloquence and selfish deceit in the name of Dharma is the sign of degeneration of Dharma."

In the past, while giving teachings I would suddenly feel embarrassed, scared or ashamed. I asked Rinpoche about this and he advised, "Meditate on Bodhicitta while giving teachings. There is nothing more effective than this. Bodhicitta is needed in both worldly and spiritual work. Today, very few practise Bodhicitta even in spiritual work, not to mention worldly work." Then I asked him how to practise Bodhicitta and he replied, "Today, some people say that Bodhicitta cannot be practised in worldly work, but this is a very narrow-minded way of thinking. Engaging in worldly work without any selfish interest – or minimum selfishness – will gradually generate an authentic altruistic mind. In this way, everything you do from today until enlightenment will become positive activity touched by Bodhicitta. This is how you should interpret the saying that the seven non-virtuous activities of the body and speech are permissible, if the intention is purely altruistic. As you practise the path, Bodhicitta will also grow. We have little Bodhicitta today because selfishness, the opposite of Bodhicitta, is strong in us. Whatever you do in life must end in the nature of Bodhicitta. So long as the eight worldly motives are present, there is no way for the activity to end in the nature of Bodhicitta. So, let alone enlightenment, one cannot hope to even become a good human. Generally, practice of the Sutra path is firm and steady. That is why the practice of Bodhicitta should be the main focus."

Then I asked, "So then, does it mean that for us Vajrayana practitioners, except for the generation and completion stages, the use of trumpets and drums, mandala drawing, torma-making, ritual dances, tunes and music, *etc.*, are not important?" He replied, "No, it does not mean that. All Vajrayana practices fall under the methods of dispelling attachment to ordinary appearances. Attachment to ordinary appearances is the main opponent of Bodhicitta. If you wonder how such mistakes are made, there are many causes, but the main cause is the grasping of body, speech and mind as being separate, and spontaneously clinging to ordinary appearances. This is the reason why the definition of foundation, path and fruit – channels as the base, wind as the path and droplet as the fruit – should not be seen as separate, but as one, and captured as the essence of the Four Empowerments.[59] In some texts it is described as the simultaneous practice of the three Vajras. Sacred dance steps, tunes and ritual practices must also be understood as part of the practice of the four empowerments of channels, wind and droplet. Otherwise, merely blowing trumpets, beating drums, tunes and mudras will be meaningless. In addition to Vajrayana practices, one must be gradually able to turn every action, such as walking, sitting or sleeping into practice."

Then I said, "So that means ritual practices, torma-making and butter sculpture, sacred dances and music, *etc.*, are also Bodhicitta practices. Is it so?" He replied, "Of course it is. It must be the supreme form of Bodhicitta practice." The term "supreme" has many meanings. My understanding was that although we regard daily activities like walking, sitting or sleeping as ordinary, and regard blowing of trumpets, beating of drums, drawing mandalas, making tormas, sacred dances, tunes and music, *etc,* as superior. All ordinary and superior activities must be turned into the practice of the state of union.

I had the tradition of daily performing smoke offerings and making offerings of tormas to the protecting deities. One day, when I went for my scripture class, Rinpoche asked me, "What is it that you chant every day?" and I told him what I chanted. He said, "It is good. But one must be able to subdue the practice deity, guardian

---

59. Four levels or stages within any empowerment according to the inner tantra: 1. the vase empowerment; 2. the secret empowerment; 3. the knowledge-wisdom empowerment; and 4. the precious word empowerment.

deity, local deity or spirit by the right view and practise. Then they will be with you even if you don't practise them. If you look at the deities and spirits as being separate from your mind, you will never be able to accomplish them, or even if you accomplish them, they will be wrathful deities. So you must understand that this is not of much use."

I asked, "I have heard the term 'subduing with view'. How does one practise this?" Rinpoche replied, "It means integrating the deity inseparably with your mind. If there is a deity that is born from the illusion of seeing a deity, or a spirit separate from your mind, the foundation of your practice is damaged and the deity or spirit cannot be subdued. Then you need the wisdom of seeing the void nature of your mind. That will subdue the deity." Then as if joking, he remained gazing for a while. Then he smiled and stayed in contemplation for some time. I felt a strange sensation of all my body hair bristling.

Rinpoche further said, "You and I should not take to propitiating deities too often, but believe them to be inseparable from our mind. Thus, we need the awareness of conviction that the support of the deities and protectors is with you all the time. It would be deplorable not to know how to propitiate the deities and protectors without using drums, cymbals, trumpets and chanting."

One day when I went for teachings, I saw Rinpoche making an offering of black tea in a small offering cup outside his window. So I said, "Now I see you too are making offerings," and he replied, "Yes. But this is slightly different. This is for getting their assistance in opening the gates of Sukhavati Pure Land and when I leave this world. I am making offerings to protector Anandakumara."

On many occasions he said, "Although I came from the *Copper-coloured Mountain* I think it is better to go to Sukhavati." I asked, "Why?" When he replied, "The Dakinis will not look after this old monk. It will be very disheartening and embarrassing if they don't open the door, lay the cushion, or do not accept me. In Sukhavati, there are other old monks like me and they will receive me," and he laughed. "Once you are in Sukhavati, you can go to see Guru Rinpoche and see and receive teachings from Buddhas in other pure lands. That is good enough," he said.

On another occasion he said, "These days, as soon as I close my eyes I see beautiful landscapes filled with meadows, flowers, trees and young boys and girls playing around. Sometimes I see domestic animals like yaks and wild animals in some places. I don't know the significance of these visions. Could it be an indication of my death?" and I replied, "It cannot be an indication of death. You must live long." He said, "Yes. It is better to live, of course. No one would like to die."

He spoke of his going to the pure land on many occasions and would often tell us pupils that he will go to Sukhavati as a joke, or during serious conversations. He said that once there was a holy Geshe in India and he predicted that Rinpoche would be reborn in the Blissful pure land and Rinpoche had told him that if his prayers are fulfilled then he would prefer to go to Sukhavati.

Before his passing away, he told his attendant monks, "I am going to Sukhavati. So you don't have to worry. Moreover, you should not look for my reincarnation." I do not know with what intention he said this at that time, but it is not possible that he would not reincarnate, because Buddha-like gurus like him who have accomplished training in working for the welfare of others, can visit the pure lands just to relax for some time, but they cannot bear to stay away from reincarnating for the benefit of the Dharma and sentient beings. They are not ordinary people like us. If we find a pleasant place we want to stay there forever, and we will try everything in order to live there permanently and never bother about helping other beings. This is the difference between them and us.

You must have faith that they can reincarnate in any form as may be appropriate. Many of us accept a reincarnation that suits our thought, or else criticize reincarnation as wrong, or as an evil spirit, thereby accumulating negative karma. The best thing to do, in case something happens that is beyond your thought, is to leave it as it is. If it is harming the Sangha, the monastery, philosophical studies or meditative practices, or a lot of beings – then you have to speak out, but criticizing simply because it is inconceivable to you is foolishness. There is no account in the history of the Dharma, Sangha or lay community benefitting from criticizing the reincarnation of one's guru, harming him or displacing him. It only causes damage to you in this life and the next, and damage to the Dharma, Sangha and the lay community. I am just saying this with the hope that you will have a new perspective.

Rinpoche passed away soon after. Early one morning, I dreamt I was walking in a place full of grass and suddenly I met Ontrul

Rinpoche below a huge rock. I asked him, "Where are you going?" and he replied that he came to see me. I said I would arrange a seat for him and he replied that there was no need. He said, "It is time to leave now, and I have to go," he affectionately patted me and, looking towards the top of the hill, he left quickly. I woke up with a sad feeling. I thought to myself, "I have not seen him or dreamt of him for many years since he left for Tibet. Today, when I saw him in my dream, I did not get the opportunity to ask for instructions or even to sit with him for a while. I am so unfortunate," and I cried for a long time and then fell asleep again. Again, I dreamt Rinpoche has come back to the same place, panting, and I hugged him and he said, "Don't think too much", then he just vanished, and I felt a cool breeze over my head and woke up suddenly. I thought this may have been an indication of his passing away. Within a week I heard the sad news from many sources and on checking, I found that he had passed away the day that I had had the dream.

Although my devotion, renunciation, diligence and wisdom are negligible, I felt happy that he showed the sign that he would compassionately take care of me in this life and the next. He passed away in his native land. I don't have clear information about the day and date of his passing away. His attendant would know that. Some may have kept notes of Rinpoche's activities. The guru and disciple – all external and internal phenomena, thoughts and actions, and feelings of happiness and sorrow are impermanent. When the saying: "Even though you wish to remain inseparable from the kind guru, you are bound to be separated," became a fact – there was nothing I could do. I received many common and uncommon teachings from a realized master like him and his kindness completely held me back from samsara.

KYABJE ZHICHEN BAIRO RINPOCHE

Without my father Bairo Rinpoche, I would not have come into contact with Ontrul Rinpoche. The contribution to Buddhism of the great translator Vairochana of Tibet, one of the emanations of Buddha Vairochana, is equal to Guru Padmasambhava. He has emanated in various forms as deemed appropriate, such as laymen, monks and khenpos. His emanations are looking after monasteries and practices of various traditions.

Bairo Rinpoche is my father only in appearance, and there is no doubt that he is Vairochana in reality. For example, everyone can see a black mole on the tip of his nose, and when I was young I used to rub it playfully. One day he asked me, "There is the syllable *Ah* on the tip of my nose. Can you see it?" I said, "It is not there" and he asked me to look again. A child's mind is devoid of hope and fear, and I remember looking again and seeing a fine white spot in the form of the syllable *Ah* within the black mole. In reality, I think that syllable represents the spontaneous embodiment of the great bliss of the exalted speech of Sambhogakaya, reflected in the form of the white syllable *Ah*, but people like me who lack the certainty of seeing the Sambhogakaya Buddha do not have the good fortune to see it, and seeing what I saw then was commendable.

It was like Asanga first seeing Maitreya Buddha in the form of a sick dog with a rotten lower body. When he actually saw Maitreya the latter asked Asanga to carry him on his back to the market square, and only one old woman saw him carrying a sick dog with a rotten lower body. Others did not even see the sick dog. So, I don't think these things should be dismissed outright.

As I became older, Bairo Rinpoche neither asked me to see, nor did I look again at the mole. Once, I spoke about it and he immediately dismissed the topic saying, "It is called black-nosed and is inauspicious. There is nothing surprising about it." He doesn't usually like talking about such topics. The footprint he left on the rock in Kathok Dorjeden is there for everyone to see. Similarly, the footprint he left on a rock when he was small is as clear as if it has been made of clay, and is displayed in the shrine of Zhichen Monastery. Although I have seen the footprints of Guru Rinpoche and many realized masters, I have not seen one as clear as this. He had also knotted a tree in front of the monastery.

When he was young, he told his attendants that he was going to play on the hill on the other side from where they were, and he asked them not to follow him for some time and he went alone. After some time, wondering what he was doing, the attendant monks went to see. They saw he had sculpted a white conch shell on the rock and had finished sculpting half the shape of a drum using a stick, and when he saw them he said, "Now it can't be done," and walked away. The white conch shell and the half shape of the drum can be seen even today. He also had playfully thrown his walking stick on a rock on the circular road of Ser Gonpo Drongri, and it stuck in the rock like in clay, and the local people took pieces of the stick as an object of faith and blessing and where they could reach it, they rubbed their hands on it. Its remains can be seen by pilgrims even today.

Later, when Rinpoche was living in Bhutan, Magistrate Lhadar, a devout follower, requested Rinpoche for an object of devotion and Rinpoche said he would give him blessed pills and asked if he had any vessel to put them in. He couldn't find any paper, so he went to the kitchen and found a small bottle and gave it to Rinpoche. Rinpoche filled it with blessed pills and gave it back to him. Lhadar couldn't find a lid for the bottle and seeing this, Bairo Rinpoche said, "Bring it to me. A way can be found." Taking the bottle he pressed the bottle's tip with his three fingers into a shape similar to the tip of a Momo and gave it back to Lhadar. Lhadar said at that he fainted out of joy and devotion and didn't remember anything. Later, he thought that if he had to take the pills there was no way he could take them out, and wondered what he should do. A few months later he again went to see Rinpoche and explained his dilemma. Rinpoche said, "Keep both the inner content and the outer holder as an object of devotion. You don't have to be in haste to open it. It is an omen of a long life for you. This happened because of your faith. This is what an object of devotion should be like. I don't like publicity. So keep it secret."

When you hear all this, some of you might feel devotion and some of you might wonder if this is true. Some of you might believe it is true and yet wonder for what reason all this is being done. The fact is that while the inner, empty, clear, unobstructed expanse remains unchanged – as a sign of accomplishment of the external visible manifestation of energy of the blissful state of awareness, mastered over many births, a realized being is able to show signs of realization naturally without any effort, while sitting, walking or standing. Also, seeing such signs of realization prove that, as explained in the texts, although objects like rocks appear real and solid, as labelled by our artificial conception of true existence, they are not as they appear. In fact these signs of accomplishment also serve the huge purpose of inspiring a strong faith in Buddhism, and ultimately help us to attain realization. It is similar to teaching the scriptures. There are stories of some devoted and wise persons realizing the nature of truth while debating on colour. Otherwise, being buried in scriptures for one's entire life would not be of much use.

These days, there are not many who show signs of realization. Even if there are any, people in our society lack wisdom and faith and will denigrate them as black magic. It is really sad. It is an indication that they have not read the text which mentions drawing milk from the painting of a cow to reverse the attachment to truth. The articulate speaker will claim that the dedicated practice of the Six Perfections with pure ethics as the foundation is itself a sign of realization, and proudly remain ready to criticize those performing miracles. This is a covert act of dishonouring all realized beings, from the Buddha to one's root guru, including the Six Ornaments and the Two Excellent Ones. You are spoiling your own path and making all your future followers lose faith in the unimaginable state. So, even if one has such thoughts they should not be expressed in front of novices. There may be realized beings among those who say such things, but in that case, they would be saying them for a greater purpose and one should not imitate such beings. If the wolf jumps where the tiger springs, then the wolf risks breaking its back.

If one has faith only in what is conceivable, and not in the unconceivable state, then studying scriptures, debating, meditating or running a monastic centre with thousands of monks and nuns will remain a superficial effort, and one can never attain the state of omniscience. Omniscience and enlightenment are all beyond our imagination. We must always check what is our goal? We build monasteries for monks and nuns which is admirable. But the real objective of a Mahayana practitioner should be to attain the state of omniscience. It is doubtful whether we know this or not. I feel it is difficult to achieve even liberation by treating superficiality as a spiritual practice, by being bloated with fame and pride and burning with envy and jealousy, so attaining the state of omniscience is out of reach.

I am speaking of our faults and not exposing the fault of others. Buddha has said again and again that exposing others' fault cannot be justified. Then does it mean I see this fault only in myself and not in others? I may see them, but treating faults in others as my fault is my main practice. Reflecting on how it is my fault, and how the fault I see in others is not the others' fault; thinking about day to day life; reading instructions and biographies of past masters; and discussing with spiritual friends, really helps the mind in a big way. I am telling you all this hoping it will help you in the same way.

As the Chinese intensified reforms, most Tibetans began to run after money and fame, showing disrespect to their own religion and spiritual teachers, and neglecting their own culture and tradition. Bairo Rinpoche said, "Guru Rinpoche had prophesied the coming of soldiers from across the border and the degeneration of Tibet's merit, and advised abandoning attachment and going to the southern border and hidden lands. I thought that the prophecy was coming true and decided to leave my homeland and go elsewhere. Whomsoever I talked to said, 'What you are saying is true.' But no one supported me. Instead they said, 'Many prayers and rituals are being performed. This will ward off the invasion.' Everyone was prepared to stay and no one was prepared to leave."

Bairo Rinpoche secretly informed Kunsang Nima, a realized master who was the root guru of both Ontrul Rinpoche and Bairo Rinpoche, about his thoughts and reasons, and he advised Rinpoche to go, saying, "I cannot leave behind the monastery, the monks and lay followers. I am also advanced in age. I will pray for us to meet in this or the next life."

Bairo Rinpoche said, "Not only was Guru Rinpoche's prophecy clear, but one could see it from people's behaviour. But except for me, no one seemed prepared to leave. Human beings are surprising." He said, "Even in that situation, some people were raising money and materials to build new monasteries. With a good intention I told them that their effort was meaningless. Some said that they understood the situation, but were building a monastery for the sake of the Dharma and beings and to accumulate merit, that they had neither worry nor regret, even if the monastery was razed tomorrow. It was amazing."

Thus he left behind the monastery, his homeland and his people. It was both physically and emotionally painful for him to do so. He said, "Even before leaving, I vowed to do whatever I could to look after the monks and lay people in this life and the next. I just did not abandon them from my heart." He was 25 years old then.

After leaving the monastery he reached Mura. He said, "I wanted to go to central Tibet via Labrang Tashi Khyil as a pilgrim, but many people came, saying they wanted to join me on the pilgrimage. At the end there were about eighty kitchens and it was difficult. Then we reached Labrang Tashi Khyil and I told the people that if they did not leave now it would be difficult once they fell into Chinese hands. But no one listened. Maybe it was because I was young. Then I sent someone to ask Gya Zhabdrung for a divination. Gya Zhabdrung's divination was highly respected at that time. His divination said, 'If you leave now, it is good both for your life and travel. Otherwise it would be very bad.' So from there on we had to separate. The people cried saying, 'If the guru is going to a distant land we may not see him again.' It was a very sad moment."

At that time, Rinpoche had a horse named Wusei and everyone saw the horse weep. I felt it was amazing that even animals, not just humans, could recognize the qualities of the body, speech and mind of a realized being. Arriving in Lhasa, Rinpoche joined the great prayer festival, Ganachakra puja and the ceremony of His Holiness the Dalai Lama's dialectical debate. Rinpoche said, "When I left the monastery I had quite a few attendants, including Drukchung, Chokyab and Thubga, but some returned home to look after their property. Most returned to the monastery. Drukchung, for example, was like my manager and he stayed back to look after my belongings. I heard he was later killed by the Chinese. I asked Khenpo Drukchung if he could help me and he immediately agreed."

Later, Khenpo Drukchung shared, "The previous Bairo called me one day and said, 'A day will come when you will have to carry my load,' and gave him sugar candy. It was a prediction that I would be able to serve this reincarnation."

From Lhasa, Rinpoche went to Mindrolling and on the way he stayed in retreat for one hundred days. Rinpoche said, "Mindrolling Monastery kindly made arrangements and showed me great respect and kindness. I received teachings on *A Guide to a Bodhisattva's Way of Life* and other instructions from the Khenpo. I received the initiation of *Garland of Views* and Vajrasattva, *etc.*, from Chung Rinpoche."

Then he stayed in retreat for a few years in the hidden land of Khempa Jong. He lived in Bhutan for thirteen or fourteen years and both the Royal Queen mother Phuntsok Choedon and the Third King Jigme Dorje became his patrons. Rinpoche always says that the Royal Queen mother and the King were very kind. In 1961, he spent a summer in Darjeeling on his way from Bhutan to Rewalsar and went to Bodhgaya on pilgrimage.

There is a history of a close connection with the Kathok Lineage during the time of the 7th and 8th Gyalwang Drukpa. Particularly, Rigzin Tshewang Norbu, who shared an inseparable state of mind with the 7th Gyalwang Drukpa, was very gracious to the Drukpa Lineage teachings. So it must be this auspicious connection that led to me, the holder of the title of the 12th Gyalwang Drukpa, to be born as the son of this holder of the Nyingma Kathok Lineage. He was in his late twenties then.

An American lady named Mrs Bedi started a school to give an opportunity to many young gurus of the New and Old Schools, with the kind intention of benefitting the Dharma and beings. It is said that Rinpoche learned the English language without much effort. Rinpoche himself says that he could not learn much because he did not have any interest in learning English. He worked as a tutor for the students. At that time, many gurus and tulkus were busy trying to go abroad. Some kind-hearted people suggested that it would be good if Rinpoche could also go abroad, because he had the skills of languages, painting, photographic development, even repairing watches and radios; a knowledge of Buddhist philosophy and culture, and secret meditation methods; and that finding a means of livelihood would not be a problem to him. But Mrs Bedi said, "If a guru like you goes abroad it would be very fortunate for people like me, but it would be a waste of your time. Places like India, Bhutan, Sikkim and Nepal are the right places for the gurus and tulkus to live in. The Dharma will benefit more by your staying here."

Rinpoche said, "Her advice was very helpful when I was undecided what to do. This enabled me to benefit the Dharma and beings a little bit." Rinpoche said just this much. But in a long life prayer composed for Rinpoche, Jamyang Khyentse Choekyi Lodoe, the embodiment of Manjushri had written, "May your body remain firm on the Vajra throne, victorious against the demonic forces, may your activities radiate the essence of teachings and, usher in festivity of the new golden age," predicting that the demonic Chinese forces would not bind him. Coming to India, Rinpoche braved the heat and cold, and with just a couple of monks to assist him, he printed the Oral Lineage and the Treasure Texts such as the instruction manuals of Dudul Dorje and Longsel, at a time when texts were hard to find. He distributed them free of charge to monasteries of all traditions. He gave initiations, oral transmissions and teachings on both the Oral Lineage and the Treasure Texts such as *Dui-Long*, *Longchen Nyingthig* and *Rinchen Terdzö*, on many occasions in Bhutan, Nepal and other countries. Rinpoche also invited Kathok

Moktsa Rinpoche, his elder brother, to give teachings and initiations to devoted disciples, gurus, tulkus, khenpos, monks and nuns. He has also done a lot for the Drukpa Lineage, as Rigzin Tshewang Norbu did in the past, but I don't need to go into those details here.

After more than forty years since the political upheaval in Tibet, Rinpoche was invited to his homeland. He visited about twenty of his monasteries and gave them ritual objects, left funds and gave all the necessary guidance. He enquired about the sacred dances, butter sculptures, mandala drawings, ritual practices, Vajrayana sadhanas and meditation practices that had suffered damage during the Cultural Revolution. When he discussed and taught over a hundred sacred dance steps in order to revive the sacred dances. Some of the elderly monks, gurus and khenpos were amazed that even after more than forty years Rinpoche remembered the old traditions vividly, and this made them cry with a mixed feeling of joy and sadness. The surprising thing is that normally he did not show much interest in reading, or the revision of the texts related to the old traditions.

When I was young, he remained a hidden yogi and rode a bicycle with me. Knowing that I liked horses, he would get hold of the Stray horses on the hill, put me on their back and take me around. He would play football with us. When all of us children were tired and would lie down on the grass, Rinpoche never seemed tired and instead would ask us if we were. Today, I feel that his actions then truly reflected the prayer, "Doing whatever is appropriate for each one, I pay homage to the Noble Avalokiteshvara."

He pretended not to know the tasks of a Vajracharya, such as sacred dances, mandala making or line drawing. Once, my monastery organized a sadhana session and I heard that the Chant Master of our monastery taught Rinpoche the practices of the Vajracharya! A similar incident happened with Dza Patrul. Once when Vajradhara Dza Patrul went as a hidden yogi, he met an elderly village monk and this elderly monk said to him, "Why does such a young and intelligent person like you is wasting his time. You must study *The Words of my Perfect Teacher* (which was composed by Dza Patrul himself)", and tried to explain the text to him. I have never seen Rinpoche perform sacred dances, make or draw mandalas. He must have done all this while giving initiations. Yet he possessed the inner quality of a memory that forgot nothing. Unlike Rinpoche, if I don't do the practices I know at least once a year I forget everything.

Rinpoche normally lived a joyful life and I believe "the open and joyful yogi" described in the Dzogchen instructions is someone like Rinpoche.

Later, when I was receiving teachings from Kyabje Trulshik Rinpoche, he said, "I do not know your father Bairo Rinpoche personally. He used to visit His Holiness Dudjom Rinpoche often. I remember he was tall and had a dark complexion. His Holiness told me that he is not only a great Dzogchen yogi but also a Treasure Revealer. Do you know of any Treasure Texts revealed by him? Have you seen one?" I replied, "I have not heard this before today, not to mention the fact that I have never seen any Treasure Texts." He folded his hands in a gesture of respect and said, "This is how a hidden yogi behaves."

The night we arrived at the holy place called Tetrapuri during a pilgrimage to Mount Kailash, Bairo Rinpoche insisted that we go to the Vajravarahi cave. I told him that we were all tired and would like to go the next day, and he said, "Okay. But just the two of us will go early in the morning. There is something important to do." The next morning at sunrise he got out of his tent and came to wake me up and said, "I am going now." I immediately went with him. It took us about half an hour to reach the cave. The caretaker had just opened the door. After prostrating he stretched his left hand into a dark rock opening behind the altar, and felt around for some time. I told him to be careful for there might be a snake or some harmful animal. He asked me not to worry and jokingly said, "I had hidden something here. I am trying to see if it is still here."

After some time he said, "It is still here. Look," and happily showed me an image of the Buddha, about the size of a finger. The throne and some of the fingers were slightly damaged. I requested him to bless me with the statue and he blessed me and prayed for a long time. I had never experienced anything like this and remained stunned for some time, not knowing what to say or do. I had a camera and asked if I could take a photo holding the statue, and with his permission I took a picture which is still with me. Then I asked him to give me the statue to keep as an object of blessing and he said, "What are you saying? This statue must be kept here. If you have a similar statue then you can leave the statue and take this one", and he didn't give it to me. Then he called the caretaker monk and, telling him to render proper service to the statue, wrapped it in a ceremonial scarf and kept it on top of the altar.

I had no authority and my guru had not given his consent, but I was concerned and worried about leaving the statue like that. Even today, when I think about it, I wonder if it is still there. Perhaps it may have already been turned into a commodity. This experience gave me new faith in what Kyabje Trulshik Rinpoche had said a few years earlier.

My father usually liked to play various games. He had a keen interest in new technical equipment. He would often jokingly say, "The old traditions and articles are good but I know all about them, so I don't have to take an interest in them. The modern machines are new and I have to learn about them. Generally people like you persist with what you know and criticize what you don't know as an unnecessary field of knowledge. If you don't take an interest, then your knowledge will not expand. It is such a waste. You must make your intellect work or else it will become dull. Don't you know Guru Rinpoche learned the art of pottery-making from a potter and carpentry from a carpenter? Like the saying, 'Train yourself in knowledge, even if you are dying tomorrow,' it is important to show interest in everything. It is a pity that you know nothing and sit idle."

His knowledge of astrology, traditional medicine, painting and poetry were flawless. Painting thangkas was like a game for him and he didn't have to concentrate. The filling of sacred incantations in statues, the making of medicinal blessed pills and mandala making were effortless practices for him. If anyone asked him about sacred dances he had complete knowledge about them. On the eve of my birth, His Holiness Dudjom Rinpoche gave a test of the sacred dances to all the gurus and tulkus present, in preparation of the *Tsechu* festival. Many Gurus, tulkus and khenpos, including Bairo Rinpoche took the test, and His Holiness told Bairo Rinpoche that he could perform any sacred dance of his choice as he had a perfect knowledge of them.

I remember many spiritual masters of the Sakya, Kagyu and Nyingma traditions gathered in our monastery many years ago. Even our Khen Rinpoche was present and they were engaged in dialectical debate. After some time, Bairo Rinpoche slowly got up and sat among those for the motion and answered all dialectical questions, to the surprise of everyone. I don't remember clearly but the subject of debate was *The Seventy Topics* from Maitreya's *Ornament of Clear Realization*. Everyone knows he is highly qualified and yet remains humble, without showing any pride, and this is his greatest quality. I believe if any of us had even a part of his knowledge we would be busy publicizing our expertise on the internet.

On returning from a visit to his monasteries in Tibet in 1980, Rinpoche began to think of building a monastery in India or Nepal. Sometimes he would say, "There are gurus, tulkus, khenpos and monks who come to me from Tibet and even from Ladakh and Bhutan. I need to build a place where they can stay for a few days." On other occasions he would say, "I need a monastery which will be like a mortuary to keep my body after my death." I said to Rinpoche, "I don't have to say this. You know building a monastery is easy, but the development of discipline, training, education and the practice of meditation need constant management. In today's time it will be difficult to find obedient and dedicated people. You have to think about this." He replied, "That is true. It will be an additional burden for you after my death. It is better to give up the idea."

A few months later my mother came to me and said, "Bairo Rinpoche has the thought of building a small monastery for Dharma in general, and for his lineage in particular. It may be a prophecy of the Dakinis. I think it will make him very happy if you approve. I also think it will be an auspicious connection. This is just my feeling." So suddenly, one day I said to Rinpoche, "If you want to build a monastery I am prepared to make the drawings." Rinpoche said, "Today you have brought good news. Then please prepare a drawing of the monastery's site plan."

Thinking of this as an offering to please the guru, I began to prepare the drawings and presented them to him. He said, "It need not be so big. It should be enough to hold my dead body," and laughed. I said, "Unless you have some special reason, you should not be so humble. Any activity in a small monastery will remain small. I have heard that before the upheaval in Tibet, no less than four-thousand monks gathered when teachings, accomplishment practices and functions were held in your main monastery in Tibet. So an auspicious omen for a similar thing happening here also should be set." He replied, "Then this is good. It is like the proverb, 'Except for oaths and sins, the bigger the better.' We will keep this drawing. The Tantra says that Buddhism will be sustained in Nepal for a long time. So I will build the monastery here."

Hence, the construction of Bairo Ling near the Boudhanath stupa in Kathmandu was started. I think it was in 1994. While we were abroad, the engineers had to reduce the building plan by one pillar for structural reasons. Otherwise, the original building plan was adhered to. All the construction and images were completed within three years and everyone said it was amazing – like a dream. Rinpoche himself would simply say, "The Guru and the Triple Gem are incontrovertible. All this happened by their grace." But I do believe that he must have received some prophecy, like my mother said.

Although these days we don't hear much about such things, the biographies of past masters tell us that gurus and Dakinis prophesied the seat of their activity and disciples to carry on their lineage. It is also mentioned that during the construction of the monastery the Dakinis, local gods, treasure gods and guardian deities assist directly and indirectly. So it is not as difficult as when an ordinary man builds his house.

As mentioned earlier, Kathok Moktsa Rinpoche conducted a hundred million recitations of Guru Rinpoche's mantra and Amitabha mantra on many occasions, in this monastery. Similarly, Moktsa Rinpoche gave initiations, transmissions and teachings of both the Oral Lineage and the Treasure Texts over many days and months. On my request, Dugey Tulku also taught *Collected Topics on Prime Cognition and Knowledge and Awareness* to the novices for a few years. Similarly, Khenpo Tsondue is also giving teachings on *Words of My Perfect Teacher* and *Letter to a Friend*. The Khenpo has, on my request, maintained the three basic codes of the practice of the Kathok tradition. Bairo Rinpoche himself has given thorough teachings on preliminary practices of the Kathok tradition and *Words of My Perfect Teacher* to new practitioners on many occasions. He also gave teachings of *Old Instructions of Longsel* for a few years continuously. Quite a few disciples at that time decided to dedicate their life to practice and some of them are at the Zhichen retreat centre near the Amitabha hermitage. This is worth rejoicing about. At such functions Bairo Ling is big enough to accommodate all. I feel it is the right size for the moment. I can't say anything for the future: it may be too small to accommodate all the practitioners or it may be too big to manage. There is no point thinking about the future.

Generally speaking, it need not be mentioned that the realized beings treat all sentient beings with love and kindness, as a mother would treat her only child. But Rinpoche has been particularly gracious to some of our monasteries. His kindness extended to Zhichen Monastery and over twenty branch monasteries, inside and outside Tibet, the two monasteries in Nepal, Bumthang Nima Lung Monastery in Bhutan where he spent many years, Hemis and Chemdey and other monasteries in Ladakh, as well as the monastery in Darjeeling where I live. He took care of everything, be it inner or external education, its economic state, sadhanas and serious sadhana sessions, all ritual practices, monastic land, building statues and reliquaries, and making costumes and masks for sacred dances and the ceremonial parasol. On the instructions of His Holiness Dudjom Rinpoche, he also spent a few years in Zangdok Palri Monastery in Kalimpong.

Personally, he has given both spiritual and worldly guidance to me since my birth. I sometimes feel proud that of all the children born to parents in this world, very few are as fortunate as me to have such parents. Everyone must, of course, feel the same way. Respecting and valuing one's parents is courteous behaviour in both the spiritual and worldly sense and it also gives you a special sense of joy and pride.

Usually, we give more importance to spirituality and less to worldly affairs. But I see worldly affairs as more important and crucial, because if the worldly conditions are poor, we get too busy trying to acquire them. In my case, for example, Bairo Rinpoche picked me up about an hour after my birth and showered me with his love and affection. Even today he says with joy, "Even at that time you knew how to hold on to your neck." I don't remember, but people told me that for many days after that, Rinpoche slept with me in his bed. Sometimes I wish there was a picture taken at that time. As I grew older he gave me everything that was necessary, while skillfully avoiding what was not necessary. From giving me food, drink and clothes to playing with me, he took care of me in every way and I think this kindness was the most important thing during that period.

As I grew up, he taught me how to respect the elders, look after those who were less fortunate and befriend the equals, and this had a positive effect and made a big difference to my attitude in life. So from this angle, worldly guidance and nurturing is most important.

Some people become cruel due to a lack of proper guidance and upbringing by their parents. It was Bairo Rinpoche who first took affectionate care of me, and thus I was able to experience such kindness, physically and mentally, until today. Some may think I am being voluble and some may think that these are the rantings of a crazy person. And those who pay no attention to the issue of upbringing may not understand this. If one does not understand the role of parents, then one might wonder what it means when you are told that parents are gracious. One will not be able to understand the importance of respecting others and that others being more valuable than oneself will remain just an expression.

If you are left alone, it will be difficult to survive and remain sustained physically and mentally. When we were born we did not inherently possess a big body, various skills, articulate speech and a lot of ideas. It is important to understand that what we are today it is because of our parents and various foods and drinks, the four elements, the natural environment, life-wind, *etc.*, and not to forget the kindness of others. If you reflect on whether the self is so important, you will understand that one should not always blindly follow selfishness.

As a little child I was fond of horses and Bairo Rinpoche bought me a foal. Later I became fond of bicycles and he bought me a tricycle, and as I grew up he bought me a small bicycle and a bigger one later. As I grew bigger and more demanding I became fond of cars. I must have been around twelve years old then, and he bought me a beautiful Fiat car. I drove it for about four or five years. Then Rinpoche bought me a Toyota car and much later a Mercedes. These are some of the bigger things he gave me as a child. He bought me different cameras, tape recorders, watches and clothes. I can't recount them all. As I mentioned earlier, he always played with me to keep me happy and never showed any exhaustion. He would always accompany me whether it was rain or shine, wind or mud. It was out of great love that he did all this, because accompanying me and playing with me proved most beneficial for me the time I was growing up. It has gone a long way with e in my entire life.

These days, many of the elders restrain children from doing this or that, or telling them not to eat this or drink that, presumably out of affection, and don't allow the child to do anything. We, the elders, don't understand that this restraint is the biggest source of sorrow for children. Some even resort to beating six or seven year old children to discipline them. There is nothing heroic about such behaviour and this is not the way to discipline a child. There are so many young people who transgress both mundane and spiritual ethics, and the parents who thrash small children quiver in front of these youths, and don't even dare to look at their faces. Parents and teachers must think properly. Torturing children indicates your lack of love and affection for others, especially for small children. I am saying all this with the hope that parents, future parents and teachers in monasteries and schools may gain a new perspective in dealing with children.

A person who cannot nurture children affectionately shows his own immaturity. As a lay man it is not enough to make a baby – he must be able to nurture him with affection by giving the child what he/she wants. As the child enters teenage years, he/she should be guided and disciplined with patience, because if not disciplined at that age he/she will become crooked and cannot be straightened later, like a dog's tail. That would be the biggest blunder committed by a parent. As the child enters adolescence, he/she should be advised by examples, all the time. Showing by example is far more effective. Parents should refrain from fighting, lying, deceptive behaviour, using abusive language or drunken behaviour in front of children, because the psychological effect on children at that age can be extreme. I can say that I was sustained solely by the moral activities of my parents; they not only nurtured me affectionately by feeding me, clothing me and playing with me as mentioned earlier. I am talking from the point of view of my daily life, not from the point of view of spiritual life. Some people used to scorn me, saying, "You cannot leave your parents, even at this grown-up age. What is wrong with you?" This scolding gave me a new understanding: it helped me appreciate the kindness of my parents and further strengthened our bond of love and affection. Bairo Rinpoche was like the pillar and beam of my life.

On the spiritual front, I received teachings, empowerments and oral transmissions. I regard him as the Guru Vajrasattva, holding me with boundless love, preventing me from falling into the abyss of samsara. This sentence says it all. I don't need to say anything more. I pray that Zhichen Vairochana, endowed with the richness of the wisdom of rejection and realization, may live long and may all his wishes be fulfilled.

KYABJE KATHOK MOKTSA RINPOCHE

At a much later date I received many teachings and empowerments of *Dui-Long* and *Nying-thig* and others, from Moktsa Rinpoche. I have not seen any detailed biography of his, and since I have not had the opportunity to spend time together with him, I do not know much about his activities. From the worldly point of view, he is my uncle and the elder brother of my father Bairo Rinpoche. He is one of the five golden throne-holders of the Kathok Lineage. I have complete faith that he has intentionally taken birth as the holder of all the oral treasure and pure vision lineage of teachings, because even though he is in his eighties, he continues untiringly, at the request of devotees, to give teachings, initiations and transmissions of the oral lineage and treasure text teachings, to tens of thousands of followers in China, India, Nepal and Tibet. This act alone generates devotion and faith in him. He gives away all the offerings he receives to the monasteries, to the poor and needy and never keeps anything for himself. It is said that his attendants sometimes have to hide some of the valuable things and robes offered to him, so that these can be used for the monastery and for Rinpoche himself later on. It need not be said that the basic practice of great Bodhisattvas like him are the six perfections. It is said that generosity and ethical conduct are important externally, and that the practice of generosity especially, is the essence of all practices. Not simply reading this in the text, but by seeing the activity of this spiritual teacher, I gained a new confidence that this is how one should practise generosity.

Once, while receiving an extensive Kilaya empowerment from the late Kyabje Trulshik Rinpoche he suddenly said to me, "You have dogs of different colours but you don't have a black dog. You must get a black dog." So, following the advice my guru I bought a black pug from the USA and named it Kilaya. Among those of us receiving an initiation of Vajrakilaya from Moktsa Rinpoche were my mother and the black pug Kilaya, now old and blind. As the ritual for inviting the deity and seeking blessings began, Kilaya jumped up with a loud bark and kept walking around where I was sitting. Moktsa Rinpoche stopped the initiation and without specifying anything said, "He saw it. It's amazing." He smiled and then continued the initiation. After the initiation my mother said, "Did you see anything. I saw something terrifying." I had not seen anything, but I had sensed a terrifying feeling. I said to my mother, "Tell me, what did you see?" and she replied, "I dare not say what I saw," and took a long breath. On my insistence she said, "I saw a dark old woman with red eyes, red and black matted hair touching the ground, with a big build, and terrifying looks, and as she shook her head clots of blood fell in every direction. She was moving around behind where you were sitting. My body felt numb at this sight." Although no one explained the significance of this, I later thought that, since Rinpoche was giving the initiation in the form of Vajrakilaya, what they saw must have been one of the many guardians surrounding him.

The dog was named Kilaya because I bought it following the advice my guru gave while receiving an extensive empowerment of Kilaya. I thought it was wonderful that Kilaya too saw the vision. The texts instruct us that realized beings or great holders of the teachings, great selfless Bodhisattvas and Vajracharyas, are the all-pervading lords of the Mandala, and even if one cannot see them as that with the naked eye, one should develop faith in them as such. I feel joy, and especially devotion, to have had the opportunity to see, hear and take as my root guru, such a great Bodhisattva in human form, as my uncle. I hope and pray that I will be able to receive more teachings and initiations from this Vajradhara.

Part of his name is Jigdral, or "fearless", and in reality too, he is free of the fear of affliction of grasping at self, and possesses the marvellous quality of thinking about the welfare of Dharma and other sentient beings all the time. Looking at the attitude and manner of people like me, I understand how marvellous the qualities of my gurus are. We only think of ourselves if we get money, and we go to a brand showroom. Most probably, we would buy the latest mobile phone, and if we have enough money we might buy the latest laptop model. If we have still more money, we might want to buy a good car – there's nothing that we don't want for ourselves. Compare this with the activity of a spiritual teacher like Moktsa Rinpoche and you feel admiration from the depth of your heart. There are some people who lead an austere life and criticize other realized beings as greedy. This is a big flaw. I think a spiritual teacher should be like Moktsa Rinpoche – looking after the welfare of others naturally and effortlessly. Working tirelessly with the motivation of gaining fame is pitiable.

CHAPTER 15

Root and Branch Teachers

> I was fortunate to receive transmissions from these Buddhas,
> These root and branch teachers.

There are different definitions of a root guru but I think the meaning will be more profound if one interprets it as the "root of practice". The root of all practices, such as learning, contemplation and prayers, meditation and yantra yoga, prostrations and circumambulation, mudras and postures and the practice of the Six Perfections is given by the root guru. Does it mean that one cannot practise without adhering to a guru? It does not mean that. However, there is no way to practise Mahayana and especially Vajrayana without adhering to a guru. Nowadays, we don't seem to give much importance to the guru. Even practitioners treat receiving instructions and blessings similar to attending a class on science or art, or like purchasing a commodity from a shopkeeper. This is not how it should be. The relationship between qualified guru and you should be maintained until enlightenment is attained.

The guru is like the foundation stone of a building: you have to remember the guru, you have to visualize the guru on the crown of your head or visualize him as the meditational deity, or understand the guru as your mind. Every level of your practice, whether it is the generating stage or the completion stage, is rooted in the guru. That is why he is called the "root guru".

I would interpret the "branch gurus" as those who have been kind in developing other aspects of knowledge in you, such as the Khenpo who bestows the ordination vow, teachers who taught you different sciences, or the teacher who taught you reading and writing. Anyway, the definition of branch gurus needs to be further investigated. Some say that there can be only one root guru. This interpretation too should be investigated further; otherwise it could create a lot of confusion. If you look at the root and branch gurus from the perspective of the primordially pure nature of the mind, without considering their physical appearance, the sound of their voice, soft or harsh behaviour; and then doubtlessly you can call your gurus – Buddha. In this sense, today I feel I was very fortunate to have had the opportunity to study under them, and that my birth as a human has not been wasted.

When I was young, I was not very attentive during teachings and perceived the teaching sessions as merely gaining knowledge and did not have any profound awareness. Kunkhyen Pema Karpo has said that perceiving the holy doctrine as mere knowledge is a mistake, and I lived with this mistaken notion for many years. Yet I made every effort to be well behaved in the presence of my teachers and gurus.

> Although I have not achieved
> Confident realization of their teachings,
> I have not displeased them.
> And although I have not had prophecies induced by trance,
> I am sure that I have received the blessings of their compassion.

As it is said that even the Buddha cannot please everyone, and although I cannot claim to have pleased all my spiritual teachers, I am confident that I have not displeased them. All of them were fond of me.

BEING MINDFUL IN THE PRESENCE OF THE TEACHERS

Some people behave immodestly in the presence of the spiritual teacher, as a show of intimacy, and I wonder if that is proper. One can also see that the spiritual teachers too, pretend to like this show of closeness and do not attempt to change such immodest behaviour. Wondering why they do so, I asked some of the spiritual teachers and found that although they did not appreciate such immodest behaviour, they pretended to like it and kept quiet because, as the texts say, "When fruitional cause is absent, nothing can be fabricated;" they felt any advice they gave would fall on deaf ears. Moreover, today people hardly give advice or affectionate guidance and there is hardly any respect for the seniors or the learned. Very few appreciate sincere advice. That is why the spiritual teachers just tolerate such immodesty and keep quiet, to avoid any negative reactions that could lead to embarrassing situations, or create discord between the teacher and disciple. Therefore, it is important to behave as properly as possible in the presence of the spiritual teacher for the benefit of this life as well as the next. Modest behaviour is important from both the spiritual and the mundane point of view.

IT IS DIFFICULT TO KEEP SECRETS TODAY

It is important to be careful in the presence not only of the spiritual teacher, but also in front of the lay people, because even if they themselves are not well mannered, they will always criticize others' behaviour and form a wrong view. Even though they do not say anything up front, I have heard them criticize monks and nuns behind their back. We do not hesitate to show our true colours in front of the lay people: we eat everything, dress oddly and behave in a disorderly manner. The lay people are neither spiritual teachers nor monks or nuns; they neither know one another well nor belong to the same race, and yet they do not leave us alone. For example, an airline pilot I knew asked me if Buddhist monks can drink, and I replied that we are not allowed to drink. Then he said many people dressed like you drink in the aircraft and he asked, "Why do they drink?" And all I could say was that I knew nothing about those who drank. Those in the garb of spiritual practitioners as well as lay Buddhist followers must always be mindful of their conduct. If such people can abstain from drinking or eating non-vegetarian food it will be of great service to the Dharma.

THE WORLD HAS BECOME SMALLER

A young journalist I know once said to me that Buddhists in the Himalayan region do not hesitate to eat meat, drink alcohol, smoke or consume tobacco. For example, in the holy 1st month of the lunar calendar, Tibetans in the settlements and monasteries place orders for large quantities of meat for Tibetan New Year. "How do you justify this?" he asked me. I just said that worldly traditions and spiritual practice are different. I could not give a proper answer.

In the past, the misconduct of one person would not have had much impact: murder and robbery could be kept secret, or only people in the close neighbourhood would know about the incident and it would takes days for the news of the incident to spread. The world has now become small. In this age, when information can be exchanged within a short time through telephones, e-mail and other modes of communication, such as air travel, it is easy to bring disrepute to your culture, religion, parents, relatives and community.

On top of that, today, unlike the past, very few people live by faith and devotion. In today's world people like to investigate, debate and reason and so it is important that those who care for the Dharma should remain mindful of their conduct.

MY LIFE AND PROPHESIES OF THE GURUS

As I said earlier, I have not displeased my spiritual teachers and khenpos from whom I received teachings. I have firm faith and confidence that they will take care of me in this life, the intermediate state and the next life. I have never been pretentious in my devotion to my gurus; and all major activities, spiritual and mundane, have been directly or indirectly prophesied by my Buddha-like gurus.

> As it is said:
> "You do not need to visualize the guru,
> You do not need to remember anything,
> For he is always in your heart."
> Although I cannot boast I have that view,
> I always remember these teachers with longing –
> Sometimes by recalling them, ordinary thought ceases.
> Recalling their qualities often increases my faith.

Whether it's the guru, parents, friends, or relatives, you need a relationship based on love and affection. If you have such a relationship, then it is natural for you to remember them and wish for their well-being. Therefore, remembering one's guru, recalling the qualities of their body, speech and mind and remembering their instructions, is very important for the disciples practising and training in the path. Those who have reached the "no more learning" stage or non-meditation stage do not have to specifically visualize the Buddha-like guru. I cannot boast of having reached that stage, but I keep remembering my gurus with longing. I have had this longing since I was young, and on many occasions I had such a strong longing that tears would fill up my eyes and the hair on my body would stand up; I would feel giddy, and I had to stop my prayers or recitations. On such occasions ordinary thoughts cease.

CONFESSION DOES BRING PEACE OF MIND

Recalling my faults with remorse, I confess and renew my vows:
Reaffirming my vows with prayer,
This is my natural style.
Apart from that, I do not have much more to say.

I recall the kindness of my spiritual teachers often, and confess all my wrong doings from the depth of my heart, and vow not to repeat them in the future. This is the focus of all my prayers and virtuous activities. I have nothing else to ask for. As a result, one becomes more open-minded and relaxed. One becomes more confident and successful in whatever one does and there is no sense of guilt. For some time in the past, my mind was misdirected and I did not think about these things much. Instead, I was distracted by gross external activities. On the outside life seemed good, but in truth I could not be sure of myself; there was a nagging sense of guilt and shame.

Thinking about my faults made me feel uncomfortable and dull; the peace of mind that I'd had earlier was missing. I am telling you my own experience – many of you may be experiencing the same feeling. The scriptures stress that we must confess and vow repeatedly, and this really is a wonderful way of bringing peace of mind. Some people try to forget their faults as a way of bringing peace of mind, they believe that reflecting on their own faults is a source of suffering, and it is better not to think about them. This can be double-edged: one can live one's life under an illusion, such as when one is drunk, this may be beneficial in a way. But people like me who reflect on their own faults and their consequences have a different view of samsara. I realized from experience that continuing on this path of reflection can bring mental satisfaction and peace of mind. I believe this sort of experience is common to ordinary beings like me who have a proper perception. If expounding the idea of forgetting one's faults means forgetting without believing in the truth, then it would mean one is creating an illusory sense of happiness.

If one would be able to forget faults in a uniquely different way, then it would be marvellous. If one would be able to forget one's faults – along with the confidence of seeing the dualism of quality; faults with non-dual sameness; all phenomena comprising of samsara and nirvana as baseless and rootless; and seeing all phenomenal existence as the Mahamudra of the Truth Body; then one would be able to completely forget the faults and be liberated. There is nothing greater than this, because one has been able to completely destroy the faults.

> In order to make favourable conditions purposeful,
> One needs the eye which discerns and does not confuse
> The actual intent of the causal and resultant vehicles.
> Being clear and applying the meanings according
> To the (particular) vehicle,
> Through deep analysis, the essence of all the teachings
> Is shown to be emptiness and compassion.
>
> The fruit of realizing this meaning comes
> As the spontaneous fulfillment of benefitting others.

In order to make life meaningful one must be able to accomplish the purpose of oneself and others. To do this, from the Buddhist point of view, one must attain the Truth Body and the Form Body simultaneously. As the prayer says, "May I accomplish the two sublime bodies, arising from the accumulation of merit and wisdom." The texts say that until this is attained it is difficult to accomplish the purpose of others and oneself completely. For this reason, the Sutra system or the Philosophical Vehicle gives importance to accumulating merit through the practice of generosity and ethics. As a consequence, at the fruitional stage, the Form Body of the Buddha is attained.

On the other hand, Vajrayana or the Resultant Vehicle gives priority to accumulating wisdom by practising the path of the Four Thorough Purifications, in addition to the practice of the Six Perfections, from the beginning. This practice, my gurus explained to me, is known as taking the fruit as the path, and leads to the attainment of the Truth Body or Wisdom Truth Body. I think if one reflects on such instructions heard from the guru, in conjunction with one's practice, then there is a profound meaning that one can understand. This is an explanation mainly of the joint practice of Sutrayana and Tantrayana.

Whatever the religion, Buddhist or non-Buddhist, if one differentiates their essence or reality distinctly, and investigates the natural state of phenomena, then, I believe, one can understand that the interpretable definition does not contradict the Sutra and Tantra teachings of the Buddha.

BUDDHISM IS SCIENTIFIC

I am not speaking with a bias as a Buddhist. Many scientists and learned people believe that there is a lot to think about in Buddhism and show new interest. What the Buddha said over 2000 years ago is now being discovered with modern technology. This is what surprises them about Buddhism, and they see Buddhism as an active and qualitatively different from other religions.

His Holiness the Dalai Lama is also keen on having discussions with scientists, realizing that collaborating with them will give exposure to the splendour of the Buddhist view and philosophy, through the use of modern technology; and thus will benefit many beings. His Holiness advised me that keeping secret the channels and energy practise, would not be of much benefit and that I should hold discussions with scientists, and let them do research with machines. These days I do hold discussions with scientists in the USA, Europe and Asia. However, I do not have permission, from the spiritual teachers from whom I have received the instructions, to show the channels and energy practice. This is why I have not been able to fully carry out the wishes of His Holiness.

Thus, if one is able to define all apparent phenomena without transgressing the words of the Buddha and, while practising the path, if one has the wisdom to follow the instructions given by the qualified kind root gurus, who have accomplished complete experiential knowledge, one will be able to do authentic practice and understand the nature of emptiness and the radiance of compassion. In this way, the essence of the teachings will not remain covered by verbal barks and inner doubts or deviate from the path of literal meaning. The ultimate meaning will be realized and the ability to spontaneously accomplish the purpose of others can be attained within one lifetime. But under the influence of lethargy, we keep on postponing practice and remain caught in an endless cycle of work.

However extensive one's learning may be, one is not able to link it with the instructions of the guru or be able to ascertain them with awareness. As a result, the meditational practices such as the generation and completion stages remain mediocre. Being deceived by the endless cycle of work is the worst deception. Even now, one must be driven by diligent effort, develop sincerity and practise meditation. One should not use past failure as an excuse to discourage oneself. If you do this, it will be a big mistake.

> Until now I have not come to that,
> Because of my endless busy work –
> So I yearn to be in a remote hermitage
> And to practise single-mindedly the Dharma I have understood.

The yearning to practise the Dharma single-mindedly is needed. Personally, from a young age I yearned to practise all that I learned from my spiritual teachers.

THE IMPORTANCE OF STAYING IN RETREAT AFTER STUDYING THE SCRIPTURES

I did a lot of meditation when I was young. After receiving initiations and instructions, I used to follow the advice of my guru and do the necessary retreat for recitations. I did retreats for six months, for a year or for a few weeks, many times. I did most of the retreats in caves, as well on the ground. Staying in a cave has its advantages. An important factor is that there is less distraction, and so doing prayers and practice deepens.

Unless you are carrying your mobile phone and laptop with you, there is no distraction in a cave. So it is best to leave behind such unnecessary articles. It is best to be alone during retreat, because then you have less distractions of attachment and aversion, and practice becomes more enhanced.

From Buddha to Indian Mahasiddhas like Nagarjuna and his spiritual sons Tilopa and Naropa, as well as Tibetan masters such as Milarepa, Tsangpa Gyare, Gyalwa Gotsangpa, Gyalwa Lorepa and Gyalwa Yangonpa etc. have all stayed in retreat alone, as in the saying, "becoming the son of the mountains, with mist as clothing." Many gurus, including gurus of our Drukpa Lineage, have stayed in retreat in such a manner. Spiritual masters of all traditions, such as Gyalwa Drikungpa, Gyalwa Longchenpa and Tsongkhapa have practised in this way. The biography of our root gurus and their root gurus reveal that they too have practised in the same way.

You will understand this if you go through the biography of Khyentse Woeser Tulpei Dorje, Drubwang Shakyashri, Khenpo Ngagga and Tripon Pema Chogyal. They were not like us: today gurus like me cannot stay in retreat unless there is a private chamber and an entourage of attendants. A great guru, I think, means the fruit is achieved by discarding distracting activities and practising solitary meditation. There is no greater guru than Milarepa, and he meditated alone in caves, without a private chamber and an entourage of attendants. Gyalwa Longchenpa and Tsongkhapa practised in a similar way.

All of them gave up the luxury of food, clothing and a name, and stayed in retreat for years. These things have to be understood, because this generates devotion to them in your mind and humbles you, and gradually it gives you the chance to train in the higher paths. I am not saying you must like them, and it would be asking too much to say that everyone should do this. It is difficult for people like us to give up the mundane world. If inner and outer conditions are absent for one to stay in retreat alone, then doing a retreat together with one or two spiritually minded friends of pure integrity is also all right.

Retreat means cutting off the boundary between the mind and distractions and for this, the border between speech and expression should be cut off. The indispensable condition for this is to first cut off the border between the physical body and distracting activities. Therefore, for novices like us it is important to cut off the boundary of the physical body.

There are some people who stay in retreat in crowded places filled with distraction. Except for realized beings who have achieved stability in meditation, it will be difficult for ordinary beings to do proper meditation in such places. In this age people like me have to hold assemblies and gatherings in the name of spiritual activities. Perhaps this can be called white distraction. Cutting off the boundary of the physical body may be difficult while staying in the monastery. It would be better to be without monks and nuns, old and young attendants, whose views and conduct you do not agree with – in short non-virtuous friends who disturb your mind, or even material things that disturb your mind, whether they be expensive or cheap things, of high quality or poor quality, necessary or unnecessary.

For example, television, computers and mobile phones do not allow your mind to rest peacefully. It is better to give them away, even if they are expensive and of high quality, or pack them up at least, during the period of retreat. If you are thinking of doing genuine practice, then it is better to discard them altogether. Whether the mind is disturbed in the form of joy or sorrow, whether one is shackled with a golden chain or an iron chain, it is the same. Your friends and these articles keep you occupied day and night, not leaving your mind in its natural condition, and waste your time. Gradually, your interest in spiritual practice wanes, you pay less and less attention to this life and the next life, the law of karma and the need to be kind-hearted. And when you look at yourself you feel sad. So recognize bad friends and bad objects and make an effort to discard them. Remain happy with spiritually-minded friends who have the same commitment and honesty. Even if you cannot do much spiritual practice, you can at least lead a relaxed and happy life. There is true happiness in the spiritual way. I have always wished to lead such a life, but my wishes have not been fulfilled completely.

> I would like to practise in a remote place
> By myself or with a Dharma friend;
> Although I do not have the favourable situation of physical seclusion,
> Whenever I have the chance, I do practise in the seclusion of my mind.

A DISOBEDIENT DISCIPLE IS A PROBLEM FOR THE SPIRITUAL TEACHER

Generally speaking, having a large group of monks and nuns as disciples looks highly notable and impressive. But having a large number of followers without spiritual intention is a source of unhappiness for a spiritual teacher like me. You cannot know the difficulties faced by us, who sit at the top. We might seem happy and impressive to you. I don't know whether telling you this will give you a new perspective, but I see no harm in sharing, since I am expressing my opinion. I do not even get the opportunity to stay in a secluded place and do some practice. Often, I have thought of giving up the distraction of followers who have no spiritual intentions, and go to a hermitage to do authentic practice. Many a time, in a crazy rush, I have done year-long and month-long retreats in caves and solitary places.

GOING TO THE MOUNTAINS, LEAVING BEHIND DISOBEDIENT DISCIPLES

Once, driven by a strong yearning for retreat, I took my dog Holy, a Saint Bernard, and one monk with me and drove away without any specific destination in mind. As I kept driving I came close to Chumig Jangchub, the holy place where Guru Rinpoche meditated, and that night we slept outside the house of a villager. I felt very happy. They gave us rice and vegetables but I don't think Holy had enough to fill his belly. The next morning I started my retreat in an open ground above the holy site, and stayed there for a few months. The monk accompanying me used to go once a week to the village below to do the shopping. The money I had was sufficient to purchase our rations, but we didn't have plates, cups, utensils, mats or blankets and so we hired these from the monastery and the villagers. My companion monk said, "In future, if Your Holiness were to go on such a trip, some preparations should be made. Going to retreat without even a cup or plate is terrible." I know he had a hard time. If my dog Holy could speak I am sure he too would have had a lot to complain about, because he also had no facilities.

Generally speaking, animals have a deep bond of love with their owners and they don't show too much distress about heat, cold, hunger or thirst. From a traditional conservative point of view, it is inappropriate to take pet animals like a dog on retreat. But from a broader point of view, so long as you have enough food to feed them, then I don't see anything wrong with taking them along. I have gone on pilgrimage taking my dog on many occasions, but that was the first time I took my dog to a retreat. Wandering carefree and staying in retreat for a couple of months makes you physically and mentally happy and gives you an inconceivably high view of phenomena. From my experience, I learned the great purpose of renunciation of the mundane world, by Buddha and past spiritual masters.

> Being amongst many "friends" who are contrary to Dharma,
> Does not provide the context for mental seclusion,
> So I wish to avoid such "retinues" with their many activities
> And just practice alone on the ultimate essence.
> Friends who are uncertain about Dharma practice,
> Disciples who are not enthusiastic about receiving teachings –

Such acquaintances damage both teacher and student,
And I never want to be in such a situation.

This is what I wish to do. Whenever I see a secluded place I wish I could pitch a tent and stay quietly in retreat here. I still feel the same way.

A SELFISH PERSON STAYING IN A SECLUDED RETREAT MAY NOT BE PURPOSEFUL

On deeper reflection, the wish to relax in a quiet place is an aspect of selfishness, and so even this thought should be ultimately abandoned. However, this way of thinking is harmless for the time being, and we regard those who stay away in seclusion as good people. From the spiritual point of view, being able to stay put in one place is preferable, because in this way one can hope gradually to be able to practise learning and contemplation. We can see that without the ability to stay in one place, there is no way to practise learning and contemplation. Carefree people who think only of mundane happiness, without any idea of practising learning or contemplation, have a great disadvantage. This carefree attitude could be the cause of falling out of human company in future – I can't say whether you will leave human company to join divine company, perhaps it is difficult.

Once Drukpa Kunleg took shelter in the home of a village householder and she offered him tea. Describing the quality of tea offered to him, he said, "The tea without the fragrance of China tea cannot be expected to have the scent of butter. Since no one will drink such tea, it is better to send it to the wall," and he splashed the tea on the wall. The householder replied, "A person untouched by the scent of mundane ethics cannot be expected to be touched by the fragrance of spiritual ethics. There is no need for you to take shelter here. You may leave the house," and expelled him from her house. There is a great teaching in what the householder said. Her saying, "A person untouched by the scent of mundane ethics cannot be expected to be touched by the fragrance of spiritual ethics" is something that practitioners like us should think about.

It is important to take mundane morals into consideration. It is not good to think about pleasure from the beginning. One needs to have the determination to face hardships in life in order to become a genuine person and a part of human society, amenable with everyone. As I said, personally I wish to live a quiet life in a remote place in the company of spiritually-minded friends. I am still investigating if I have the thought of the welfare of other beings deep inside me: sometimes I feel I have the thought for others and sometimes I feel I am being selfish. Nothing seems certain. But having non-spiritually-minded friends doesn't serve much purpose.

A SELFISH SPIRITUAL PRACTITIONER IS NOT GOOD

Spiritual wisdom is the treasure of a person like me and it is non-spiritually-minded friends who will diminish this treasure. The term "spiritually-minded" should be understood to mean kind-hearted; and kind-hearted person would be less selfish and think only of the well-being of other beings all the time. If you have such a quality, then you become a good human being, even if you don't accomplish much else. If, by being in the company of such a person you acquire a similar nature, then all your practice becomes practical; especially for a person like me who engages in the activities of a guru, it becomes easier to do things. Since such a person is less selfish, he listens to any guidance he is given and even carries it out as much as he can. In this way, we are able to mutually benefit each other and live cordially with affection.

Living without any spiritual thoughts is a different way of life. But having friends who pretend to be spiritual but who have no spiritual intentions, and only pursue selfish interests without thinking of the well-being of other beings, or disciples who pretend to receive teachings but do not listen to the words, remember the meaning, or intellectually try to understand the depth of the teachings, waste the time of both theirs and the teacher's. This becomes a problem for both the teacher and disciples. I have become wary of such disciples and followers and do not want the company of such people.

> At first they see the guru as a Buddha,
> Then they see the guru as a helpful human;
> Finally they see the guru as their enemy, and use harsh words of abuse:
> I want to avoid such disciples and go into a remote place.

There are disciples who, without any investigation, on the first meeting say, "How fortunate we are to have met such a Buddha-like guru like you," and seem amazed. Then they will say, "I will offer everything, my body and wealth, to you", and generously offer money and other material things. They even pretend to give much help and assistance. After a few years they will talk about how knowledgeable the guru is, how ethically pure he is, what a large following and the number of monasteries he has, how fine his character is and how patient; but they gradually stop making material offerings and assistance. Finally, they will look at the guru as an adversary and say how eloquently he deceives people, what a fraud he is and how all their wealth has been usurped by the guru and this has turned them into a pauper, and they will tell lie after lie to denigrate the guru. If the guru is humble, they will say all this to the guru directly, but if the guru is grand with a large following, he will not dare to say such things to the guru on his face. He will speak ill of him behind his back. So there is no point in having such disciples.

THE PROBLEM OF FOLLOWING A GURU WITHOUT GENUINE DEVOTION

A few years ago, an acquaintance and a practitioner who had studied Buddhism a little, came to me. One day, he spoke a lot about my qualities, and prostrating with reverence; he took out ten thousand US dollars, a photograph of his house and some other stuff and said, "I am offering this to you. You can do whatever you want with the house. The ownership deeds can be changed later. This money is a symbol of my wealth. I will offer all my wealth and property to you later." When I told him, "You should not do this. You have to live in this mundane world and you will face problems later." He seemed sad and was getting angry and very insistent and so I said, "All right then. Leave it here for the time being." He came to see me frequently but I remained impartial and did not give him any special treatment.

After a year or two he called and asked me to return all the money and things he had given me and said he was coming in a week's time and that everything should be given back to him then. I said, "Of course. I have kept the money separately, the photo of your house and all the articles you gave me. Even if I am not here, you can come and take them." So he came in my absence and took everything back. Later, I heard that he had told other people that I was shameless, and that however good he was to me I showed no appreciation and that I was greedy.

THE FAULT OF REPEATEDLY SPEAKING OF A GURU'S QUALITY

There are different types of people among disciples, but one can be certain that a disciple who speaks frequently of the guru's qualities does not have true devotion. Those who have genuine devotion do not normally speak about the guru's qualities unless asked. Such people are dedicated and sincere and have no reason to flatter. These days such people are rare to find. The disciple who is sycophantic and flatters the guru is really wasting his time. Many are frauds and cheats. So I genuinely feel it is better to leave behind such disciples and go to a secluded place to practise.

> Expert in praising if it benefits oneself,
> Clever in avoiding what benefits others,
> Clever in sowing seeds which break Samaya –
> I wish to avoid such friends and go to a remote place.

As mentioned earlier, the friend one needs to have should be someone who is spiritually minded – in the sense that the person is not selfish, but considers the welfare of others. Any person, male or female, monk or layperson, with such thoughts, should be befriended.

BAD FRIENDS SHOULD BE DISCARDED

Having the wrong type of friend can be a big mistake. A friend – good looking or ugly, articulate or not, humble or not, who only seeks selfish pleasure, will feign sickness, pretend to be incompetent even though he is competent, pretend to have no money even though he has money and stays away when it comes to doing something for others. But when it comes to selfish gains, the same person will speak a lot, claim competence and pretend to be altruistic. Such a person will create discord between the guru and disciples and sow the seeds of breaking Samaya among disciples. One should discard the company of such friends and go to practise in a secluded place.

IDENTIFYING A SECLUDED HERMITAGE

There are many types of secluded places. A place where there is no controversy can be called a secluded place. For a spiritual practitioner, a place without attachment and aversion to worldly activities is a secluded place. One has to leave and escape from any temporary or long-term disturbance, or from the person causing such a problem. I feel there is no other way except to leave the person causing the disturbance.

Some of my spiritual friends say that such people can be changed by giving advice and one has to be patient with such people. But I don't think I am capable of doing that. It is my belief that in today's time, wasting time by giving patient advice, scolding or pointing out faults will not yield any result. Then should such people be abandoned completely? No. Of course not! One must always remember them in one's prayers. Prayers are powerful and I believe sooner or later will have a positive effect on them. One may not be able to give help immediately. But faith in prayers is one of our key features.

As I said earlier, a secluded place can be interpreted in different ways. Generally, it is understood to mean a hermitage in rocky mountains or grassy hills, but it is important to see if the place is secluded. Although today, outer seclusion is the sole consideration, for a dedicated practitioner, but inner seclusion is more important. For people like us, it is difficult to maintain inner seclusion without outer seclusion, and yet the main objective should be to achieve inner seclusion. Spending months and years in a remote place may earn you a name, but will be meaningless if you remain attached to the outer seclusion without inner seclusion. I think you can have some understanding if you look at a hermitage and a secluded place from four logical positions.

Therefore, one must always make the effort to achieve seclusion within one's mind. Experience has taught me that it is possible to achieve inner seclusion, whether you are in a hermitage or in a town. From this perspective, one does not need to follow literally the advice given in the texts to "abandon the friend and go to a secluded place", and carry one's rations and leave the friend with sadness. But today, most of us do not pay much attention to accomplishing seclusion or solitude, and this is one reason why the meditation lineage is degenerating.

BOTH THE GURU AND THE DISCIPLE SHOULD BE QUALIFIED

The desire for a name is making us suffer. The distractive activities with a gathering of indifferent people may seem alright. But from the point of the altruistic mind of enlightenment, it is not right. Having a large following may earn you a name, but if the disciples see the guru as a human being or a leader and see spiritual friends as servants, there is not much need for such followers. As for the guru, if he is someone who has achieved the superior ground endowed with the six liberations, then the larger the following, the greater will his activities be for the benefit of other beings and for a longer duration. If the guru gives teachings it is well and good, and even if he does not give teachings, it is not necessary. In such a case the disciple does not need any special devotion to the guru, because he attains liberation just by seeing the guru or hearing his name, or the seed of liberation is sown, say the Sutras and Tantras.

But gurus like me are of little use to the type of modern disciples mentioned earlier. Honestly speaking, I think the pretence of receiving teachings reciting prayers staying in monastic confines reverence and humility, is a self-brought problem for the disciples who do not have devotion or faith. I do not think there is any need for such pretension. Objectively speaking, if there is a disciple, who has devotion based on logical understanding, then he might gain some benefit, and as for the guru, his efforts will not go waste. The texts have given clear explanations about this and I have a strong immutable view on this issue.

FAKE GURU AND FAKE DISCIPLE

Maybe I am being conservative and hard-headed. Whatever it may be, you as disciples must use your intellect and reflect on this issue. When you cannot identify between the real gurus and fake gurus and between true disciples and fake disciples, it becomes a headache for both the gurus and disciples. I often think that this is not the right way of living this short life, from both the spiritual as well as the mundane point of view.

Unless I am hoping for fame, I do not need the entourage of today,
And unless they are looking for misery, they do not need a teacher like me.

I have already explained the meaning of this.

As long as it is not the time to benefit others
It is not right to have disciples:
This is repeatedly said in the Sutras and Tantras.

Therefore I wish to live in a remote place.
I wish to observe the real nature of things free from thought.
I wish to crush the shell of deluded ideas.
I wish to contemplate measureless compassion.
I wish to realize Buddha nature which is naturally present.

Ever since I was a child, staying alone was something I liked the most. I like being away from people I hardly know or acquaintances who are neither spiritual nor worldly friends, and particularly smooth-talking, evil-minded monks or lay people, male or female, who pretend to be devoted in front of me, but hold wrong views behind my back. When I stay aloof like this, some people say that I am being snobbish, and as offerings dwindle, the monks and staff members say that my staying inside alone is a big loss to the monastery. Some have told this to me directly and some indirectly.

ONE IS HAPPIER STAYING ALONE

People today are apprehensive about being left alone and I wonder why they feel so. We have all come into this world alone and we have to leave alone. I think most people do not understand the joy of staying alone and regard it as some kind of suffering. We are confused by the sight of good couples living together for many years, and all the family members seem happy and fine living together. Not knowing how much distance the fox has travelled, we get angry at it when we see the fox attack and eat the sheep. Similarly, we do not understand that the accumulation of merit and purification accomplished through many years of practice is a special achievement, and we get attracted by what is visible, and follow the mundane way of life.

Speaking from the worldly perspective, after struggling for years as the saying goes, "By giving the flesh of your face to others, feeding fish to the dog, working like a dog at night and a human during the day, you may achieve something, but then you have to check what you have achieved is satisfactory."

You have to reflect on what I mean by saying, "There is happiness in staying in seclusion", because some of you might misunderstand it as meaning that one should stay alone and that there is no happiness in living among a crowd of people. It is not like this. Happiness is something you get when your mind is free. I had many opportunities to live in seclusion, thanks to my root gurus. We call this "staying in retreat" or staying "cut-off". Whether you are really cut-off or not, you can do more prayers and virtuous practices and this gives you mental satisfaction. If you can control your mind and appreciate happiness when you stay alone – not to mention when you are in a crowd – then there is a feeling of delight.

These days, people live in crowded places and are so distracted that they don't know how time passes. Being in this state of numbness may give them a sense of happiness. But due to a lack of freedom of their minds, they feel lonely, dark, scared, empty, unhappy or desolate when they are left alone and this is not correct. I remember feeling scared when I stayed in solitary retreat; and I found that the place of your retreat and the company you have makes a big difference. In some solitary places I wished to stay for months and years, while at other places I didn't want to stay for more than a couple of weeks. This was a clear indication of my lack of control over my mind.

BEING HAPPY WHEREVER YOU ARE

For any practitioner, the ability to stay alone and be happy is regarded as a great quality, and I realized that this was true from my own experiences. Irrespective of the duration of retreat, one needs to be unaffected by heat, cold or the comfortableness of the place. A lay person should be able to remain happy amongst friends, as well as while staying alone. Anyway, if you are free, would you not be happier and more comfortable? There are some people who are attached to being alone and cannot go out in a crowd and do not wish to mix with others. This is a fault and is recognized as a disease. So you need some ability, both mental and physical, to release and restrain, and to go, as well as to stay away. From the spiritual point of view, without such ability, the complete practice of the altruistic mind of enlightenment will be difficult. From the mundane point of view, you will be causing a lot of problems to your children, spouse and near and dear ones.

YOU MUST MEND YOURSELF

People like me, recognized as a guru born for the welfare of others, must remain secluded in order to study the teachings one has received on Mahamudra, Dzogchen and the Middle Path. Reflect on their meaning, learn other fields of knowledge as well, and complete the recitation of mantras, *etc.*, until one attains the power to work for the welfare of other beings. Even from my childhood, I knew that one should have sufficient knowledge that is required for the work of a guru – such as divination, astrology, the power of mantra and meditative stabilization, line-drawing and the use of powdered colour in mandalas, *etc.* Without such a knowledge, the good intention of benefitting others cannot be put to practical use. For example, the Buddha and the kind spiritual masters have said in the scriptures, that keeping disciples and followers without reaching a certain level of warmth of feeling would be a grave risk to both the guru and disciples.

One can understand this from one's own experience, without needing the support of scriptural quotations. For example, it would be dangerous for someone to pretend to be a doctor without knowing anything about medicines. Isn't it the same? When will one know that it is time to work for the benefit of others? Since you know your mind, you must be able to appraise yourself. You should not deceive yourself, because once you start to deceive yourself, you will begin deceiving others as well.

So speaking from experience, one should check whether one is capable of benefitting other sentient beings, including humans. Without deceiving yourself, you should know that the fame of articulate speech and sweet-talking is like the sound of a waterfall, or like an echo in an empty house, and will not take you much further. You should care for yourself, look inwards and mend your ways.

There are many ways of mending oneself. From the Buddhist perspective, one should follow the methods explained in Vinaya,

Sutra and Abhidharma, *etc.*, to purify delusory thoughts and the faults of speech and body that generate these thoughts. Practise impartial compassion for humans and all beings, and understand that the ultimate nature of all phenomena is beyond conception, and maintain the natural state that cuts off all fabrication.

The ultimate goal of all this is to attain the natural state of Buddhahood. Attaining Buddhahood is not like winning a competition or making a profit in business. Some people today tend to practise the Dharma as an entertainment or for fame and material gain. You must pray and dedicate whatever merit is gained from practicing, for the well-being of others. I also do this from the depth of my heart. Such prayers and dedication is of immense benefit to you.

From the worldly point of view, for your own happiness, first you have to become a good human being, even if you cannot generate an altruistic mind. To become a good human being it is important to first understand the difference between a good and a bad human being.

VIOLENCE HAS BECOME A TREND TODAY

Perhaps today, people either do not know the difference between a good or a bad human being, or do not care much about it. Being a good human being is not a key theme of discussion in the world today, so people have no interest in it. The key theme of discussion and the main topic of news is killing, robbing and violence.

Recently I went to the market to do some shopping. Two young men were quarrelling. Initially, only a few people were around them, but in less than ten minutes a huge crowd gathered from nowhere. Forgetting their shopping and without really knowing what they were arguing about, the crowd started to encourage the youths to fight. Before a physical fight broke out between the two, a kind man intervened and brought peace. But most of the people present started shouting at one of the youths, instigating him, and this made the two get into a physical fight. Both of them got injured and were later taken away by the police. I looked at the faces of the people and they looked happy – smiling with satisfaction and speaking loudly. No one seemed unhappy that such an unnecessary incident had taken place. This was my observation.

It is a trend now that people eagerly participate in demonstrations or they indulge in plundering and looting if you pay them. When reporters ask the demonstrators about their feelings, many of them say that they are happy to come to the city for the first time in their lives to demonstrate. Very few are aware of the political objective of the demonstrations, or what the organizing party has done for the welfare of the people. People do not hesitate to beat or break or destroy property as soon as they hear the slogan to do so. Very few people sincerely work for peace. Since most people in the world are more interested in violence, they don't care about being good. One becomes a good person by respecting others. Oppressing others and making them suffer makes you a bad person.

Genuine self-interest is achieved by giving up selfishness and working for the welfare of others. This is a spiritual explanation. Even if you don't believe in religion, the law of cause and effect should be enough to make you understand this. Since I am a Buddhist, you might think that I am speaking from the Buddhist perspective. But however I may explain things, you should be able to understand by reflecting on your own experiences of everyday life. For example, you cannot be happy when your family members are unhappy. So, to make yourself happy you have to keep your family happy and satisfied. If your partner is unhappy you cannot be happy, because the partner will not let you be happy. If you think in this way, you will realize that it is important to first keep your partner and family members happy.

> I should not practise Dharma for fame or profit,
> And should dedicate the merit of doing practice to all beings.
> Whether or not it is difficult depends on one's attitude –
> If a decision is made, it is easier.

Many people say what I have just said. Spiritual teachers have often said this. However, very few of the speakers and listeners are able to practise it. Isn't that true? The merit accumulated and ascetic practices done by the Buddha-like gurus in their past lives, as mentioned in their biographies, can be understood only by those who believe in life after death. In this life alone, they have spent years and months in ascetic practices for the welfare of other beings, in both spiritual and worldly ways, and to accumulate merit. This in itself is amazing.

A PLEDGE SHOULD BE TAKEN BEFORE DOING ANYTHING

For novices like us, it is difficult to accept or carry out everything we say, but it is important to do whatever is possible. It is important to take a pledge first. Some people say it is better not to pledge because if you make one you have to keep it, and that is why some people hesitate to receive vows. I think many people have such a misconception in their minds. Some people have told me with pride, "I don't eat meat, drink alcohol, kill, tell lies or steal, but I have not taken any vows for all this." I think it needs to be checked whether this is the right way of doing things, from both the spiritual and mundane point of view, for the present and for the long term. The great Bodhisattvas keep all their vows without fail. Novices training in the path of Bodhisattva are like small children taking their first step. They fall and get up. There is a saying, "First mount the horse of pledge while training in the path; use the whip of diligence to inspire you while learning the knowledge, and use the horse-shoe of patience when virtue diminishes." This is how one should practise. So if you take control of yourself, make up your mind and take the pledge, then it may not be so difficult.

CHAPTER 16

❖

Appearances as Example

> I have too many opinions;
> It is impossible to write them all down.
> Since so many past teachers have said,
> "All appearance and existence should be seen as a teaching,"
> I need to really think about the meaning of this.
> Even though I do not have the sharpest of minds.
> Yet knowing my own emotions create both pleasure and pain,
> With conditions and companions always changing,
> Impermanence and suffering, karma and its results,
> Interdependence and the union of appearance and emptiness –
> These I know as true teachers, showing what's real.
> These I know as true teachers, pointing out defects.
> These I know as true teachers, crushing arrogance.
> These I know as true teachers, driving one towards Dharma.
> These I know as true teachers, causing compassion to grow.
>
> When I sometimes have a bit of insight about this,
> According to my training, I feel this is truly
> Receiving the guru's blessings.
> So to the gurus I intensely pray
> And am quite happy when I feel their kindness.

The decisive mind itself is the real great teacher. It is the root of everything. Generally speaking, from abandoning the ten non-virtuous deeds to accomplishing the Truth Body of Buddha, every effort has to be made with decisiveness. Like the proverb says, 'You cannot stitch with a double-tipped needle', with a hesitant mind you cannot achieve anything in this life or the next.

A DECISIVE AND BELIEVING MIND

From the Buddhist point of view, when you practice the two truths taught by the Buddha you have to do it with full faith. When you meditate on the image of the Buddha, if you meditate with decisiveness, discarding the thought that you are meditating on something else, then you achieve an appropriate result. Similarly, you have to be certain about the infallibility of the law of karma. You cannot just make do with having a faithful mind as the base, because it lies within the frame of Conventional Truth.

After an in-depth investigation and reflection, you need the mind to believe and decide that all phenomena that we see, touch, hear or think about are mere appearances, and in reality do not exist as they appear. With such wisdom, if you reflect on the happiness and suffering experienced by your physical body due to your karma and afflictions, the joy and sorrow caused by foes and friends, hope and fear, attachment and aversion, the cause and effect of happiness and suffering, and the impermanence of phenomena, you realize that the infallibility of the two truths is the essence of the sublime doctrine, and the instructions of past masters to perceive all phenomenal appearances as teachings, will not remain empty words, for then you will see them as teachers of the ultimate truth.

When you look from the perspective of the real nature of emptiness, you realize all that you have done and are doing, or all that you have thought and are thinking, is corrupted by the fault of dualistic perception, and you will understand that the phenomenal existences are true teachers pointing out the faults. If you reflect on the infallibility of cause and effect from the point of dependent origination, you understand it as the teacher that tames all negative thoughts, such as pride, arrogance and the eight worldly concerns present in our mind-stream. Therefore, I believe them to be the sole spiritual teacher that inspires you to do authentic practice with diligent effort.

I lament the fact that sentient beings like us, not knowing the infallible nature of emptiness and dependent origination, engage in non-virtuous activities and suffer the consequences of the vicious cycle of samsara. This situation itself is the true teacher of the practice of genuine compassion. Such minor spiritual thoughts arise in me often, and I am confident that this is the result of the blessings of my gurus entering my mind-stream.

Due to this confidence, I pray to my gurus and knowing their kindness, I feel joy and devotion. It inspires enthusiasm in me to follow whatever instructions the Buddha-like guru has given me to the best of my capability. This becomes the cause of further development of all qualities.

> Apart from this, receiving a guru's "blessing"
> Is merely like the pleasure of sex
> Or the bliss of being drunk or dizzy,

> And this kind of "blessing" is not useful.
> I have never received a blessing like this from my teachers
> And do not expect to in the future.

That is the meaning of receiving the guru's blessings. Other than that, instead of practising the Dharma with the hope of physical pleasure, such as sexual or mental pleasure, as when drunk or fainting and becoming unconscious, it is better to indulge in eating meat, drinking or sex for the pleasure that you seek. It may not be correct to say such things and I apologize for expressing my opinion. After accumulating virtue, by paying homage to the gurus and the three reliquaries and visiting holy places, many people expect to make money, find a girl friend or a boyfriend or conceive a child. This is completely wrong.

It is wrong to expect such results, and I see no reason why the Dharma should be used for such ends. I do not think my Buddha-like gurus would give such blessings. I have never hoped for such results. As mentioned above, I see no reason to wear the mask of Dharma or use Dharma for such petty things. This is what I always feel and so I have written it. Since whatever comes to my mind is written here, it is called *My Crazy Tale*. There is no eloquence in deceiving others or beating around the bush – it is a straight-forward narration of the thoughts that came to my mind.

CHAPTER 17

The Ultimate Great Bliss

In fact, all appearance arises as the bliss state;
And the essence of this bliss being emptiness,
How can the net of attachment and aversion trap it?
How can the lasso rope of grasping and clinging tie it up?

CAN THOSE WITH MONASTIC VOWS PRACTICE THE TANTRIC PATH OF GREAT BLISS?

As I said earlier, great bliss is not like sexual pleasure that dogs, pigs, horses, donkeys and humans and non-humans experience. Whatever the method followed, great bliss ultimately means the state of Buddhahood. Once this state is attained, the appearances that we see as truly existent are seen as primordially empty by nature, and all sound and thoughts that arise are realized as empty. In short, happiness and suffering, hope and fear, attachment and aversion, are all sealed by emptiness. In other words, the method of wavering appearances is set to equipoise by the wisdom of emptiness, and manifests as the union state of inherent great bliss.

Another thing that needs to be understood is the term 'eliminate' – an important practice of Vajrayana. The flickering, grasping at attachment towards appearances as the truth, that does not leave our minds in peace, and makes us do all that we do in our lives, is called the inner foe by the common path. The sword of the primordial nature of emptiness cuts off the dualistic appearance of high and low, good and bad, long and short and big and small and turns into the primordially pure and primordially perfected state, in the sphere of great equipoise, or balance. In other words, the sword of wisdom eliminates the web of attachment to conceptual thought.

Most of us think of great bliss as simply an improvement of physical pleasure and mental peace over an extended period. It is doubtful whether it means just this. The instruction manuals of past spiritual masters, that are available, have given clear explanations. Perhaps one will understand better by studying them thoroughly, learning and contemplating.

By studying the scriptures and from experiential knowledge of practice, one can understand that "union" does not simply mean copulation and 'elimination' should not be understood to simply mean taking the lives of others. So, thinking from this angle, I see no reason why the fully ordained monks and monastics who observe the

Vinaya, should not take the form of great Tantric yogis and Yoginis known as three-fold Vajra holder.

For whatever reason, I have heard that an ordained monk cannot practice Vajrayana, and I wonder about the motivation of spreading such a rumour. Since Vajrayana is the essence of Buddhism, I am worried this might cause some problem to Vajrayana teachings. Generally speaking, Vajrayana teaching has suffered much degeneration. Like the Chinese eating a snake, many gurus and khenpos have plucked the top, taken from the middle and cut off the tail, and today all that remains are a few glittering aspects, such as sacred music, sacred dance-steps, drawing, and the use of coloured powder for mandalas

When practitioners do not practice properly, the wrong practice spreads, causing damage to the doctrine in general. Even in the past some of the educated people held wrong views about Vajrayana. It is said that when Atisha visited Tibet he was not given the opportunity to teach Vajrayana. When people talk of "reforming and restoring Buddhism", most people feel uncomfortable with the Vajrayana teachings. Therefore, in order to not harm Buddhism in general and in order to enhance it, I think steps should be taken to promote the study of the Tantras, instead of talking about banning them.

We claim to be the followers of the Nalanda tradition of Nagarjuna, other scholars and Mahasiddhas. Naropa and Maitripa are counted among our guru lineage. They are all Indians and no one can say they did not practise Vajrayana. In Tibet too, there were many scholars and siddhas, such as the trio of Abbot, Acharya and Dharma king: Marpa, Mila, Gampopa; Rongsom Choesang, Longchen Rabjam, Je Tsongkhapa; Lingre, Gyare and Drukpa Kunleg. Drukpa Kunleg is a Mahasiddha respected by all traditions. I have heard that he is highly respected by the Gelugpas. I have also heard that in Labrang Tashi Khyil, thirteen volumes of the *Hundred Thousand Verses of Prajnaparamita* are placed on his throne in reverence, and this was treated as a place of worship until the Chinese invasion. This is why it is said that scholars respect scholars.

Those who do not know the reason, treat gurus like Drukpa Kunleg as a comedian, a source of jokes and entertainment. Unrivalled siddhas like Gyalwa Gotsangpa, Gyalwa Yangonpa and Gyalwa Lorepa are like heroes of our guru lineage. As their followers, we have to study their biographies. Most of them were in the form of fully-ordained monks. Therefore, one must look inward and reflect on the saying that fully-ordained monks can't practice Vajrayana. One should not be carried away by rumour.

I don't have to tell you that it is important to first study and contemplate. Most of you have studied the scriptures. Many of you are familiar with Vajrayana practice. Many of you have completed the *Four Foundation* practices of Mahamudra many times. This is very good. Some of you are familiar with channel and wind practices. So, if you sustain whatever experience of bliss you have with the seal of the Middle Way view of emptiness, then it helps immensely in gaining ground in practice. If you cannot embrace the view of emptiness, then the bliss becomes grasping and results in birth as an animal in the next life, or in this life you become greedy. This further leads to a growth of anger and brutality and ultimately you become worse than an ordinary human being. Some may criticize what I have said above. But in my view, there is no way to attain the state of Buddhahood other than with the view expounded by Nagarjuna.

CHAPTER 18

Crazy Thoughts

> Common bliss binds one through attachment and grasping –
> Even dogs and pigs have this kind.
> Common emptiness is like the empty cup.
> But real emptiness means there's nothing whatsoever
> To establish [as empty],
> And yet the internal pulsing of
> Real emptiness vibrates everywhere:
> This is the union of emptiness and clarity, as I understand it.

Some familiarity with learning, and contemplating the profound view of emptiness, naturally reduces grasping to what is apparent as the truth, and clinging to attachment and aversion. Otherwise, as explained earlier, the experience of bliss infused by attachment and grasping can cause a lot of problems. For example, grasping bliss is present even in dogs and pigs during copulation. Dogs especially, suffer both physically and mentally, engaging in dog fights because of this grasping. Many lose their lives. In the case of humans it is present at the time of drinking alcohol and in sleep. You all know of instances where people fight when they are drunk, and kill each other. There are many tales of how people have been deceived by such bliss.

Similarly, nothingness is like an empty house, or a land without water, or an empty cup without tea in it. If you consider this to be the Middle Way view of emptiness, then it is a big mistake. So then, what is this "emptiness" that we value so much? As mentioned earlier, there is no need to remain confused with the idea of emptiness with a limited scope, because all phenomenal appearance, although appearing to be real, on further investigation has no identifiable essence. And so Buddha called it empty. I think on this basis, because however extensively I try to clear my doubts there is no other conclusion. But a person like me cannot make a conclusive statement on this topic. "Ascertain with scriptural citations and reasoning", means one has to think, use one's intellect and investigate thoroughly. One cannot say what would be the result of the investigation, because it depends on wisdom. Therefore, you need the scriptural citation as background support. It is important to use your intelligence.

Whether you find something or not, the final meaning you understand at that time is firm and unchangeable, different from what others say and the meaning understood by reading the texts. I have a little experience in this matter and so I wish to share my thoughts with you. But when it comes to actual explaining it is difficult to explain, like not finding the right word. It is a funny situation. Perhaps it is like the scriptural description, "It is inexpressible in words and beyond the scope of intellectual faculty," or it could be that I am ignorant about the wording. I don't know. In brief, the self-manifestation or character of the empty nature of all phenomena has been described as clear in every way, and manifestable in any possible way. So not only the feeling is bliss, but even appearance manifests as bliss. Such accomplishment is empty, with no identifiable essence, and the mind that is capable of thinking so many things and learning so much, abiding as lucid awareness, is also without substance. I think this is how the term "union" that we talk so much about should be understood.

A qualified guru with experience may explain these things, using appropriate expressions. Otherwise, whatever gurus like me say, it would be a sort of embellishment with direct perception and inferential reasoning of the inherent conception of "I", without anything to learn or contemplate on, and so takes us further from the essential nature of suchness, and thereby cause us to lose faith in the inconceivable application of the meaning of the true nature. Thus, you don't accept the views of Nagarjuna and lose the opportunity to understand emptiness and dependent origination. Then you have no choice but to insist that what exists has to be seen and what can't be seen cannot exist, or even if you don't say so, that would be what you believe in your mind. So ultimately, one has to rely on the blessings of the guru to understand the inconceivable and inexpressible meaning which is like a mute person tasting jaggery.[60]

MISTAKING THE MARVELLOUS AND DISTINCTIVE BLISS

A RE TSAR!
The bliss state is amazing!

---

60. Jaggery is a type of raw sugar, and this expression refers to an inability to express joy or delight, just like a mute person not being able to explain his/her delight or the experience.

> But the union [of bliss and emptiness] is even more amazing!
> Well, actually it is not so amazing.
> We should really wonder about our assumptions,
> For the really amazing thing is our habit of inquiry:

As mentioned earlier, generally when we talk about bliss, we think only in terms of happiness and suffering and cannot perceive anything more profound beyond that. So some people wear the mask of Vajrayana, to eat meat, drink and keep female company, in the pursuit of pleasure. For example, I heard that in some remote places some people indulge in outrageous activities – like killing goats, the meat and making blood offerings – which go against Buddhist tenets, in the name of propitiating the oath-bound protector. It is normal to have a partner for physical pleasure, but keeping a partner as a spiritual practice of the great bliss, having many children and becoming unintentionally caught in the vicious cycle of samsara, is what Guru Rinpoche described as "the time when Vajrayana strays towards paganism". Such behaviour is a serious damage for Vajrayana teachings. Therefore, it is important to contemplate the proper meaning of "bliss".

On proper reflection, "the state of bliss" is amazing. It is an essential state – enough if you have it and indispensable if you don't have it – for all of us practising Vajrayana sincerely, with the hope of attaining enlightenment within one life time. Ultimately, it means the union of emptiness and bliss. Instructions of the past masters tell us to "keep bliss as the foundation, purify the path with emptiness and finish with the fruit of union." So when you gain certainty even with just a dry understanding, one can experience numbness of body and be stunned into speechlessness, with nothing to pin-point in your thoughts; a hundred or thousand times more amazing than the bliss discussed earlier. Although this is how it commonly appears to us, it seems there is nothing so amazing from the point of its innate state. Those of us ignorant of the state of things, find it uniquely amazing. Yet what is really amazing is our way of thinking, which is defiled by ignorance and our daily activities incited by it.

> We perceive as dual the non-dual state.
> We perceive as separate the unified state.
> We perceive as existing things which don't exist
> And we perceive as non-existing things which do exist!

We perceive the primordially non-dual state as dual. Without reflecting on the meaning of the union of vision and emptiness; sound and emptiness; clarity and emptiness; awareness and emptiness; and their non-dual nature, we hold a dualistic view. Being attached to the conception of self and the conception of true existence, we see non-existent phenomena as everlasting and unchangeable. Realities like cause and effect and life after death are seen as non-existent. Thus, disregarding the law of karma, we engage in activities that damage ourselves and others in this and the next life, such as murder, suicide and deceit.

> Existing and non-existing things are creations of the mind.
> And these magical things are truly amazing.

When I think how people do not contemplate on the existence and non-existence of phenomena, but believe what exists as non-existence, and reject its existence, I find the magical creations of the mind truly amazing. However, nothing can be done until you reach the stage of the exhaustion of reality.

> Their ultimate view is the extreme of eternalism;
> Their meditation is trapped in the shell of clinging;
> Their conduct according to the eight worldly dharmas is quite active –
> Such yogis are truly amazing!

Pretending to be learned, we actively take the view to eternalism, and on that basis give various definitions, shackling one with conceptual thoughts. Since the view cannot go beyond that limit, contemplation and meditation remain trapped in the shell of a number of concepts such as, the conception of self, the conception of existence and non-existence, good and bad happiness, eternalism and impermanence and pure and impure. Since the quality of meditation is mediocre, the conduct remains fraudulent, influenced by the eight worldly motivations and attachment and aversion. Very few amongst us may actually think of deceiving others, but due to the wrong view or wrong way of thinking, the conduct becomes deceitful. Yogis or spiritual practitioners like us in this form are the most amazing among all the hypocrites.

> We are the real magicians,
> For in actual fact nothing exists.
> Pleasure and pain are created by attraction and aversion,
> Grasping attractions magically creates things,

Generally when we say "realized being endowed with magical powers" we refer to Buddha, to Bodhisattvas, to realized beings, to yogis or yoginis who have attained a superior ground or level. But we ordinary beings are the real magicians – not the Buddhas, gurus and realized beings – because we believe that phenomena, which has no innate existence, to be existent. Not understanding the non-existence of "I" we are attached to the concept of "I", and this gives rise to desire and attachment. We believe that the feelings and manifestations such as: happiness and suffering; like and dislike; hope and fear that arise due to desire and attachment; are truly existent. Thus we are confused, believing the non-existent to be existent and the existent to be non-existent, simply because we are unable to see that.

> And if we analyse this thoroughly,
> We cannot be certain that even we exist.

Like the proverb, "If you lose the needle you cannot trust your head." If you analyse the mundane world thoroughly, it is difficult to trust yourself. On occasions I have spent hours in thought and I have remained sleepless at night, thinking about phenomena, making me wonder if I was going crazy.

> I laugh when I think about daytime happenings;
> I laugh when I think about continual change;
> I laugh when I think about attachment and aversion;
> I laugh when I think about pleasure and pain –
> Maybe I am possessed by demons, I'm not sure.
>
> I call on you, my teachers – regard me with compassion!
> I sincerely wish to receive your blessings.

When I think about the reality of phenomena, I get a different perception of people and feel like laughing. I feel like laughing when I think about the day time, the sun and the moon and the continual change of seasons. Similarly, when I think about the emotions of desire and aversion, I feel like laughing, wondering about the need to desire or hate anything. It is really funny.

HOW DO DESIRE AND ATTACHMENT ARISE?

If you think that the feeling of happiness gives rise to desire, you have to reflect on the happiness that you desire and the suffering that you do not want. And then you find all this laughable. But if you leave the feeling as it is without investigation, then there is an indescribable sense of happiness that is seemingly existent. When grasping permeates this feeling, you start running after it and this is what the insects, animals, practitioners like me, rulers, ministers or people of fame. are habituated to doing. This habit is the cause of all problems. There is occasional enjoyment also, but ultimately it is difficult to achieve the happiness one expects. All this is my opinion and observation. I sometimes feel that I may be going crazy, because I have not heard of anyone continually thinking loudly on this issue, day and night. Of course, there may be people who do so secretly. So I mean it when I say, "Maybe I am possessed by demons, I'm not sure. I call on you, my teachers – regard me with compassion! I sincerely wish to receive your blessings."

I used to have this thought since I was very young.

NATURAL DEVELOPMENT OF IRREVERSIBLE FAITH

At such moments, remembering the qualities of the body, speech, mind and kindness of the spiritual masters who had given me instructions, and introduced me to the true natural state, I recall involuntarily, on many occasions, folding my hands and reciting whatever prayers came to mind with tears in my eyes. There was nothing else that I could do. Whenever I analysed the ultimate nature of phenomena, I used to feel an authentic devotion churning my mind-stream, as described in the texts on the ultimate meaning. Then I could feel a new sense, of only devotion to my spiritual masters, who showed me the ultimate truth, and spiritual friends despite their beating, harsh words of scolding, or show of anger. Simultaneously, I would feel less interested in mundane phenomena and this sometimes caused inconvenience. For example, I think my conduct in dealing with other people was not satisfactory. I have been told this directly and I have also heard that some people were disappointed with my behaviour.

In brief, the attitude of a spiritual practitioner should have the determination to sacrifice his/her life for all beings to have happiness and be free from suffering at that moment, and must always be smartly prepared to provide what is needed for the well-being of anyone. In the long run, one must train in the path, as the qualified Buddha-like gurus have done, have less attachment for this life, and always have a deep aspiration for the blessing of mental and physical happiness – for all beings – in the next life. If one has such an aspiration, then the Mahayana practice becomes complete.

Many practitioners of Buddhism among us today, lack the idea of seeking blessings, and even those who seek blessings, pray with a deep selfish motivation. I think very few have an altruistic motivation without relying on karma and its ripening, and this is causing the degeneration of Mahayana teachings. I think generally people do not understand the meaning of seeking blessings. There are different definitions of blessing, and it is important that Buddhists understand the Buddhist definition of blessings, but many do not know it.

As a result, all followers of different traditions of Buddhism, including Vajrayana, pray in front of the reliquary of Buddha in a way that is not the practice of any of the three yanas, but is almost similar to the practice of non-Buddhists. I remember speaking about this a few times earlier, and so I will not go into details here today. Monks and nuns who know the prayers must seek oral transmission and teachings on prayers, such as *Aspirational Prayers for Auspicious Deeds* – the king of prayers – and *Prayer of Maitreya* and learn and contemplate a little bit. None of us care much about this.

Many people talk of how much they have studied the treatises of Indian and Tibetan masters, but they don't seem to have given any thought to the content of the prayers that are recited. I don't think it is enough to know how to recite the prayers. As I said earlier, a Mahayana follower has to train through prayers to become a Mahayana practitioner, but judging by our manner I think it will be difficult to complete the path through prayers.

The following are all prayers. What I normally pray for in my mind has been written down. I don't think they require an explanation: the literal meaning will suffice.

> Please regard your child's long desire.
> Please bless me with the resolve [to attain realization].

Those born in the desire realm have an innate attachment to sense-pleasure, and this is bound by clinging, and this in turn inflames the affliction of desire, leading to unbearable suffering day and night. So, it is a prayer to the gurus to regard with compassion all beings like me, going through such suffering. Desire and attachment are generally to be discarded. Yet in Vajrayana, they have to be carried as the path. The essential meaning of this is explained as "not being bound by fixation" in all the Tantras. But as you study, contemplate and meditate perfectly, you may realize the inexpressible nature of all gross and subtle emotions in one's mind-stream.

The word "Please" used here externally, indicates my appeal to my qualified Buddha-like gurus, Buddhas and Bodhisattvas in the ten directions to come to my rescue. Internally, it is an appeal to the great wisdom, or great intelligence that is devoid of grasping and attachment, or the wisdom attained through learning, reflecting and meditation. It is an appeal for the blessing of this wisdom to completely fill my being, so that I am able to gain an unmistaken understanding of the immutable meaning of dependent origination of all phenomenal appearances; a correct understanding of the true nature of boundless emptiness; and reach the conclusion of the great equanimity.

> Please bless me to have a steady and smooth mind,

At the moment, one may have the intention of working for the welfare of others, but one's action and conduct follow the wrong path. Harmful thoughts arise, leading to negative action. For example, you make up your mind not to tell lies, but circumstances force you to lie. When you are fasting, it becomes difficult to continue the practice for an entire day. I am telling you my experience and don't mean to belittle you all. So please don't misunderstand me. Generally, one has to accept that "a vow is compounded phenomena and will disintegrate", but when you analyse why all the positive vows disintegrate, while the negative vows remain intact as if carved on rocks, you understand that we have been accustomed to the wrong thoughts and actions life after life, and so are drawn towards them implicitly. I am saying this from the point of someone accepting life after death. Having a steady and smooth mind or "serviceable mind" means having control over the mind and being able to drive our minds towards positive actions and thereby, make progress towards a higher and higher path.

CHAPTER 19

Supplication

> So that for this life and those to follow,
> As a true practitioner whose heart and mind are in accord,
> The special intention [to help others] is spontaneously present.
> May I be able to benefit measureless beings.
>
> Without the toxic stains of a competitive mind,
> Without the intoxicating liquor of anger and lust,
> May I be able to practice the peaceful and soothing Dharma.
> May I be able to give teachings diligently.
>
> Through listening and thinking and examining,
> Especially about those teachings I practice,
> May I be able to precisely determine their meaning;
> Raising the victorious banner of ultimate practice,
> May I be able to accomplish great service to the Dharma.

These are the supplications that I genuinely make in my mind daily – for this life, the next life and the intermediate state. It is a simple prayer and there is no need for explanation. I feel that all of us should bear the last stanza in mind. Whatever activity you take up, spiritual or educational, one has to clear all doubts, through study and contemplation, without the motivation of competition or fame. Without being proud and arrogant with understanding the meaning correctly, one should be able to raise the victory banner of practice, by practising what one has learned. "May I be able to serve the society as best as I can" is my prayer. This applies to non-Buddhists also.

If you are born into a non-Buddhist family, you must thoroughly study and analyse the religion and its philosophy. Although I cannot comment on the view, I am sure you can learn a lot about kindness, compassion and morality. This will help you become an intelligent, good human. You will stand out as an exemplary person in the society and be able to do a lot for the welfare of others. Therefore, I believe you should pray to become an excellent Buddhist or non-Buddhist. Otherwise you will be involved in negative activities, like taking the life of innocent animals, creating social disturbances and other immoral conduct, unheard and unseen before.

Any act that harms or takes the life of innocent beings, done in the name of any religion, is definitely contrary to the tenet of any religion. When practitioners and scholars misunderstand the meaning, it becomes a big blunder, and furthermore, the followers too make the mistake of barbaric conduct, instead of the right conduct, for thousands of years. Like the proverb, "The mistake of a scholar remains an absolute mistake."

This is the way I pray, all the time,
And I request all of you to support my prayers.
These are my insane suggestions,
These are my crazy ways of thinking,
The shapes of a madman's musings.

The words are boring,
And the composition is lousy.
So there is nothing admirable here
For all those learned ones.

Since there is no mix of the eight worldly dharmas,
It is difficult to satisfy worldly-minded people.
This chatter is neither for the learned, nor for the worldly –
It is only suitable for crazies like me.

By spreading this kind of nonsense
May all innumerable beings be freed from their endless activities.
May they reach the state free from birth.
This, my own tale, is a lunatic's sketch, drawn from the heart,
I wrote down whatever came to mind, without distortion.
It has nothing to do with "benefitting beings";
It is pure gossip.

This was done in the Maratika Cave (in Nepal)
Known as Great Bliss Dharmadhatu
By one holding the name Kyabgon Drukpa XII,
Commonly called Padma Wangchen,
At the age of twenty-eight.
On the 25th day, the feast-day of the dakinis,
I wrote this during a break in my practice.
May it transmit the auspicious
Union of bliss and emptiness!

My Crazy Tale is a narration of my thoughts without any embellishment, at the request of my friend. It is pure idle talk, without expectations of fame or recognition as a spiritual activity. It was written during a break in the retreat session on the day of Dakinis at Yingchuk Dechen Phug, east of the holy place Maratika, at the age of 28 years, by Jigme Padma Wangchen – holder of the title of 12th Gyalwang Drukpa. May the great bliss of union bring auspiciousness all around!

The random thoughts that arise in the mind of a yogi like me, is entitled *My Crazy Tale*. It was written many years back – over twenty years ago. It is important to know that one is aging. I check myself to find out if I have made any mental progress since then. I have become older and there is no way to avoid old age. Finally, one has to die. Even animals grow old and the proverbial saying is, "Even diamond hills age". As humans capable of speaking and understanding, our aging should be meaningful. This is called aging with wisdom.

Everyone, believers and non-believers, should have served the purpose of being born and living in this world. Even death should be meaningful. This is what I feel. In short, while you are alive you should be able to do great work for the happiness of the society, so that your work is recognized by the world, and even when you die you leave behind your contributions to humanity. You must be able to leave, with happiness for this life and the next life, having fulfilled the purpose of life for yourself and others, unrivalled – spiritually and mundanely.

Today, I am concluding the explanation of *My Crazy Tale* that I have been giving at different places over the years at the request of my pupils. *My Crazy Tale* was composed over twenty years ago at Maratika Cave, the holy place of Guru Rinpoche, where I stayed in retreat for one year and six months, on the instructions of my root Guru Vajradhara Trulshik Rinpoche.

Thank you.